"I've written in the fields of adventure, space opera, parallel worlds, pocket universes, psychological, political, sexual, and biological pastiche, parody, religious, horror, time travel, ESP, "biographical," Cthulhu mythos, metaphysical, ecological, and Marxian. The last term refers to Groucho, Chico, and Harpo, not Karl..."

Berkley books by Philip José Farmer

THE BOOK OF PHILIP JOSÉ FARMER
DARE
INSIDE • OUTSIDE
NIGHT OF LIGHT
A WOMAN A DAY

THE RIVERWORLD SERIES:

TO YOUR SCATTERED BODIES GO
THE FABULOUS RIVERBOAT
THE DARK DESIGN
THE MAGIC LABYRINTH
RIVERWORLD AND OTHER STORIES

THE BOOK OF
PHILIP JOSÉ FARMER

PHILIP JOSE FARMER

BERKLEY BOOKS, NEW YORK

To My Sister, Joan

This Berkley book has been completely reset
in a type face designed for easy reading,
and was printed from new film.

THE BOOK OF
PHILIP JOSÉ FARMER

A Berkley Book/published by arrangement with
the author

PRINTING HISTORY
Daw edition/July 1973
Revised Berkley edition/February 1982

All rights reserved.
Copyright © 1973 by Philip José Farmer.
Revised and additional material copyright © 1982 by Philip José Farmer.
Father's in the Basement, copyright © 1972, by Damon Knight.
Reprinted by permission of the author and Berkley Publishing
Corporation. First published in *Orbit 11*.
Towards the Beloved City. From *Signs and Wonders* (Fleming H.
Revell), by permission of Roger Elwood, Editor.
The Freshman, copyright © 1979 by Philip José Farmer.
The Last Rise of Nick Adams, copyright © 1978 by Philip José Farmer.
Uproar in Acheron, copyright © 1962 by Philip José Farmer.
Cover art by James Warhola.
This book may not be reproduced in whole or in part,
by mimeograph or any other means, without permission.
For information address: Berkley Publishing Corporation,
200 Madison Avenue, New York, New York 10016.

ISBN: 0-425-05298-2

A BERKLEY BOOK® TM 757,375
PRINTED IN THE UNITED STATES OF AMERICA

TABLE OF CONTENTS

PREFACE *vii*

MY SISTER'S BROTHER *1*

SKINBURN *52*

THE ALLEY MAN *66*

FATHER'S IN THE BASEMENT *109*

TOWARD THE BELOVED CITY *117*

POLYTROPICAL PARAMYTHS *140*

DON'T WASH THE CARATS *142*

THE SUMERIAN OATH *146*

ONLY WHO CAN MAKE A TREE? *153*

THE LAST RISE OF NICK ADAMS *165*

THE FRESHMAN *177*

UPROAR IN ACHERON *195*

AN EXCLUSIVE INTERVIEW WITH LORD GREYSTOKE
  210

**SEXUAL IMPLICATIONS OF
   THE CHARGE OF THE LIGHT BRIGADE**   *223*

**THE OBSCURE LIFE AND HARD TIMES OF
   KILGORE TROUT**   *227*

THANKS FOR THE FEAST BY LESLIE A. FIEDLER   *240*

NOTES ON PHILIP JOSÉ FARMER   *242*

PREFACE

This collection is a reprint of *The Book of Philip José Farmer*, published in 1973 in softcover in the States and in hardcover in England in 1976. However, for this edition the forewords, where needing it, have been revised and updated. And since three stories, "Totem and Taboo," "The Voice of the Sonar in My Vermiform Appendix," and "Brass and Gold" have been recently reprinted in other collections, I have replaced them with "The Last Rise of Nick Adams," "The Freshman," and a non-science-fiction tale, "Uproar in Acheron."

The title of this book implies a broad spectrum of my works, samples from each of the many fields of the vast genre of science-fiction in which I've worked. (Played, rather.)

Unfortunately, I can't include every field. I've written stories in many: adventure, space opera, parallel worlds, pocket universes, psychological, political, sexual, biological, pastiche, parody, religious, horror, time travel, ESP, "biographical," Cthulhu mythos, metaphysical, ecological, and Marxian. The last term refers to Groucho, Chico, and Harpo, not Karl, and could be applied to my polytropical paramyths. To include one sample of each would make a book twice as long as this, maybe three times as long. Also, some of the samples would have to be novels.

Thus, the stories and extracts herein are samples of the spectrum, not the complete spectrum.

MY SISTER'S BROTHER

Of all my shorter fiction, this is, after my "Riders of the Purple Wage," my favorite. A curious story, it has a curious history. It first went to John Campbell, then editor of *Astounding* (now *Analog*). He rejected it with the message that it made him nauseated, not because it was a bad story but because of its vivid biological details and its premises. He believed that the readers of *Astounding* would react as he did. I wasn't surprised; this wasn't the first story of mine that had sickened John.

Sadly, because I liked *Astounding*'s word rates, I mailed it out to a lesser-paying market. I bypassed Horace Gold, editor of *Galaxy*, an equally good payer, because Horace's editorial stomach was, I knew from experience, no stronger than John's. John was supposed to be a flaming reactionary, and Horace was supposed to be a flaming liberal. Actually, both were individuals, proteans who would wriggle out of the grasp of anyone who tried to hold them down while pinning a label on them. In this case, the compelling reason for rejection was their fear of their readers' reactions.

Bob Mills, editor of *The Magazine of Fantasy and Science Fiction*, also bounced it. He liked it but thought it too strong for his readers. However, Leo Margulies was planning a new science fiction magazine, *Satellite*, and, hearing of "My Sister's Brother," then titled "Open to Me, My Sister," asked Bob if he could read it. He purchased it, and the story, retitled "The Strange Birth," was set up in galley sheets and illustrated for the first issue. But Leo's plans collapsed; *Satellite* though, was canceled.

Bob Mills, meanwhile, had changed his mind. He

would take a chance on it. He paid the difference between Leo's check to me and his and published it with my original title. Most of the readers were less queasy than any of the editors would have expected. This was in 1960, when the gears of the *Zeitgeist* were shifting into overdrive. The makeup of the general readership had changed somewhat; there were many more flexible-minded people than in the 1950's.

I'll note that the reactions of the editors who rejected this story, or, in the case of Gold, would have, are similar to the reactions of the protagonist to the strange society of Mars and the even stranger visitor to Mars, "Martia." This story is a hardcore science fiction tale, but it is also about an Earthman's hangups, extraterrestrial ecosystems, sexobiological structures, and religion.

Also, when the story was written, Hawaii was not yet the fiftieth state. But it seemed likely.

Also, the reproductive-phallic system of Martia's people is an original concept, just as Jeannette Rastignac's was in *The Lovers*. At the time I wrote the two stories, I was in my sexobiological phase. Which may come again, no pun intended.

Come to think of it, the phase did descend upon me again briefly in the 60's when I wrote the novels *Image of the Beast* and *Blown*.

The sixth night on Mars, Lane wept.

He sobbed loudly while tears ran down his cheeks. He smacked his right fist into the palm of his left hand until the flesh burned. He howled with loneliness. He swore the most obscene and blasphemous oaths he knew.

After a while, he quit weeping, He dried his eyes, downed a shot of Scotch, and felt much better.

He wasn't ashamed because he had bawled like a woman. After all, there had been a Man who had not been ashamed to weep. He could dissolve in tears the grinding stones within; he was the reed that bent before the wind, not the oak that toppled, roots and all.

Now, the weight and the ache in his breast gone, feeling almost cheerful, he made his scheduled report over the transceiver to the circum-Martian vessel five hundred and eight miles overhead. Then he did what men must do any place in the universe. Afterward, he lay down in the bunk and opened the one personal book he had been allowed to bring along, an anthology of the world's greatest poetry.

He read here and there, running, pausing for only a line or two, then completing in his head the thousand-times murmured lines. Here and there he read, like a bee tasting the best of the nectar....

> *It is the voice of my beloved that knocketh, saying,*
> *Open to me, my sister, my love, my dove,*
> > *my undefiled ...*
>
> *We have a little sister,*
> *And she hath no breasts;*
> *What shall we do for our sister*
> *In the day when she shall be spoken for?*
>
> *Yea, though I walk through the valley of the shadow of*
> > *death,*
> *I will fear no evil for Thou art with me ...*
>
> *Come live with me and be my love*
> *And we shall all the pleasures prove ...*
>
> *It lies not in our power to love or hate*
> *For will in us is over-ruled by fate ...*
>
> *With thee conversing, I forget all time,*
> *All seasons, and their change, all please alike ...*

He read on about love and man and woman until he had almost forgotten his troubles. His lids drooped; the book fell from his hand. But he roused himself, climbed out of the bunk, got down on his knees, and prayed that he be forgiven and that his blasphemy and despair be understood. And he prayed that his four lost comrades be found safe and sound. Then he climbed back into the bunk and fell asleep.

At dawn he woke reluctantly to the alarm clock's ringing. Nevertheless, he did not fall back into sleep but rose, turned on the transceiver, filled a cup with water and instant, and dropped in a heat pill. Just as he finished the coffee, he heard Captain Stroyansky's voice from the 'ceiver. Stroyansky spoke with barely a trace of Slavic accent.

"Cardigan Lane? You awake?"

"More or less. How are you?"

"If we weren't worried about all of you down there, we'd be fine."

"I know. Well, what are your orders?"

"There is only one thing to do, Lane. You must go look for the others. Otherwise, you cannot get back up to us. It takes at least two more men to pilot the rocket."

"Theoretically, one man can pilot the beast," replied Lane. "But it's uncertain. However, that doesn't matter. I'm leaving at once to look for the others. I'd do that even if you ordered otherwise."

Stroyansky chuckled. Then he barked like a seal. "The success of the expedition is more important than the fate of four men. Theoretically, anyway. But if I were in your shoes, and I'm glad I'm not, I would do the same. So, good luck, Lane."

"Thanks," said Lane. "I'll need more than luck. I'll also need God's help. I suppose He's here, even if the place does look God forsaken."

He looked through the transparent double plastic walls of the dome.

"The wind's blowing about twenty-five miles an hour. The dust is covering the tractor tracks. I have to get going before they're covered up entirely. My supplies are all packed; I've enough food, air, and water to last me six days. It makes a big package, the air tanks and the sleeping tent bulk large. It's over a hundred Earth pounds, but here only about forty. I'm also taking a rope, a knife, a pickax, a flare pistol, half a dozen flares. And a walkie-talkie.

"It should take me two days to walk the thirty miles to the spot where the tracs last reported. Two days to look around. Two days to get back."

"You be back in five days!" shouted Stroyansky. "That's an order! It shouldn't take you more than one day to scout around. Don't take chances. Five days!"

And then, in a softer voice, "Good luck, and, if there is a God, may He help you!"

Lane tried to think of things to say, things that might go down with the *Doctor Livingstone, I presume*, category. But all he could say was, "So long."

Twenty minutes later, he closed behind him the door to the dome's pressure lock. He strapped on the towering pack and began to walk. But when he was about fifty yards from the base, he felt compelled to turn around for one long look at what he might never see again. There, on the yellow-red felsite plain, stood the pressurized bubble that was to have been the home of the five men for a year. Nearby squatted the glider that had brought them down, its enormous wings spreading far, its skids covered with the forever-blowing dust.

Straight ahead of him was the rocket, standing on its fins, pointing toward the blue-black sky, glittering in the Martian sun, shining with promise of power, escape from Mars, and return to the orbital ship. It had come down to the surface of Mars on the back of the glider in a hundred-and-twenty-mile an hour landing. After it had dropped the two six-ton caterpillar tractors it carried, it had been pulled off the glider and tilted on end by winches pulled by those very tractors. Now it waited for him and for the other four men.

"I'll be back," he murmured to it. "And if I have to, I'll take you up by myself."

He began to walk, following the broad double tracks left by the tank. The tracks were faint, for they were two days old, and the blowing silicate dust had almost filled them. The tracks made by the first tank, which had left three days ago, were completely hidden.

The trail led northwest. It left the three-mile wide plain between two hills of naked rock and entered the quarter-mile corridor between two rows of vegetation. The rows ran straight and parallel from horizon to horizon, for miles behind him and miles ahead.

Lane, on the ground and close to one row, saw it for what it was. Its foundation was an endless three-foot high tube, most of whose bulk, like an iceberg's, lay buried in the ground. The curving sides were covered with blue-green lichenoids that grew on every rock or projection. From the spine of the tube, separated at regular intervals, grew the trunks of plants. The trunks were smooth shiny blue-green pillars two feet thick and six feet high. Out of their tops spread radially many pencil-thin branches, like bats' fingers. Between the fingers stretched a blue-green membrane, the single tremendous leaf of the umbrella tree.

When Lane had first seen them from the glider as it hurtled over them, he had thought they looked like an army of giant hands uplifted to catch the sun. Giant they were, for each rib-supported leaf measured fifty feet across. And hands they were, hands to beg for and catch the rare gold of the tiny sun. During the day, the ribs on the side nearest the moving sun dipped toward the ground, and the furthest ribs tilted upward. Obviously, the daylong maneuver was designed to expose the complete area of the membrane to the light, to allow not an inch to remain in shadow.

It was to be expected that strange forms of plant life would be found here. But structures built by animal life were not expected. Especially when they were so large and covered an eighth of the planet.

These structures were the tubes from which rose the trunks of the umbrella trees. Lane had tried to drill through the rocklike side of the tube. So hard was it, it had blunted one drill and had done a second no good before he had chipped off a small piece. Contented for the moment with that, he had taken it to the dome, there to examine it under a microscope. After an amazed look, he had whistled. Embedded in the cement-like mass were plant cells. Some were partially destroyed; some, whole.

Further tests had shown him that the substance was composed of cellulose, a lignin-like stuff, various nucleic acids, and unknown materials.

He had reported his discovery and also his conjecture to the orbital ship. Some form of animal life had, at some time, chewed up and partially digested wood and then had regurgitated it as a cement. The tubes had been fashioned from the cement.

The following day he intended to go back to the tube and blast a hole in it. But two of the men had set out in a tractor on a field exploration. Lane, as radio operator for that day, had stayed in the dome. He was to keep in contact with the two, who were to report to him every fifteen minutes.

The tank had been gone about two hours and must have been about thirty miles away, when it had failed to report. Two hours later, the other tank, carrying two men, had followed the prints of the first party. They had gone about thirty miles from base and were maintaining continuous radio contact with Lane.

"There's a slight obstacle ahead," Greenberg had said. "It's a tube coming out at right angles from the one we've been paralleling. It has no plants growing from it. Not much of a rise, not much of a drop on the other side, either. We'll make it easy."

Then he had yelled.

That was all.

My Sister's Brother

Now, the day after, Lane was on foot, following the fading trail. Behind him lay the base camp, close to the junction of the two *canali* known as Avernus and Tartarus. He was between two of the rows of vegetation which formed Tartarus, and he was traveling northeastward, toward the Sirenum Mare, the so-called Siren Sea. The Mare, he supposed, would be a much broader group of tree-bearing tubes.

He walked steadily while the sun rose higher and the air grew warmer. He had long ago turned off his suit-heater. This was summer and close to the equator. At noon the temperature would be around seventy degrees Fahrenheit.

But at dusk, when the temperature had plunged through the dry air to zero, Lane was in his sleeping tent. It looked like a cocoon, being sausage-shaped and not much larger than his body. It was inflated so he could remove his helmet and breathe while he warmed himself from the battery-operated heater and ate and drank. The tent was also very flexible; it changed its cocoon shape to a triangle while Lane sat on a folding chair from which hung a plastic bag and did that which every man must do.

During the daytime he did not have to enter the sleeping tent for this. His suit was ingeniously contrived so he could unflap the rear section and expose the necessary area without losing air or pressure from the rest of his suit. Naturally, there was no thought of tempting the teeth of the Martian night. Sixty seconds at midnight were enough to get a severe frostbite where one sat down.

Lane slept until half an hour after dawn, ate, deflated the tent, folded it, stowed it, the battery, heater, food-box, and folding chair into his pack, threw away the plastic sack, shouldered the pack, and resumed his walk.

By noon the tracks faded out completely. It made little difference, for there was only one route the tanks could have taken. That was the corridor between the tubes and the trees.

Now he saw what the two tanks had reported. The trees on his right began to look dead. The trunks and leaves were brown, and the ribs drooped.

He began walking faster, his heart beating hard. An hour passed, and still the line of dead trees stretched as far as he could see.

"It must be about here," he said out loud to himself.

Then he stopped. Ahead was an obstacle.

It was the tube of which Greenberg had spoken, the one that

ran at right angles to the other two and joined them.

Lane looked at it and thought that he could still hear Greenberg's despairing cry.

That thought seemed to turn a valve in him so that the immense pressure of loneliness, which he had succeeded in holding back until then, flooded in. The blue-black of the sky became the blackness and infinity of space itself, and he was a speck of flesh in an immensity as large as Earth's land area, a speck that knew no more of this world than a newborn baby knows of his.

Tiny and helpless, like a baby....

No, he murmured to himself, not a baby. Tiny, yes. Helpless, no. Baby, no. I am a man, a man, an Earthman....

Earthman: Cardigan Lane. Citizen of the U.S.A. Born in Hawaii, the fiftieth state. Of mingled German, Dutch, Chinese, Japanese, Negro, Cherokee, Polynesian, Portuguese, Russian-Jewish, Irish, Scotch, Norwegian, Finnish, Czech, English, and Welsh ancestry. Thirty-one years old. Five foot six. One hundred and sixty pounds. Brown-haired. Blue-eyed. Hawk-featured, M.D. and Ph.D. Married. Childless. Methodist. Sociable mesomorphic mesovert. Radio ham. Dog breeder. Deer hunter. Skin diver. Writer of first-rate but far from great poetry. All contained in his skin and his pressure suit, plus a love of companionship and life, an intense curiosity, and a courage. And now very much afraid of losing everything except his loneliness.

For some time he stood like a statue before the three-foot high wall of the tube. Finally, he shook his head violently, shook off his fear like a dog shaking off water. Lightly, despite the towering pack on his back, he leaped up onto the top of the tube and looked on the other side, though there was nothing he had not seen before jumping.

The view before him differed from the one behind in only one respect. This was the number of small plants that covered the ground. Or rather, he thought, after taking a second look, he had never seen these plants this size before. They were foot-high replicas of the huge umbrella trees that sprouted from the tubes. And they were not scattered at random, as might have been expected if they had grown from seeds blown by the wind. Instead, they grew in regular rows, the edges of the plants in one row separated from the other by about two feet.

His heart beat even faster. Such spacing must mean they were planted by intelligent life. Yet intelligent life seemed very improbable, given the Martian environment.

Possibly some natural condition might have caused the seeming artificiality of this garden. He would have to investigate.

Always with caution, though. So much depended on him: the lives of the four men, the success of the expedition. If this one failed, it might be the last. Many people on Earth were groaning loudly because of the cost of Space Arm and crying wildly for results that would mean money and power.

The field, or garden, extended for about three hundred yards. At its far end there was another tube at right angles to the two parallel ones. And at this point the giant umbrella plants regained their living and shining blue-green color.

The whole setup looked to Lane very much like a sunken garden. The square formation of the high tubes kept out the wind and most of the felsite flakes. The walls held the heat within the square.

Lane searched the top of the tube for bare spots where the metal plates of the caterpillar tractors' treads would have scraped off the lichenoids. He found none but was not surprised. The lichenoids grew phenomenally fast under the summertime sun.

He looked down at the ground on the garden side of the tube, where the tractors had presumably descended. Here there were no signs of the tractors' passage, for the little umbrellas grew up to within two feet of the edge of the tube, and they were uncrushed. Nor did he find any tracks at the ends of the tube where it joined the parallel rows.

He paused to think about his next step and was surprised to find himself breathing hard. A quick check of his air gauge showed him that the trouble wasn't an almost empty tank. No, it was the apprehension, the feeling of eeriness, of something *wrong,* that was causing his heart to beat so fast, to demand more oxygen.

Where could two tractors and four men have gone? And what could have caused them to disappear?

Could they have been attacked by some form of intelligent life? If that had happened, the unknown creatures had either carried off the six-ton tanks, or driven them away, or else forced the men to drive them off.

Where? How? By whom?

The hairs on the back of his neck stood up.

"Here is where it must have happened," he muttered to

himself. "The first tank reported seeing this tube barring its way and said it would report again in another ten minutes. That was the last I heard from it. The second was cut off just as it was on top of the tube. Now, what happened? There are no cities on the surface of Mars, and no indications of underground civilization. The orbital ship would have seen openings to such a place through its telescope...."

He yelled so loudly that he was deafened as his voice bounced off the confines of his helmet. Then he fell silent, watching the line of basketball-size blue globes rise from the soil at the far end of the garden and swiftly soar into the sky.

He threw back his head until the back of it was stopped by the helmet and watched the rising globes as they left the ground, swelling until they seemed to be hundreds of feet across. Suddenly, like a soap bubble, the topmost one disappeared. The second in line, having reached the height of the first, also popped. And the others followed.

They were transparent. He could see some white cirrus clouds through the blue of the bubbles.

Lane did not move but watched the steady string of globes spurt from the soil. Though startled, he did not forget his training. He noted that the globes, besides being semitransparent, rose at a right angle to the ground and did not drift with the wind. He counted them and got to forty-nine when they ceased appearing.

He waited for fifteen minutes. When it looked as if nothing more would happen, he decided that he must investigate the spot where the globes seemed to have popped out of the ground. Taking a deep breath, he bent his knees and jumped out into the garden. He landed lightly about twelve feet out from the edge of the tube and between two rows of plants.

For a second he did not know what was happening, though he realized that something was wrong. Then he whirled around. Or tried to do so. One foot came up, but the other sank deeper.

He took one step forward, and the forward foot also disappeared into the thin stuff beneath the red-yellow dust. By now the other foot was too deep in to be pulled out.

Then he was hip-deep and grabbing at the stems of the plants to both sides of him. They uprooted easily, coming out of the soil, one clenched in each hand.

He dropped them and threw himself backward in the hope he could free his legs and lie stretched out on the jellylike stuff. Perhaps, if his body presented enough of an area, he could keep from sinking. And, after a while, he might be able to work his way to the ground near the tube. There, he hoped, it would be firm.

His violent effort succeeded. His legs came up out of the sticky semiliquid. He lay spread-eagled on his back and looked up at the sky through the transparent dome of his helmet. The sun was to his left; when he turned his head inside the helmet he could see the sun sliding down the arc from the zenith. It was descending at a slightly slower pace than on Earth, for Mars's day was about forty minutes longer. He hoped that, if he couldn't regain solid ground, he could remain suspended until evening fell. By then this quagmire would be frozen enough for him to rise and walk up on it. Provided that he got up before he himself was frozen fast.

Meanwhile, he would follow the approved method of saving oneself when trapped in quicksand. He would roll over quickly, once, and then spread-eagle himself again. By repeating this maneuver, he might eventually reach that bare strip of soil at the tube.

The pack on his back prevented him from rolling. The straps around his shoulders would have to be loosened.

He did so, and at the same time felt his legs sinking. Their weight was pulling them under, whereas the air tanks in the pack, the air tanks strapped to his chest, and the bubble of his helmet gave buoyancy to the upper part of his body.

He turned over on his side, grabbed the pack, and pulled himself up on it. The pack, of course, went under. But his legs were free, though slimy with liquid and caked with dust. And he was standing on top of the narrow island of the pack.

The thick jelly rose up to his ankles while he considered two courses of action.

He could squat on the pack and hope that it would not sink too far before it was stopped by the permanently frozen layer that must exist....

How far? He had gone down hip-deep and felt nothing firm beneath his feet. And...He groaned. The tractors! Now he knew what had happened to them. They had gone over the tube and down into the garden, never suspecting that the solid-seeming surface covered this quagmire. And down they had plunged, and it had been Greenberg's horrified realization of what lay beneath the dust that had made him cry out, and then the stuff had closed over the tank and its antenna, and the transmitter, of course, had been cut off.

He must give up his second choice because it did not exist. To get to the bare strip of soil at the tube would be useless. It would be as unfirm as the rest of the garden. It was at that point that the tanks must have fallen in.

Another thought came to him: that the tanks must have disturbed the orderly arrangement of the little umbrellas close to the tube. Yet there was no sign of such a happening. Therefore, somebody must have rescued the plants and set them up again.

That meant that somebody might come along in time to rescue him.

Or to kill him, he thought.

In either event, his problem would be solved.

Meanwhile, he knew it was no use to make a jump from the pack to the strip at the tube. The only thing to do was to stay on top of the pack and hope it didn't sink too deeply.

However, the pack did sink. The jelly rose swiftly to his knees, then his rate of descent began slowing. He prayed, not for a miracle but only that the buoyancy of the pack plus the tank on his chest would keep him from going completely under.

Before he had finished praying, he had stopped sinking. The sticky stuff had risen no higher than his breast and had left his arms free.

He gasped with relief but did not feel overwhelmed with joy. In less than four hours the air in his tank would be exhausted. Unless he could get another tank from the pack, he was done for.

He pushed down hard on the pack and threw his arms up in the air and back in the hope his legs would rise again and he could spread-eagle. If he could do that, then the pack, relieved of his weight, might rise to the surface. And he could get another tank from it.

But his legs, impeded by the stickiness, did not rise far enough, and his body, shooting off in reaction to the kick, moved a little distance from the pack. It was just far enough so that when the legs inevitably sank again, they found no platform on which to be supported. Now he had to depend entirely on the lift of his air tank.

It did not give him enough to hold him at his former level; this time he sank until his arms and shoulders were nearly under, and only his helmet stuck out.

He was helpless.

Several years from now the second expedition, if any, would

perhaps see the sun glinting off his helmet and would find his body stuck like a fly in glue.

If that does happen, he thought, I will at least have been of some use; my death will warn them of this trap. But I doubt if they'll find me. I think that Somebody or Something will have removed me and hidden me.

Then, feeling an inrush of despair, he closed his eyes and murmured some of the words he had read that last night in the base, though he knew them so well it did not matter whether he had read them recently or not.

> *Yea, though I walk through the valley of the shadow of death, I will fear no evil; for Thou art with me..*

Repeating that didn't lift the burden of hopelessness. He felt absolutely alone, deserted by everybody, even by his Creator. Such was the desolation of Mars.

But when he opened his eyes, he knew he was not alone. He saw a Martian.

A hole had appeared in the wall of the tube to his left. It was a round section about four feet across, and it had sunk in as if it were a plug being pulled inward, as indeed it was.

A moment later a head popped out of the hole. The size of a Georgia watermelon, it was shaped like a football and was as pink as a baby's bottom. Its two eyes were as large as coffee cups and each was equipped with two vertical lids. It opened its two parrot-like beaks, ran out a very long tubular tongue, withdrew the tongue, and snapped the beak shut. Then it scuttled out from the hole to reveal a body also shaped like a football and only three times as large as its head. The pinkish body was supported three feet from the ground on ten spindly spidery legs, five on each side. Its legs ended in broad round pads on which it ran across the jelly-mire surface, sinking only slightly. Behind it streamed at least fifty others.

These picked up the little plants that Lane had upset in his struggles and licked them clean with narrow round tongues that shot out at least two feet. They also seemed to communicate by touching their tongues, as insects do with antennae.

As he was in the space between two rows, he was not involved in the setting up of the dislodged plants. Several of them ran their tongues over his helmet, but these were the only ones that paid him any attention. It was then that he began to stop dreading that they might attack him with their powerful-looking beaks. Now he broke into a sweat at the idea that they might ignore him completely.

That was just what they did. After gently embedding the thin roots of the plantlets in the sticky stuff, they raced off toward the hole in the tube.

Lane, overwhelmed with despair, shouted after them, though he knew they couldn't hear him through his helmet and the thin air even if they had hearing organs.

"Don't leave me here to die!"

Nevertheless, that was what they were doing. The last one leaped through the hole, and the entrance stared at him like the round black eye of Death itself.

He struggled furiously to lift himself from the mire, not caring that he was only exhausting himself.

Abruptly, he stopped fighting and stared at the hole.

A figure had crawled out of it, a figure in a pressure-suit.

Now he shouted with joy. Whether the figure was Martian or not, it was built like a member of Homo sapiens. It could be presumed to be intelligent and therefore curious.

He was not disappointed. The suited being stood up on two hemispheres of shiny red metal and began walking toward him in a sliding fashion. Reaching him, it handed him the end of a plastic rope it was carrying under its arm.

He almost dropped it. His rescuer's suit was transparent. It was enough of a shock to see clearly the details of the creature's body, but the sight of the two heads within the helmet caused him to turn pale.

The Martian slidewalked to the tube from which Lane had leaped. It jumped lightly from the two bowls on which it had stood, landed on the three-foot high top of the tube, and began hauling Lane out from the mess. He came out slowly but steadily and soon was scooting forward, gripping the rope. When he reached the foot of the tube, he was hauled on up until he could get his feet in the two bowls. It was easy to jump from them to a place beside the biped.

It unstrapped two more bowls from its back, gave them to Lane, then lowered itself on the two in the garden. Lane followed it across the mire.

Entering the hole, he found himself in a chamber so low he had to crouch. Evidently, it had been constructed by the dekapeds and not by his companion for it, too, had to bend its back and knees.

Lane was pushed to one side by some dekapeds. They picked

up the thick plug, made of the same gray stuff as the tube walls, and sealed the entrance with it. Then they shot out of their mouths strand after strand of gray spiderwebby stuff to seal the plug.

The biped motioned Lane to follow, and it slid down a tunnel which plunged into the earth at a forty-five degree angle. It illuminated the passage with a flashlight which it took from its belt. They came into a large chamber which contained all of the fifty dekapeds. These were waiting motionless. The biped, as if sensing Lane's curiosity, pulled off its glove and held it before several small vents in the wall. Lane removed his glove and felt warm air flowing from the holes.

Evidently this was a pressure chamber, built by the ten-legged things. But such evidence of intelligent engineering did not mean that these things had the individual intelligence of a man. It could mean group intelligence such as Terrestrial insects possess.

After a while, the chamber was filled with air. Another plug was pulled; Lane followed the dekapeds and his rescuer up another forty-five degree tunnel. He estimated that he would find himself inside the tube from which the biped had first come. He was right. He crawled through another hole into it.

And a pair of beaks clicked as they bit down on his helmet!

Automatically, he shoved at the thing, and under the force of his blow the dekaped lost its bite and went rolling on the floor, a bundle of thrashing legs.

Lane did not worry about having hurt it. It did not weigh much, but its body must be tough to be able to plunge without damage from the heavy air inside the tube into the almost-stratospheric conditions outside.

However, he did reach for the knife at his belt. But the biped put its hand on his arm and shook one of its heads.

Later, he was to find out that the seeming bite must have been an accident. Always—with one exception—the leggers were to ignore him.

He was also to find that he was lucky. The leggers had come out to inspect their garden because, through some unknown method of detection, they knew that the plantlets had been disturbed. The biped normally would not have accompanied them. However, today, its curiosity aroused because the leggers had gone out three times in three days, it had decided to investigate.

The biped turned out its flashlight and motioned to Lane to

follow. Awkwardly, he obeyed. There was light, but it was dim, a twilight. Its source was the many creatures that hung from the ceiling of the tube. These were three feet long and six inches thick, cylindrical, pinkish-skinned, and eyeless. A dozen frondlike limbs waved continuously, and their motion kept air circulating in the tunnel.

Their cold firefly glow came from two globular pulsing organs which hung from both sides of the round loose-lipped mouth at the free end of the creature. Slime drooled from the mouth, and dripped onto the floor or into a narrow channel which ran along the lowest part of the sloping floor. Water ran in the six-inch deep channel, the first native water he had seen. The water picked up the slime and carried it a little way before it was gulped up by an animal that lay on the bottom of the channel.

Lane's eyes adjusted to the dimness until he could make out the water-dweller. It was torpedo-shaped and without eyes or fins. It had two openings in its body; one obviously sucked in water, the other expelled it.

He saw at once what this meant. The water at the North Pole melted in the summertime and flowed into the far end of the tube system. Helped by gravity and by the pumping action of the line of animals in the channel, the water was passed from the edge of the Pole to the equator.

Leggers ran by him on mysterious errands. Several, however, halted beneath some of the downhanging organisms. They reared up on their hind five legs and their tongues shot out and into the open mouths by the glowing balls. At once, the fireworm—as Lane termed it—its cilia waving wildly, stretched itself to twice its former length. Its mouth met the beak of the legger, and there was an exchange of stuff between their mouths.

Impatiently, the biped tugged at Lane's arm. He followed it down the tube. Soon they entered a section where pale roots came down out of holes in the ceiling and spread along the curving walls, gripping them, then becoming a network of many thread-thin rootlets that crept across the floor and into the water of the channel.

Here and there a dekaped chewed at a root and then hurried off to offer a piece to the mouths of the fireworms.

After walking for several minutes, the biped stepped across the stream. It then began walking as closely as possible to the wall, meanwhile looking apprehensively at the other side of the tunnel, where they had been walking.

Lane also looked but could see nothing at which to be alarmed. There was a large opening at the base of the wall which evidently led into a tunnel. This tunnel, he presumed, ran underground into a room or rooms, for many leggers dashed in and out of it. And about a dozen, larger than average, paced back and forth like sentries before the hole.

When they had gone about fifty yards past the opening, the biped relaxed. After it had led Lane along for ten minutes, it stopped. Its naked hand touched the wall. He became aware that the hand was small and delicately shaped, like a woman's.

A section of the wall swung out. The biped turned and bent down to crawl into the hole, presenting buttocks and legs femininely rounded, well shaped. It was then that he began thinking of it as a female. Yet the hips, though padded with fatty tissue, were not broad. The bones were not widely separated to make room to carry a child. Despite their curving, the hips were relatively as narrow as a man's.

Behind them, the plug swung shut. The biped did not turn on her flashlight, for there was illumination at the end of the tunnel. The floor and walls were not of the hard gray stuff nor of packed earth. They seemed vitrified, as if glassed by heat.

She was waiting for him when he slid off a three-foot high ledge into a large room. For a minute he was blinded by the strong light. After his eyes adjusted, he searched for the source of light but could not find it. He did observe that there were no shadows in the room.

The biped took off her helmet and suit and hung them in a closet. The door slid open as she approached and closed when she walked away.

She signaled that he could remove his suit. He did not hesitate. Though the air might be poisonous, he had no choice. His tank would soon be empty. Moreover, it seemed likely that the atmosphere contained enough oxygen. Even then he had grasped the idea that the leaves of the umbrella plants, which grew out of the top of the tubes, absorbed sunlight and traces of carbon dioxide. Inside the tunnels, the roots drew up water from the channel and absorbed the great quantity of carbon dioxide released by the dekapeds. Energy of sunlight converted gas and liquid into glucose and oxygen, which were given off in the tunnels.

Even here, in this deep chamber which lay beneath and to one side of the tube, a thick root penetrated the ceiling and spread its thin white web over the walls. He stood directly beneath the fleshy growth as he removed his helmet and took his first breath of Martian air. Immediately afterward, he jumped. Something wet had dropped on his forehead. Looking up, he saw that the root was excreting liquid from a large pore. He wiped the drop off with his finger and tasted it. It was sticky and sweet.

Well, he thought, the tree must normally drop sugar in water. But it seemed to be doing so abnormally fast, because another drop was forming.

Then it came to him that perhaps this was so because it was getting dark outside and therefore cold. The umbrella trees might be pumping the water in their trunks into the warm tunnels. Thus, during the bitter subzero night, they'd avoid freezing and swelling up and cracking wide open.

It seemed a reasonable theory.

He looked around. The place was half living quarters, half biological laboratory. There were beds and tables and chairs and several unidentifiable articles. One was a large black metal box in a corner. From it, at regular intervals, issued a stream of tiny blue bubbles. They rose to the ceiling, growing larger as they did so. On reaching the ceiling they did not stop or burst but simply penetrated the vitrification as if it did not exist.

Lane now knew the origin of the blue globes he had seen appear from the surface of the garden. But their purpose was still obscure.

He wasn't given much time to watch the globes. The biped took a large green ceramic bowl from a cupboard and set it on a table. Lane eyed her curiously, wondering what she was going to do. By now he had seen that the second head belonged to an entirely separate creature. Its slim four-foot length of pinkish skin was coiled about her neck and torso; its tiny flat-faced head turned toward Lane; its snaky light blue eyes glittered. Suddenly, its mouth opened and revealed toothless gums, and its bright red tongue, mammalian, not at all reptilian, thrust out at him.

The biped, paying no attention to the worm's actions, lifted it from her. Gently, cooing a few words in a soft many-voweled language, she placed it in the bowl. It settled inside and looped around the curve, like a snake in a pit.

The biped took a pitcher from the top of a box of red plastic. Though the box was not connected to any visible power source, it seemed to be a stove. The pitcher contained warm water which she poured into the bowl, half filling it. Under the shower, the worm closed its eyes as if it were purring soundless ecstasy.

Then the biped did something that alarmed Lane.

She leaned over the bowl and vomited into it.

He stepped toward her. Forgetting the fact that she couldn't understand him, he said, "Are you sick?"

She revealed human-looking teeth in a smile meant to reassure him, and she walked away from the bowl. He looked at the worm, which had its head dipped into the mess. Suddenly, he felt sick, for he was sure that it was feeding off the mixture. And he was equally certain that she fed the worm regularly with regurgitated food.

It didn't cancel his disgust to reflect that he shouldn't react to her as he would to a Terrestrial. He knew that she was totally alien and that it was inevitable that some of her ways would repel, perhaps even shock him. Rationally, he knew this. But if his brain told him to understand and forgive, his belly said to loathe and reject.

His aversion was not much lessened by a close scrutiny of her as she took a shower in a cubicle set in the wall. She was about five feet tall and slim as a woman should be slim, with delicate bones beneath rounded flesh. Her legs were human; in nylons and high heels they would have been exciting—other things being equal. However, if the shoes had been toeless, her feet would have caused much comment. They had four toes.

Her long beautiful hands had five fingers. These seemed nailless, like the toes, though a closer examination later showed him they did bear rudimentary nails.

She stepped from the cubicle and began toweling herself, though not before she motioned to him to remove his suit and also to shower. He stared intently back at her until she laughed a short embarrassed laugh. It was feminine, not at all deep. Then she spoke.

He closed his eyes and was hearing what he had thought he would not hear for years: a woman's voice. Hers was extraordinary: husky and honeyed at the same time.

But when he opened his eyes, he saw her for what she was. No woman. No man. What? It? No. The impulse to think *her*, *she*, was too strong.

This, despite her lack of mammaries. She had a chest, but no nipples, rudimentary or otherwise. Her chest was a man's, muscled under the layer of fat which subtly curved to give the impression that beneath it...budding breasts?

No, not this creature. She would never suckle her young. She did not even bear them alive, if she *did* bear. Her belly was smooth, undimpled with a navel.

Smooth also was the region between her legs, hairless, unbroken, as innocent of organ as if she were a nymph painted for some Victorian children's book.

It was that sexless joining of the legs that was so horrible. Like the white belly of a frog, thought Lane, shuddering.

At the same time, his curiosity became even stronger. How did this thing mate and reproduce?

Again she laughed and smiled with fleshy pale-red humanly everted lips and wrinkled a short, slightly uptilted nose and ran her hand through thick straight red-gold fur. It was fur, not hair, and it had a slightly oily sheen, like a water-dwelling animal's.

The face itself, though strange, could have passed for human, but only passed. Her cheekbones were very high and protruded upward in an unhuman fashion. Her eyes were dark blue and quite human. This meant nothing. So were an octopus' eyes.

She walked to another closet, and as she went away from him he saw again that though the hips were curved like a woman's they did not sway with the pelvic displacement of the human female.

The door swung momentarily open, revealed the carcasses of several dekapeds, minus their legs, hanging on hooks. She removed one, placed it on a metal table, and out of the cupboard took a saw and several knives and began cutting.

Because he was eager to see the anatomy of the dekaped, he approached the table. She waved him to the shower. Lane removed his suit. When he came to the knife and ax he hesitated, but, afraid she might think him distrustful, he hung up the belt containing his weapons beside the suit. However, he did not take off his clothes because he was determined to view the inner organs of the animal. Later, he would shower.

The legger was not an insect, despite its spidery appearance. Not in the Terrestrial sense, certainly. Neither was it a vertebrate. Its smooth hairless skin was an animal's, as lightly pigmented as a blond Swede's. But, though it had an endoskeleton, it had no backbone. Instead, the body bones formed a round cage. Its thin ribs radiated from a cartilaginous collar which adjoined the back of the head. The ribs curved outward, then in, almost meeting at the posterior. Inside the cage were ventral lung sacs, a relatively large heart, and liver-like and kidney-like organs. Three arteries, instead of the mammalian two, left the heart. He couldn't be sure with such a hurried examination, but it looked as if the dorsal aorta, like some Terrestrial reptiles, carried both pure and impure blood.

There were other things to note. The most extraordinary was that, as far as he could discern, the legger had no digestive system. It seemed to lack both intestines and anus unless you would define as an intestine a sac which ran straight through from the throat halfway into the body. Further, there was nothing he could identify as reproductive organs, though this did not mean that it did not possess them. The creature's long tubular tongue, cut open by the biped, exposed a canal running down the length of tongue from its open tip to the bladder at its base. Apparently these formed part of the excretory system.

Lane wondered what enabled the legger to stand the great pressure differences between the interior of the tube and the Martian surface. At the same time he realized that this ability was no more wonderful than the biological mechanism which gave whales and seals the power to endure without harm the enormous pressures a half mile below the sea's surface.

The biped looked at him with round and very pretty blue eyes, laughed, and then reached into the chopped open skull and brought out the tiny brain.

"Hauaimi," she said slowly. She pointed to her head, repeated, *"Hauaimi,"* and then indicated his head. *"Hauaimi."*

Echoing her, he pointed at his own head. *"Hauaimi.* Brain."

"Brain," she said, and she laughed again.

She proceeded to call out the organs of the legger which corresponded to hers. Thus, the preparations for the meal passed swiftly as he proceeded from the carcass to other objects in the room. By the time she had fried the meat and boiled strips of the membranous leaf of the umbrella plant, and also added from cans various exotic foods, she had exchanged at least forty words with him. An hour later, he could remember twenty.

There was one thing yet to learn. He pointed to himself and said, "Lane."

Then he pointed to her and gave her a questioning look.

"Mahrseeya," she said.

"Martia?" he repeated. She corrected him, but he was so struck by the resemblance that always afterward he called her that. After a while, she would give up trying to teach him the exact pronunciation.

Martia washed her hands and poured him a bowlful of water. He used the soap and towel she handed him, then walked to the table where she stood waiting. On it was a bowl of thick soup, a plate of fried brains, a salad of boiled leaves and some unidentifiable vegetables, a plate of ribs with thick dark legger meat, hard-boiled eggs, and little loaves of bread.

Martia gestured for him to sit down. Evidently her code did not allow her to sit down before her guest did. He ignored his chair, went behind her, put his hand on her shoulder, pressed down, and with the other hand slid her chair under her. She turned her head to smile up at him. Her fur slid away to reveal one lobeless pointed ear. He scarcely noticed it, for he was too intent on the half-repulsive, half heart-quickening sensation he got when he touched her skin. It had not been the skin itself that caused that, for she was soft and warm as a young girl. It had been the *idea* of touching her.

Part of that, he thought as he seated himself, came from her nakedness. Not because it revealed her sex but because it revealed her lack of it. No breasts, no nipples, no navel, no pubic fold or projection. The absence of these seemed wrong, very wrong, unsettling. It was a shameful thing that she had nothing of which to be ashamed.

That's a queer thought, he said to himself. And for no reason, he became warm in the face.

Martia, unnoticing, poured from a tall bottle a glassful of dark wine. He tasted it. It was exquisite, no better than the best Earth had to offer but as good.

Martia took one of the loaves, broke it into two pieces, and handed him one. Holding the glass of wine in one hand and the bread in the other, she bowed her head, closed her eyes, and began chanting.

He stared at her. This was a prayer, a grace-saying. Was it the prelude to a sort of communion, one so like Earth's it was startling?

Yet, if it were, he needn't be surprised. Flesh and blood, bread and wine: the symbolism was simple, logical, and might even be universal.

However, it was possible that he was creating parallels that did not exist. She might be enacting a ritual whose origin and meaning were like nothing of which he had ever dreamed.

If so, what she did next was equally capable of misinterpretation. She nibbled at the bread, sipped the wine, and then plainly invited him to do the same. He did so. Martia took a third and empty cup, spat a piece of wine-moistened bread into the cup, and indicated that he was to imitate her.

After he did, he felt his stomach draw in on itself. For she mixed the stuff from their mouths with her finger and then offered it to him. Evidently, he was to put the finger in his mouth and eat from it.

So the action was both physical and metaphysical. The bread and the wine were the flesh and blood of whatever divinity she worshiped. More, she, being imbued with the body and the spirit of the god, now wanted to mingle hers and that of the god's with his.

What I eat of the god's, I become. What you eat of me, you become. What I eat of you, I become. Now we three are become one.

Lane, far from being repelled by the concept, was excited. He knew that there were probably many Christians who would have refused to share in the communion because the ritual did not have the same origins or conform to theirs. They might even have thought that by sharing they were subscribing to an alien god. Such an idea Lane considered to be not only narrow-minded and inflexible, but illogical, uncharitable, and ridiculous. There could be but one Creator; what names the creature gave to the Creator did not matter.

Lane believed sincerely in a personal god, one who took note of him as an individual. He also believed that mankind needed redeeming and that a redeemer had been sent to Earth. And if other worlds needed redeeming, then they too would have gotten or would get a redeemer. He went perhaps further than most of his fellow religionists, for he actually made an attempt to practice love for mankind. This had given him somewhat of a reputation as a fanatic among his acquaintances and friends. However, he had been restrained enough not to make himself too much of a nuisance, and his genuine warmheartedness had made him welcome in spite of his eccentricity.

Six years before, he had been an agnostic. His first trip into space had converted him. The overwhelming experience had made him realize shatteringly what an insignificant being he was, how awe-inspiringly complicated and immense was the universe, and how much he needed a framework within which to be and to become.

The strangest feature about his conversion, he thought afterward, was that one of his companions on that maiden trip had been a devout believer who, on returning to Earth, had renounced his own sect and faith and become a complete atheist.

He thought of this as he took her proffered finger in his mouth and sucked the paste off it.

Then obeying her gestures, he dipped his own finger into the bowl and put it between her lips.

She closed her eyes and gently mouthed the finger. When he began to withdraw it, he was stopped by her hand on his wrist. He did not insist on taking the finger out, for he wanted to avoid offending her. Perhaps a long time interval was part of the rite.

But her expression seemed so eager and at the same time so ecstatic, like a hungry baby just given the nipple, that he felt uneasy. After a minute, seeing no indication on her part that she meant to quit, he slowly but firmly pulled the finger loose. She opened her eyes and sighed, but she made no comment. Instead, she began serving his supper.

The hot thick soup was delicious and invigorating. Its texture was somewhat like the plankton soup that was becoming popular on hungry Earth, but it had no fishy flavor. The brown bread reminded him of rye. The legger meat was like wild rabbit, though it was sweeter and had an unidentifiable tang. He took only one bite of the leaf salad and then frantically poured wine down his throat to wash away the burn. Tears came to his eyes, and he coughed until she spoke to him in an alarmed tone. He smiled back at her but refused to touch the salad again. The wine not only cooled his mouth, it filled his veins with singing. He told himself he should take no more. Nevertheless, he finished his second cup before he remembered his resolve to be temperate.

By then it was too late. The strong liquor went straight to his head; he felt dizzy and wanted to laugh. The events of the day, his near-escape from death, the reaction to knowing his comrades were dead, his realization of his present situation, the tension caused by his encounters with the dekapeds, and his unsatisfied curiosity about Martia's origins and the location of others of her kind, all these combined to produce in him a half-stupor, half-exuberance.

He rose from the table and offered to help Martia with the dishes. She shook her head and put the dishes in a washer. In the meantime, he decided that he needed to wash off the sweat, stickiness, and body odor left by two days of travel. On opening the door to the shower cubicle, he found that there wasn't room enough to hang his clothes in it. So, uninhibited by fatigue and wine, also mindful that Martia, after all, was *not* a female, he removed his clothes.

Martia watched him, and her eyes became wider with each garment shed. Finally, she gasped and stepped back and turned pale.

"It's not that bad," he growled, wondering what had caused her reaction. "After all, some of the things I've seen around here aren't too easy to swallow."

She pointed with a trembling finger and asked him something in a shaky voice.

Perhaps it was his imagination, but he could swear she used the same inflection as would an English speaker.

"Are you sick? Are the growths malignant?"

He had no words with which to explain, nor did he intend to illustrate function through action. Instead, he closed the door of the cubicle after him and pressed the plate that turned on the water. The heat of the shower and the feel of the soap, of grime and sweat being washed away, soothed him somewhat, so that he could think about matters he had been too rushed to consider.

First, he would have to learn Martia's language or teach her his. Probably both would happen at the same time. Of one thing he was sure. That was that her intentions toward him were, at least at present, peaceful. When she had shared communion with him, she had been sincere. He did not get the impression that it was part of her cultural training to share bread and wine with a person she intended to kill.

Feeling better, though still tired and a little drunk, he left the cubicle. Reluctantly, he reached for his dirty shorts. Then he smiled. They had been cleaned while he was in the shower. Martia, however, paid no attention to his smile of pleased surprise but, grim-faced, she motioned to him to lie down on the bed and sleep. Instead of lying down herself, however, she picked up a bucket and began crawling up the tunnel. He decided to follow her, and, when she saw him, she only shrugged her shoulders.

On emerging into the tube, Martia turned on her flashlight. The tunnel was in absolute darkness. Her beam playing on the ceiling, showed that the glowworms had turned out their lights. There were no leggers in sight.

She pointed the light at the channel so he could see that the jetfish were still taking in and expelling water. Before she could turn the beam aside, he put his hand on her wrist and with his other hand lifted a fish from the channel. He had to pull it loose with an effort, which was explained when he turned the torpedo-shaped creature over and saw the column of flesh hanging from its belly. Now he knew why the reaction of the propelled water did not shoot them backward. The ventral-foot acted as a suction pad to hold them to the floor of the channel.

Somewhat impatiently, Martia pulled away from him and began walking swiftly back up the tunnel. He followed her until she came to the opening in the wall which had earlier made her so apprehensive. Crouching, she entered the opening, but before she had gone far she had to move a tangled heap of leggers to one side. There were the large great-beaked ones he had seen guarding the entrance. Now they were asleep at the post.

If so, he reasoned, then the thing they guarded against must also be asleep.

What about Martia? How did she fit into their picture? Perhaps she didn't fit into their picture at all. She was absolutely alien, something for which their instinctual intelligence was not prepared and which, therefore, they ignored. That would explain why they had paid no attention to him when he was mired in the garden.

Yet there must be an exception to that rule. Certainly Martia had not wanted to attract the sentinels' notice the first time she had passed the entrance.

A moment later he found out why. They stepped into a huge chamber which was at least two hundred feet square. It was as dark as the tube, but during the walking period it must have been very bright because the ceiling was jammed with glowworms.

Martia's flash raced around the chamber, showing him the piles of sleeping leggers. Then, suddenly, it stopped. He took one look, and his heart raced, and the hairs on the back of his neck rose.

Before him was a worm three feet high and twenty feet long.

Without thinking, he grabbed hold of Martia to keep her from coming closer to it. But even as he touched her, he dropped his hand. She must know what she was doing.

Martia pointed the flash at her own face and smiled as if

My Sister's Brother

to tell him not to be alarmed. And she touched his arm with a shyly affectionate gesture.

For a moment, he didn't know why. Then it came to him that she was glad because he had been thinking of her welfare. Moreover, her reaction showed she had recovered from her shock at seeing him unclothed.

He turned from her to examine the monster. It lay on the floor, asleep, its great eyes closed behind vertical slits. It had a huge head, football-shaped like those of the little leggers around it. Its mouth was big, but the beaks were very small, horny warts on its lips. The body, however, was that of a caterpillar worm's, minus the hair. Ten little useless legs stuck out of its side, too short even to reach the floor. Its side bulged as if pumped full of gas.

Martia walked past the monster and paused by its posterior. Here she lifted up a fold of skin. Beneath it was a pile of a dozen leathery-skinned eggs, held together by a sticky secretion.

"Now I've got it," muttered Lane. "Of course. The egg-laying queen. She specializes in reproduction. That is why the others have no reproductive organs, or else they're so rudimentary I couldn't detect them. The leggers are animals, all right, but in some things they resemble Terrestrial insects.

"Still, that doesn't explain the absence also of a digestive system."

Martia put the eggs in her bucket and started to leave the room. He stopped her and indicated he wanted to look around some more. She shrugged and began to lead him around. Both had to be careful not to step on the dekapeds, which lay everywhere.

They came to an open bin made of the same gray stuff as the walls. Its interior held many shelves, on which lay hundreds of eggs. Strands of the spiderwebby stuff kept the eggs from rolling off.

Nearby was another bin that held water. At its bottom lay more eggs. Above them minnow-sized torpedo shapes flitted about in the water.

Lane's eyes widened at this. The fish were not members of another genus but were the larvae of the leggers. And they could be set in the channel not only to earn their keep by pumping water which came down from the North Pole but to grow until they were ready to metamorphose into the adult stage.

However, Martia showed him another bin which made him partially revise his first theory. This bin was dry, and the eggs were laid on the floor. Martia picked one up, cut its tough skin open with her knife, and emptied its contents into one hand.

Now his eyes did get wide. This creature had a tiny cylindrical body, a suction pad at one end, a round mouth at the other, and two globular organs hanging by the mouth. A young glowworm.

Martia looked at him to see if he comprehended. Lane held out his hands and hunched his shoulders with an I-don't-get-it air. Beckoning, she walked to another bin to show him more eggs. Some had been ripped from within, and the little fellows whose hard beaks had done it were staggering around weakly on ten legs.

Energetically, Martia went through a series of charades. Watching her, he began to understand.

The embryos that remained in the egg until they fully developed went through three main metamorphoses: the jetfish stage, the glowworm stage, and finally the baby dekaped stage. If the eggs were torn open by the adult nurses in one of the first two stages, the embryo remained fixed in that form, though it did grow larger.

What about the queen? he asked her by pointing to the monstrously egg-swollen body.

For answer, Martia picked up one of the newly-hatched. It kicked its many legs but did not otherwise protest, being, like all its kind, mute. Martia turned it upside down and indicated a slight crease in its posterior. Then she showed him the same spot on one of the sleeping adults. The adult's rear was smooth, innocent of the crease.

Martia made eating gestures. He nodded. The creatures were born with rudimentary sexual organs, but these never developed. In fact, they atrophied completely unless the young were given a special diet, in which case they matured into egg-layers.

But the picture wasn't complete. If you had females, you had to have males. It was doubtful if such highly developed animals were self-fertilizing or reproduced parthenogenetically.

Then he remembered Martia and began doubting. She gave no evidence of reproductive organs. Could her kind be self-reproducing? Or was she a martin, her natural fulfillment diverted by diet?

It didn't seem likely, but he couldn't be sure that such things were not possible in her scheme of Nature.

Lane wanted to satisfy his curiosity. Ignoring her desire to get out of the chamber, he examined each of the five baby dekapeds. All were potential females.

Suddenly Martia, who had been gravely watching him, smiled and took his hand, and led him to the rear of the room. Here, as they approached another structure, he smelled a strong odor which reminded him of clorox.

Closer to the structure, he saw that it was not a bin but a hemispherical cage. Its bars were of the hard gray stuff, and they curved up from the floor to meet at the central point. There was no door. Evidently the cage had been built around the thing in it, and its occupant must remain until he died.

Martia soon showed him why this thing was not allowed freedom. It—he—was sleeping, but Martia reached through the bars and struck it on the head with her fist. The thing did not respond until it had been hit five more times. Then, slowly, it opened its sidewise lids to reveal great staring eyes, bright as fresh arterial blood.

Martia threw one of the eggs at the thing's head. Its beak opened swiftly, the egg disappeared, the beak closed, and there was a noisy gulp.

Food brought it to life. It sprang up on its ten long legs, clacked its beak, and lunged against the bars again and again.

Though in no danger, Martia shrank back before the killer's lust in the scarlet eyes. Lane could understand her reaction. It was a giant, at least two feet higher than the sentinels. Its back was on a level with Martia's head; its beaks could have taken her head in between them.

Lane walked around the cage to get a good look at its posterior. Puzzled, he made another circuit without seeing anything of maleness about it except its wild fury, like that of a stallion locked in a barn during mating season. Except for its size, red eyes, and a cloaca, it looked like one of the guards.

He tried to communicate to Martia his puzzlement. By now, she seemed to anticipate his desires. She went through another series of pantomimes, some of which were so energetic and comical that he had to smile.

First, she showed him two eggs on a nearby ledge. These were larger than the others and were speckled with red spots. Supposedly, they held male embryos.

Then she showed him what would happen if the adult male got loose. Making a face which was designed to be ferocious but only amused him, clicking her teeth and clawing with her hands, she imitated the male running amok. He would kill everybody in sight. Everybody, the whole colony, queen, workers, guards, larvae, eggs, bite off their heads, mangle them, eat them all up, all, all. And out of the slaughterhouse he would charge into the tube and kill every legger he met, devour the jetfish, drag down the glowworms from the ceiling, rip them apart, eat them, eat the roots of the trees. Kill, kill, kill, eat, eat, eat!

That was all very well, sighed Lane. But how did...?

Martia indicated that, once a day, the workers rolled, literally rolled the queen across the room to the cage. There they arranged her so that she presented her posterior some few inches from the bars and the enraged male. And the male, though he wanted to do nothing but get his beak into her flesh and tear her apart, was not master of himself. Nature took over; his will was betrayed by his nervous system.

Lane nodded to show he understood. In his mind was a picture of the legger that had been butchered. It had had one sac at the internal end of the tongue. Probably the male had two, one to hold excretory matter, the other to hold seminal fluid.

Suddenly Martia froze, her hands held out before her. She had laid the flashlight on the floor so she could act freely; the beam splashed on her paling skin.

"What is it?" said Lane, stepping toward her.

Martia retreated, holding out her hands before her. She looked horrified.

"I'm not going to harm you," he said. However, he stopped so she could see he didn't mean to get any closer to her.

What was bothering her? Nothing was stirring in the chamber itself besides the male, and he was behind her.

Then she was pointing, first at him and then at the raging dekaped. Seeing this unmistakable signal of identification, he comprehended. She had perceived that he, like the thing in the cage, was male, and now she perceived structure and function in him.

What he didn't understand was why that should make her so frightened of him. Repelled, yes. Her body, its seeming lack of sex, had given him a feeling of distaste bordering on nausea. It was only natural that she should react similarly to his body. However, she had seemed to have gotten over her first shock.

Why this unexpected change, this horror of him?

Behind him, the beak of the male clicked as it lunged against the bars.

The click echoed in his mind.

Of course, the monster's lust to kill!

Until she had met him, she had known only one male creature. That was the caged thing. Now, suddenly, she had equated him with the monster. A male was a killer.

Desperately, because he was afraid that she was about to run in panic out of the room, he made signs that he was not like this monster; he shook his head no, no, no. He wasn't, he wasn't, he wasn't!

Martia, watching him intently, began to relax. Her skin regained its pinkish hue. Her eyes became their normal size. She even managed a strained smile.

To get her mind off the subject, he indicated that he would like to know why the queen and her consort had digestive systems, though the workers did not. For answer, she reached up into the downhanging mouth of the worm suspended from the ceiling. Her hand, withdrawn, was covered with secretion. After smelling her fist, she gave it to him to sniff also. He took it, ignoring her slight and probably involuntary flinching when she felt his touch.

The stuff had an odor such as you would expect from pre-digested food.

Martia then went to another worm. The two light organs of this one were not colored red, like the others, but had a greenish tint. Martia tickled its tongue with her finger and held out her cupped hands. Liquid trickled into the cup.

Lane smelled the stuff. No odor. When he drank the liquid, he discovered it to be a thick sugar water.

Martia pantomimed that the glowworms acted as the digestive systems for the workers. They also stored food away for them. The workers derived part of their energy from the glucose excreted by the roots of the trees. The proteins and vegetable matter in their diet originated from the eggs and from the leaves of the umbrella plant. Strips of the tough membranous leaf were brought into the tubes by harvesting parties which ventured forth in the daytime. The worms partially digested the eggs, dead leggers, and leaves and gave it back in the form of a soup. The soup, like the glucose, was swallowed by the workers and passed through the walls of their throats or into the long straight sac which connected the throat to the larger blood vessels. The waste products were excreted through the skin or emptied through the canal in the tongue.

Lane nodded and then walked out of the room. Seemingly relieved, Martia followed him. When they had crawled back into her quarters, she put the eggs in a refrigerator and poured two glasses of wine. She dipped her finger in both, then touched the finger to her lips and to his. Lightly, he touched the tip with his tongue. This, he gathered, was one more ritual, perhaps a bedtime one, which affirmed that they were at one and at peace. It might be that it had an even deeper meaning, but if so, it escaped him.

Martia checked on the safety and comfort of the worm in the bowl. By now it had eaten all its food. She removed the worm, washed it, washed the bowl, half filled it with warm sugar water, placed it on the table by the bed, and put the creature back in. Then she lay down on the bed and closed her eyes. She did not cover herself and apparently did not expect him to expect a cover.

Lane, tired though he was, could not rest. Like a tiger in its cage, he paced back and forth. He could not keep out of his mind the enigma of Martia nor the problem of getting back to base and eventually to the orbital ship. Earth must know what had happened.

After half an hour of this, Martia sat up. She looked steadily at him as if trying to discover the cause of his sleeplessness. Then, apparently sensing what was wrong, she rose and opened a cabinet hanging down from the wall. Inside were a number of books.

Lane said, "Ah, maybe I'll get some information now!" and he leafed through them all. Wild with eagerness, he chose three and piled them on the bed before sitting down to peruse them.

Naturally, he could not read the texts, but the three had many illustrations and photographs. The first volume seemed to be a child's world history.

Lane looked at the first few pictures. Then he said, hoarsely, "My God, you're no more Martian than I am!"

Martia, startled by the wonder and urgency in his voice, came over to his bed and sat down by him. She watched while he turned the pages over until he reached a certain photo. Unexpectedly, she buried her face in her hands, and her body shook with deep sobs.

Lane was surprised. He wasn't sure why she was in such grief. The photo was an aerial view of a city on her home planet—or some planet on which her people lived. Perhaps it was the city in which she had—somehow—been born.

It wasn't long, however, before her sorrow began to stir a response in him. Without any warning he, too, was weeping.

Now he knew. It was loneliness, appalling loneliness, of the kind he had known when he had received no more word from the men in the tanks and he had believed himself the only human being on the face of this world.

After a while, the tears dried. He felt better and wished she would also be relieved. Apparently she perceived his sympathy, for she smiled at him through her tears. And in an irresistible gust of rapport and affection she kissed his hand and then stuck two of his fingers in her mouth. This, he thought, must be her way of expressing friendship. Or perhaps it was gratitude for his presence. Or just sheer joy. In any event, he thought, her society must have a high oral orientation.

"Poor Martia," he murmured. "It must be a terrible thing to have to turn to one as alien and weird as I must seem. Especially to one who, a little while ago, you weren't sure wasn't going to eat you up."

He removed his fingers but, seeing her rejected look, he impulsively took hers in his mouth.

Strangely, this caused another burst of weeping. However, he quickly saw that it was happy weeping. After it was over, she laughed softly, as if pleased.

Lane took a towel and wiped her eyes and held it over her nose while she blew.

Now, strengthened, she was able to point out certain illustrations and by signs give him clues to what they meant.

This child's book started with an account of the dawn of life on her planet. The planet revolved around a star that, according to a simplified map, was in the center of the Galaxy.

Life had begun there much as it had on Earth. It had developed in its early stages on somewhat the same lines. But there were some rather disturbing pictures of primitive fish life. Lane wasn't sure of his interpretation, however, for these took much for granted.

They did show plainly that evolution there had picked out biological mechanisms with which to advance different from those on Earth.

Fascinated, he traced the passage from fish to amphibian to reptile to warm-blooded but non-mammalian creature to an upright ground-dwelling apelike creature to beings like Martia.

Then the pictures depicted various aspects of this being's

prehistoric life. Later, the invention of agriculture, working of metals, and so on.

The history of civilization was a series of pictures whose meaning he could seldom grasp. One thing was unlike Earth's history. There was a relative absence of warfare. The Rameseses, Genghis Khans, Attilas, Caesars, Hitlers, seemed to be missing.

But there was more, much more. Technology advanced much as it had on Earth, despite a lack of stimulation from war. Perhaps, he thought, it had started sooner than on his planet. He got the impression that Martia's people had evolved to their present state much earlier than Homo sapiens.

Whether that was true or not, they now surpassed man. They could travel almost as fast as light, perhaps faster, and had mastered interstellar travel.

It was then that Martia pointed to a page which bore several photographs of Earth, obviously taken at various distances by a spaceship.

Behind them an artist had drawn a shadowy figure, half-ape, half-dragon.

"Earth means this to you?" Lane said. *"Danger? Do not touch?"*

He looked for other photos of Earth. There were many pages dealing with other planets but only one of his home. That was enough.

"Why are you keeping us under distant surveillance?" said Lane. "You're so far ahead of us that, technologically speaking, we're Australian aborigines. What're you afraid of?"

Martia stood up, facing him. Suddenly, viciously, she snarled and clicked her teeth and hooked her hands into claws.

He felt a chill. This was the same pantomime she had used when demonstrating the mindless kill-craziness of the caged male legger.

He bowed his head. "I can't really blame you. You're absolutely correct. If you contacted us, we'd steal your secrets. And then, look out! We'd infest all of space!"

He paused, bit his lip, and said, "Yet we're showing some signs of progress. There's not been a war or a revolution for fifteen years; the UN has been settling problems that would once have resulted in a world war; Russia and the U.S. are still armed but are not nearly as close to conflict as they were when I was born. Perhaps...?

"Do you know, I bet you've never seen an Earthman in the

flesh before. Perhaps you've never seen a picture of one, or if you did, they were clothed. There are no photos of Earth people in these books. Maybe you knew we were male and female, but that didn't mean much until you saw me taking a shower. And the suddenly revealed parallel between the male dekaped and myself horrified you. And you realized that this was the only thing in the world that you had for companionship. Almost as if I'd been shipwrecked on an island and found the other inhabitant was a tiger.

"But that doesn't explain what you are doing here, alone, living in these tubes among the indigenous Martians. Oh, how I wish I could talk to you!

"With thee conversing," he said, remembering those lines he had read the last night in the base.

She smiled at him, and he said, "Well, at least you're getting over your scare. I'm not such a bad fellow, after all, heh?"

She smiled again and went to a cabinet and from it took paper and pen. With them, she made one simple sketch after another. Watching her agile pen, he began to see what had happened.

Her people had had a base for a long time—a long long time—on the side of the Moon the Terrestrials could not see. But when rockets from Earth had first penetrated into space, her people had obliterated all evidences of the base. A new one had been set up on Mars.

Then, as it became apparent that a Terrestrial expedition would be sent to Mars, that base had been destroyed and another one set up on Ganymede.

However, five scientists had remained behind in these simple quarters to complete their studies of the dekapeds. Though Martia's people had studied these creatures for some time, they still had not found out how their bodies could endure the differences between tube pressure and that in the open air. The four believed that they were breathing hot on the neck of this secret and had gotten permission to stay until just before the Earthmen landed.

Martia actually was a native, in the sense that she had been born and raised here. She had been seven years here, she indicated, showing a sketch of Mars in its orbit around the sun and then holding up seven fingers.

That made her about fourteen Earth years old, Lane estimated. Perhaps these people reached maturity a little faster than his. That is, if she were mature. It was difficult to tell.

Horror twisted her face and widened her eyes as she showed him what had happened the night before they were to leave for Ganymede.

The sleeping party had been attacked by an uncaged male legger.

It was rare that a male got loose. But he occasionally managed to escape. When he did, he destroyed the entire colony, all life in the tube wherever he went. He even ate the roots of the trees so that they died, and oxygen ceased to flow into that section of the tunnel.

There was only one way a forewarned colony could fight a rogue male—a dangerous method. That was to release their own male. They selected the few who would stay behind and sacrifice their lives to dissolve the bars with an acid secretion from their bodies while the others fled. The queen, unable to move, also died. But enough of her eggs were taken to produce another queen and another consort elsewhere.

Meanwhile, it was hoped that the males would kill each other or that the victor would be so crippled that he could be finished off by the soldiers.

Lane nodded. The only natural enemy of the dekapeds was an escaped male. Left unchecked, they would soon crowd the tubes and exhaust food and air. Unkind as it seemed, the escape of a male now and then was the only thing that saved the Martians from starvation and perhaps extinction.

However that might be, the rogue had been no blessing in disguise for Martia's people. Three had been killed in their sleep before the other two awoke. One had thrown herself at the beast and shouted to Martia to escape.

Almost insane with fear, Martia had nevertheless not allowed panic to send her running. Instead, she had dived for a cabinet to get a weapon.

—A weapon, thought Lane. I'll have to find out about that.

Martia acted out what had happened. She had gotten the cabinet door open and reached in for the weapon when she felt the beak of the rogue fastening on her leg. Despite the shock, for the beak cut deeply into the blood vessels and muscles, she managed to press the end of the weapon against the male's body. The weapon did its work, for the male dropped on the floor. Unfortunately, the beaks did not relax but held their terrible grip on her thigh, just above the knee.

Here Lane tried to interrupt so he could get a description of what the weapon looked like and of the principle of its operation. Martia, however, ignored his request. Seemingly, she did not understand his question, but he was sure that she did not care to reply. He was not entirely trusted, which was understandable. How could he blame her? She would be a fool to be at ease with such an unknown quantity as himself. That is, if he were unknown. After all, though she did not know him well personally, she knew the kind of people from whom he came and what could be expected from them. It was surprising that she had not left him to die in the garden, and it was amazing that she had shared that communion of bread and wine with him.

Perhaps, he thought, it is because she was so lonely and any company was better than nothing. Or it might be that she acted on a higher ethical plane than most Earthmen and she could not endure the idea of leaving a fellow sentient being to die, even if she thought him a bloodthirsty savage.

Or she might have other plans for him, such as taking him prisoner.

Martia continued her story. She had fainted and some time later had awakened. The male was beginning to stir, so she had killed him this time.

One more item of information, thought Lane. The weapon is capable of inflicting degrees of damage.

Then, though she kept passing out, she had dragged herself to the medicine chest and treated herself. Within two days she was up and hobbling around, and the scars were beginning to fade.

They must be far ahead of us in everything, he thought. According to her, some of her muscles had been cut. Yet they grew together in a day.

Martia indicated that the repair of her body had required an enormous amount of food during the healing. Most of her time had been spent in eating and sleeping. Reconstruction, even if it took place at a normal accelerated rate, still required the same amount of energy.

By then the bodies of the male and of her companions were stinking with decay. She had had to force herself to cut them up and dispose of them in the garbage burner.

Tears welled in her eyes as she recounted this, and she sobbed.

Lane wanted to ask her why she had not buried them, but he reconsidered. Though it might not be the custom among her kind to bury the dead, it was more probable that she wanted to destroy all evidence of their existence before Earthmen came to Mars.

Using signs, he asked her how the male had gotten into the room despite the gate across the tunnel. She indicated that the gate was ordinarily closed only when the dekapeds were awake or when her companions and she were sleeping. But it had been the turn of one of their number to collect eggs in the queen's chamber. As she reconstructed it, the rogue had appeared at that time and killed the scientist there. Then, after ravening among the still-sleeping colony, it had gone down the tube and there had seen the light shining from the open tunnel. The rest of the story he knew.

Why, he pantomimed, why didn't the escaped male sleep when all his fellows did? The one in the cage evidently slept at the same time as his companions. And the queen's guards also slept in the belief they were safe from attack.

Not so, replied Martia. A male who had gotten out of a cage knew no law but fatigue. When he had exhausted himself in his eating and killing, he lay down to sleep. But it did not matter if it was the regular time for it or not. When he was rested, he raged through the tubes and did not stop until he was again too tired to move.

So then, thought Lane, that explains the area of dead umbrella plans on top of the tube by the garden. Another colony moved into the devastated area, built the garden on the outside, and planted the young umbrellas.

He wondered why neither he nor the others of his group had seen the dekapeds outside during their six days on Mars. There must be at least one pressure chamber and outlet for each colony, and there should be at least fifteen colonies in the tubes between this point and that near his base. Perhaps the answer was that the leaf-croppers only ventured out occasionally. Now that he remembered it, neither he nor anyone else had noticed any holes on the leaves. That meant that the trees must have been cropped some time ago and were now ready for another harvesting. If the expedition had only waited several days before sending out men in tracs, it might have seen the dekapeds and investigated. And the story would have been different.

There were other questions he had for her. What about the vessel that was to take them to Ganymede? Was there one hidden on the outside, or was one to be sent to pick them up? If one was to be sent, how would the Ganymedan base be contacted? Radio? Or some—to him—inconceivable method?

My Sister's Brother

The blue globes! he thought. Could they be means of transmitting messages?

He did not know or think further about them because fatigue overwhelmed him, and he fell asleep. His last memory was that of Martia leaning over him and smiling at him.

When he awoke reluctantly, his muscles ached, and his mouth was as dry as the Martian desert. He rose in time to see Martia drop out of the tunnel, a bucket of eggs in her hand. Seeing this, he groaned. That meant she had gone into the nursery again, and that he had slept the clock around.

He stumbled up and into the shower cubicle. Coming out much refreshed, he found breakfast hot on the table. Martia conducted the communion rite, and then they ate. He missed his coffee. The hot soup was good but did not make a satisfactory substitute. There was a bowl of mixed cereal and fruit, both of which came out of a can. It must have had a high energy content, for it made him wide awake.

Afterward, he did some setting-up exercises while she did the dishes. Though he kept his body busy, he was thinking of things unconnected with what he was doing.

What was to be his next move?

His duty demanded that he return to the base and report. What news he would send to the orbital ship! The story would flash from the ship back to Earth. The whole planet would be in an uproar.

There was one objection to his plan to take Martia back with him.

She would not want to go.

Halfway in a deep knee bend, he stopped. What a fool he was! He had been too tired and confused to see it. But if she had revealed that the base of her people was on Ganymede, she did not expect him to take the information back to his transmitter. It would be foolish on her part to tell him unless she were absolutely certain that he would be able to communicate with no one.

That must mean that a vessel was on its way and would arrive soon. And it would not only take her but him. If he was to be killed, he would be dead now.

Lane had not been chosen to be a member of the first Mars expedition because he lacked decision. Five minutes later, he had made up his mind. His duty was clear. Therefore, he would carry it out, even if it violated his personal feelings toward Martia and caused her injury.

First, he'd bind her. Then he would pack up their two pressure suits, the books, and any tools small enough to carry so they might later be examined on Earth. He would make her march ahead of him through the tube until they came to the point opposite his base. There they would don their suits and go out to the dome. And as soon as possible the two would rise on the rocket to the orbital ship. This step was the most hazardous, for it was extremely difficult for one man to pilot the rocket. Theoretically, it could be done. It had to be done.

Lane tightened his jaw and forced his muscles to quit quivering. The thought of violating Martia's hospitality upset him. Still, she had treated him so well for a purpose not altogether altruistic. For all he knew, she was plotting against him.

There was a rope in one of the cabinets, the same flexible rope with which she had pulled him from the mire. He opened the door of the cabinet and removed it. Martia stood in the middle of the room and watched him while she stroked the head of the blue-eyed worm coiled about her shoulders. He hoped she would stay there until he got close. Obviously, she carried no weapon on her nor indeed anything except the pet. Since she had removed her suit, she had worn nothing.

Seeing him approaching her, she spoke to him in an alarmed tone. It didn't take much sensitivity to know that she was asking him what he intended to do with the rope. He tried to smile reassuringly at her and failed. This was making him sick.

A moment later, he was violently sick. Martia had spoken loudly one word, and it was as if it had struck him in the pit of his stomach. Nausea gripped him, his mouth began salivating, and it was only by dropping the rope and running into the shower that he avoided making a mess on the floor.

Ten minutes later, he felt thoroughly cleaned out. But when he tried to walk to the bed, his legs threatened to give way. Martia had to support him.

Inwardly, he cursed. To have a sudden reaction to the strange food at such a crucial moment! Luck was not on his side.

That is, if it was chance. There had been something so strange and forceful about the manner in which she pronounced that word. Was it possible that she had set up in him—hypnotically or otherwise—a reflex to that word? It would, under the conditions, be a weapon more powerful than a gun.

He wasn't sure, but it did seem strange that his body had accepted the alien food until that moment. Hypnotism did not really seem to be the answer. How could it be so easily used on him since he did not know more than twenty words of her language?

Language? Words? They weren't necessary. If she had given him a hypnotic drug in his food, and then had awakened him during his sleep, she could have dramatized how he was to react if she wanted him to do so. She could have given him the key word, then have allowed him to go to sleep again.

He knew enough hypnotism to know that that was possible. Whether his suspicions were true or not, it was a fact that he had laid flat on his back. However, the day was not wasted. He learned twenty more words, and she drew many more sketches for him. He found out that when he had jumped into the mire of the garden he had literally fallen into the soup. The substance in which the young umbrella trees had been planted was a zoogloea, a glutinous mass of one-celled vegetables and somewhat larger anaerobic animal life that fed on the vegetables. The heat from the jam-packed water-swollen bodies kept the garden soil warm and prevented the tender plants from freezing even during the forty degrees below zero Fahrenheit of the midsummer nights.

After the trees were transplanted into the roof of the tube to replace the dead adults, the zoogloea would be taken piecemeal back to the tube and dumped into the channel. Here the jetfish would strain out part and eat part as they pumped water from the polar end of the tube to the equatorial end.

Toward the end of the day, he tried some of the zoogloea soup and managed to keep it down. A little later, he ate some cereal.

Martia insisted on spooning the food for him. There was something so feminine and tender about her solicitude that he could not protest.

"Martia," he said, "I may be wrong. There can be good will and rapport between our two kinds. Look at us. Why, if you were a real woman, I'd be in love with you.

"Of course, you may have made me sick in the first place. But if you did, it was a matter of expediency, not malice. And now you are taking care of me, your enemy. Love thy enemy. Not because you have been told you should but because you do."

She, of course, did not understand him. However, she replied in her own tongue, and it seemed to him that her voice had the same sense of sympático.

As he fell asleep, he was thinking that perhaps Martia and he would be the two ambassadors to bring their people together in peace. After all, both of them were highly civilized, essentially pacifistic, and devoutly religious. There was such a thing as the brotherhood, not only of man, but of all sentient beings throughout the cosmos, and...

Pressure on his bladder woke him up. He opened his eyes. The ceiling and walls expanded and contracted. His wristwatch was distorted. Only by extreme effort could he focus his eyes enough to straighten the arms on his watch. The piece, designed to measure the slightly longer Martian day, indicated midnight.

Groggily, he rose. He felt sure that he must have been drugged and that he would still be sleeping if the bladder pain hadn't been so sharp. If only he could take something to counteract the drug, he could carry out his plans now. But first he had to get to the toilet.

To do so, he had to pass close to Martia's bed. She did not move but lay on her back, her arms flung out and hanging over the sides of the bed, her mouth open wide.

He looked away, for it seemed indecent to watch when she was in such a position.

But something caught his eye—a movement, a flash of light like a gleaming jewel in her mouth.

He bent over her, looked, and recoiled in horror.

A head rose from between her teeth.

He raised his hand to snatch at the thing but froze in the posture as he recognized the tiny pouting round mouth and little blue eyes. It was the worm.

At first, he thought Martia was dead. The thing was not coiled in her mouth. Its body disappeared into her throat.

Then he saw her chest was rising easily and that she seemed to be in no difficulty.

Forcing himself to come close to the worm, though his stomach muscles writhed and his neck muscles quivered, he put his hand close to its lips.

Warm air touched his fingers, and he heard a faint whistling.

Martia was breathing through it!

Hoarsely, he said, "God!" and he shook her shoulder. He did not want to touch the worm because he was afraid that it might do something to injure her. In that moment of shock he had forgotten that he had an advantage over her, which he should use.

Martia's lids opened; her large gray-blue eyes stared blankly.

"Take it easy," he said soothingly.

She shuddered. Her lids closed, her neck arched back, and her face contorted.

He could not tell if the grimace was caused by pain or something else.

"What is this—this monster?" he said. "Symbiote? Parasite?"

He thought of vampires, of worms creeping into one's sleeping body and there sucking blood.

Suddenly, she sat up and held out her arms to him. He seized her hands, saying, "What is it?"

Martia pulled him toward her, at the same time lifting her face to his.

Out of her open mouth shot the worm, its head pointed toward his face, its little lips formed into an O.

It was reflex, the reflex of fear that made Lane drop her hands and spring back. He had not wanted to do that, but he could not help himself.

Abruptly, Martia came wide awake. The worm flopped its full length from her mouth and fell into a heap between her legs. There it thrashed for a moment before coiling itself like a snake, its head resting on Martia's thigh, its eyes turned upward to Lane.

There was no doubt about it. Martia looked disappointed, frustrated.

Lane's knees, already weak, gave way. However, he managed to continue to his destination. When he came out, he walked as far as Martia's bed, where he had to sit down. His heart was thudding against his ribs, and he was panting hard.

He sat behind her, for he did not want to be where the worm could touch him.

Martia made motions for him to go back to his bed and they would all sleep. Evidently, he thought, she found nothing alarming in the incident.

But he knew he could not rest until he had some kind of explanation. He handed her paper and pen from the bedside table and then gestured fiercely. Martia shrugged and began sketching while Lane watched over her shoulder. By the time she had used up five sheets of paper, she had communicated her message.

His eyes were wide, and he was even paler.

So—Martia *was* a female. Female at least in the sense that she carried eggs—and, at times, young—within her.

And there was the so-called worm. So called? What could he call it? It could not be designated under one category. It was many things in one. It was a larva. It was a phallus. It was also her offspring, of her flesh and blood.

But not of her genes. It was not descended from her.

She had given birth to it, yet she was not its mother. She was neither one of its mothers.

The dizziness and confusion he felt was not caused altogether by his sickness. Things were coming too fast. He was thinking furiously, trying to get this new information clear, but his thoughts kept going back and forth, getting nowhere.

"There's no reason to get upset," he told himself. "After all, the splitting of animals into two sexes is only one of the ways of reproduction tried on Earth. On Martia's planet Nature—God—has fashioned another method for the higher animals. And only He knows how many other designs for reproduction He has fashioned on how many other worlds."

Nevertheless, he was upset.

This worm, no, this larva, this embryo outside its egg and its secondary mother... well, call it, once and for all, larva, because it did metamorphose later.

This particular larva was doomed to stay in its present form until it died of old age.

Unless Martia found another adult of the Eeltau.

And unless she and this other adult felt affection for each other.

Then, according to the sketch she'd drawn, Martia and her friend, or lover, would lie down or sit together. They would, as lovers do on Earth, speak to each other in endearing, flattering, and exciting terms. They would caress and kiss much as Terrestrial man and woman do, though on Earth it was not considered complimentary to call one's lover Big Mouth.

Then, unlike the Terran custom, a third would enter the union to form a highly desired and indeed indispensable and eternal triangle.

The larva, blindly, brainlessly obeying its instincts, aroused by mutual fondling by the two, would descend tail first into the throat of one of the two Eeltau. Inside the body of the lover a fleshy valve would open to admit the slim body of the larva.

Its open tip would touch the ovary of the host. The larva, like an electric eel, would release a tiny current. The hostess would go into an ecstasy, its nerves stimulate electrochemically. The ovary would release an egg no larger than a pencil dot. It would disappear into the open tip of the larva's tail, there to begin a journey up a canal toward the center of its body, urged on by the contraction of muscle and whipping of cilia.

Then the larva slid out of the first hostess' mouth and went tail first into the other, there to repeat the process. Sometimes the larva garnered eggs, sometimes not, depending upon whether the ovary had a fully developed one to release.

When the process was successful, the two eggs moved toward each other but did not quite meet.

Not yet.

There must be other eggs collected in the dark incubator of the larva, collected by pairs, though not necessarily from the same couple of donors.

These would number anywhere from twenty to forty pairs.

Then, one day, the mysterious chemistry of the cells would tell the larva's body that it had gathered enough eggs.

A hormone was released, the metamorphosis begun. The larva swelled enormously, and the mother, seeing this, placed it tenderly in a warm place and fed it plenty of predigested food and sugar water.

Before the eyes of its mother, the larva then grew shorter and wider. Its tail contracted; its cartilaginous vertebrae, widely separated in its larval stage, shifted closer to each other and hardened, A skeleton formed, ribs, shoulders. Legs and arms budded and grew and took humanoid shape. Six months passed, and there lay in its crib something resembling a baby of Homo sapiens.

From then until its fourteenth year, the Eeltau grew and developed much as its Terran counterpart.

Adulthood, however, initiated more strange changes. Hormone released hormone until the first pair of gametes, dormant these fourteen years, moved together.

The two fused, the chromatin of one uniting with the chromatin of the other. Out of the two—a single creature, wormlike, four inches long, was released into the stomach of its hostess.

Then, nausea. Vomiting. And so, comparatively painlessly, the bringing forth of a genetically new being.

It was this worm that would be both fetus and phallus and

would give ecstasy and draw into its own body the eggs of loving adults and would metamorphose and become infant, child, and adult.

And so on and so on.

He rose and shakily walked to his own bed. There he sat down, his head bowed, while he muttered to himself.

"Let's see now. Martia gave birth to, brought forth, or up, this larva. But the larva actually doesn't have any of Martia's genes. Martia was just the hostess for it.

"However, if Martia has a lover, she will, by means of this worm, pass on her heritable qualities. This worm will become an adult and bring forth, or up, Martia's child."

He raised his hands in despair.

"How do the Eeltau reckon ancestry? How keep track of their relatives? Or do they care? Wouldn't it be easier to consider your foster mother, your hostess, your real mother? As, in the sense of having borne you, she is?

"And what kind of sexual code do these people have? It can't, I would think, be much like ours. Nor is there any reason why it should be.

"But who is responsible for raising the larva and child? Its pseudo-mother? Or does the lover share in the duties? And what about property and inheritance laws? And, and..."

Helplessly, he looked at Martia.

Fondly stroking the head of the larva, she returned his stare. Lane shook his head.

"I was wrong. Eeltau and Terran couldn't meet on a friendly basis. My people would react to yours as to disgusting vermin. Their deepest prejudices would be aroused, their strongest taboos would be violated. They could not learn to live with you or consider you even faintly human.

"And as far as that goes, could you live with us? Wasn't the sight of me naked a shock? Is that reaction a part of why you don't make contact with us?"

Martia put the larva down and stood up and walked over to him and kissed the tips of his fingers. Lane, though he had to fight against visibly flinching, took her fingers and kissed them. Softly, he said to her, "Yet... individuals could learn to respect each other, to have affection for each other. And masses are made of individuals."

He lay back on the bed. The grogginess, pushed aside for a while by excitement, was coming back. He couldn't fight off sleep much longer.

My Sister's Brother

"Fine noble talk," he murmured. "But it means nothing. Eeltau don't think they should deal with us. And we are, unknowingly, pushing out toward them. What will happen when we are ready to make the interstellar jump? War? Or will they be afraid to let us advance even to that point and destroy us before then? After all, one cobalt bomb..."

He looked again at Martia, at the not-quite-human yet beautiful face, the smooth skin of the chest, abdomen, and loins, innocent of nipple, navel, or labia. From far off she had come, from a possibly terrifying place across terrifying distances. About her, however, there was little that was terrifying and much that was warm, generous, companionable, attractive.

As if they had waited for some key to turn, and the key had been turned, the lines he had read before falling asleep the last night in the base came again to him.

> *It is the voice of my beloved that knocketh, saying,*
> *Open to me, my sister, my love, my dove,*
> *my undefiled...*
>
> *We have a little sister,*
> *And she hath no breasts:*
> *What shall we do for our sister*
> *In the day when she shall be spoken for?*
>
> *With thee conversing, I forget all time,*
> *All seasons, and their change, all please alike.*

"With thee conversing," he said aloud. He turned over so his back was to her, and he pounded his fist against the bed.

"Oh dear God, why couldn't it be so?"

A long time he lay there, his face pressed into the mattress. Something had happened; the overpowering fatigue was gone; his body had drawn strength from some reservoir. Realizing this, he sat up and beckoned to Martia, smiling at the same time.

She rose slowly and started to walk to him, but he signaled that she should bring the larva with her. At first, she looked puzzled. Then her expression cleared, to be replaced by understanding. Smiling delightedly, she walked to him, and though he knew it must be a trick of his imagination, it seemed to him that she swayed her hips as a woman would.

She halted in front of him and then stooped to kiss him full on the lips. Her eyes were closed.

He hesitated for a fraction of a second. She—no, it, he told himself—looked so trusting, so loving, so womanly, that he could not do it.

"For Earth!" he said fiercely and brought the edge of his palm hard against the side of her neck.

She crumpled forward against him, her face sliding into his chest. Lane caught her under the armpits and laid her facedown on the bed. The larva, which had fallen from her hand onto the floor, was writhing about as if hurt. Lane picked it up by its tail and, in a frenzy that owed its violence to the fear he might not be able to do it, snapped it like a whip. There was a crack as the head smashed into the floor and blood spurted from its eyes and mouth. Lane placed his heel on the head and stepped down until there was a flat mess beneath his foot.

Then, quickly, before she could come to her senses and speak any words that would render him sick and weak, he ran to a cabinet. Snatching a narrow towel out of it, he ran back and gagged her. After that he tied her hands behind her back with the rope.

"Now, you bitch!" he panted. "We'll see who comes out ahead! You would do that with me, would you! You deserve this; your monster deserves to die!"

Furiously he began packing. In fifteen minutes he had the suits, helmets, tanks, and food rolled into two bundles. He searched for the weapon she had talked about and found something that might conceivably be it. It had a butt that fitted to his hand, a dial that might be a rheostat for controlling degrees of intensity of whatever it shot, and a bulb at the end. The bulb, he hoped, expelled the stunning and killing energy. Of course, he might be wrong. It could be fashioned for an entirely different purpose.

Martia had regained consciousness. She sat on the edge of the bed, her shoulders hunched, her head drooping, tears running down her cheeks and into the towel around her mouth. Her wide eyes were focused on the smashed worm by her feet.

Roughly, Lane seized her shoulder and pulled her upright. She gazed wildly at him, and he gave her a little shove. He felt sick within him, knowing that he had killed the larva when he did not have to do so and that he was handling her so violently because he was afraid, not of her, but of himself. If he had been disgusted because she had fallen into the trap he set for her, he was so because he, too, beneath his disgust, had wanted to commit that act of love. Commit, he thought, was the right word. It contained criminal implications.

Martia whirled around, almost losing her balance because of her tied hands. Her face worked, and sounds burst from the gag.

"Shut up!" he howled, pushing her again. She went sprawling and only saved herself from falling on her face by dropping on her knees. Once more, he pulled her to her feet, noting as he did so that her knees were skinned. The sight of the blood, instead of softening him, enraged him even more.

"Behave yourself, or you'll get worse!" he snarled.

She gave him one more questioning look, threw back her head, and made a strange strangling sound. Immediately, her face took on a bluish tinge. A second later, she fell heavily on the floor.

Alarmed, he turned her over. She was choking to death.

He tore off the gag and reached into her mouth and grabbed the root of her tongue. It slipped away and he seized it again, only to have it slide away as if it were a live animal that defied him.

Then he had pulled her tongue out of her throat; she had swallowed it in an effort to kill herself.

Lane waited. When he was sure she was going to recover, he replaced the gag around her mouth. Just as he was about to tie the knot at the back of her neck, he stopped. What use would it be to continue this? If allowed to speak, she would say the word that would throw him into retching. If gagged, she would swallow her tongue again.

He could save her only so many times. Eventually, she would succeed in strangling herself.

The one way to solve his problem was the one way he could not take. If her tongue were cut off at the root, she could neither speak nor kill herself. Some men might do it; he could not.

The only other way to keep her silent was to kill her.

"I can't do it in cold blood," he said aloud. "So, if you want to die, Martia, then you must do it by committing suicide. That, I can't help. Up you go. I'll get your pack, and we'll leave."

Martia turned blue and sagged to the floor.

"I'll not help you this time!" he shouted, but he found himself frantically trying to undo the knot.

At the same time, he told himself what a fool he was. Of course! The solution was to use her own gun on her. Turn the rheostat to a stunning degree of intensity and knock her out whenever she started to regain consciousness. Such a course would mean he'd have to carry her and her equipment, too, on the thirty-mile walk down the tube to an exit near his base. But he could do it. He'd rig up some sort of travois. He'd do it! Nothing could stop him. And Earth...

At that moment, hearing an unfamiliar noise, he looked up. There were two Eeltau in pressure suits standing there, and another crawling out of the tunnel. Each had a bulb-tipped handgun in her hand.

Desperately, Lane snatched at the weapon he carried in his belt. With his left hand he twisted the rheostat on the side of the barrel, hoping that this would turn it on full force. Then he raised the bulb toward the group....

He woke flat on his back, clad in his suit, except for the helmet, and strapped to a stretcher. His body was helpless, but he could turn his head. He did so, and saw many Eeltau dismantling the room. The one who had stunned him with her gun before he could fire was standing by him.

She spoke in English that held only a trace of foreign accent. "Settle down, Mr. Lane. You're in for a long ride. You'll be more comfortably situated once we're in our ship."

He opened his mouth to ask her how she knew his name but closed it when he realized she must have read the entries in the log at the base. And it was to be expected that some Eeltau would be trained in Earth languages. For over a century their sentinel spaceships had been tuning in to radio and TV.

It was then that Martia spoke to the captain. Her face was wild and reddened with weeping and marks where she had fallen.

The interpreter said to Lane, *"Mahrseeya* asks you to tell her why you killed her... baby. She cannot understand why you thought you had to do so."

"I cannot answer," said Lane. His head felt very light, almost as if it were a balloon expanding. And the room began slowly to turn around.

"I will tell her why," answered the interpreter. "I will tell her that it is the nature of the beast."

"That is not so!" cried Lane. "I am no vicious beast. I did what I did because I had to! I could not accept her love and still remain a man! Not the kind of man..."

"Mahrseeya," said the interpreter, "will pray that you be forgiven the murder of her child and that you will someday,

My Sister's Brother

under our teaching, be unable to do such a thing. She herself, though she is stricken with grief for her dead baby, forgives you. She hopes the time will come when you will regard her as a—sister. She thinks there is some good in you."

Lane clenched his teeth together and bit the end of his tongue until it bled while they put his helmet on. He did not dare to try to talk, for that would have meant he would scream and scream. He felt as if something had been planted in him and had broken its shell and was growing into something like a worm. It was eating him, and what would happen before it devoured all of him he did not know.

SKINBURN

It makes no difference in the story itself, but devotees of old pulp-magazine fiction might deduce Kent Lane's identity from his fire opal ring and his name. The surname implies, of course, that his parents were never married. I have plans for Lane, who will carry on his distinguished father's career, though in a less violent manner.

This story is about Love, which means that it is also about Hate. One of the themes that run through much of my work is that for every advantage you gain there is a disadvantage, that the gods, or whoever, require payment, that the universe in all its aspects, which include the human psyche, is governed by a check and balance system.

"Your skin tingles every time you step outdoors?" Dr. Mills said. "And when you stand under the skylight in your apartment? But only now and then when you're standing in front of the window, even if the sunlight falls on you?"

"Yes," Kent Lane said. "It doesn't matter whether or not it's night or day, the skies are cloudy or clear, or the skylight is open or closed. The tingling is strongest on the exposed parts of my body, my face and hands or whatever. But the tingling spreads from the exposed skin to all over my body, though it's much weaker under my clothes. And the tingling eventually arouses vaguely erotic feelings."

The dermatologist walked around him. When he had completed his circuit, he said, "Don't you ever tan?"

"No, I just peel and blister. I usually avoid burning by staying out of the sun as much as possible. But that isn't doing

Skinburn

me any good now, as you can see. I look as if I'd been on the beach all day. That makes me rather conspicuous, you know. In my work, you can't afford to be conspicuous."

The doctor said, "I know."

He meant that he was aware that Lane was a private detective. What he did not know was that Lane was working on a case for a federal government agency. CACO—Coordinating Authority for Cathedric Organizations—was short of competent help. It had hired, after suitable security checks, a number of civilian agents. CACO would have hired only the best, of course, and Lane was among these.

Lane hesitated and then said, "I keep getting these phone calls."

The doctor said nothing. Lane said, "There's nobody at the other end. He, or she, hangs up just as soon as I pick the phone up."

"You think the skinburn and the phone calls are related?"

"I don't know. But I'm putting all unusual phenomena into one box. The calls started a week after I'd had a final talk with a lady who'd been chasing me and wouldn't quit. She has a Ph.D. in bioelectronics and is a big shot in the astronautics industry. She's brilliant, charming, and witty, when she wants to be, but very plain in face and plane in body and very nasty when frustrated. And so..."

He was, he realized, talking too much about someone who worked in a top-secret field. Moreover, why would Mills want to hear the sad story of Dr. Sue Brackwell's unrequited love for Kent Lane, private eye? She had been hung up on him for some obscure psychological reason and, in her more rational moments, had admitted that they could never make it as man and wife, or even as man and lover, for more than a month, if that. But she was not, outside of the laboratory, always rational, and she would not take no from her own good sense or from him. Not until he had gotten downright vicious over the phone two years ago.

Three weeks ago, she had called him again. But she had said nothing to disturb him. After about five minutes of light chitchat about this and that, including reports on their health, she had said good-bye, making it sound like an *ave atque vale*, and had hung up. Perhaps she had wanted to find out for herself if the sound of his voice still thrilled her. Who knew?

Lane became aware that the doctor was waiting for him to finish the sentence. He said, "The thing is, these phone calls occurred at first when I was under the skylight and making love. So I moved the bed to a corner where nobody could possibly see it from the upper stories of the Parmenter Building next door.

"After that, the phone started ringing whenever I took a woman into my apartment, even if it was just for a cup of coffee. It'd be ringing before I'd get the door open, and it'd ring at approximately three-minute intervals thereafter. I changed my phone number twice, but it didn't do any good. And if I went to the woman's apartment instead, her phone started ringing."

"You think this lady scientist is making these calls?"

"Never! It's not her style. It must be a coincidence that the calls started so soon after our final conversation."

"Did your women also hear the phone?"

Lane smiled and said, "Audiohallucinations? No. They heard the phone ringing, too. One of them solved the problem by tearing her phone out. But I solved mine by putting in a phone jack and disconnecting the phone when I had in mind another sort of connection."

"That's all very interesting, but I fail to see what it has to do with your skin problem."

"Phone calls aside," Lane said, "could the tingling, the peeling and blistering, and the mild erotic reaction be psychosomatic?"

"I'm not qualified to say," Mills said. "I can, however, give you the name of a doctor whose specialty is recommending various specialists."

Lane looked at his wristwatch. Rhoda should be about done with her hairdresser. He said, "So far, I'm convinced I need a dermatologist, not a shrink. I was told you're the best skin doctor in Washington and perhaps the best on the East Coast."

"The world, actually," Dr. Mills said. "I'm sorry. I can do nothing for you at this time. But I do hope you'll inform me of new developments. I've never had such a puzzling, and, therefore, interesting, case."

Lane used the phone in the ground-floor lobby to call his fiancée's hairdresser. He was told that Rhoda had just left but that she would pick him up across the street from the doctor's building.

He got out of the building just in time to see Rhoda drive his MG around the corner, through a stoplight, and into the path of a pickup truck. Rhoda, thrown out by the impact (she was careless about using her safety belt), landed in front of a Cadillac. Despite its locked brakes, it slid on over her stomach.

Lane had seen much as an adviser in Vietnam and as a member of the San Francisco and Brooklyn police departments. He thought he was tough, but the violent and bloody deaths of Leona and Rhoda within four months was too much. He stood motionless, noting only that the tingling was getting warmer and spreading over his body. There was no erotic reaction, or, if there were, he was too numb to feel it. He stood there until a policeman got the nearest doctor, who happened to be Mills, to come out and look at him. Mills gave Lane a mild sedative, and the cop sent him home in a taxi. But Lane was at the morgue an hour later, identified Rhoda, and then went to the precinct station to answer some questions.

He went home prepared to drink himself to sleep, but he found two CACO agents, Daniels and Lyons, waiting for him. They seemed to have known about Rhoda's death almost as quickly as he, and so he knew that they had been shadowing him or Rhoda. He answered some of their questions and then told them that the idea that Leona and Rhoda might be spies was not worth a second's consideration. Besides, if they were working for SKIZO, or some other outfit, why would SKIZO, or whoever, kill their own agents?

"Or did CACO kill them?" Lane said.

The two looked at him as if he were unspeakably stupid.

"All right," Lane said. "But there's absolutely no evidence to indicate that their deaths were caused by anything but pure accident. I know it's quite a coincidence..."

Daniels said, "CACO had both under surveillance, of course. But CACO saw nothing significant in the two women's behavior. However, that in itself is suspicious, you know. Negative evidence demands a positive inquiry."

"That maxim demands the investigation of the entire world," Lane said.

"Nevertheless," Lyons said, "SKIZO must've spotted you by now. They'd have to be blind not to. Why in hell don't you stay out from under sunlamps?"

"It's a skin problem," Lane said. "As you must know, since you've undoubtedly bugged Dr. Mills's office."

"Yeah, we know," Daniels said. "Frankly, Lane, we got two tough alternatives to consider. Either you're going psycho, or else SKIZO is on to you. Either way..."

"You're thinking in two-valued terms only," Lane said.

"Have you considered that a third party, one with no connection at all with SKIZO, has entered the picture?"

Daniels cracked his huge knuckles and said, "Like who?"

"Like whom, you mean. How would I know? But you'll have to admit that it's not only possible but highly probable."

Daniels stood up. Lyons jumped up. Daniels said, "We don't have to admit anything. Come along with us, Lane."

If CACO thought he was lying, CACO would see to it that he was never seen again. CACO was mistaken about him, of course, but CACO, like doctors, buried mistakes.

On leaving the apartment building, Lane immediately felt the warm tingling on his face and hands and, a few seconds later, the spreading of the warmth to his crotch. He forgot about that a moment later when Daniels shoved him as he started to get into the back seat of the CACO automobile. He turned and said, "Keep your dirty hands off me, Daniels! Push me, and I may just walk off. You might have to shoot me to stop me, and you wouldn't want to do that in broad daylight, would you?"

"Try it and find out," Daniels said. "Now shut up and get in or get knocked in. You know we're being observed. Maybe that's why you're making a scene."

Lane got into the back seat with Lyons, and Daniels drove them away. It was a hot June afternoon, and evidently the CACO budget did not provide for cars with air-conditioning. They rode with the windows down while Lyons and Daniels asked him questions. Lane answered all truthfully, if not fully, but he was not concentrating on his replies. He noticed that when he hung his hand out of the window, it felt warm and tingling.

Fifteen minutes later, the big steel doors of an underground garage clanged shut behind him. He was interrogated in a small room below the garage. Electrodes were attached to his head and body, and various machines with large staring lenses were fixed on him while he was asked a series of questions. He never found out what the interpreters of the machines' graphs and meters thought about his reactions to the questions. Just as the electrodes were being detached, Smith, the man who had hired Lane for CACO, entered. Smith had a peculiar expression. He called the interrogators to one side and spoke to them in a low voice. Lane caught something about "a telephone call." A minute later, he was told he could go home. But he was to keep in touch, or, rather, keep himself available

Skinburn

for CACO. For the time being, he was suspended from service.

Lane wanted to tell Smith that he was quitting CACO, but he had no desire to be "detained" again. Nobody quit CACO; it let its employees go only when it felt like it.

Lane went home in a taxi and had just started to pour himself a drink when the doorman called up.

"Feds, Mr. Lane. They got proper ID's."

Lane sighed, downed his Scotch and, a few minutes later, opened the door. Lyons and two others, all holding .45 automatic pistols, were in the hall.

Lyons had a bandage around his head and some BandAids on one cheek and his chin. Both eyes were bloodshot.

"You're under arrest, Lane," Lyons said.

In the chair in the interrogation room, attached once again to various machines, Lane answered everything a dozen times over. Smith personally conducted the questioning, perhaps because he wanted to make sure that Lyons did not attack Lane.

It took Lane ten hours to piece together what had happened from occasional comments by Smith and Lyons. Daniels and Lyons had followed Lane when he had been released from CACO HQ. Trailing Lane by a block, Daniels had driven through a stoplight and into the path of a hot rod doing fifty miles an hour. Daniels had been killed. Lyons had escaped with minor injuries to the body but a large one to the psyche. For no logical reason, he blamed Lane for the accident.

After the interrogation, Lane was taken to a small padded room, given a TV dinner, and locked in. Naked, he lay down on the padded floor and slept. Three hours later, two men woke him up and handed him his clothes and then conducted him to Smith's office.

"I don't know what to do with you," Smith said. "Apparently, you're not lying. Or else you've been conditioned somehow to give the proper—or perhaps I should say, improper—responses and reactions. It's possible, you know, to fool the machines, what with all the conscious control of brain waves, blood pressure, and so on being taught at universities and by private individuals."

"Yes, but you know that I haven't had any such training," Lane said. "Your security checks show that."

Smith grunted and looked sour.

"I can only conclude," he said, "from the data that I have, that you are involved in counterespionage activity."

Lane opened his mouth to protest, but Smith continued,

"Innocently, however. For some reason, you have become the object of interest, perhaps even concern, to some foreign outfit, probably Commie, most probably SKIZO, CACO's worst enemy. Or else you are the focus of some wildly improbable coincidences."

Lane couldn't think of anything to say to that. Smith said, "You were released the first time because I got a phone call from a high authority, a very high authority, telling me to let you go. By telling, I mean ordering. No reasons given. That authority doesn't have to give reasons.

"But I made the routine checkback, and I found out that the authority was fake. Somebody had pretended to be him. And the code words and the voice were exactly right. So, somehow, somebody, probably SKIZO, has cracked our code and can duplicate voices so exactly that even a voiceprint check can't tell the difference between the fake and the genuine. That's scary, Lane."

Lane nodded to indicate that he agreed it was scary. He said, "Whoever is doing this must have a damn good reason to reveal that he knows all this stuff. Why would a foreign agent show such a good hand just to get me out of your clutches—uh, custody? I can't do anyone, foreign agent or not, any good. And by revealing that they know the code words and can duplicate voices, they lose a lot. Now the code words will be changed, and the voices will be double-checked."

Smith drummed his fingers on the desktop and then said, "Yes, we know. But this extraordinary dermal sensitivity... these automobile accidents..."

"What did Lyons report about his accident?"

"He was unaware of anything wrong until Daniels failed to slow down on approaching the stoplight. He hesitated to say anything, because Daniels did not like backseat drivers, although Lyons was, as a matter of fact, in the front seat. Finally, he was unable to keep silent, but it was too late. Daniels looked up at the signal and said, 'What in hell you talking about?' and then the other car hit them."

Lane said, "Apparently Daniels thought the signal was green."

"Possibly. But I believe that there is some connection between the phone calls you got while with your women and the one I got from the supposed high authority."

"How could there be?" Lane said. "Why would this, this person, call me up just to ruin my lovemaking?"

Smith's face was as smooth as the face on a painting, but his fingers drummed a tattoo of desperation. No wonder. A case which could not even give birth to a hypothesis, let alone a theory, was the ultimate in frustration.

"I'm letting you go again, only this time you'll be covered with my agents like the North Pole is with snow in January," Smith said.

Lane did not thank him. He took a taxi back to his apartment, again feeling the tingling and warmth and mildly erotic sensations on the way to the taxi and on the way out of it.

In his rooms, he contemplated his future. He was no longer drawing pay from CACO, and CACO would not permit him to go to work for anybody else until this case was cleared up. In fact, Smith did not want him to leave his apartment unless it was absolutely necessary. Lane was to stay in it and force the unknown agency to come to him. So how was he to support himself? He had enough money to pay the rent for another month and buy food for two weeks. Then he would be eligible for welfare. He could defy Smith and get a job at nondetective work, say, a carryout boy at a grocery store or a car salesman. He had experience in both fields. But times were bad, and jobs of any kind were scarce.

Lane became angry. If CACO was keeping him from working, then it should be paying him. He phoned Smith, and, after a twelve-minute delay, during which Smith was undoubtedly checking back that it was really Lane phoning, Smith answered.

"I should pay you for doing nothing? How could I justify that on the budget I got?"

"That's your problem."

Lane looked up, because he had carried the phone under the skylight and his neck started tingling. Whoever was observing him at this moment had to be doing it from the Parmenter Building. He called Smith back and, after a ten-minute delay, got him.

"Whoever's laying a tap-in beam on me is doing it from any of the floors above the tenth. I don't think he could angle in from a lower floor."

"I know," Smith said. "I've had men in the Parmenter Building since yesterday. I don't overlook anything, Lane."

Lane had intended to ask him why he had overlooked the fact that they were undoubtedly being overheard at this moment. He did not do so because it struck him that Smith wanted their conversations to be bugged. He was keen to appear overconfident so that SKIZO, or whoever it was, would move again. Lane was the cheese in the trap. However, anybody who threatened Lane seemed to get hurt or killed, and Smith, from Lane's viewpoint, was threatening him.

During the next four days, Lane read Volume IV of the Durants' *The Story of Civilization,* drank more than he should have, exercised, and spent a half hour each day, nude, under the skylight. The result of this exposure was that the skin burned and peeled all over his body. But the sexual titillation accompanying the dermal heat made the pain worth it. If the sensations got stronger each day, he'd be embarrassing himself, and possibly his observers, within a week.

He wondered if the men at the other end of the beam (or beams) had any idea of the gratuitous sexuality their subject felt. They probably thought that he was just a horny man with horny thoughts. But he knew that his reaction was unique, a result of something peculiar in his metabolism or his pigment or his whatever. Others, including Smith, had been under the skylight, and none had felt anything unusual.

The men investigating the Parmenter Building had detected nothing suspicious beyond the fact that there was nothing suspicious.

On the seventh day, Lane phoned Smith. "I can't take this submarine existence any longer. And I have to get a job or starve. So, I'm leaving. If your storm troopers try to stop me, I'll resist. And you can't afford to have a big stink raised."

In the struggle that followed, Lane and the two CACO agents staggered into the area beneath the skylight. Lane went down, as he knew he would, but he felt that he had to make some resistance or lose his right to call himself a man. He stared up into the skylight while his hands were cuffed. He was not surprised when the phone rang, though he could not have given a reasonable explanation of why he expected it.

A third agent, just entering, answered. He talked for a moment, then turned and said, "Smith says to let him go. And we're to come on home. Something sure made him change his mind."

Lane started for the door after his handcuffs were unlocked. The phone rang again. The same man as before answered it. Then he shouted at Lane to stop, but Lane kept on going, only to be halted by two men stationed at the elevator.

Lane's phone was being monitored by CACO agents in the basement of the apartment building. They had called up to report that Smith had not given that order. In fact, no one had actually called in from outside the building. The call had come from somewhere within the building.

Smith showed up fifteen minutes later to conduct the search throughout the building. Two hours later, the agents were told to quit looking. Whoever had made that call imitating Smith's voice and giving the new code words had managed, somehow, to get out of the building unobserved.

"SKIZO, or whoever it is, must be using a machine to simulate my voice," Smith said. "No human throat could do it well enough to match voiceprints."

Voices!

Lane straightened up so swiftly that the men on each side of him grabbed his arms.

Dr. Sue Brackwell!

Had he really talked to her that last time, or was someone imitating her voice, too? He could not guess why; the mysterious Whoever could be using her voice to advance whatever plans he had. Sue had said that she just wanted to talk for old times' sake. Whoever was imitating her might have been trying to get something out of him, something that would be a clue to... to what? He just did not know.

And it was possible that this Whoever had talked to Sue Brackwell, imitating his, Lane's voice.

Lane did not want to get her into trouble, but he could not afford to leave any possible avenue of investigation closed. He spoke to Smith about it as they went down the elevator. Smith listened intently, but he only said, "We'll see."

Glumly, Lane sat on the back seat between two men, also glum, as the car traveled through the streets of Washington. He looked out the window and through the smog saw a billboard advertising a rerun of *The Egg and I*. A block later, he saw another billboard, advertising a well-known brand of beer. SKY-BLUE WATERS, the sign said, and he wished he were in the land of sky-blue waters, fishing and drinking beer.

Again, he straightened up so swiftly that the two men grabbed him.

"Take it easy," he said. He slumped back down, and they removed their hands. The two advertisements had been a sort of free association test, provided only because the car had driven down this route and not some other it might easily have taken. The result of the conjunction of the two billboards might or might not be validly linked up with the other circuits that had been forming in the unconscious part of his mind. But he now had a hypothesis. It could be developed into a theory which could be tested against the facts. That is, it could be if he were given a chance to try it.

Smith heard him out, but he had only one comment. "You're thinking of the wildest things you can so you'll throw us off the track."

"What track?" Lane said. He did not argue. He knew that Smith would go down the trail he had opened up. Smith could not afford to ignore anything, even the most farfetched of ideas.

Lane spent a week in the padded cell. Once, Smith entered to talk to him. The conversation was brief.

"I can't find any evidence to support your theory," Smith said.

"Is that because even CACO can't get access to certain classified documents and projects at Lackalas Astronautics?" Lane said.

"Yeah. I was asked what my need to know was, and I couldn't tell them what I really was trying to find out. The next thing I'd know, I'd be in a padded cell with regular sessions with a shrink."

"And so, because you're afraid of asking questions that might arouse suspicions of your sanity, you'll let the matter drop?"

"There's no way of finding out if your crazy theory has any basis."

"Love will find a way," Lane said.

Smith snorted, spun around, and walked out.

That was at 11 A.M. At 12:03, Lane looked at his wristwatch (since he was no longer compelled to go naked) and noted that lunch was late. A few minutes afterward, an Air Force jet fighter on a routine flight over Washington suddenly dived down and hit CACO HQ at close to 1000 mph. It struck the massive stone building at the end opposite Lane's cell. Even so, it tore through the fortress-like outer walls and five rooms before stopping.

Lane, in the second subfloor, would not have been hit if the wreck had traveled entirely through the building. However, flames began to sweep through, and guards unlocked his door and got him outside just in time. On orders transmitted via radio, his escorts put him into a car to take him across the city to another CACO base. Lane was stiff with shock, but he reacted quickly enough when the car started to go through a red light. He was down on the floor and braced when the car and the huge Diesel met. The others were not killed. They were not, however, in any condition to stop him. Ten minutes later, he was in his apartment.

Dr. Sue Brackwell was waiting for him under the skylight. She had no clothes on; even her glasses were off. She looked very beautiful; it was not until much later that he remembered that she had never been beautiful or even passably pretty. He could not blame his shock for behaving the way he did, because the tingling and the warmth dissolved that. He became very alive, so much so that he loaned sufficient life to the thing that he pulled down to the floor. Somewhere in him existed the knowledge that "she" had prepared this for him and that no man might ever experience this certain event again. But the knowledge was so far off that it influenced him not at all.

Besides, as he had told Smith, love would find a way. He was not the one who had fallen in love. Not at first. Now, he felt as if he were in love, but many men, and women, feel that way during this time.

Smith and four others broke into the apartment just in time to rescue Lane. He was lying on the floor and was as naked and red as a newborn baby. Smith yelled at him, but he seemed to be deaf. It was evident that he was galloping with all possible speed in a race between a third-degree burn and an orgasm. He obviously had a partner, but Smith could neither see nor hear her.

The orgasm might have won if Smith had not thrown a big pan of cold water on Lane.

Two days afterward, Lane's doctor permitted Smith to enter the hospital room to see his much-bandaged and somewhat-sedated patient. Smith handed him a newspaper turned to page two. Lane read the article, which was short and all about EVE. EVE—Ever Vigilant Eye—had been a stationary-orbit surveillance satellite which had been sent up over the East Coast two years ago. EVE had exploded for unknown reasons, and the accident was being investigated.

"That's all the public was told," Smith said. "I finally got through to Brackwell and the other bigwigs connected with EVE. But either they were under orders to tell me as little as possible or else they don't have all the facts themselves. In any event, it's more than just a coincidence that she—EVE, I mean—blew up just as we were taking you to the hospital."

Lane said, "I'll answer some of your questions before you

ask them. One, you couldn't see the holograph because she must've turned it off just before you got in. I don't know whether it was because she heard you coming or because she knew, somehow, that any more contact would kill me. Or maybe her alarms told her that she had better stop for her own good. But it would seem that she didn't stop or else did try to stop but was too late.

"I had a visitor who told me just enough about EVE so I wouldn't let my curiosity carry me into dangerous areas after I got out of here. And it won't. But I can tell you a few things and know it won't get any further.

"I'd figured out that Brackwell was the master designer of the bioelectronics circuit of a spy satellite. I didn't know that the satellite was called EVE or that she had the capability to beam in on ninety thousand individuals simultaneously. Or that the beams enabled her to follow each visually and tap in on their speech vibrations. Or that she could activate phone circuits with a highly variable electromagnetic field projected via the beam.

"My visitor said that I was not, for an instant, to suppose that EVE had somehow attained self-consciousness. That would be impossible. But I wonder.

"I also wonder if a female designer-engineer-scientist could, unconsciously, of course, design female circuits? Is there some psychic influence that goes along with the physical construction of computers and associated circuits? Can the whole be greater than the parts? Is there such a thing as a female gestalt in a machine?"

"I don't go for that metaphysical crap," Smith said.

"What does Brackwell say?"

"She says that EVE was simply malfunctioning."

"Perhaps man is a malfunctioning ape," Lane said. "But could Sue have built her passion for me into EVE? Or given EVE circuits which could evolve emotion? EVE had self-repairing capabilities, you know, and was part protein. I know it sounds crazy. But who, looking at the first apeman, would have extrapolated Helen of Troy?

"And why did she get hung up on me, one out of the ninety thousand she was watching? I had a dermal supersensitivity to the spy beam. Did this reaction somehow convey to EVE a feeling, or a sense, that we were in rapport? And did she then become jealous? It's obvious that she modulated the beams she'd locked on Leona and Rhoda so that they saw green where

Skinburn 65

the light was really red and did not see oncoming cars at all.

"And she worked her modulated tricks on Daniels and that poor jet pilot, too."

"What about that holograph of Dr. Brackwell?"

"EVE must've been spying on Sue, also, on her own creator, you might say. Or—and I don't want you to look into this, because it won't do any good now—Sue may have set all this up in the machinery, unknown to her colleagues. I don't mean that she put in extra circuits. She couldn't get away with that; they'd be detected immediately, and she'd have to explain them. But she could have put in circuits which had two purposes, the second of which was unknown to her colleagues. I don't know.

"But I do know that it was actually Sue Brackwell who called me that last time and not EVE. And I think that it was this call that put into EVE's mind, if a machine can have a mind in the human sense, to project the much-glamorized holograph of Sue. Unless, of course, my other theory is correct, and Sue herself was responsible for that."

Smith groaned and then said, "They'll never believe me if I put all this in a report. For one thing, will they believe that it was only free association that enabled you to get *eye in the sky* from 'The egg and I' and 'Sky-blue waters'? I doubt it. They'll think you had knowledge you shouldn't have had and you're concealing it with that incredible story. I wouldn't want to be in your shoes. But then, I don't want to be in my shoes.

"But why did EVE blow up? Lackalas says that she could be exploded if a destruct button at control center was pressed. The button, however, was not pressed."

"You dragged me away just in time to save my life. But EVE must have melted some circuits. She died of frustration—in a way, that is."

"What?"

"She was putting out an enormous amount of energy for such a tight beam. She must have overloaded."

Smith guffawed and said, "She was getting a charge out of it, too? Come on!"

Lane said, "Do you have any other explanation?"

THE ALLEY MAN

This seems to have called forth either cries of "Bravo!" or "Abomination of abominations!"

Philip Klass (William Tenn) admired it and said that if it had been sent to *Playboy* (where he was an editor at the time), it probably would have sold there. If I remember correctly, it came in second to Keyes's "Flowers for Algernon" (both appeared in *The Magazine of Fantasy and Science-Fiction*) in the 1960 Hugo contest. Afterward, I heard from about a dozen people that they would have voted for it, but didn't bother to vote at all, because they assumed it would win.

I have no doubt, however, that the better story won. If Keyes is Cellini, I'm Gutzon Borglum.

In any event, there must have been some who had the same reaction as Jim Harmon, well-known nostalgic, and Avram Davidson, a highly erudite fantasist and a philanthropist, who thought that "The Alley Man" was a stench in the nostrils of Heaven.

Read it and decide.

An independent New York producer began making it into a movie but he ran out of money. Another producer wanted to pick up an option on it, but he called me a week after I'd made the deal with the first party. So much for square eggs.

Now that the use of four-letter words and explicit description of sexual intercourse are permitted in books, I could have dropped the original euphemisms, such as "shirt" and "figuring," from the text. But I don't see that substituting real-life language adds anything. In fact, the original terms give Old Man's speech an extra paleolithic patina.

* * *

"The man from the puzzle factory was here this morning," said Gummy. "While you was out fishin."

She dropped the piece of wiremesh she was trying to tie with string over a hole in the rusty window screen. Cursing, grunting like a hog in a wallow, she leaned over and picked it up. Straightening, she slapped viciously at her bare shoulder.

"Figurin skeeters! Must be a million outside, all tryin to get away from the burnin garbage."

"Puzzle factory?" said Deena. She turned away from the battered kerosene-burning stove over which she was frying sliced potatoes and perch and bullheads caught in the Illinois River, half a mile away.

"Yeah!" snarled Gummy. "You heard Old Man say it. Nuthouse. Booby hatch. So . . . this cat from the puzzle factory was named John Elkins. He gave Old Man all those tests when they had him locked up last year. He's the skinny little guy with a moustache 'n never lookin you in the eye 'n grinnin like a skunk eatin a shirt. The cat who took Old Man's hat away from him 'n woun't give it back to him until Old man promised to be good. Remember now?"

Deena, tall, skinny, clad only in a white terrycloth bathrobe, looked like a surprised and severed head stuck on a pike. The great purple birthmark on her cheek and neck stood out hideously against her paling skin.

"Are they going to send him back to the State hospital?" she asked.

Gummy, looking at herself in the cracked full-length mirror nailed to the wall, laughed and showed her two teeth. Her frizzy hair was a yellow brown, chopped short. Her little blue eyes were set far back in tunnels beneath two protruding ridges of bone; her nose was very long, enormously wide, and tipped with a broken-veined bulb. Her chin was not there, and her head bent forward in a permanent crook. She was dressed only in a dirty once-white slip that came to her swollen knees. When she laughed, her huge breasts, resting on her distended belly, quivered like bowls of fermented cream. From her expression, it was evident that she was not displeased with what she saw in the broken glass.

Again she laughed. "Naw, they din't come to haul him away. Elkins just wanted to interduce this chick he had with him. A cute little brunette with big brown eyes behint real thick glasses. She looked just like a collidge girl, 'n she was. This chick has got a B.M. or somethin in sexology. . . ."

"Psychology?"

"Maybe it was societyology...."

"Sociology?"

"Umm. Maybe. Anyway, this foureyed chick is doin a study for a foundation. She wants to ride aroun with Old Man, see how he collects his junk, what alleys he goes up 'n down, what his, uh, habit patterns is, 'n learn what kinda bringin up he had...."

"Old Man'd never do it!" burst out Deena. "You know he can't stand the idea of being watched by a False Folker!"

"Umm. Maybe. Anyway, I tell em Old Man's not goin to like their slummin on him, 'n they say quick they're not slummin, it's for science. 'N they'll pay him for his trouble. They got a grant from the foundation. So I say maybe that'd make Old Man take another look at the color of the beer, 'n they left the house...."

"You *allowed* them in the house? Did you hide the birdcage?"

"Why hide it? His hat wasn't in it."

Deena turned back to frying her fish, but over her shoulder she said, "I don't think Old Man'll agree to the idea, do you? It's rather degrading."

"You *kiddin?* Who's lower'n Old Man? A snake's belly, maybe. Sure, he'll agree. He'll have an eye for the foureyed chick, sure."

"Don't be absurd," said Deena. "He's a dirty stinking one-armed middle-aged man, the ugliest man in the world."

"Yeah, it's the uglies he's got, for sure. 'N he smells like a goat that fell in a outhouse. But it's the smell that gets em. It got me, it got you, it got a whole stewpotful a others, includin that high society dame he used to collect junk off of...."

"Shut up!" spat Deena. "This girl must be a highly refined and intelligent girl. She'd regard Old Man as some sort of ape."

"You know them apes," said Gummy, and she went to the ancient refrigerator and took out a cold quart of beer.

Six quarts of beer later, Old Man had still not come home. The fish had grown cold and greasy, and the big July moon had risen. Deena, like a long lean dirty-white nervous alley cat on top of a backyard fence, patrolled back and forth across the shanty. Gummy sat on the bench made of crates and hunched over her bottle. Finally, she lurched to her feet and turned on the battered set. But, hearing a rattling and pounding of a loose motor in the distance, she turned it off.

The Alley Man

The banging and popping became a roar just outside the door. Abruptly, there was a mighty wheeze, like an old rusty robot coughing with double pneumonia in its iron lungs. Then, silence.

But not for long. As the two women stood paralyzed, listening apprehensively, they heard a voice like the rumble of distant thunder.

"Take it easy, kid."

Another voice, soft, drowsy, mumbling.

"Where . . . we?"

The voice like thunder, "Home, sweet home, where we rest our dome."

Violent coughing.

"It's this smoke from the burnin garbage, kid. Enough to make a maggot puke, ain't it? Lookit! The smoke's risin t'ward the full moon like the ghosts a men so rotten even their spirits're carryin the contamination with em. Hey, li'l chick, you din't know Old Man knew them big words like contamination, didja? That's what livin on the city dump does for you. I hear that word all a time from the big shots that come down inspectin the stink here so they kin get away from the stink a City Hall. I ain't no illiterate. I got a TV set. Hor, hor, hor!"

There was a pause, and the two women knew he was bending his knees and tilting his torso backward so he could look up at the sky.

"Ah, you lovely lovely moon, bride a The Old Guy In The Sky! Some day to come, rum-a-dum-a-dum, one day I swear it, Old Woman a The Old Guy In The Sky, if you help me find the longlost headpiece a King Paley that I and my fathers been lookin for for fifty thousand years, so help me, Old Man Paley'll spread the freshly spilled blood a a virgin a the False Folkers out acrosst the ground for you, so you kin lay down in it like a red carpet or a new red dress and wrap it aroun you. And then you won't have to crinkle up your lovely shinin nose at me and spit your silver spit on me. Old Man promises that, just as sure as his good arm is holdin a daughter a one a the Falsers, a virgin, I think, and bringin her to his home, however humble it be, so we shall see. . . ."

"Stoned out a his head," whispered Gummy.

"My God, he's bringing a girl in here!" said Deena. *"The girl!"*

"Not the *collidge* kid?"

"Does the idiot want to get lynched?"

The man outside bellowed, "Hey, you wimmen, get off your fat asses and open the door 'fore I kick it in! Old Man's home with a fistful a dollars, a armful a sleepin lamb, and a gutful a beer! Home like a conquerin hero and wants service like one, too!"

Suddenly unfreezing, Deena opened the door.

Out of the darkness and into the light shuffled something so squat and blocky it seemed more a tree trunk come to life than a man. It stopped, and the eyes under the huge black homburg hat blinked glazedly. Even the big hat could not hide the peculiar lengthened-out bread-loaf shape of the skull. The forehead was abnormally low; over the eyes were bulging arches of bone. These were tufted with eyebrows like Spanish moss that made even more cavelike the hollows in which the little blue eyes lurked. Its nose was very long and very wide and flaring-nostriled. The lips were thin but pushed out by the shoving jaws beneath them. Its chin was absent, and head and shoulders joined almost without intervention from a neck, or so it seemed. A corkscrew forest of rusty-red hairs sprouted from its open shirt front.

Over his shoulder, held by a hand wide and knobbly as a coral branch, hung the slight figure of a young woman.

He shuffled into the room in an odd bent-kneed gait, walking on the sides of his thick-soled engineer's boots. Suddenly, he stopped again, sniffed deeply, and smiled, exposing teeth thick and yellow, dedicated to biting.

"Jeez, that smells good. It takes the old garbage stink right off. Gummy! You been sprinklin yourself with that perfume I found in a ash heap up on the bluffs?"

Gummy, giggling, looked coy.

Deena said, sharply, "Don't be a fool, Gummy. He's trying to butter you up so you'll forget he's bringing this girl home."

Old Man Paley laughed hoarsely and lowered the snoring girl upon an Army cot. There she sprawled out with her skirt around her hips. Gummy cackled, but Deena hurried to pull the skirt down and also to remove the girl's thick shell-rimmed glasses.

"Lord," she said, "how did this happen? What'd you do to her?"

"Nothin," he growled, suddenly sullen.

He took a quart of beer from the refrigerator, bit down on the cap with teeth thick and chipped as ancient gravestones, and tore it off. Up went the bottle, forward went his knees, back went his torso and he leaned away from the bottle, and down went the amber liquid, gurgle, gurgle, glub. He belched, then roared. "There I was, Old Man Paley, mindin my own figurin business, packin a bunch a papers and magazines I found, and here comes a blue fifty-one Ford sedan with Elkins, the doctor jerk from the puzzle factory. And this little foureyed chick here, Dorothy Singer. And..."

"Yes," said Deena. "We know who they are, but we didn't know they went after you."

"Who asked you? Who's tellin this story? Anyway, they tole me what they wanted. And I was gonna say no, but this little collidge broad says if I'll sign a paper that'll agree to let her travel aroun with me and even stay in our house a couple a evenins, with us actin natural, she'll pay me fifty dollars. I says yes! Old Guy In The Sky! That's a hundred and fifty quarts a beer! I got principles, but they're washed away in a roarin foamin flood of beer.

"I says yes, and the cute little runt give me the paper to sign, then advances me ten bucks and says I'll get the rest seven days from now. Ten dollars in my pocket! So she climbs up into the seat a my truck. And then this figurin Elkins parks his Ford and says he thinks he ought a go with us to check on if everythin's gonna be OK."

"He's not foolin Old Man. He's after Little Miss Foureyes. Everytime he looks at her, the lovejuice runs out a his eyes. So, I collect junk for a couple a hours, talkin all the time. And she is scared a me at first because I'm so figurin ugly and strange. But after a while she busts out laughin. Then I pulls the truck up in the alley back a Jack's Tavern on Ames Street. She asks me what I'm doin. I says I'm stoppin for a beer, just as I do every day. And she says she could stand one, too. So..."

"You actually went inside with her?" asked Deena.

"Naw. I was gonna try, but I started gettin the shakes. And I hadda tell her I coun't do it. She asks me why. I say I don't know. Ever since I quit bein a kid, I kin't. So she says I got a... somethin like a fresh flower, what is it?"

"Neurosis?" said Deena.

"Yeah. Only I call it a taboo. So Elkins and the little broad go into Jack's and get a cold six-pack, and brin it out, and we're off...."

"So?"

"So we go from place to place, though always stayin in

alleys, and she thinks it's funnier'n hell gettin loaded in the backs a taverns. Then I get to seein double and don't care no more and I'm over my fraidies, so we go into the Circle Bar. And get in a fight there with one a the hillbillies in his sideburns and leather jacket that hangs out there and tries to take the foureyed chick home with him."

Both the women gasped, "Did the cops come?"

"If they did, they was late to the party. I grab this hillbilly by his leather jacket with my one arm—the strongest arm in this world—and throw him clean acrosst the room. And when his buddies come after me, I pound my chest like a figurin gorilla and make a figurin face at em, and they all of a sudden get their shirts up their necks and go back to listenin to their hillbilly music. And I pick up the chick—she's laughin so hard she's chokin—and Elkins, white as a sheet out a the laundromat, after me, and away we go, and here we are."

"Yes, you fool, here you are!" shouted Deena. "Bringing that girl here in that condition! She'll start screaming her head off when she wakes up and sees you!"

"Go figure yourself!" snorted Paley. "She was scared a me a first, and she tried to stay upwind a me. But she got to *likin* me. I could tell. And she got so she liked my smell, too. I knew she would. Don't all the broads? These False wimmen ki't say no once they get a whiff of us. Us Paleys got the gift in the blood."

Deena laughed and said, "You mean you have it in the head. Honest to God, when are you going to quit trying to forcefeed me with that bull? You're insane!"

Paley growled. "I tole you not never to call me nuts, not never!" and he slapped her across the cheek.

She reeled back and slumped against the wall, holding her face and crying, "You ugly stupid stinking ape, you hit me, the daughter of people whose boots you aren't fit to lick. *You* struck *me!*"

"Yeah, and ain't you glad I did," said Paley in tones like a complacent earthquake. He shuffled over to the cot and put his hand on the sleeping girl.

"Uh, feel that. No sag there, you two flabs."

"You beast!" screamed Deena. "Taking advantage of a helpless little girl!"

Like an alley cat, she leaped at him with claws out.

Laughing hoarsely, he grabbed one of her wrists and twisted it so she was forced to her knees and had to clench her teeth

The Alley Man

to keep from screaming with pain. Gummy cackled and handed Old Man a quart of beer. To take it, he had to free Deena. She rose, and all three, as if nothing had happened, sat down at the table and began drinking.

About dawn a deep animal snarl awoke the girl. She opened her eyes but could make out the trio only dimly and distortedly. Her hands, groping around for her glasses, failed to find them.

Old Man, whose snarl had shaken her from the high tree of sleep, growled again. "I'm tellin you, Deena, I'm tellin you, don't laugh at Old Man, don't laugh at Old Man, and I'm tellin you again, three times, don't laugh at Old Man!"

His incredible bass rose to a high-pitched scream of rage.

"Whassa matter with your figurin brain? I show you proof after proof, and you sit there in all your stupidity like a silly hen that sits down too hard on its eggs and breaks em but won't get up and admit she's squattin on a mess. I—I—Paley—Old Man Paley—kin prove I'm what I say I am, a Real Folker."

Suddenly, he propelled his hand across the table toward Deena.

"Feel them bones in my lower arm! Them two bones ain't straight and dainty like the arm bones a you False Folkers. They're thick as flagpoles, and they're curved out from each other like the backs a two tomcats outbluffin each other over a fishhead on a garbage can. They're built that way so's they kin be real strong anchors for my muscles, which is bigger'n False Folkers'. Go ahead, feel em.

"And look at them brow ridges. Like the tops a those shell-rimmed spectacles all them intellekchooalls wear. Like the spectacles this collidge chick wears.

"And feel the shape a my skull. It ain't a ball like yours but a loaf a bread."

"Fossilized bread!" sneered Deena. "Hard as a rock, through and through."

Old Man roared on, "Feel my neck bones if you got the strength to feel through my muscles! They're bent forward, not—"

"Oh, I know you're an ape. You can't look overhead to see if that was a bird or just a drop of rain without breaking your back."

"Ape, hell! I'm a Real Man! Feel my heel bone! Is it like yours? No, it ain't! It's built diff'runt, and so's my whole foot!"

"Is that why you and Gummy and all those brats of yours have to walk like chimpanzees?"

"Laugh, laugh, laugh!"

"I am laughing, laughing, laughing. Just because you're a freak of nature, a monstrosity whose bones all went wrong in the womb, you've dreamed up this fantastic myth about being descended from the Neanderthals...."

"Neanderthals!" whispered Dorothy Singer. The walls whirled about her, looking twisted and ghostly in the halflight, like a room in Limbo.

"... all this stuff about the lost hat of Old King," continued Deena, "and how if you ever find it you can break the spell that keeps you so-called Neanderthals on the dumpheaps and in the alleys, is garbage, and not very appetizing...."

"And you," shouted Paley, "are headin for a beatin!"

"Thass what she wants," mumbled Gummy. "Go ahead. Beat her. She'll get her jollies off, 'n quit needlin you. 'N we kin all get some shuteye. Besides, you're gonna wake up the chick."

"That chick is gonna get a wakin up like she never had before when Old Man gets his paws on her," rumbled Paley. "Guy In The Sky, ain't it somethin she should a met me and be in this house? Sure as an old shirt stinks, she ain't gonna be able to tear herself away from me.

"Hey, Gummy, maybe she'll have a kid for me, huh? We ain't had a brat aroun here for ten years. I kinda miss my kids. You gave me six that was Real Folkers, though I never was sure about that Jimmy, he looked too much like O'Brien. Now you're all dried up, dry as Deena always was, but you kin still raise em. How'd you like to raise the collidge chick's kid?"

Gummy grunted and swallowed beer from a chipped coffee mug. After belching loudly, she mumbled, "Don't know. You're crazier'n even I think you are if you think this cute little Miss Foureyes'd have anythin to do with you. 'N even if she was out of her head enough to do it, what kind a life is this for a brat? Get raised in a dump? Have a ugly old maw 'n paw? Grow up so ugly nobody'd have nothin to do with him 'n smellin so strange all the dogs'd bite him?"

Suddenly, she began blubbering.

"It ain't only Neanderthals has to live on dumpheaps. It's the crippled 'n sick 'n the stupid 'n the queer in the head that has to live here. 'N they become Neanderthals just as much as us Real Folk. No diff'runce, no diff'runce. We're all ugly

The Alley Man

'n hopeless 'n rotten. We're all Neander..."

Old Man's fist slammed the table.

"Name me no names like that! That's a *G'yaga* name for us Paleys—Real Folkers. Don't let me never hear that other name again! It don't mean a man; it means somethin like a high-class gorilla."

"Quit looking in the mirror!" shrieked Deena.

There was more squabbling and jeering and roaring and confusing and terrifying talk, but Dorothy Singer had closed her eyes and fallen asleep again.

Some time later, she awoke. She sat up, found her glasses on a little table beside her, put them on, and stared about her.

She was in a large shack built of odds and ends of wood. It had two rooms, each about ten feet square. In the corner of one room was a large kerosene-burning stove. Bacon was cooking in a huge skillet; the heat from the stove made sweat run from her forehead and over her glasses.

After drying them off with her handkerchief, she examined the furnishings of the shack. Most of it was what she had expected, but three things surprised her. The bookcase, the photograph on the wall, and the birdcage.

The bookcase was tall and narrow and of some dark wood, badly scratched. It was crammed with comic books, Blue Books, and Argosies, some of which she supposed must be at least twenty years old. There were a few books whose ripped backs and waterstained covers indicated they'd been picked out of ash heaps. Haggard's *Allan and the Ice Gods*, Wells's *Outline of History*, Vol. I, and his, *The Croquet Player*. Also *Gog and Magog, A Prophecy of Armageddon* by the Reverend Caleb G. Harris. Burroughs' *Tarzan the Terrible* and *In the Earth's Core*. Jack London's *Beyond Adam*.

The framed photo on the wall was that of a woman who looked much like Deena and must have been taken around 1890. It was very large, tinted in brown, and showed an aristocratic handsome woman of about thirty-five in a high-busted velvet dress with a high neckline. Her hair was drawn severely back to a knot on top of her head. A diadem of jewels was on her breast.

The strangest thing was the large parrot cage. It stood upon a tall support which had nails driven through its base to hold it to the floor. The cage itself was empty, but the door was locked with a long narrow bicycle lock.

Her speculation about it was interrupted by the two women calling to her from their place by the stove.

Deena said, "Good morning, Miss Singer. How do you feel?"

"Some Indian buried his hatchet in my head," Dorothy said. "And my tongue is molting. Could I have a drink of water, please?"

Deena took a pitcher of cold water out of the refrigerator, and from it filled up a tin cup.

"We don't have any running water. We have to get our water from the gas station down the road and bring it here in a bucket."

Dorothy looked dubious, but she closed her eyes and drank.

"I think I'm going to get sick," she said. "I'm sorry."

"I'll take you to the outhouse," said Deena, putting her arm around the girl's shoulder and heaving her up with surprising strength.

"Once I'm outside," said Dorothy faintly, "I'll be all right."

"Oh, I know," said Deena. "It's the odor. The fish, Gummy's cheap perfume, Old Man's sweat, the beer. I forgot how it first affected me. But it's no better outside."

Dorothy didn't reply, but when she stepped through the door, she murmured, "Ohh!"

"Yes, I know," said Deena. "It's awful, but it won't kill you...."

Ten minutes later, Deena and a pale and weak Dorothy came out of the ramshackle outhouse.

They returned to the shanty, and for the first time Dorothy noticed that Elkins was sprawled face-up on the seat of the truck. His head hung over the end of the seat, and the flies buzzed around his open mouth.

"This is horrible," said Deena. "He'll be very angry when he wakes up and finds out where he is. He's such a respectable man."

"Let the heel sleep it off," said Dorothy. She walked into the shanty, and a moment later Paley clomped into the room, a smell of stale beer and very peculiar sweat advancing before him in a wave.

"How you feel?" he growled in a timbre so low the hairs on the back of her neck rose.

"Sick. I think I'll go home."

"Sure. Only try some a the hair."

He handed her a half-empty pint of whiskey. Dorothy re-

The Alley Man

luctantly downed a large shot chased with cold water. After a brief revulsion, she began feeling better and took another shot. She then washed her face in a bowl of water and drank a third whiskey.

"I think I can go with you now," she said. "But I don't care for breakfast."

"I ate already," he said. "Let's go. It's ten-thirty accordin to the clock on the gas station. My alley's prob'ly been cleaned out by now. Them other ragpickers are always moochin in on my territory when they think I'm stayin home. But you kin bet they're scared out a their pants every time they see a shadow cause they're afraid it's Old Man and he'll catch em and squeeze their guts out and crack their ribs with this one good arm."

Laughing a laugh so hoarse and unhuman it seemed to come from some troll deep in the caverns of his bowels, he opened the refrigerator and took another beer.

"I need another to get me started, not to mention what I'll have to give that damn balky bitch, Fordiana."

As they stepped outside, they saw Elkins stumble toward the outhouse and then fall headlong through the open doorway. He lay motionless on the floor, his feet sticking out of the entrance. Alarmed, Dorothy wanted to go after him, but Paley shook his head.

"He's a big boy; he kin take care a hisself. We got to get Fordiana up and goin."

Fordiana was the battered and rusty pickup truck. It was parked outside Paley's bedroom window so he could look out at any time of the night and make sure no one was stealing parts or even the whole truck.

"Not that I ought a worry about her," grumbled Old Man. He drank three-fourths of the quart in four mighty gulps, then uncapped the truck's radiator and poured the rest of the beer down it.

"She knows nobody else'll give her beer, so I think that if any a these robbin figurers that live on the dump or at the shacks aroun the bend was to try to steal anythin off'n her, she'd honk and backfire and throw rods and oil all over the place so's her Old Man could wake up and punch the figurin shirt off a the thievin figurer. But maybe not. She's a female. And you kin't trust a figurin female."

He poured the last drop down the radiator and roared, "There! Now don't you dare *not* turn over. You're robbin me a the good beer I could be havin! If you so much as backfire,

Old Man'll beat hell out a you with a sledgehammer!"

Wide-eyed but silent, Dorothy climbed onto the ripped open front seat beside Paley. The starter whirred, and the motor sputtered.

"No more beer if you don't work!" shouted Paley.

There was a bang, a fizz, a sput, a *whop, whop, whop,* a clash of gears, a monstrous and triumphant showing of teeth by Old Man, and they were bumpbumping over the rough ruts.

"Old man knows how to handle all them bitches, flesh or tin, two-legged, four-legged, wheeled. I sweat beer and passion and promise em a kick in the tailpipe if they don't behave, and that gets em all. I'm so figurin ugly I turn their stomachs. But once they get a whiff a the out-a-this-world stink a me, they're done for, they fall prostrooted at my big hairy feet. That's the way it's always been with us Paley men and the *G'yaga* wimmen. That's why their menfolks fear us, and why we got into so much trouble."

Dorothy did not say anything, and Paley fell silent as soon as the truck swung off the dump and onto U.S. Route 24. He seemed to fold up into himself, to be trying to make himself as inconspicuous as possible. During the three minutes it took the truck to get from the shanty to the city limits, he kept wiping his sweating palm against his blue workman's shirt.

But he did not try to release the tension with oaths. Instead, he muttered a string of what seemed to Dorothy nonsense rhymes.

"Eenie, meenie, minie, moe. Be a good Guy, help me go. Hoola boola, teenie weenie, ram em, damn em, figure em, duck em, watch me go, don't be a shmoe. Stop em, block em, sing a go go go."

Not until they had gone a mile into the city of Onaback and turned from 24 into an alley did he relax.

"Whew! That's torture, and I been doin it ever since I was sixteen, some years ago. Today seems worse'n ever, maybe cause you're along. *G'yaga* men don't like it if they see me with one a their wimmen, specially a cute chick like you."

Suddenly, he smiled and broke into a song about being covered all over "with sweet violets, sweeter than all the roses." He sang other songs, some of which made Dorothy turn red in the face though at the same time she giggled. When they crossed a street to get from one alley to another, he cut off his singing, even in the middle of a phrase, and resumed it on the other side.

The Alley Man

Reaching the west bluff, he slowed the truck to a crawl while his little blue eyes searched the ash heaps and garbage cans at the rears of the houses. Presently, he stopped the truck and climbed down to inspect his find.

"Guy In The Sky, we're off to a flyin start! Look!—some old grates from a coal furnace. And a pile a coke and beer bottles, all redeemable. Get down, Dor'thy—if you want to know how us ragpickers make a livin, you gotta get in and sweat and cuss with us. And if you come acrosst any hats, be sure to tell me."

Dorothy smiled. But when she stepped down from the truck, she winced.

"What's the matter?"

"Headache."

"The sun'll boil it out. Here's how we do this collectin, see? The back end a the truck is boarded up into five sections. This section here is for the iron and the wood. This, for the paper. This, for the cardboard. You get a higher price for the cardboard. This, for rags. This, for bottles we kin get a refund on. If you find any int'restin books or magazines, put em on the seat. I'll decide if I want to keep em or throw em in with the old paper."

They worked swiftly, and then drove on. About a block later, they were interrupted at another heap by a leaf of a woman, withered and blown by the winds of time. She hobbled out from the back porch of a large three-storied house with diamond-shaped panes in the windows and doors and cupolas at the corners. In a quavering voice she explained that she was the widow of a wealthy lawyer who had died fifteen years ago. Not until today had she made up her mind to get rid of his collection of law books and legal papers. These were all neatly cased in cardboard boxes not too large to be handled.

Not even, she added, her pale watery eyes flickering from Paley to Dorothy, not even by a poor one-armed man and a young girl.

Old Man took off his homburg and bowed.

"Sure, ma'am, my daughter and myself'd be glad to help you out in your housecleanin."

"Your daughter?" croaked the old woman.

"She don't look like me a tall," he replied. "No wonder. She's my foster daughter, poor girl, she was orphaned when she was still fillin her diapers. My best friend was her father. He died savin my life, and as he laid gaspin his life away in my arms, he begged me to take care a her as if she was my own. And I kept my promise to my dyin friend, may his soul rest in peace. And even if I'm only a poor ragpicker, ma'am, I been doin my best to raise her to be a decent Godfearin obedient girl."

Dorothy had to run around to the other side of the truck where she could cover her mouth and writhe in an agony of attempting to smother her laughter. When she regained control, the old lady was telling Paley she'd show him where the books were. Then she started hobbling to the porch.

But Old Man, instead of following her across the yard, stopped by the fence that separated the alley from the backyard. He turned around and gave Dorothy a look of extreme despair.

"What's the matter?" she said. "Why're you sweating so? And shaking? And you're so pale."

"You'd laugh if I tole you, and I don't like to be laughed at."

"Tell me. I won't laugh."

He closed his eyes and began muttering. "Never mind, it's in the mind. Never mind, you're just fine." Opening his eyes, he shook himself like a dog just come from the water.

"I kin do it. I got the guts. All them books're a lotta beer money I'll lose if I don't go down into the bowels a hell and get em. Guy in The Sky, give me the guts a a goat and the nerve a a pork dealer in Palestine. You know Old Man ain't got a yellow streak. It's the wicked spell a the False Folkers workin on me. Come on, let's go, go, go."

And sucking in a deep breath, he stepped through the gateway. Head down, eyes on the grass at his feet, he shuffled toward the cellar door where the old lady stood peering at him.

Four steps away from the cellar entrance, he halted again. A small black spaniel had darted from around the corner of the house and begun yapyapping at him.

Old Man suddenly cocked his head to one side, crossed his eyes, and deliberately sneezed.

Yelping, the spaniel fled back around the corner, and Paley walked down the steps that led to the cool dark basement. As he did so, he muttered, "That puts the evil spell on em figurin dogs."

When they had piled all the books in the back of the truck, he took off his homburg and bowed again.

"Ma'am, my daughter and myself both thank you from the rockbottom a our poor but humble hearts for this treasure trove you give us. And if ever you've anythin else you don't want, and a strong back and a weak mind to carry it out... well, please remember we'll be down this alley every Blue Monday and Fish Friday about time the sun is three-quarters acrosst the sky. Providin it ain't rainin cause The Old Guy In The Sky is cryin in his beer over us poor mortals, what fools we be."

Then he put his hat on, and the two got into the truck and chugged off. They stopped by several other promising heaps before he announced that the truck was loaded enough. He felt like celebrating; perhaps they should stop off behind Mike's Tavern and down a few quarts. She replied that perhaps she might manage a drink if she could have a whiskey. Beer wouldn't set well.

"I got some money," rumbled Old Man, unbuttoning with slow clumsy fingers his shirt pocket and pulling out a roll of worn tattered bills while the truck's wheels rolled straight in the alley ruts.

"You brought me luck, so Old Man's gonna pay today through the hose, I mean, nose, har, har, har!"

He stopped Fordiana behind a little neighborhood tavern. Dorothy, without being asked, took the two dollars he handed her and went into the building. She returned with a can opener, two quarts of beer, and a half pint of V.O.

"I added some of my money. I can't stand cheap whiskey."

They sat on the running board of the truck, drinking, Old Man doing most of the talking. It wasn't long before he was telling her of the times when the Real Folk, the Paleys, had lived in Europe and Asia by the side of the woolly mammoths and the cave lion.

"We worshiped The Old Guy In The Sky who says what the thunder says and lives in the east on the tallest mountain in the world. We faced the skulls a our dead to the east so they could see The Old Guy when he came to take them to live with him in the mountain.

"And we was doin fine for a long long time. Then, out a the east come them motherworshipin False Folk with their long straight legs and long straight necks and flat faces and thundermug round heads and their bows and arrows. They claimed they was sons a the goddess Mother Earth, who was a virgin. But we claimed the truth was that a crow with stomach trouble sat on a stump and when it left the hot sun hatched em out.

"Well, for a while we beat em hands-down because we was

stronger. Even one a our wimmen could tear their strongest man to bits. Still, they had that bow and arrow, they kept pickin us off, and movin in and movin in, and we kept movin back slowly, till pretty soon we was shoved with our backs against the ocean.

"Then one day a big chief among us got a bright idea. 'Why don't we make bows and arrows, too?' he said. And so we did, but we was clumsy at makin and shootin em cause our hands was so big, though we could draw a heavier bow'n em. So we kept gettin run out a the good huntin grounds.

"There was one thin might a been in our favor. That was, we bowled the wimmen a the Falsers over with our smell. Not that we smell good. We stink like a pig that's been makin love to a billy goat on a manure pile. But, somehow, the wimmen folk a the Falsers was all mixed up in their chemistry, I guess you'd call it, cause they got all excited and developed round-heels when they caught a whiff a us. If we'd been left alone with em, we could a Don Juan'd them Falsers right off a the face a the earth. We would a mixed our blood with theirs so much that after a while you coun't tell the diff'runce. Specially since the kids lean to their pa's side in looks, Paley blood is so much stronger.

"But that made sure there would always be war tween us. Specially after our king, Old King Paley, made love to the daughter a the Falser king, King Raw Boy, and stole her away.

"Gawd, you should a seen the fuss then! Raw Boy's daughter flipped over Old King Paley. And it was her give him the bright idea a callin in every able-bodied Paley that was left and organizin em into one big army. Kind a puttin all our eggs in one basket, but it seemed a good idea. Every man big enough to carry a club went out in one big mob on Operation False Folk Massacre. And we ganged up on every little town a them mother-worshipers we found. And kicked hell out a em. And roasted the men's hearts and ate em. And every now and then took a snack off the wimmen and kids, too.

"Then, all of a sudden, we come to a big plain. And there's a army a them False Folk, collected by Old King Raw Boy. They outnumber us, but we feel we kin lick the world. Specially since the magic strength a the *G'yaga* lies in their wimmen folk, cause they worship a woman god, The Old Woman In The Earth. And we've got their chief priestess, Raw Boy's daughter.

"All our own personal power is collected in Old King Paley's

The Alley Man

hat—his magical headpiece. All a us Paleys believed that a man's strength and his soul was in his headpiece.

"We bed down the night before the big battle. At dawn there's a cry that'd wake up the dead. It still sends shivers down the necks a us Paley's fifty thousand years later. It's King Paley roarin and cryin. We ask him why. He says that that dirty little sneakin little hoor, Raw Boy's daughter, has stole his headpiece and run off with it to her father's camp.

"Our knees turn weak as nearbeer. Our manhood is in the hands a our enemies. But out we go to battle, our witch doctors out in front rattlin their gourds and whirlin their bullroarers and prayin. And here comes the *G'yaga* medicine men doin the same. Only thing, their hearts is in their work cause they got Old King's headpiece stuck on the end a a spear.

"And for the first time they use dogs in war, too. Dogs never did like us any more'n we like em.

"And then we charge into each other. Bang! Wallop! Crash! Smash! Whack! Owwwrrroooo! And they kick hell out a us, do it to us. And we're never again the same, done forever. They had Old King's headpiece and with it our magic, cause we'd all put the soul a us Paleys in that hat.

"The spirit and power a us Paleys was prisoners cause that headpiece was. And life became too much for us Paleys. Them as wasn't slaughtered and eaten was glad to settle down on the garbage heaps a the conquerin Falsers and pick for a livin with the chickens, sometimes comin out second best.

"But we knew Old King's headpiece was hidden somewhere, and we organized a secret society and swore to keep alive his name and to search for the headpiece if it took us forever. Which it almost has, it's been so long.

"But even though we was doomed to live in shantytowns and stay off the streets and prowl the junkpiles in the alleys, we never gave up hope. And as time went on some a the nocounts a the *G'yaga* came down to live with us. And we and they had kids. Soon, most a us had disappeared into the bloodstream a the low-class *G'yaga*. But there's always been a Paley family that tried to keep their blood pure. No man kin do no more, kin he?"

He glared at Dorothy. "What d'ya think a that?"

Weakly, she said, "Well, I've never heard anything like it."

"Gawdamighty!" snorted Old Man. "I give you a history longer'n a hoor's dream, more'n fifty thousand years a history, the secret story a a longlost race. And all you kin say is that you never heard nothin like it before."

He leaned toward her and clamped his huge hand over her thigh.

"Don't flinch from me!" he said fiercely. "Or turn your head away. Sure, I stink, and I offend your dainty figurin nostrils and upset your figurin delicate little guts. But what's a minute's whiff a me on your part compared to a lifetime on my part a havin all the stinkin garbage in the universe shoved up my nose, and my mouth filled with what you woun't say if your mouth was full a it? What do you say to that, huh?"

Coolly, she said, "Please take your hand off me."

"Sure, I din't mean nothin by it. I got carried away and forgot my place in society."

"Now, look here," she said earnestly. "That has nothing at all to do with your so-called social position. It's just that I don't allow anybody to take liberties with my body. Maybe I'm being ridiculously Victorian, but I want more than just sensuality. I want love, and—"

"OK, I get the idea."

Dorothy stood up and said, "I'm only a block from my apartment. I think I'll walk on home. The liquor's given me a headache."

"Yeah," he growled "You sure it's the liquor and not me?"

She looked steadily at him. "I'm going, but I'll see you tomorrow morning. Does that answer your question?"

"OK," he grunted. "See you. Maybe."

She walked away very fast.

Next morning, shortly after dawn, a sleepy-eyed Dorothy stopped her car before the Paley shanty. Deena was the only one home. Gummy had gone to the river to fish, and Old Man was in the outhouse. Dorothy took the opportunity to talk to Deena, and found her, as she had suspected, a woman of considerable education. However, although she was polite, she was reticent about her background. Dorothy, in an effort to keep the conversation going, mentioned that she had phoned her former anthropology professor and asked him about the chances of Old Man being a genuine Neanderthal. It was then that Deena broke her reserve and eagerly asked what the professor had thought.

"Well," said Dorothy, "he just laughed. He told me it was an absolute impossibility that a small group, even an inbred group isolated in the mountains, could have kept their cultural and genetic identity for fifty thousand years.

"I argued with him. I told him Old Man insisted he and his kind had existed in the village of Paley in the mountains of the Pyrenees until Napoleon's men found them and tried to draft them. Then they fled to America, after a stay in England. And his group was split up during the Civil War, driven out of the Great Smokies. He, as far as he knows, is the last purebreed, Gummy being a half or quarter-breed.

"The professor assured me that Gummy and Old Man were cases of glandular malfunctioning, of acromegaly. That they may have a superficial resemblance to the Neanderthal man, but a physical anthropologist could tell the difference at a glance. When I got a little angry and asked him if he wasn't taking an unscientific and prejudiced attitude, he became rather irritated. Our talk ended somewhat frostily.

"But I went down to the university library that night and read everything on what makes *Homo Neanderthalensis* different from *Homo sapiens*."

"You almost sound as if you believe Old Man's private little myth is the truth," said Deena.

"The professor taught me to be convinced only by the facts and not to say anything is impossible," replied Dorothy. "If he's forgotten his own teachings, I haven't."

"Well, Old Man is a persuasive talker," said Deena. "He could sell the devil a harp and halo."

Old Man, wearing only a pair of blue jeans, entered the shanty. For the first time Dorothy saw his naked chest, huge, covered with long redgold hairs so numerous they formed a matting almost as thick as an orangutan's. However, it was not his chest but his bare feet at which she looked most intently. Yes, the big toes were widely separated from the others, and he certainly tended to walk on the outside of his feet.

His arm, too, seemed abnormally short in proportion to his body.

Old Man grunted a good morning and didn't say much for a while. But after he had sweated and cursed and chanted his way through the streets of Onaback and had arrived safely at the alleys of the west bluff, he relaxed. Perhaps he was helped by finding a large pile of papers and rags.

"Well, here we go to work, so don't you dare to shirk. Jump, Dor'thy! By the sweat a your brow, you'll earn your brew!"

When that load was on the truck, they drove off. Paley said,

"How you like this life without no strife? Good, huh? You like alleys, huh?"

Dorothy nodded. "As a child, I liked alleys better than streets. And they still preserve something of their first charm for me. They were more fun to play in, so nice and cozy. The trees and bushes and fences leaned in at you and sometimes touched you as if they had hands and liked to feel your face to find out if you'd been there before, and they remembered you. You felt as if you were sharing a secret with the alleys and the things of the alleys. But streets, well, streets were always the same, and you had to watch out the cars didn't run you over, and the windows in the houses were full of faces and eyes, poking their noses into your business, if you can say that eyes had noses."

Old Man whooped and slapped his thigh so hard it would have broke if it had been Dorothy's.

"You must be a Paley! We feel that way, too! We ain't allowed to hang aroun streets, so we make our alleys into little kingdoms. Tell me, do you sweat just crossin a street from one alley to the next?"

He put his hand on her knee. She looked down at it but said nothing, and he left it there while the truck putputted along, its wheels following the ruts of the alley.

"No, I don't feel that way at all."

"Yeah? Well, when you was a kid, you wasn't so ugly you hadda stay off the streets. But I still wasn't too happy in the alleys because a them figurin dogs. Forever and forever they was barkin and bitin at me. So I took to beatin the bejesus out a them with a big stick I always carried. But after a while I found out I only had to look at em in a certain way. Yi, yi, yi, they'd run away yapping, like that old black spaniel did yesterday. Why? Cause they knew I was sneezin evil spirits at em. It was then I began to know I wasn't human. A course, my old man had been tellin me that ever since I could talk.

"As I grew up I felt every day that the spell a the *G'yaga* was gettin stronger. I was gettin dirtier and dirtier looks from em on the streets. And when I went down the alleys, I felt like I really *belonged* there. Finally, the day came when I coun't cross a street without gettin sweaty hands and cold feet and a dry mouth and breathin hard. That was cause I was becomin a full-grown Paley, and the curse a the *G'yaga* gets more powerful as you get more hair on your chest."

"Curse?" said Dorothy. "Some people call it a neurosis."

"It's a curse."

Dorothy didn't answer. Again, she looked down at her knee, and this time he removed his hand. He would have had to do it, anyway, for they had come to a paved street.

On the way down to the junk dealer's, he continued the same theme. And when they got to the shanty, he elaborated upon it.

During the thousands of years the Paley lived on the garbage piles of the *G'yaga*, they were closely watched. So, in the old days, it had been the custom for the priests and warriors of the False Folk to descend on the dumpheap dwellers whenever a strong and obstreperous Paley came to manhood. And they had gouged out an eye or cut off his hand or leg or some other member to ensure that he remembered what he was and where his place was.

"That's why I lost this arm," Old Man growled, waving the stump. "Fear a the *G'yaga* for the Paley did this to me."

Deena howled with laughter and said, "Dorothy, the truth is that he got drunk one night and passed out on the railroad tracks, and a freight train ran over his arm."

"Sure, sure, that's the way it was. But it coun't a happened if the Falsers din't work through their evil black magic. Nowadays, stead a cripplin us openly, they use spells. They ain't got the guts anymore to do it themselves."

Deena laughed scornfully and said, "He got all those psychopathic ideas from reading those comics and weird tale magazines and those crackpot books and from watching that TV program, *Alley Oop and the Dinosaur*. I can point out every story from which he's stolen an idea."

"You're a liar!" thundered Old Man.

He struck Deena on the shoulder. She reeled away from the blow, then leaned back toward him as if into a strong wind. He struck her again, this time across her purple birthmark. Her eyes glowed, and she cursed him. And he hit her once more, hard enough to hurt but not to injure.

Dorothy opened her mouth as if to protest, but Gummy lay a fat sweaty hand on her shoulder and lifted her finger to her own lips.

Deena fell to the floor from a particularly violent blow. She did not stand up again. Instead, she got to her hands and knees and crawled toward the refuge behind the big iron stove. His naked foot shoved her rear so that she was sent sprawling on her face, moaning, her long stringy black hair falling over her face and birthmark.

Dorothy stepped forward and raised her hand to grab Old Man. Gummy stopped her, mumbling, "'S all right. Leave em alone."

"Look at that figurin female bein happy!" snorted Old Man. "You know why I *have* to beat the hell out a her, when all I want is peace and quiet? Cause I look like a figurin caveman, and they're supposed to beat their hoors silly. That's why she took up with me."

"You're an insane liar," said Deena softly from behind the stove, slowly and dreamily nursing her pain like the memory of a lover's caresses. "I came to live with you because I'd sunk so low you were the only man that'd have me."

"She's a retired high society mainliner, Dor'thy," said Paley. "You never seen her without a longsleeved dress on. That's cause her arms're full a holes. It was me that kicked the monkey off a her back. I cured her with the wisdom and magic a the Real Folk, where you coax the evil spirit out by talkin it out. And she's been livin with me ever since. Kin't get rid a her.

"Now, you take that toothless bag there. I ain't never hit her. That shows I ain't no woman-beatin bastard, right? I hit Deena cause she likes it, wants it, but I don't ever hit Gummy.... Hey, Gummy, that kind a medicine ain't what you want, is it?"

And he laughed his incredibly hoarse *hor, hor, hor*.

"You're a figurin liar," said Gummy, speaking over her shoulder because she was squatting down, fiddling with the TV controls. "You're the one knocked most a my teeth out."

"I knocked out a few rotten stumps you was gonna lose anyway. You had it comin cause you was runnin aroun with that O'Brien in his green shirt."

Gummy giggled and said, "Don't think for a minute I quit goin with that O'Brien in his green shirt just cause you slapped me aroun a little bit. I quit cause you was a better man 'n him."

Gummy giggled again. She rose and waddled across the room toward a shelf which held a bottle of her cheap perfume. Her enormous brass earrings swung, and her great hips swung back and forth.

"Look at that," said Old Man. "Like two bags a mush in a windstorm."

The Alley Man

But his eyes followed them with kindling appreciation, and, on seeing her pour that reeking liquid over her pillow-sized bosom, he hugged her and buried his huge nose in the valley of her breasts and sniffed rapturously.

"I feel like a dog that's found an old bone he buried and forgot till just now," he growled. "Arf, arf, arf!"

Deena snorted and said she had to get some fresh air or she'd lose her supper. She grabbed Dorothy's hand and insisted she take a walk with her. Dorothy, looking sick, went with her.

The following evening, as the four were drinking beer around the kitchen table, Old Man suddenly reached over and touched Dorothy affectionately. Gummy laughed, but Deena glared. However, she did not say anything to the girl but instead began accusing Paley of going too long without a bath. He called her a flatchested hophead and said that she was lying, because he had been taking a bath every day. Deena replied that, yes he had, ever since Dorothy had appeared on the scene. An argument raged. Finally, he rose from the table and turned the photograph of Deena's mother so it faced the wall.

Wailing, Deena tried to face it outward again. He pushed her away from it, refusing to hit her despite her insults—even when she howled at him that he wasn't fit to lick her mother's shoes, let alone blaspheme her portrait by touching it.

Tired of the argument, he abandoned his post by the photograph and shuffled to the refrigerator.

"If you dare turn her aroun till I give the word, I'll throw her in the creek. And you'll never see her again."

Deena shrieked and crawled onto her blanket behind the stove and there lay sobbing and cursing him softly.

Gummy chewed tobacco and laughed while a brown stream ran down her toothless jaws. "Deena pushed him too far that time."

"Ah, her and her figurin mother," snorted Paley. "Hey, Dor'thy, you know how she laughs at me cause I think Fordiana's got a soul. And I put the evil eye on em hounds? And cause I think the salvation a us Paleys'll be when we find out where Old King's hat's been hidden?

"Well, get a load a this. This here intellekchooall purple-faced dragon, this retired mainliner, this old broken-down nag for a monkey-jockey, she's the sooperstishus one. She thinks her mother's a god. And she prays to her and asks forgiveness and asks what's gonna happen in the future. And when she thinks nobody's aroun, she talks to her. Here she is, worshipin her mother like The Old Woman In The Earth, who's The Old Guy's enemy. And she knows that makes The Old Guy sore. Maybe that's the reason he ain't allowed me to find the longlost headpiece a Old King, though he knows I been lookin in every ash heap from here to Godknowswhere, hopin some fool G'yaga would throw it away never realizin what it was.

"Well, by all that's holy, that pitcher stays with its ugly face on the wall. Aw, shut up, Deena, I wanna watch *Alley Oop*."

Shortly afterward, Dorothy drove home. There she again phoned her sociology professor. Impatiently, he went into more detail. He said that one reason Old Man's story of the war between the Neanderthals and the invading *Homo sapiens* was very unlikely was that there was evidence to indicate that *Homo sapiens* might have been in Europe before the Neanderthals— it was very possible the *Homo Neanderthalensis* was the invader.

"Not invader in the modern sense," said the professor. "The influx of a new species or race or tribe into Europe during the Paleolithic would have been a sporadic migration of little groups, an immigration which might have taken a thousand to ten thousand years to complete.

"And it is more than likely that *Neanderthalensis* and *sapiens* lived side by side for millennia with very little fighting between them because both were too busy struggling for a living. For one reason or another, probably because he was outnumbered, the Neanderthal was absorbed by the surrounding peoples. Some anthropologists have speculated that the Neanderthals were blonds and that they had passed their light hair directly to North Europeans.

"Whatever the guesses and surmises," concluded the professor, "it would be impossible for such a distinctly different minority to keep its special physical and cultural characteristics over a period of half a hundred millennia. Paley has concocted this personal myth to compensate for his extreme ugliness, his inferiority, his feelings of rejection. The elements of the myth came from the comic books and TV.

"However," concluded the professor, "in view of your youthful enthusiasm and naïveté, I will consider my judgment if you bring me some physical evidence of his Neanderthaloid origin. Say you could show me that he had a taurodont tooth. I'd be flabbergasted, to say the least."

"But, Professor," she pleaded, "why can't you give him a personal examination? One look at Old Man's foot would convince you, I'm sure."

"My dear, I am not addicted to wild-goose chases. My time is valuable."

That was that. The next day, she asked Old Man if he had ever lost a molar tooth or had an X-ray made of one.

"No," he said. "I got more sound teeth than brains. And I ain't gonna lose em. Long as I keep my headpiece, I'll keep my teeth and my digestion and my manhood. What's more, I'll keep my good sense, too. The loose-screw tighteners at the State Hospital really gave me a good goin-over, fore and aft, up and down, in and out, all night long, don't never take a hotel room right by the elevator. And they proved I wasn't hatched in a cuckoo clock. Even though they tore their hair and said somethin must be wrong. Specially after we had that row about my hat. I woun't let them take my blood for a test, you know, because I figured they was going to mix it with water—*G'yaga* magic—and turn my blood to water. Somehow, that Elkins got wise that I hadda wear my hat—cause I woun't take it off when I undressed for the physical, I guess— and he snatched my hat. And I was done for. Stealin it was stealin my soul; all Paleys wears their souls in their hats. I hadda get it back. So I ate humble pie; I let em poke and pry all over and take my blood."

There was a pause while Paley breathed in deeply to get power to launch another verbal rocket. Dorothy, who had been struck by an idea, said, "Speaking of hats, Old Man, what does this hat that the daughter of Raw Boy stole from King Paley look like? Would you recognize it if you saw it?"

Old Man stared at her with wide blue eyes for a moment before he exploded.

"Would I recognize it? Would the dog that sat by the railroad tracks recognize his tail after the locomotive cut it off? Would you recognize your own blood if somebody stuck you in the guts with a knife and it pumped out with every heartbeat? Certainly, I would recognize the hat a Old King Paley! Every Paley at his mother's knees gets a detailed description a it. You want to hear about the hat? Well, hang on, chick, and I'll describe every hair and bone a it."

Dorothy told herself more than once that she should not be doing this. If she was trusted by Old Man, she was, in one sense, a false friend. But, she reassured herself, in another sense she was helping him. Should he find the hat, he might blossom forth, actually tear himself loose from the taboos that bound him to the dumpheap, to the alleys, to fear of dogs, to the conviction he was an inferior and oppressed citizen. Moreover, Dorothy told herself, it would aid her scientific studies to record his reactions.

The taxidermist she hired to locate the necessary materials and fashion them into the desired shape was curious, but she told him it was for an anthropological exhibit in Chicago and that it was meant to represent the headpiece of the medicine man of an Indian secret society dedicated to phallic mysteries. The taxidermist sniggered and said he'd give his eyeteeth to see those ceremonies.

Dorothy's intentions were helped by the run of good luck Old Man had in his alleypicking while she rode with him. Exultant, he swore he was headed for some extraordinary find; he could feel his good fortune building up.

"It's gonna hit," he said, grinning with his huge widely spaced gravestone teeth. "Like lightnin."

Two days later, Dorothy rose even earlier than usual and drove to a place behind the house of a well-known doctor. She had read in the society column that he and his family were vacationing in Alaska, so she knew they wouldn't be wondering at finding a garbage can already filled with garbage and a big cardboard box full of cast-off clothes. Dorothy had brought the refuse from her own apartment to make it seem as if the house were occupied. The old garments, with one exception, she had purchased at a Salvation Army store.

About nine that morning, she and Old Man drove down the alley on their scheduled route.

Old Man was first off the truck; Dorothy hung back to let him make the discovery.

Old Man picked the garments out of the box one by one.

"Here's a velvet dress Deena kin wear. She's been complainin she hasn't had a new dress in a long time. And here's a blouse and skirt big enough to wrap aroun an elephant. Gummy kin wear it. And here..."

He lifted up a tall conical hat with a wide brim and two balls of felted horsemane attached to the band. It was a strange headpiece, fashioned of roan horsehide over a ribwork of split bones. It must have been the only one of its kind in the world,

The Alley Man

and it certainly looked out of place in the alley of a mid-Illinois city.

Old Man's eyes bugged out. Then they rolled up, and he fell to the ground, as if shot. The hat, however, was still clutched in his hand.

Dorothy was terrified. She had expected any reaction but this. If he had suffered a heart attack, it would, she thought, be her fault.

Fortunately, Old Man had only fainted. However, when he regained consciousness, he did not go into ecstasies as she had expected. Instead, he looked at her, his face gray and said, "It kin't be! It must be a trick The Old Woman In The Earth's playing on me so she kin have the last laugh on me. How could it be the hat a Old King Paley's? Woun't the *G'yaga* that been keepin it in their famley all these years know what it is?"

"Probably not," said Dorothy. "After all, the *G'yaga*, as you call them, don't believe in magic anymore. Or it might be that the present owner doesn't even know what it is."

"Maybe. More likely it was thrown out by accident durin housecleanin. You know how stupid them wimmen are. Anyway, let's take it and get goin. The Old Guy In The Sky might a had a hand in fixin up this deal for me, and if he did, it's better not to ask questions. Let's go."

Old Man seldom wore the hat. When he was home, he put it in the parrot cage and locked the cage door with the bicycle lock. At nights, the cage hung from the stand; days, it sat on the seat of the truck. Old Man wanted it always where he could see it.

Finding it had given him a tremendous optimism, a belief he could do anything. He sang and laughed even more than he had before, and he was even able to venture out onto the streets for several hours at a time before the sweat and shakings began.

Gummy, seeing the hat, merely grunted and made a lewd remark about its appearance. Deena smiled grimly and said, "Why haven't the horsehide and bones rotted away long ago?"

"That's just the kind a question a *G'yaga* dummy like you'd ask," said Old Man, snorting. "How kin the hat rot when there's a million Paley souls crowded into it, standin room only? There ain't even elbow room for germs. Besides, the horsehide and the bones're jampacked with the power and the glory a all the Paleys that died before our battle with Raw Boy, and all the souls that died since. It's seethin with soul-energy, the lid held on it by the magic a the *G'yaga*."

"Better watch out it don't blow up 'n wipe us all out," said Gummy, sniggering.

"Now you have the hat, what are you going to do with it?" asked Deena.

"I don't know. I'll have to sit down with a beer and study the situation."

Suddenly, Deena began laughing shrilly.

"My God, you've been thinking for fifty thousand years about this hat, and now you've got it, you don't know what to do about it! Well, I'll tell you what you'll do about it! You'll get to thinking big, all right! You'll conquer the world, rid it of all False Folk, all right! You fool! Even if your story isn't the raving of a lunatic, it would still be too late for you! You're alone! The last! One against two billion! Don't worry, World, this ragpicking Rameses, this alley Alexander, this junkyard Julius Caesar, he isn't going to conquer you! No, he's going to put on his hat, and he's going forth! To do what?

"To become a wrestler on TV, that's what! That's the height of his halfwit ambition—to be billed as the One-Armed Neanderthal, the Awful Apeman. That is the culmination of fifty thousand years ha, ha, ha!"

The others looked apprehensively at Old Man, expecting him to strike Deena. Instead, he removed the hat from the cage, put it on, and sat down at the table with a quart of beer in his hand.

"Quit your cacklin, you old hen," he said. "I got my thinkin cap on!"

The next day Paley, despite a hangover, was in a very good mood. He chattered all the way to the west bluff and once stopped the truck so he could walk back and forth on the street and show Dorothy he wasn't afraid.

Then, boasting he could lick the world, he drove the truck up an alley and halted it by the backyard of a huge but somewhat run-down mansion. Dorothy looked at him curiously. He pointed to the jungle-thick shrubbery that filled a corner of the yard.

"Looks like a rabbit coun't get in there, huh? But Old Man knows thins the rabbits don't. Folly me."

Carrying the caged hat, he went to the shrubbery, dropped to all threes, and began inching his way through a very narrow passage. Dorothy stood looking dubiously into the tangle until a hoarse growl came from its depths.

"You scared? Or is your fanny too broad to get through here?"

"I'll try anything once," she announced cheerfully. In a short time she was crawling on her belly, then had come suddenly into a little clearing. Old Man was standing up. The cage was at his feet, and he was looking at a red rose in his hand.

She sucked in her breath. "Roses! Peonies! Violets!"

"Sure, Dor'thy," he said, swelling out his chest. "Paley's Garden a Eden, his secret hothouse. I found this place a couple a years ago, when I was lookin for a place to hide if the cops was lookin for me or I just wanted a place to be alone from everybody, including myself.

"I planted these rosebushes in here and these other flowers. I come here every now and then to check on em, spray em, prune em. I never take any home, even though I'd like to give Deena some. But Deena ain't no dummy, she'd know I was gettin em out a a garbage pail. And I just din't want to tell her about this place. Or anybody."

He looked directly at her as if to catch every twitch of a muscle in her face, every repressed emotion.

"You're the only person besides myself knows about this place." He held out the rose to her. "Here. It's yours."

"Thank you. I am proud, really proud, that you've shown this place to me."

"Really are? That makes me feel good. In fact, great."

"It's amazing. This, this spot of beauty. And... and..."

"I'll finish it for you. You never thought the ugliest man in the world, a dumpheaper, a man that ain't even a man or a human bein, a—I hate that word—a Neanderthal, could appreciate the beauty of a rose. Right? Well, I growed these because I loved em.

"Look, Dor'thy. Look at this rose. It's round, not like a ball but a flattened roundness...."

"Oval."

"Sure. And look at the petals. How they fold in on one another, how they're arranged. Like one ring a red towers protectin the next ring a red towers. Protectin the gold cup on the inside, the precious source a life, the treasure. Or maybe that's the golden hair a the princess a the castle. Maybe. And look at the bright green leaves under the rose. Beautiful, huh? The Old Guy knew what he was doin when he made these. He was an artist then.

"But he must a been sufferin from a hangover when he shaped me, huh? His hands was shaky that day. And he gave up after a while and never bothered to finish me but went on down to the corner for some a the hair a the dog that bit him."

Suddenly, tears filled Dorothy's eyes.

"You shouldn't feel that way. You've got beauty, sensitivity, a genuine feeling, under..."

"Under this?" he said, pointing his finger at his face. "Sure. Forget it. Anyway, look at these green buds on these baby roses. Pretty, huh? Fresh with promise a the beauty to come. They're shaped like the breasts a young virgins."

He took a step forward her and put his arm around her shoulders.

"Dor'thy."

She put both her hands on his chest and gently tried to shove herself away.

"Please," she whispered, "please, don't. Not after you've shown me how fine you really can be."

"What do you mean?" he said, not releasing her. "Ain't what I want to do with you just as fine and beautiful a thin as this rose here? And if you really feel for me, you'd want to let your flesh say what your mind thinks. Like the flowers when they open up for the sun."

She shook her head. "No. It can't be. Please. I feel terrible because I can't say yes. But I can't. I—you—there's too much diff—"

"Sure, we're diff'runt. Goin in diff'runt directions and then, comin roun the corner—bam!—we run into each other, and we wrap our arms aroun each other to keep from fallin."

He pulled her to him so her face was pressed against his chest.

"See!" he rumbled. "Like this. Now, breathe deep. Don't turn your head. Sniff away. Lock yourself to me, like we was glued and nothin could pull us apart. Breathe deep. I got my arm aroun you, like these trees roun these flowers. I'm not hurtin you: I'm givin you life and protectin you. Right? Breathe deep."

"Please," she whimpered. "Don't hurt me. Gently..."

"Gently it is. I won't hurt you. Not too much. That's right, don't hold yourself stiff against me, like you're stone. That's right, melt like butter. I'm not forcin you, Dor'thy, remember that. You want this, don't you?"

"Don't hurt me," she whispered. "You're so strong, oh my God, so strong."

For two days, Dorothy did not appear at the Paleys'. The third morning, in an effort to fire her courage, she downed two double shots of V.O. before breakfast. When she drove to the dumpheap, she told the two women that she had not been feeling well. But she had returned because she wanted to finish her study, as it was almost at an end and her superiors were anxious to get her report.

Paley, though he did not smile when he saw her, said nothing. However, he kept looking at her out of the corners of his eyes when he thought she was watching him. And though he took the hat in its cage with him, he sweated and shook as before while crossing the streets. Dorothy sat staring straight ahead, unresponding to the few remarks he did make. Finally, cursing under his breath, he abandoned his effort to work as usual and drove to the hidden garden.

"Here we are," he said. "Adam and Eve returnin to Eden."

He peered from beneath the bony ridges of his brows at the sky. "We better hurry in. Looks as if The Old Guy got up on the wrong side a the bed. There's gonna be a storm."

"I'm not going in there with you," said Dorothy. "Not now or ever."

"Even after what we did, even if you said you loved me, I still make you sick?" he said. "You sure din't act then like Old Ugly made you sick."

"I haven't been able to sleep for two nights," she said tonelessly. "I've asked myself a thousand times why I did it. And each time I could only tell myself I didn't know. Something seemed to leap from you to me and take me over. I was powerless."

"You certainly wasn't paralyzed," said Old Man, placing his hand on her knee. "And if you was powerless, it was because you wanted to be."

"It's no use talking," she said. "You'll never get a chance again. And take your hand off me. It makes my flesh crawl."

He dropped his hand.

"All right. Back to business. Back to pickin people's piles a junk. Let's get out a here. Forget what I said. Forget this garden, too. Forget the secret I told you. Don't tell nobody. The dumpheapers'd laugh at me. Imagine Old Man Paley, the one-armed candidate for the puzzle factory, the fugitive from the Old Stone Age, growin peonies and roses! Big laugh, huh?"

Dorothy did not reply. He started the truck and, as they emerged onto the alley, they saw the sun disappear behind the clouds. The rest of the day, it did not come out, and Old Man and Dorothy did not speak to each other.

As they were going down Route 24 after unloading at the junkdealer's, they were stopped by a patrolman. He ticketed Paley for not having a chauffeur's license and made Paley follow him downtown to court. There Old Man had to pay a fine of twenty-five dollars. This, to everybody's amazement, he produced from his pocket.

As if that weren't enough, he had to endure the jibes of the police and the courtroom loafers. Evidently he had appeared in the police station before and was known as *King Kong, Alley Oop,* or just plain Chimp. Old Man trembled, whether with suppressed rage or nervousness Dorothy could not tell. But later, as Dorothy drove him home, he almost frothed at the mouth in a tremendous outburst of rage. By the time they were within sight of his shanty, he was shouting that his life savings had been wiped out and that it was all a plot by the *G'yaga* to beat him down to starvation.

It was then that the truck's motor died. Cursing, Old Man jerked the hood open so savagely that one rusty hinge broke. Further enraged by this, he tore the hood completely off and threw it away into the ditch by the roadside. Unable to find the cause of the breakdown, he took a hammer from the toolchest and began to beat the sides of the truck.

"I'll make her go, go, go!" he shouted. "Or she'll wish she had! Run, you bitch, purr, eat gasoline, rumble your damn belly and eat gasoline but run, run, run! Or your ex-lover, Old Man, sells you for junk, I swear it!"

Undaunted, Fordiana did not move.

Eventually, Paley and Dorothy had to leave the truck by the ditch and walk home. And as they crossed the heavily traveled highway to get to the dumpheap, Old Man was forced to jump to keep from getting hit by a car.

He shook his fist at the speeding auto.

"I know you're out to get me!" he howled. "But you won't! You been tryin for fifty thousand years, and you ain't made it yet! We're still fightin!"

The Alley Man

At that moment, the black sagging bellies of the clouds overhead ruptured. The two were soaked before they could take four steps. Thunder bellowed, and lightning slammed into the earth on the other end of the dumpheap.

Old Man growled with fright, but seeing he was untouched, he raised his fist to the sky.

"OK, OK, so you got it in for me, too. I get it. OK, OK!"

Dripping, the two entered the shanty, where he opened a quart of beer and began drinking. Deena took Dorothy behind a curtain and gave her a towel to dry herself with and one of her white terrycloth robes to put on. By the time Dorothy came out from behind the curtain, she found Old Man opening his third quart. He was accusing Deena of not frying the fish correctly, and when she answered him sharply, he began accusing her of every fault, big or small, real or imaginary, of which he could think. In fifteen minutes, he was nailing the portrait of her mother to the wall with its face inward. And she was whimpering behind the stove and tenderly stroking the spots where he had struck her. Gummy protested, and he chased her out into the rain.

Dorothy at once put her wet clothes on and announced she was leaving. She'd walk the mile into town and catch the bus.

Old Man snarled, "Go! You're too snotty for us, anyway. We ain't your kind, and that's that."

"Don't go," pleaded Deena. "If you're not here to restrain him, he'll be terrible to us."

"I'm sorry," said Dorothy. "I should have gone home this morning."

"You sure should," he growled. And then he began weeping, his pushed-out lips fluttering like a bird's wings, his face twisted like a gargoyle's.

"Get out before I forget myself and throw you out," he sobbed.

Dorothy, with pity on her face, shut the door gently behind her.

The following day was Sunday. That morning, her mother phoned her she was coming down from Waukegan to visit her. Could she take Monday off?

Dorothy said yes, and then, sighing, she called her supervisor. She told him she had all the data she needed for the Paley report and that she would begin typing it out.

Monday night, after seeing her mother off on the train, she

decided to pay the Paleys a farewell visit. She could not endure another sleepless night filled with fighting the desire to get out of bed again and again, to scrub herself clean, and the pain of having to face Old Man and the two women in the morning. She felt that if she said goodbye to the Paleys, she could say farewell to those feelings, too, or, at least, time would wash them away more quickly.

The sky had been clear, star-filled, when she left the railroad station. By the time she had reached the dumpheap clouds had swept out from the west, and a blinding rainstorm was deluging the city. Going over the bridge, she saw by the lights of her headlamps that the Kickapoo Creek had become a small river in the two days of heavy rains. Its muddy frothing current roared past the dump and on down to the Illinois River, a half mile away.

So high had it risen that the waters lapped at the doorsteps of the shanties. The trucks and jalopies parked outside them were piled high with household goods, and their owners were ready to move at a minute's notice.

Dorothy parked her car a little off the road, because she did not want to get it stuck in the mire. By the time she had walked to the Paley shanty, she was in stinking mud up to her calves, and night had fallen.

In the light streaming from a window stood Fordiana, which Old Man had apparently succeeded in getting started. Unlike the other vehicles, it was not loaded.

Dorothy knocked on the door and was admitted by Deena. Paley was sitting in the ragged easy chair. He was clad only in a pair of faded and patched blue jeans. One eye was surrounded by a big black, blue, and green bruise. The horsehide hat of Old King was firmly jammed onto his head, and one hand clutched the neck of a quart of beer as if he were choking it to death.

Dorothy looked curiously at the black eye but did not comment on it. Instead, she asked him why he hadn't packed for a possible flood.

Old Man waved the naked stump of his arm at her.

"It's the doins a The Old Guy In The Sky. I prayed to the old idiot to stop the rain, but it rained harder'n ever. So I figure it's really The Old Woman In The Earth who's kickin up this rain. The Old Guy's too feeble to stop her. He needs strength. So... I thought about pouring out the blood a a virgin to him, so he kin lap it up and get his muscles back with that. But I give that up, cause there ain't no such thin anymore, not within a hundred miles a here, anyway.

"So... I been thinkin about goin outside and doin the next best thing, that is pourin a quart or two a beer out on the ground for him. What the Greeks call pourin a liberation to the Gods...."

"Don't let him drink none a that cheap beer," warned Gummy. "This rain fallin on us is bad enough. I don't want no god pukin all over the place."

He hurled the quart at her. It was empty, because he wasn't so far gone he'd waste a full or even half-full bottle. But it was smashed against the wall, and since it was worth a nickel's refund, he accused Gummy of malicious waste.

"If you'd a held still, it woun't a broke."

Deena paid no attention to the scene. "I'm pleased to see you, child," she said. "But it might have been better if you had stayed home tonight."

She gestured at the picture of her mother, still nailed face inward. "He's not come out of his evil mood yet."

"You kin say that again," mumbled Gummy. "He got a pistolwhippin from that young Limpy Doolan who lives in that packinbox house with the Jantzen bathin suit ad pasted on the side, when Limpy tried to grab Old King's hat off a Old Man's head just for fun."

"Yeah, he tried to grab it," said Paley. "But I slapped his hand hard. Then he pulls a gun out a his coat pocket with the other hand and hit me in this eye with its butt. That don't stop me. He sees me comin at him like I'm late for work, and he says he'll shoot me if I touch him again. My old man din't raise no silly sons, so I don't charge him. But I'll get him sooner or later. And he'll be limpin in both legs, if he walks at all.

"But I don't know why I never had nothin but bad luck ever since I got this hat. It ain't supposed to be that way. It's supposed to be bringin me all the good luck the Paleys ever had."

He glared at Dorothy and said, "Do you know what? I had good luck until I showed you that place, you know, the flowers. And then, after you know what, everythin went sour as old milk. What did you do, take the power out a me by doin what you did? Did The Old Woman In The Earth send you to me so you'd draw the muscle and luck and life out a me if I found the hat when Old Guy placed it in my path?"

He lurched up from the easy chair, clutched two quarts of beer from the refrigerator to his chest, and staggered toward the door.

"Kin't stand the smell in here. Talk about *my* smell. I'm sweet violets, compared to the fish a some a you. I'm goin out where the air's fresh. I'm goin out and talk to The Old Guy In The Sky, hear what the thunder has to say to me. He understands me; he don't give a damn if I'm a ugly old man that's ha'f-ape."

Swiftly, Deena ran in front of him and held out her claws at him like a gaunt, enraged alley cat.

"So that's it! You've had the indecency to insult this young girl! You evil beast!"

Old Man halted, swayed, carefully deposited the two quarts on the floor. Then he shuffled to the picture of Deena's mother and ripped it from the wall. The nails screeched; so did Deena.

"What are you going to do?"

"Somethin I been wantin to do for a long long time. Only I felt sorry for you. Now I don't. I'm gonna throw this idol a yours into the creek. Know why? Cause I think she's a delegate a The Old Woman In The Earth, Old Guy's enemy. She's been sent here to watch on me and report to Old Woman on what I was doin. And you're the one brought her in this house."

"Over my dead body you'll throw that in the creek!" screamed Deena.

"Have it your way," he growled, lurching forward and driving her to one side with his shoulder.

Deena grabbed at the frame of the picture he held in his hand, but he hit her over the knuckles with it. Then he lowered it to the floor, keeping it from falling over with his leg while he bent over and picked up the two quarts in his huge hand. Clutching them, he squatted until his stump was level with the top part of the frame. The stump clamped down over the upper part of the frame, he straightened, holding it tightly, lurched toward the door, and was gone into the driving rain and crashing lightning.

Deena stared into the darkness for a moment, then ran after him.

Stunned, Dorothy watched them go. Not until she heard Gummy mumbling, "They'll kill each other," was Dorothy able to move.

She ran to the door, looked out, turned back to Gummy.

"What's got into him?" she cried. "He's so cruel, yet I know he has a soft heart. Why must he be this way?"

"It's you," said Gummy. "He thought it din't matter how he looked, what he did, he was still a Paley. He thought his sweat would get you like it did all em chicks he was braggin about, no matter how uppity the sweet young thin was. 'N you hurt him when you din't dig him. Specially cause he thought more a you 'n anybody before.

"Why'd you think life's been so miserable for us since he found you? What the hell, a man's a man, he's always got the eye for the chicks, right? Deena din't see that. Deena hates Old Man. But Deena kin't do without him, either...."

"I have to stop them," said Dorothy, and she plunged out into the black and white world.

Just outside the door, she halted, bewildered. Behind her, light streamed from the shanty, and to the north was a dim glow from the city of Onaback. But elsewhere was darkness. Darkness, except when the lightning burned away the night for a dazzling frightening second.

She ran around the shanty toward the Kickapoo, some fifty yards away—she was sure that they'd be somewhere by the bank of the creek. Halfway to the stream, another flash showed her a white figure by the bank.

It was Deena in her terrycloth robe, Deena now sitting up in the mud, bending forward, shaking with sobs.

"I got down on my knees," she moaned. "To him, to him. And I begged him to spare my mother. But he said I'd thank him later for freeing me from worshiping a false goddess. He said I'd kiss his hand."

Deena's voice rose to a scream. "And then he did it! He tore my blessed mother to bits! Threw her in the creek! I'll kill him! I'll kill him!"

Dorothy patted Deena's shoulder. "There, there. You'd better get back to the house and get dry. It's a bad thing he's done, but he's not in his right mind. Where'd he go?"

"Toward that clump of cottonwoods where the creek runs into the river."

"You go back," said Dorothy. "I'll handle him. I can do it."

Deena seized her hand.

"Stay away from him. He's hiding in the woods now. He's

dangerous, dangerous as a wounded boar. Or as one of his ancestors when they were hurt and hunted by ours."

"Ours?" said Dorothy. "You mean you believe his story?"

"Not all of it. Just part. That tale of his about the mass invasion of Europe and King Paley's hat is nonsense. Or, at least it's been distorted through God only knows how many thousands of years. But it's true he's at least part Neanderthal. Listen! I've fallen low, I'm only a junkman's whore. Not even that, now—Old Man never touches me anymore, except to hit me. And that's not his fault, really. I ask for it; I want it.

"But I'm not a moron. I got books from the library, read what they said about the Neanderthal. I studied Old Man carefully. And I *know* he must be what he says he is. Gummy, too—she's at least a quarter-breed."

Dorothy pulled her hand out of Deena's grip.

"I have to go. I have to talk to Old Man, tell him I'm not seeing him anymore."

"Stay away from him," pleaded Deena, again seizing Dorothy's hand. "You'll go to talk, and you'll stay to do what I did. What a score of others did. We let him make love to us because he isn't human. Yet, we found Old Man as human as any man, and some of us stayed after the lust was gone because love had come in."

Dorothy gently unwrapped Deena's fingers from her hand and began walking away.

Soon she came to the group of cottonwood trees by the bank where the creek and the river met and there she stopped.

"Old Man!" she called in a break between the rolls of thunder. "Old Man! It's Dorothy!"

A growl as of a bear disturbed in his cave answered her, and a figure like a tree trunk come to life stepped out of the inkiness between the cottonwoods.

"What you come for?" he said, approaching so close to her that his enormous nose almost touched hers. "You want me just as I am, Old Man Paley, descendant a the Real Folk—Paley, who loves you? Or you come to give the batty old junkman a tranquillizer so you kin take him by the hand like a lamb and lead him back to the slaughterhouse, the puzzle factory, where they'll stick a ice pick back a his eyeball and rip out what makes him a man and not an ox."

"I came . . ."

"Yeah?"

"For this!" she shouted, and she snatched off his hat and raced away from him, toward the river.

Behind her rose a bellow of agony so loud she could hear it even above the thunder. Feet splashed as he gave pursuit.

Suddenly, she slipped and sprawled facedown in the mud. At the same time, her glasses fell off. Now it was her turn to feel despair, for in this halfworld she could see nothing without her glasses except the lightning flashes. She must find them. But if she delayed to hunt for them, she'd lose her headstart.

She cried out with joy, for her groping fingers found what they sought. But the breath was knocked out of her, and she dropped the glasses again as a heavy weight fell upon her back and half stunned her. Vaguely, she was aware that the hat had been taken away from her. A moment later, as her senses came back into focus, she realized she was being raised into the air. Old Man was holding her in the crook of his arm, supporting part of her weight on his bulging belly.

"My glasses. Please, my glasses. I need them."

"You won't be needin em for a while. But don't worry about em. I got em in my pants pocket. Old Man's takin care a you."

His arm tightened around her so she cried out with pain.

Hoarsely, he said, "You was sent down by the *G'yaga* to get that hat, wasn't you? Well, it din't work cause The Old Guy's stridin the sky tonight, and he's protectin his own."

Dorothy bit her lip to keep from telling him that she had wanted to destroy the hat because she hoped that that act would also destroy the guilt of having made it in the first place. But she couldn't tell him that. If he knew she had made a false hat, he would kill her in his rage.

"No. Not again," she said. "Please. Don't. I'll scream. They'll come after you. They'll take you to the State Hospital and lock you up for life. I swear I'll scream."

"Who'll hear you? Only The Old Guy, and he'd get a kick out a seein you in this fix cause you're a Falser and you took the stuffin right out a my hat and me with your Falser Magic. But I'm gettin back what's mine and his, the same way you took it from me. The door swings both ways."

He stopped walking and lowered her to a pile of wet leaves.

"Here we are. The forest like it was in the old days. Don't worry. Old Man'll protect you from the cave bear and the bull a the woods. But who'll protect you from Old Man, huh?"

Lightning exploded so near that for a second they were

blinded and speechless. Then Paley shouted, "The Old Guy's whoopin it up tonight, just like he used to do! Blood and murder and wickedness're ridin the howlin night air!"

He pounded his immense chest with his huge fist.

"Let The Old Guy and The Old Woman fight it out tonight. They ain't goin to stop us. Dor'thy. Not unless that hairy old god in the clouds is going to fry me with his lightnin, jealous a me cause I'm havin what he kin't."

Lightning rammed against the ground from the charged skies, and lightning leaped up to the clouds from the charged earth. The rain fell harder than before, as if it were being shot out of a great pipe from a mountain river and pouring directly over them. But for some time the flashes did not come close to the cottonwoods. Then, one ripped apart the night beside them, deafened and stunned them.

And Dorothy, looking over Old Man's shoulder, thought she would die of fright because there was a ghost standing over them. It was tall and white, and its shroud flapped in the wind, and its arms were raised in a gesture like a curse.

But it was a knife that it held in its hand.

Then, the fire that rose like a cross behind the figure was gone, and night rushed back in.

Dorothy screamed. Old Man grunted, as if something had knocked the breath from him.

He rose to his knees, gasped something unintelligible, and slowly got to his feet. He turned his back to Dorothy so he could face the thing in white. Lightning flashed again. Once more Dorothy screamed, for she saw the knife sticking out of his back.

Then the white figure had rushed toward Old Man. But instead of attacking him, it dropped to its knees and tried to kiss his hand and babbled for forgiveness.

No ghost. No man. Deena, in her white terrycloth robe.

"I did it because I love you!" screamed Deena.

Old Man, swaying back and forth, was silent.

"I went back to the shanty for a knife, and I came here because I knew what you'd be doing, and I didn't want Dorothy's life ruined because of you, and I hated you, and I wanted to kill you. But I don't really hate you."

Slowly, Paley reached behind him and gripped the handle of the knife. Lightning made everything white around him, and by its brief glare the women saw him jerk the blade free of his flesh.

Dorothy moaned, "It's terrible, terrible. All my fault, all my fault."

She groped through the mud until her fingers came across the Old Man's jeans and its backpocket, which held her glasses. She put the glasses on, only to find that she could not see anything because of the darkness. Then, and not until then, she became concerned about locating her own clothes. On her hands and knees she searched through the wet leaves and grass. She was about to give up and go back to Old Man when another lightning flash showed the heap to her left. Giving a cry of joy, she began to crawl to it.

But another stroke of lightning showed her something else. She screamed and tried to stand up but instead slipped and fell forward on her face.

Old Man, knife in hand, was walking slowly toward her.

"Don't try to run away!" he bellowed. "You'll never get away! The Old Guy'll light thins up for me so you kin't sneak away in the dark. Besides, your white skin shines in the night, like a rotten toadstool. You're done for. You snatched away my hat so you could get me out here defenseless, and then Deena could stab me in the back. You and her are Falser witches, I know damn well!"

"What do you think you're doing?" asked Dorothy. She tried to rise again but could not. It was as if the mud had fingers around her ankles and knees.

"The Old Guy's howlin for the blood a *G'yaga* wimmen. And he's gonna get all the blood he wants. It's only fair. Deena put the knife in me, and The Old Woman got some a my blood to drink. Now it's your turn to give The Old Guy some a yours."

"Don't!" screamed Deena. "Don't! Dorothy had nothing to do with it! And you can't blame me, after what you were doing to her!"

"She's done everythin to me. I'm gonna make the last sacrifice to Old Guy. Then they kin do what they want to me. I don't care. I'll have had one moment a bein a real Real Folker."

Deena and Dorothy both screamed. In the next second, lightning broke the darkness around them. Dorothy saw Deena hurl herself on Old Man's back and carry him downward. Then, night again.

There was a groan. Then, another blast of light. Old Man was on his knees, bent almost double but not bent so far Dorothy could not see the handle of the knife that was in his chest.

"Oh, Christ!" wailed Deena. "When I pushed him, he must have fallen on the knife. I heard the bone in his chest break. Now he's dying!"

Paley moaned. "Yeah, you done it now, you sure paid me back, din't you? Paid me back for my takin the monkey off a your back and supportin you all these years."

"Oh, Old Man," sobbed Deena, "I didn't mean to do it. I was just trying to save Dorothy and save you from yourself. Please! Isn't there anything I can do for you?"

"Sure you kin. Stuff up the two big holes in my back and chest. My blood, my breath, my real soul's flowin out a me. Guy In the Sky, what a way to die! Kilt by a crazy woman!"

"Keep quiet," said Dorothy. "Save your strength. Deena, you run to the service station. It'll still be open. Call a doctor."

"Don't go, Deena," he said. "It's too late. I'm hangin onto my soul by its big toe now; in a minute I'll have to let go, and it'll jump out a me like a beagle after a rabbit.

"Dor'thy, Dor'thy, was it the wickedness a The Old Woman put you up to this? I must a meant something to you... under the flowers... maybe it's better... I felt like a god, then... not what I really am... a crazy old junkman... a alley man.... Just think a it... fifty thousand years behint me... older'n Adam and Eve by far... now, this...."

Deena began weeping. He lifted his hand, and she seized it.

"Let loose," he said faintly. "I was gonna knock hell outta you for blubberin... just like a Falser bitch... kill me... then cry... you never did 'preciate me... like Dorothy...."

"His hand's getting cold," murmured Deena.

"Deena, bury that damn hat with me... least you kin do.... Hey, Deena, who you goin to for help when you hear that monkey chitterin outside the door, huh? Who...?"

Suddenly, before Dorothy and Deena could push him back down, he sat up. At the same time, lightning hammered into the earth nearby and it showed them his eyes, looking past them out into the night.

He spoke, and his voice was stronger, as if life had drained back into him through the holes in his flesh.

"Old Guy's givin me a good send-off. Lightnin and thunder. The works. Nothin cheap about him, huh? Why not? He knows this is the end a the trail for me. The last a his worshipers... last a the Paleys...."

He sank back and spoke no more.

FATHER'S IN THE BASEMENT

Nowadays, Gothic has degenerated into a word meaning a shuddery tale wherein a lovely young woman, not too bright, is trapped in a huge shuddery old mansion with a handsome young man, sometimes middle-aged, who's suffering from the delusion he's Lord Byron or Rochester (not Jack Benny's). Also in the house are various other creatures, an old housekeeper or butler who is usually evil, or a young and handsome housekeeper who is usually evil, out to get the heroine and the hero in one way or another, a lost will, a mad wife locked up in a room in one wing of the crumbling castle, and various kindly victims.

In the old days, it meant a long novel, usually in three volumes, always taking place in an old castle or monastery with secret passages in the walls, ghosts, vampires, poisoners, trapdoors, and various monsters.

This Gothic isn't like any of the above.

The typewriter had clattered for three and a half days. It must have stopped now and then, but never when Millie was awake. She had fallen asleep perhaps five times during that period, though something always aroused her after fifteen minutes or so of troubled dreams.

Perhaps it was the silence that hooked her and drew her up out of the thick waters. As soon as she became fully conscious, however, she heard the clicking of the typewriter start up.

The upper part of the house was almost always clean and neat. Millie was only eleven, but she was the only female in the household, her mother having died when Millie was nine.

Millie never cleaned the basement because her father forbade it.

The big basement room was his province. There he kept all his reference books, and there he wrote at a long desk. This room and the adjoining furnace-utility room constituted her father's country (he even did the washing), and if it was a mess to others, it was order to him. He could reach into the chaos and pluck out anything he wanted with no hesitation.

Her father was a free-lance writer, a maker of literary soups, a potboiler cook. He wrote short stories and articles for men's and women's magazines under male or female names, science fiction novels, trade magazine articles, and an occasional Gothic. Sometimes he got a commission to write a novel based on a screenplay.

"I'm the poor man's Frederick Faust," her father had said many times. "I won't be remembered ten years from now. Not by anyone who counts. I want to be remembered, baby, to be reprinted through the years as a classic, to be written of, talked of, as a great writer. And so..."

And so, on the left side of his desk, in a file basket, was half a manuscript, three hundred pages. Pop had been working on it, on and off, mostly off, for fifteen years. It was to be his masterpiece, the one book that would transcend all his hackwork, the book that would make the public cry "Wow!" the one book by him that would establish him as a Master ("Capital M, baby!"). It would put his name in the *Encyclopaedia Brittanica;* he would not take up much space in it; a paragraph was all he asked.

He had patted her hand and said, "And so when you tell people your name, they'll say, 'You aren't the daughter of the great Brady X. Donaldson? You are? Fantastic! And what was he really like, your father?'"

And then, reaching out and stroking her pointed chin, he had said, "I hope you can be proud of having a father who wrote at least one great book, baby. But of course, you'll be famous in your own right. You have unique abilities, and don't you ever forget it. A kid with your talents has to grow up into a famous person. I only wish that I could be around...."

He did not go on. Neither of them cared to talk about his heart "infraction," as he insisted on calling it.

She had not commented on his remark about her "abilities." He was not aware of their true breadth and depth, nor did she want him to be aware.

Father's in the Basement

The phone rang. Millie got up out of the chair and walked back and forth in the living room. The typewriter had not even hesitated when the phone rang. Her father was stopping for nothing, and he might not even have heard the phone, so intent was he. This was the only chance he would ever get to finish his Work ("Capital W, baby!"), and he would sit at his desk until it was done. Yet she knew that he could go on like this only so long before falling apart.

She knew who was calling. It was Mrs. Coombs, the secretary of Mr. Appleton, the principal of Dashwood Grade School. Mrs. Coombs had called every day. The first day, Millie had told Mrs. Coombs that she was sick. No, her father could not come to the phone because he had a deadline schedule to meet. Millie had opened the door to the basement and turned the receiver of the phone so that Mrs. Coombs could hear the heavy and unceasing typing.

Millie spoke through her nose and gave a little cough now and then, but Mrs. Coombs's voice betrayed disbelief.

"My father knows I have this cold, and so he doesn't see why he should be bothered telling anybody that I have it. He knows I have it. No, it's not bad enough to go to the doctor for it. No, my father will not come to the phone now. You wouldn't like it if he had to come to the phone now. You can be sure of that.

"No, I can't promise you he'll call before five, Mrs. Coombs. He doesn't want to stop while he's going good, and I doubt very much he'll be stopping at five. Or for some time after, if I know my father. In fact, Mrs. Coombs, I can't promise anything except that he won't stop until he's ready to stop."

Mrs. Coombs had made some important-sounding noises, but she finally said she'd call back tomorrow. That is, she would unless Millie was at school in the morning, with a note from her father, or unless her father called in to say that she was still sick.

The second day, Mrs. Coombs had phoned again, and Millie had let the ringing go on until she could stand it no longer.

"I'm sorry, Mrs. Coombs, but I feel lots worse. And my father didn't call in, and won't, because he is still typing. Here, I'll hold the phone to the door so you can hear him."

Millie waited until Mrs. Coombs seemed to have run down.

"Yes, I can appreciate your position, Mrs. Coombs, but he won't come, and I won't ask him to. He has so little time left, you know, and he has to finish this one book, and he isn't listening to any such thing as common sense or...No, Mrs. Coombs, I'm not trying to play on your sympathies with his talk about his heart trouble.

"Father is going to sit there until he's done. He said this is his lifework, his only chance for immortality. He doesn't believe in life after death, you know. He says that a man's only chance for immortality is in the deeds he does or the works of art he produces.

"Yes, I know it's a peculiar situation, and he's a peculiar man, and I should be at school."

And you, Mrs. Coombs, she thought, you think I'm a very peculiar little girl, and you don't really care that I'm not at school today. In fact, you like it that I'm not there because you get the chills every time you see me.

"Yes, Mrs. Coombs, I know you'll have to take some action, and I don't blame you for it. You'll send somebody out to check; you have to do it because the rules say you have to, not because you think I'm lying.

"But you can hear my father typing, can't you? You surely don't think that's a recording of a typist, do you?"

She shouldn't have said that, because now Mrs. Coombs would be thinking exactly that.

She went into the kitchen and made more coffee. Pop had forbidden her coffee until she was fourteen, but she needed it to keep going. Besides, he wouldn't know anything about it. He had told her, just before he had felt the first pain, that he could finish the Work in eighty-four to ninety-six hours if he were uninterrupted and did not have to stop because of exhaustion or another attack.

"I've got it all composed up here," he had said, pointing a finger at his temple. "It's just a matter of sitting down and staying down, and that's what I'm going to do, come hell or high water, come infraction or infarction. In ten minutes, I'm going down into my burrow, and I'm not coming back up until I'm finished."

"But, Pop," Millie had said, "I don't see how you can. Exercise or excitement is what brings on an attack...."

"I got my pills, and I'll rest if I have to and take longer," he had said. "So it takes two weeks? But I don't think it will. Listen, Millie," and he had taken her hand in his and looked into her eyes as if they were binoculars pointing into a fourth dimension, "I'm depending on you more than on my pills or even on myself. You'll not let anybody or anything interfere, will you? I know I shouldn't ask you to stay home from school, but this is more important than school. I really need you. I can't afford to put this off any longer. I don't have the time. You know that."

He released her hand and started toward the basement door, saying, "This is it; here goes," when his face had twisted and he had grabbed his chest.

But that had not stopped him.

The phone rang. It was, she knew, Mrs. Coombs again.

Mrs. Coombs's voice was as thin as river ice in late March.

"You tell your father that officers will be on their way to your house within a few minutes. They'll have a warrant to enter."

"You're causing a lot of trouble and for no good reason," Millie said. "Just because you don't like me. . . ."

"Well, I never!" Mrs. Coombs said. "You know very well that I'm doing what I have to and, in fact, I've been overly lenient in this case. There's no reason in the world why your father can't come to the phone. . . ."

"I told you he had to finish his novel," Millie said. "That's all the reason he needs."

She hung up the phone and then stood by the door for a moment, listening to the typing below. She turned and looked through the kitchen door at the clock on the wall. It was almost twelve. She doubted that anybody would come during the lunch hour, despite what Mrs. Coombs said. That gave her—her father, rather—another hour. And then she would see what she could do.

She tried to eat but could get down only half the liverwurst and lettuce sandwich. She wrapped the other half and put it back into the refrigerator. She looked at herself in the small mirror near the wall clock. She, who could not afford to lose an ounce, had shed pounds during the past three and a half days. As if they were on scales, her cheekbones had risen while her eyes had sunk. The dark brown irises and the bloodshot whites of her eyes looked like two fried eggs with ketchup that someone had thrown against a wall.

She smiled slightly at the thought, but it hurt her to see her face. She looked like a witch and always would.

"But you're only eleven!" her father had boomed at her.

"Is it a tragedy at eleven because the boys haven't asked you for a date yet? My God, when I was eleven, we didn't ask girls for dates. We hated girls!"

Yet his Great Work started with the first-love agonies of a boy of eleven, and he had admitted long ago that the boy was himself.

Millie sighed again and left the mirror. She cleaned the front room but did not use the vacuum cleaner because she wanted to hear the typewriter keys. The hour passed, and the doorbell rang.

She sat down in a chair. The doorbell rang again and again. Then there was silence for a minute, followed by a fist pounding on the door.

Millie got up from the chair but went to the door at the top of the basement steps and opened it. She breathed deeply, made a face, went down the wooden steps and around the corner at the bottom and looked down the long room with its white-painted cement blocks and pine paneling. She could not see her father because a tall and broad dark-mahogany bookcase in the middle of the room formed the back of what he called his office. The chair and desk were on the other side, but she could see the file basket on the edge of the desk. Her practiced eye told her that the basket held almost five hundred pages, not counting the carbon copies.

The typewriter clattered away. After a while, she went back up the steps and across to the front door. She opened the peephole and looked through. Two of the three looked as if they could be plainclothesmen. The third was the tall, beefy, red-faced truant officer.

"Hello, Mr. Tavistock," she said through the peephole. "What can I do for you?"

"You can open the door and let me in to talk to your father," he growled. "Maybe he can explain what's been going on, since you won't."

"I told Mrs. Coombs all about it," Millie said. "She's a complete ass, making all this fuss about nothing."

"That's no way for a lady to talk, Millie," Mr. Tavistock said. "Especially an eleven-year-old. Open the door. I got a warrant."

He waved a paper in his huge hand.

"My father'll have you in court for trampling on his civil rights," Millie said. "I'll come to school tomorrow. I promise. But not today. My father mustn't be bothered."

"Let me in now, or we break the door down!" Mr. Tavistock shouted. "There's something funny going on, Millie, otherwise your father would've contacted the school long ago!"

"You people always think there's something funny about me, that all!" Millie shouted back.

"Yeah, and Mrs. Coombs fell down over the wastebasket and wrenched her back right after she phoned you," Tavistock said. "Are you going to open that door?"

It would take them only a minute or so to kick the door open even if she chained it. She might as well let them in. Still, two more minutes might be all that were needed.

She reached for the knob and then dropped her hand. The typing had stopped.

She walked to the top of the basement steps.

"Pop! Are you through?"

She heard the squeaking of the swivel chair, then a shuffling sound. The house shook, and there was a crash as someone struck the door with his body. A few seconds later, another crash was followed by the bang of the door against the inner wall. Mr. Tavistock said, "All right, boys! I'll lead the way!"

He sounded as if he were raiding a den of bank robbers, she thought.

She went around the corner to the front room and said, "I think my father is through."

"In more ways than one, Millie," Mr. Tavistock said.

She turned away and walked back around the corner, through the door and out onto the landing. Her father was standing at the bottom of the steps. His color was very bad and he looked as if he had gained much weight, though she knew that that was impossible.

He looked up at her from deeply sunken eyes, and he lifted the immense pile of sheets with his two hands.

"All done, Pop?" Millie said, her voice breaking.

He nodded slowly.

Millie heard the three men come up behind her. Mr. Tavistock leaned over her and said, "Whew!"

Millie turned and pushed at him. "Get out of my way! He's finished it!"

Mr. Tavistock glared, but he moved to one side. She walked to a chair and sat down heavily. One of the detectives said, "You look awful, Millie. You look like you haven't slept for a week."

"I don't think I'll ever be able to sleep," she said. She

breathed deeply and allowed her muscles to go loose. Her head lolled as if she had given up control over everything inside her.

There was a thumping noise from the basement. Mr. Tavistock cried out, "He's fainted!" The shoes of the three men banged on the steps as they ran down. A moment later Mr. Tavistock gave another cry. Then all three men began talking at once.

Millie closed her eyes and wished she could quit trembling. Some time later, she heard the footsteps. She did not want to open her eyes, but there was no use putting it off.

Mr. Tavistock was pale and shaking. He said, "My God! He looks, he smells like..."

One of the detectives said, "His fingertips are worn off, the bones are sticking out, but there wasn't any bleeding."

"I got him through," Millie said. "He finished it. That's all that counts."

TOWARD THE BELOVED CITY

This was written for an anthology of religious science fiction, *Signs and Wonders*, Fleming H. Revell, edited by Roger Elwood (1972). Revell is a house specializing in books on religion. I developed it as I would any science fiction story, that is, first, "What if . . . ?" and, second, a rigid extrapolation from the basic premise. What if the Book of Revelations were true? What then?

Elwood said that Revell liked this unsentimental story very much, and he himself said that he had not really understood Revelations until he read "Toward the Beloved City." I've been a reader of the Bible most of my life, and when I was a child had vivid and terrifying nightmares about the Last Judgments.

Note the plural.

The western sky was as red as if it had broken a vein. In a sense, it had, Kelvin Norris thought.

The Earth had broken open, too, and it was this which had created the bloody sunsets. The Pacific and Mediterranean coasts had shaken many times with a violence unknown since the days of creation. Old volcanoes had spouted, and new ones had reared up. It would be twenty years before all the dust would settle. It would have been a hundred years if it had not been for the great nightly rains, rains which nevertheless did not succeed in making the atmosphere wet, at least, not along the Mediterranean coast. By noon the air was as dry as an old camel bone, and at sunset the sky was red with light reflected from the dust that would not die.

A thousand years would have to pass before the dust of human affairs would settle. Meanwhile, this land was tawny and broken, like the body of a dead lion torn by hyenas. And the sun, rising after last night's violent rain, had been another lion. But it lived, and its breath turned the skin of men and women to leather and burned the bones of the dead to white. Even now, sinking toward the horizon, it lapped greedily at the moisture in Kelvin Norris's skin.

He was riding a horse, the only one he had seen alive since he and his party had landed near the submerged city of Tunis. There were many bones of horses and other animals, killed in the quakes or by tidal waves or bombings or gunfights or by disease or by starving men, for food. Bones of men also lay everywhere. The crows and ravens and kites were, however, numerous, though swiftly losing their fat now. Kelvin knew the taste of their stringy carrion-smelling flesh very well.

The party had traveled on foot from the California mountains across the continent, had built from wreckage a small sailing ship with an auxiliary engine, sailed across the Atlantic to England and from there down along the newly created coasts of France and Portugal, through the straits of Gibraltar (past the great tumbled rock), and then had been wrecked by a storm on the shore of what was left of Tunisia.

Three days ago, Anna Silvich had shot a scrawny goat; that had kept them from collapsing with hunger. Then Kelvin had found the white stallion, which was amazingly sleek and healthy. Its presence, so well-fed, in these bleak and deserted environs, seemed a miracle. Some of the party said that it *was* a miracle. Perhaps this was the very horse on which the rider called Faithful and True had led the hosts of Heaven to victory over the Beast and the Antichrist.

But Kelvin said that he did not think that was likely, though it could be one of the horses ridden by one of the hosts that had followed the Faithful and True into the final battle. However, if a miracle were to be performed, it would be just as easy to transport them, teleport them rather, in the closing of an eye, the scratching of a nose, instead of letting them slog along by boat and foot. But this was not to be; they were alone. He hastened to add as the others frowned, that he meant that the party would never be alone, of course, in the sense that He was always with them. What he had meant was that they could not just sit down and expect some sort of celestial welfare.

That morning, Kelvin had taken a rifle and thirty bullets, all he had for a .32 caliber gun, a goatskin waterbag containing distilled water (which became red-colored two hours afterward), and a leather sling and some stones, and had ridden into the hills. The countryside here had been stripped by the cataclysms, but, in the past three years, some plants had re-established themselves. There were still hares and rodents and lizards and the little desert foxes in this area. He hoped to get some of these with his sling. The .32 was for protection only or in case he should, by some chance, find larger game.

He had tied the horse to a bush and had gone on foot into the tumbled and deeply fissured hills. He smashed a lizard with a stone from his sling and dropped it into the bag hanging from his belt. A few minutes later, he killed a raven with a stone. And then, under a deep shelf of rock, he found the ashes of a recent fire and some thoroughly scraped sheep and rat bones. There were no tracks in this rocky wilderness for him to follow, but he went down three long fissures searching for signs of the fire-builder. Reluctantly, he gave up looking and returned to the place where he had tied the horse. His tightening belly and his weakness told him that he would have to give permission for the horse to be butchered. It would hurt him to kill such a fine animal, but the party would then have plenty of meat for a few days.

The ringing of iron shoes on rocks warned him before he left the mouth of the fissure. Crouching, he looked around a boulder. A woman with short curly auburn hair, dressed in a ragged and dirty green coverall, was riding his horse away.

He did not want to shoot her or to make the horse bolt because of the shot. He put the rifle down and ran out after her while he took a stone from the bag at his belt and fitted it into the sling. She turned her head to look behind her just as the stone gave her a glancing blow on her back, near the spine. She screamed and fell forward off the horse; it reared and then galloped off.

Kelvin approached her with the rifle pointed at her. She seemed to be armed with only a knife, but he had learned long ago not to trust to appearances. At the moment, she did not look as if she could use a hidden weapon, even if she had one. She was sitting up, leaning on one arm, and groaning. The skin on her arms and legs and on one side of her face was torn.

"Any broken bones?" he said.

She shook her head and moaned, "Oh, no! But I think you almost broke my back. It really hurts."

"I'm sorry," he said, "but you were stealing my horse. Now, take out your knife slowly and throw it over to one side. Gently."

She obeyed and then slowly got to her feet. At his orders, she stripped and turned around twice so that he could make sure that she had no weapons taped to her. After he inspected the coverall, he threw it back to her, and she put it back on.

"Have you got anything to eat?" she said.

"The dinner ran away," he said. "What's your name and what are you doing here? And are you a Christian?"

There had been a time when he would not have asked that last question. He had assumed that all those who had bowed to the Beast and allowed it to put its mark on them had been killed either during the series of cataclysms that had almost wrecked the Earth or during the war afterward. But it had long been evident that he had misread the Revelation of John.

"I'm Dana Webster of Beverly, Yorkshire, and I was in a party which was going to the beloved city. But they're all dead now, mostly of starvation, though some were killed by heathens. I found the horse, and I took it because I wanted to get away from whomever owned it, far away, where I could eat the horse without worrying about being tracked down."

She did have a slight English accent, he noted. And her remark about the heathens implied that she was Christian. But she could retract the statement, or rationalize it, if it turned out that she had given the wrong answer. After all, she had no way of knowing that he was really a Christian.

He handed her his canteen, and she drank deeply before giving it back. "It tastes wonderful, even if it does look like blood," she said. "Do you suppose it'll ever get its natural color back? I mean, its lack of color."

"I don't know," he said.

"There's a lot we don't know, isn't there?"

"We'll know when we get to the beloved city," he said. "Let's go."

She turned and walked ahead of him. He carried the rifle in the crook of his elbow, but he was ready to use it at any time. They trudged along silently while the sun dropped through its pool of red. Once, he thought he saw the east begin to lighten, and he stopped, giving a soft cry. She halted and then turned slowly so that he would not misinterpret her movement.

"What is it?" she said.

"I thought...I hoped...no...I was mistaken. I thought

Toward the Beloved City

that the east was beginning to light up with His glory and that He was surely coming. But my nerves were playing tricks on me. Nerves plus hunger."

"Even if you saw a glory wrapping the world," she said, "how do you know that it would be Him? How could you be certain that it was He and not the Antichrist?"

He goggled at her for a moment and then said, "The Antichrist and the Beast went into the flaming lake!"

"What Beast? I thought the Beast was the world government? You surely don't mean that mythical monster that Gurets was supposed to have locked up in a room in his palace? As for the flaming lake, has anyone ever seen it? I know no one who has. Do you? Actually, all we know is what we've heard by word of mouth or the very little that comes over our radio receivers, supposedly from the beloved city. And where is the beloved city? Well, actually, there isn't any, as the broadcaster admits. There is a site somewhere in what used to be mountainous Israel where the faithful will gather and where the beloved city will be built by the faithful under the supervision of, I presume, angels.

"But how do you know that all this is true or why we're being led, somewhat like sheep into a chute, toward the beloved city? And if there is a flaming lake, and God knows there are plenty all over the world now, how do you know that the Antichrist went into it? Wouldn't the Antichrist, or whoever is supposed to be the Antichrist, have spread this tale about to make the faithful think it was safe to come to Israel?"

"You must be a heathen!" Kelvin said. "Telling a lie like that!"

"Do you see any numbers on my hand?" she said. "And if you looked at my forehead with a polarizer, you wouldn't see any numbers there, either. And if you care to, you can look at my scalp. You won't see any scars there because my head wasn't opened and there's no transceiver there for the Beast to activate any time it wants to press a button."

"We'll see about that when we get to camp," he said.

"I'm not telling lies," she said. "I'm just speculating, as any Christian should. Remember, the Serpent is very cunning and full of guile. What better way to fight those who believe in God than to pose as Christ returned?"

Kelvin did not like the path down which his mind was walking. There should be no more uncertainties; all should be hard and final.

Things were not what he had thought they would be. Not that he was reproaching God even in his thoughts. But things just had not worked out as he had assumed they would. And his assumptions had been based on a lifetime of reading the Scriptures.

"Were you one of those martyred by the Beast?" he said.

Dana Webster had started walking again. She did not stop to reply but slowed down so that he was only a step behind and a step to one side of her.

"Do you mean, was I one of those whose heads were rayed off and who was then resurrected? No, I wasn't, though I could easily claim to be one and no one could prove that I was lying. Most of my brothers and sisters were killed, but I was lucky. I got away to a hideout up on Mount Skiddaw, in Cumberland. The Beast's search parties were getting close to my cave when the meteorites fell and the quakes started and everything was literally torn to shreds."

"God's intervention," he said. "Without His help, we would all have perished."

"Somebody's intervention."

"What do you mean by *somebody?*"

"Extraterrestrials," she said. "Beings from a planet of some far-off star. Beings far advanced beyond man—in science, at least."

The ideas from her were coming too fast. "Could Extraterrestrials resurrect the dead?" he said.

"I don't know why not," she said. "Scientists have said that we would be able to do it in a hundred years or so, maybe sooner. Of course, that would require some means of recording the total molecular makeup and electromagnetic radiation patterns of an individual. That would someday be possible, according to the scientists. And then, using the recordings, the dead person could be duplicated with an energy-matter converter. This was also theoretically possible."

"But the person would be duplicated, not resurrected," he said. "He would not be the same person!"

"No, but he would think he was."

"What good would that do?"

"How do I know what superbeings have in their superminds? Do you know what's being planned for you by God?"

He was becoming very angry, and he did not wish to be so. He said, "I think we'd better stop talking and save our strength."

"For that matter," she said, "what sense is there in two

resurrections or in having a millennium? Why lock up Satan for a thousand years and then release him to lead the heathens against the Christians again, only to lock him up again and then hold the final judgment?"

He did not answer, and she said nothing more for a long time. After an hour, they came down out of the jumbled and shattered hills, and Kelvin saw the white horse eating some long brown grass growing from between tiny cracks in the rocks. They approached slowly while Kelvin called out softly to him. The animal trotted off, however, when Kelvin was only forty feet away from him. He aimed his rifle at it; he could not let this much meat get away now on the slim chance that he might catch it later on.

Dana Webster said, "Don't shoot it! I'll get him!" She called out loudly. The horse wheeled, snorting, and ran up to her and nuzzled her. She patted it and smiled at Kelvin. "I have a feeling for animals," she said. "Rather, there's a good feeling between me and them. An ESP of some sort, sympathetic vibrations, call it what you will."

"Beauty and the beast."

She quit smiling. "The Beast?"

"I didn't mean that. But your power over animals..."

"Don't tell me you believe in witchcraft? Good God! And I'm not swearing when I say that. Don't you believe in love? He feels it. And I feel such a traitor getting him back, because he'll probably be eaten."

An hour later, they led the horse, worn-out from carrying the two humans, into camp near the sea. The sentinels had challenged them, and Kelvin had given the proper countersigns. They passed them and entered a depression on a jagged but low hill. All around them was the mouth-watering odor of frying fish. The four men who had put out into the red-tinged waters, in the small, lightweight, collapsible boat had been fortunate. Or blessed by God. They had not expected to catch anything at all, because the fish life had been frighteningly depleted. When St. John had predicted that a third of the seas would be destroyed, he had underestimated. Rather, underpredicted.

Dana Webster pointed at the thirteen large fish frying in the dural pans over the fires. She said, "Does that mean we won't have to slaughter the horse?"

"Not now, anyway," he said.

"I'm so glad."

Kelvin was glad, too, but he was not impressed by her love for it. He had known too many butchers of children who were very much concerned about humane treatment for dogs and cats.

The men and women waiting for them were lean and dark with the sun and wind and were ridged, as if they were pieces of mahogany carved by windblown sand. They shone with something of a great strength derived from certainty. They had been through the persecutions and the cataclysms and the battles against the slaves of the Beast after the Beast's power had been broken by the cataclysms. "Blessed and holy is he who shares in the first resurrection! Over such the second death has no power, but they shall be priests of God and of Christ and they shall reign with him a thousand years."

However, Kelvin thought, the statement that the second death will have no power over them apparently meant that those who had resisted the Beast for love of God would not be judged again. But they *could* die, and those who died would not return to the Earth until the thousand years had passed. And then they would rise with the other dead in their new bodies and witness the final judgment. It was then that those faithful who had died before the time of the Beast would be given new bodies and the others would go to whatever fate awaited them. The Alpha and Omega, the final kingdom, would come.

All this had gone into the shaping of their bodies and the expression of face and eye. They were saints now, and nothing could ever change that. But saints could be hungry and thirsty and get very tired and become discouraged. And they would kill if they must.

There were no children here nor had any of the party seen anyone under seven during their journey across the continent and the seas. Their time would come at the end of the millennium.

"What do we have here?" Anna Silvich said.

Anna was a tall gray-eyed blonde who would have been beautiful under softer conditions. Now her flesh was pared away so that the bones seemed very near and the white skin was dark and cracked. Despite this, Kelvin had felt very attracted to her. He intended to ask her to be his wife after they reached the beloved city. He could have married her before this, if she would have him, since any of the party could conduct the ceremony. They were all priests now. But he did not want to do anything that would take his mind off the most important object: getting to the beloved city.

"We have here one who claims she is a Christian," Kelvin said.

Anna took a pencil-shaped plastic object from her shirt-pocket, pointed it at Dana Webster's forehead, and slid a section of the object forward.

"See?" Webster said. "I don't have the mark of the Beast."

Anna stepped forward and seized the woman's hair and pulled her head down. Kelvin started to protest against the unnecessary roughness, but he decided not to. He would see how Webster reacted; perhaps she might get angry enough to trip herself up. Anna released the woman's hair and said, "No scars there. But that doesn't mean anything. If I had a microscope or even a magnifying glass..."

Dana Webster said nothing but looked scornful. If she were upset or angry about her treatment, however, she did not allow it to interfere with her appetite. She ate the fish and the biscuits and canned peaches. The latter two items had been found in the ruins of a house by Sherborn, a little man who had a nose for buried or concealed food.

Kelvin had given the prayer of thankfulness before they ate, but he felt he should say more afterward. "God has been good and given us enough today to restore our strength. We can face tomorrow with the certain knowledge that He will provide more. It's evident from today's catch that there are still fish in the Mediterranean. There must be enough to keep us fed until we get to the beloved city."

Dana Webster, he noticed, said amen to that just as the others did. That could mean nothing except that she was playing her role of Christian, if she was indeed playing. She could be sincere. On the other hand, there were her remarks while they were traveling campward. He asked her what she had meant by *Extraterrestrials*.

She looked around at the dark faces with their protruding cheekbones and hollow cheeks and the darkly rimmed but fire-bright eyes. "I should have kept these doubts—or, rather, speculations—to myself," she said. "I should've waited until we got to the beloved city. Then everything would be straightened out. One way or another. Of course, by then it might be too late for us. I hate to say anything about this because you'll think I'm a heathen. But I have a mind, and I must speak it. Isn't that the Christian way?"

"We're not slaves of the Beast, if that's what you mean," Anna said. "We won't kill somebody because they differ somewhat from us on certain theological matters. Of course, we won't listen to blasphemy. But then you won't blaspheme if you're a Christian."

"It's easy to see you don't like me. Anna Silvich," Webster said. "Of course, that doesn't mean you're not a Christian. You can love mankind but dislike a particular person for one or another reason. Even if she is a fellow believer. Still, that doesn't mean that you're excused from examining yourself and finding out why you can't love me."

Anna said, with only a slight quaver of anger, "Yes, I don't like you. There is something about you... some... odor..."

"Of brimstone, I suppose?" Dana Webster said.

"God forgive me if I'm wrong," Anna said. "But you know what we've all been through. The betrayals, the spies, the prisons, seeing our children and mates tortured and then beheaded, our supposed friends turning their backs on us or turning us in, the terrible, terrible things done to us. But you know this, whether you're what you say you are or a Judas. However, you are right in reproaching me for one thing. I shouldn't say you stink of the devil unless I really have proof. But..."

"But you have said so and therefore you've stained me in everybody's thoughts," Dana said. "Couldn't you have waited until you were certain, instead of maliciously, and most unchristianly, stigmatizing me?"

"Somehow, we've strayed from the original question," Kelvin said. "What do you mean, Dana, by *Extraterrestrials?*"

She looked around at the faces in the firelight and then at the shadows outside as if there were things in the shadows. "I know you won't even want to consider what I'm going to speculate about. You're too tired in body and mind, too numb with the horrors of the persecution and the cataclysms and the battles that followed, to think about one more battle, or series of battles. But do I have to remind you that men have been looking for the apocalypse for two thousand years? And that there have been many times when men claimed that it was not only at hand but had actually begun?

"There have been times when men who spoke with authority, or seeming authority, proclaimed that the end of the world was at hand. But they were all mistaken, deceived by themselves or by the Enemy. Which may be the same. I mean, the Enemy may be the enemy within ourselves, not an entity, a unique person with an objective existence outside of us. The point is, what if we're being fooled again? Not self-deceived, as in the past, but deceived by an outside agency? By Extraterrestrials who are using weapons against Earth, weapons which far surpass ours? And now we're being asked to gather at the so-called beloved city, asked to come in and surrender. Why? Perhaps we're to form the basis of the future slave population for these beings?"

There was a long silence afterward. Anna Silvich broke it by crying, "You have convicted yourself, woman! You are trying to put doubts into our hearts, to destroy our faith! You are a heathen!"

Kelvin held his hands up for silence, and, when that did not work, shouted at Anna and the others to shut up. When the uproar had died, he said, "What evidence do you have that your Extraterrestrials exist, Dana?"

"Exactly the same evidence you have that this is the beginning of the millennium," she said. "The difference is my interpretation. Try to look at the situation, and our theories, objectively. And remember that the Antichrist fooled many, probably including some right here, when he claimed to be Christ. He has been exposed and, supposedly defeated for all time. Or, at least until the final battle a thousand years from now. But think. Could it be Satan himself who was trying his final trick on us? Or could it be that Extraterrestrials who knew of the longing of the faithful for the millennium have caused this pseudomillennium to occur? And..."

"Or perhaps it is Satan who is using the Extraterrestrials?" Anna said scornfully.

"It could be," Dana Webster said.

"Just a minute," Kelvin said. "I can't for the life of me, the soul of me, I should say, imagine why these Extraterrestrials should bring the faithful back to life? What reason could they have to do that?"

"Have you seen any of the resurrected?" Dana Webster said. "Is there anybody in this group who has seen one of them? Or, perhaps, some among you were killed and then brought back to life?"

Kelvin said, "It's true that no one here was restored to life. But it is not true that none of us have seen a resurrected person. I myself talked with a man who had been killed for his faith, though he was given the chance to deny God and become a slave of the Beast after seeing his wife and children raped and tortured and then beheaded. But he refused and so he was roasted over the fire and his head cut off. But he awoke at the bottom of the grave which had been opened for him, and he crawled out and was with a number of others who had been brought back to life. His wife and children were not among them, but he was sure that he would find them. I had no reason to doubt him, since I had known him from childhood."

"What do you think of that, Webster?" Anna said.

"But you did not see him killed, nor did you see him resurrected, isn't that right?" Webster said. "How do you know that he did not in actuality deny God and become a slave of the Beast? How do you know that his story about his resurrection was not a lie, that he wasn't lying so he could pass himself off as a Christian, since he had fallen among Christians? Indeed, it would be wise of the Enemy, whether Satan or Extraterrestrial, to send out spies with these lying stories so they could deceive the Christians."

Kelvin had to admit to himself that he had no proof of his friend's story and that what Webster postulated could be true. But he did not think that she was right. Some things had to be taken on faith. On the other hand, the Antichrist had fooled many, including himself at first. He gestured impatiently and said, "All this talk! We'll take you with us to the city and, when we get there, we'll find out the truth about everything."

"Why take her along?" Anna said. "She's convicted herself out of her own mouth with her lies, and she'll be an extra mouth to feed...."

"Anna!" Kelvin said. "That's not loving...."

"The time has come and gone for loving your enemies!" Anna said. "The new times are here; there is no room for tolerance of heathens. And we can't take her along, because she'll be lying to us with her tales of Extraterrestrials and other subtleties designed to make us fall into error! And we haven't anyone to ask what we should do with her. We have to make up our own minds and act on our decision, hard though it may seem."

Dana Webster gave a little start. Even by the firelight, she could be seen to pale. She pointed past Anna and said, quietly but with a tremor in her voice, "Why don't you ask him what to do?"

They spun around, their hands going for their weapons. But the tall man in white robes and with short hair as white as newly washed wool had his hands high up in the air so they could see he was unarmed. He was smiling; his teeth were very white in the firelight, and his eyes were shining with the reflected light. The eyes of no human being shone like those; they were like a lion's. Nor could any human being have crept by the sentinels and appeared so suddenly. The breeze, which Kelvin had suddenly felt just before Webster had spoken, must have been the air displaced by the emergence of this man... person... from nowhere. Kelvin felt his skin grow cold over his scalp and the back of his neck. He was scared, yet he was glad. At last someone to tell them what was happening and what they must do had come.

The man slowly lowered his hands. He was very handsome and very clean and had a beautiful well-proportioned body, quite in contrast to the ragged, dirty, scruffy bunch, scarred and skinny and stinking. The man slowly opened his robes so that they could see that he had no concealed weapons beneath them. They could also see that he was sexless. And, now that Kelvin was coming out of the shock of the sudden appearance, he saw that *he* was a misnomer. The being's features were effeminate. But the total impression the being gave was more masculine than feminine, and so Kelvin continued to think of the person as he.

He said, "You may call me Jones. I'll take up only a few minutes of your time."

Kelvin recognized the deep rich voice. It was the same voice that came to them from time to time, over their transistor receivers. It was the voice that had told the faithful all over the world to start out for the beloved city. It had also told a little about what was expected from the faithful when they did get to the beloved city. Only one thing was clear. The new citizens would have much hard work to do for a long, long time.

"We would be honored, and very happy, if you would stay for more than a few minutes... Mr. Jones," Kelvin said. "We have many questions. We also have a crucial problem here."

The angel looked at Dana Webster, but he did not lose his smile. "I don't know what your problem is with her, but I'm sure you'll do the right thing," he said. "As for your questions, most of them will have to wait. I'm busy just now. We have a thousand years to get ready for, and that will pass quickly enough for those who will live through it."

It was difficult to get up enough courage to argue with an angel, but Kelvin had not survived because of lack of courage. He said, "Why do we have to get to the beloved city on our own? We've suffered enough, I would think, and several of our party have been killed by heathens or in accidents. That doesn't seem to jibe with what we read in St. John the Divine...."

Jones raised a long slim hand on the back of which were many white woolly hairs. He said, still smiling, "I don't know the answer to that, any more than I know why there is a first death and then a second death or why all the heathens weren't killed or why they will flourish and propagate once more. Some of whom, by the way, will be your children and grandchildren to the two hundred and fiftieth generation, to your sorrow, though not to your everlasting sorrow. Don't ask me why. I know more than you, but I don't know everything. I am content to wait until the obscurities and ambiguities and seeming paradoxes are straightened out. And you will have to wait. Unless you are killed, of course, and spared the thousand years of struggle."

"We are as subject as ever to the whims of chance!" Kelvin said. "I thought..."

"You thought you'd have everything programmed, everything certain and easy," Jones said. "Well, God has always dealt with this world on a statistical basis, excepting certain people and events. And, generally speaking, He will continue to do so until the second death. Then, my friend, He will deal with every bit of matter in this world, and the souls that inhabit certain material forms, on a specific and individual basis. And that will be the difference between the world as it has been, and the new, unfluctuating, and unchanging world as it will be after the second death. Not that He is not aware of every atom now and what it is doing. But in the unchanging time to come, He will have His hand upon all matter and all souls, and nothing will evolve or change. You might say that, up to now, and until the thousand years are over, He has respected Heisenberg's principle of uncertainty." Jones looked at each intently, still smiling, and then said, "Actually, I'm here in my office—one of many—of requisitioner. I'm taking your horse, which is needed at the city."

"Why don't you just create some horses and leave this one with us?" Anna said. "We need it for food."

"There's other food to be had," Jones said. "This horse is destined to be the father of many hundreds of thousands. As far as I know, the only new creations will be after the second death, when you fortunate ones will be given new bodies. Something like the one I'm using."

That answered one question. There would be no sex in the

new Earth and the new Heaven. And why should there be? There would be no more babies, and the ecstasy of beholding God's face would far transcend any fleshly delights. Despite this, Kelvin felt a panic. He would be castrated. Then he told himself that he would have to get over that reaction. There would be compensations which would make the loss of his sex seem trivial and, perhaps, a cause for rejoicing. Nor would he be any less a man, that is, a human being.

Anna said, loudly, "There is one thing you should know so you can report it to your superiors, even if you won't do anything about it here!"

Jones raised his woolly white eyebrows and said, "Superiors? I have only two, and I won't have to report to them. They know what's going on at every second."

Anna was checked, but she rallied after a moment's silence. She said, "Forgive me if I'm presuming. But you should know that this woman here claims that all this, that is, the events of the past four years, have been caused by Extraterrestrials! She says we're being fooled! It's all a trick of things from outer space or whatever they come from! What do you say to that?"

Jones smiled and said, "Well, angels *are* Extraterrestrial beings, though not all Extraterrestrials are angels. As I said, it's your problem. You're grown up now, though still, of course, children of God. I go now. God bless you." Jones mounted the horse and rode out of sight down a defile. Kelvin climbed up onto the shoulder of a high hill to watch him ride out. He heard the bang, like a large balloon exploding, as the air rushed in to fill the vacuum left by a suddenly unoccupied space.

After five minutes, he climbed back down.

"If he wanted the horse, why didn't he just take it?" Anna said. "Surely he could have done it without leaving the city."

"Perhaps teleportation requires that the teleporter has to be physically present to do the work." Dana said.

"Teleportation?" Anna said. "That was an angel, you fool. Angels don't have to resort to teleportation."

"Teleportation is only a term used to describe a phenomenon," Dana said. "It's the same whether it's brought about by an angel or an Extraterrestrial."

"And you're a heathen," Anna said. "That angel must think we're a fine bunch of featherbrains if we can't see what's so obvious. He was laughing at us because we were so stupid."

"He could have been laughing because I told you the truth

and you wouldn't believe it," Dana Webster said.

"And if he was one of your creatures from outer space, why didn't he just wipe us out," Anna said, "or just teleport us to the city? It would be so easy for him."

"I don't know," Dana Webster said. "Maybe they're giving us some sort of test so they can decide where to assign us for some sort of job. Those who survive the terrible journey to the city get some sort of booby prize. Or become the studs and mares of a new breed of superslaves. I don't know."

The effect of her words was stronger then Kelvin liked. Too many looked as if they were seriously considering her speculations.

It rained heavily that night, as it had for almost every night for three years. Everybody was soaked, but no one came down with colds or pneumonia or any respiratory disease. Yet, many had been subject to colds and allergic to pollen or suffering from various degrees of emphysema before the cataclysms had begun. Something had rid them of all diseases, in fact, and Kelvin pointed this out that morning. He indicated it as evidence that they would all be free of body infirmities and ailments, and would not age for a thousand years. Yet microorganisms continued to do their work on dead bodies. Meat got spoiled; dead animals, and humans, rotted. Surely, this discrimination was God-given. Why should the Enemy, or Extraterrestrials, give human beings immunity from disease?

"I don't know," Dana Webster said. "We'll find out. Also, have the heathens been given this same immunity? If they have, then surely God is not responsible for the immunity, that is, He is not responsible for the dispensation of immunity. He, of course, is primarily responsible for anything that happens, in that it can't happen unless He permits it."

Kelvin expected her to bring up the question of why a good God would permit evil in the first place, but she did not push that time-waster on them.

The days and nights, the burning under the sun and the cold soaking at night, went on and on. A thousand miles of desert along the sea behind them and another thousand to go.

Dana Webster had more than done her share. She was a genius at catching lizards and finding large quantities of locusts and stunning birds and the little desert foxes with her slings. The items she brought to the community pot were not attractive, but they were nutritious and filled the belly. Even Anna had to admit that the party had eaten better since Webster joined them. But Anna also pointed out that Webster's very gift at hunting could be due to a strange power she had over animals. And who knew but that this was because she was herself one of the slaves of the Beast. Ex-slaves rather, since the Beast was now in the lake of burning brimstone. But the ex-slaves were still dedicated to evil, of course.

Kelvin had become irritated at Dana Webster's attitude, since he was now very attracted to her. In fact, he told himself during a fit of honesty, he was in love with her. He did not tell Dana, of course, because he could never marry her if she were a heathen. There had been a time when Christians had married heathens, but that must never be again. There was no doubt anymore about the line between good and evil. That is, as far as marriage went, there was no doubt about the lines. But there was still doubt about the honesty and the motives of people. And he was not sure what Dana Webster was. Sometimes, she talked so close to blasphemy that he felt repelled. Or uneasy. And he was uneasy because she seemed to be making some sense. At other times, he thought that she was truly a Christian but one who did not trust appearances and so was perhaps oversuspicious. But, in this world of untrustworthy appearances, could a person be overly suspicious?

Whatever the truth, he now yearned for this woman as he had yearned for none, not even Anna, since his wife had betrayed him. Was there something still evil in him, something that attracted him to women who had enlisted for Satan? But he had been attracted to Anna, and surely she was not on the Enemy's side? Nor did he have any proof that Dana was with the Enemy.

It did not seem likely that some residue of evil still lay deep within him. He had refused to go along with the Beast, and he had survived the cataclysms and the overthrow of the Beast, and so the second death had no power over him. He had been judged once and for all.

But could it be that he still needed refining, that there were elements of evil in him, and that the thousand years were to be used to purge him? Was that why the millennium must be? So that the surviving Christians could be purged of all evil? What, then, would purge those who had died and who would arise at the second judgment and be given new bodies? Why did they not have to go through the fire of a thousand years?

One night, Dana, who had been silent about her theories of the reality of the situation for a long time, proposed a new theory. "Those prophets who came closest to predicting the future as it really develops are those whose minds have an inborn computer. They don't truly prophesy, in the sense that they can actually look into the future. No, their minds, unconsciously, of course, compute the highest probabilities, and it is the most likely course of events that they predict. Or choose, rather. Your true prophet has a gift which is not a clairvoyance but is the selection of what is most probable. He sees the *in potentio* as actualized, though vaguely and in large general terms. His vision must necessarily be cast into symbolic images because he can't understand what he sees. He can't because he is a creature of the present, and the future contains many unfamiliar things."

"But John saw what was revealed by God," Anna said. "God would not reveal a probability; He would show only a certainty."

Dana shrugged and said, "Sometimes, a prophet will get two probable futures mixed up. He'll not be able to differentiate between the most likely and the next most likely. He sees the future as one, but in reality he is witnessing a part of one probable future inserted in the continuum of another probable future. That is why, perhaps, John saw two resurrections, the millennium, and so forth. He saw two or more futures all mixed up. Only true events will straighten out what future is really the most probable. Do you follow me?"

"And I suppose he may have seen Extraterrestrials and thought they were angels?" Anna said.

"It's possible."

Anna stood up and cried, "She is saying all these confusing things to lead us astray!"

"But you can't be led astray," Dana Webster said. "Only the heathen can now be led astray."

"Not if your theory is right," Anna said, and then she stared at Webster in an obvious confusion.

The entire party was upset. The next night, seeing that the situation had not improved, even though Dana had refused to talk about her theories anymore, Kelvin held a conference. After he had Dana taken to one side, he said to the others, "We may be saints, but we're certainly not behaving as such. Now, I've heard some of you, especially Anna, say that Dana should be killed. You don't even want just to kick her out of our party, because she might then find some heathens and lead them to attack us. Or because she may be the mother of heathens, and such should not be allowed to breed.

"Anna, would you be the one to shoot her in cold blood if we decided that she should die?"

"It wouldn't be in cold blood!" Anna said.

"Would it be in hate then? With an unchristian desire to shed blood?"

"At one time," Anna said, "it would have been a sin to hate. But the first death has come, and the old order has passed away, and the new one has come. There is no more returning of lost sheep to the field. Once a heathen, always a heathen. That is the way it is now."

"The old order will not pass away until the second death," Kelvin said. "I quote you Revelation 21:4: 'Now God's home is with men! He will live with them and they shall be His people. God Himself will be with them. . . . He will wipe away all tears from their eyes. There will be no more death, no more grief, crying, or pain. The old things have disappeared.' And don't forget what John says in 20:13, '. . . and all were judged according to what they had done.' If we kill Dana Webster, we will be judged by what we have done, which will be, in my opinion, murder."

"But you said we won't be judged again!" Anna said. "And remember what that angel said. Whatever we do, it will be the right thing!"

Kelvin was silent for a while. Everything was so tangled and shadowy, not bright and straight as it was supposed to be after the Beast had been put away. Or had they misunderstood the real meaning of the Revelation. What was it supposed to be? John had not said so or even implied it. Kelvin, like so many, had just assumed it.

It was then that Anna said that they would all starve if Dana Webster had to be fed, and that she should be killed before she could say another word of her blasphemous speculations.

"We have eaten better since Dana joined us," Kelvin said. "You know that to be true, Anna, so why do you lie? Listen, all of you, whatever else is not clear in this hot and dusty world, two things are. It is by these two that we must live, and by these two that we must die. One is, love God. The other is, love your fellow man. As long as Dana claims to be a Christian, then we must treat her as one until we get proof to the contrary."

"Many of us were delivered into the hands of the torturer and the butcher because of that," Anna said.

"So be it," Kelvin said. "But that is the way it must be. We take her along to the beloved city, and when we're there, then we'll find out."

Anna walked away. Others were not happy about his decision but, in these hard and dangerous times, there was no room for committee action. Like it or not, survival depended upon the quick rule of one good man.

Dana, smiling, though still pale, came up to him and kissed him on the lips. Kelvin felt a spasm of desire for her, but he pushed her away, though gently. He could not marry her now, or perhaps, ever. Not until they got to the city would he find out what was or was not permitted. And if he allowed his desire to overrule his good sense and he married her now, the group would believe, perhaps rightly, that he had put his self above the good of the whole.

Nevertheless, he did not get to sleep that night, and he found himself straining through the darkness toward Dana, as if his soul itself were trying to lift his body up and propel it through the air to her. The rains fell, and he huddled under the shelf of rock and wished he had her warm body inside the blanket with him. After a while, he prayed himself to sleep.

He awoke to shouting, screams, curses, the sound of the edge of steel striking flesh, and then shots from those of his party who had awakened in time.

Kelvin got off one shot, saw the dark figure before him fall, and something struck his head. He awoke shortly after dawn with a headache like a hot stone in his brain. His hands were tied behind him, and his feet were hobbled. Six of the attackers, all in ragged black and gold uniforms of the soldiers of the Beast, were standing over the survivors of his party. Little Jessica Crenwell lay on her back, unconscious and groaning, and apparently not long for life. Dana Webster rose from beside Crenwell and walked toward him. She seemed unhurt. And she carried a rifle.

He suppressed a groan and said, "So Anna was right."

But she was not, as he had expected, pleased.

"I had nothing to do with these," she said, gesturing at the sullen-faced heathen. "At least, I did not tell them to attack. They have ruined my plans to enter your beloved city with your party. Now I'll have to find another party of fools or somehow manage to convince the city's guardians that I am what I claim to be. And that won't be easy."

"I don't understand," he said, wincing from the pain involved in talking. "If you meant to palm yourself off as a Christian, why did you argue so vehemently that this was a false apocalypse? Why your theory of the Extraterrestrials?"

She smiled then, and she said, "Long before we reached the city, I would have pretended to have converted wholly to your way of thinking. I would have repented my errors. You would then accept me far more easily, because I would have seemed to have been confused and hurt by my traumatic experiences but would have been cured, shown the right way. And then you wouldn't have had much hesitation about marrying me, would you?"

"To be honest, no. I would have rejoiced at your change and leaped at the chance to marry you. But I would have done so only if you had made it plain that you really wanted me."

"And I would have arranged it so that you would not have been able to hold out," she said. "And then, as your wife, as one of the faithful band, I would have started planting my little seeds of doubt here and there, watering them on the sly, and all the time determining the weaknesses and the strengths of the city for the day when we attack."

"We?"

"We have been chosen by the new rulers of Earth as the favored executives, the herders of the swine. We were approached before all this began, told what would happen, and given our duties. And it was all as they said it would be. They are your true prophets, my friend, not some old half-crazy man on an island. They knew that the stresses inside the Earth would bring us the greatest quakes the Earth has ever known, and they knew that a group of large asteroids was heading for the Earth. Why shouldn't they, since they launched the asteroids ages ago, and since they have devices to store up energy in the Earth and to trigger it off whenever they care to do so."

"They?" Kelvin said, and he felt the stone in his brain become bigger and hotter.

"They are from a planet which orbits a star in Andromeda. They are the true rulers of this universe, or destined to be such. They can travel through interstellar space at speeds far exceeding those of light. But there is another race which has the same powers, and an evil race which has been the eon-long enemy of the Andromedans."

Kelvin groaned, partly from the agony in his head and partly from the agony in his soul.

"Your story sounds vaguely familiar," he said. "And I'm

not referring to the science fiction stories we used to read before the Beast suppressed them."

"It's in the Bible," she said, "but in a rather distorted form. I wasn't lying when I said that some men could compute the most probable future. To some extent, that is, on a broad and unspecific scale, of course. However, the Arcturans were going to seize Earth and take over when the Andromedans struck. The Arcturans are those you think of as angels. They are the ones preparing to build the beloved city, which will be a fortress to hold Earth—they think."

Kelvin said, "Satan may be locked up, but surely his aides are loose. But they won't be able to do anything really drastic for a long, long time. Not for a thousand years."

She laughed and said, "You still insist on believing your old cast-off myth?"

"It is you who believe in the myth, though it is new," he said. "You have to rationalize. You have to believe that the evil spirits are not spirits but beings from another star. And they, of course, must be the good ones, because no one really allies himself with what he admits is an evil cause. No, somehow, the cause must be a good one, no matter what evil it does. And we Christians, of course, are the evil ones. The Enemy has to think of himself as good."

The other heathens were walking toward him. They held knives and cigarette lighters.

Dana Webster said, "I must go now. I have work to do. I leave you to these. They'd be angry if I frustrated them by killing you. I need them, so they'll get their way now. I'm sorry, in a way, since I don't like torture. But there are times when it must be used."

"That's the difference between me and you, between us and your kind," Kelvin said. "I pity you, Dana Webster, I pity you from the deepest part of my being. I wish even now that you could see the light, that you could love God, know God as I know Him. But it is too late. The thousand years have started, and your end is foretold.

"And if I scream, *when* I scream, I should say, and if I beg for mercy from these things that have no mercy, and if I scream at them to get it over with—well, no matter how long it seems, it will be over. And then I will arise in a new body, and the old order will have passed away, and there will be no death any longer or any grief or pain."

"You nauseating egotistic fool!" she said.

"Time will tell which of us is a fool," he said. "But time has already told which of us is for man and God."

As death came, a smile passed, fleetingly, over his face—a smile Dana Webster would not, indeed, could not understand.

POLYTROPICAL PARAMYTHS

"Many—turning beyond—myths" is the literal translation from the ancient Greek. Perhaps the noun should have been "mythoparas." From "mythos," which I don't have to explain, and *-para*, from Latin *parere*, to give birth to. They're a form of fun-therapy for me and perhaps for the reader. They're symptoms of something in my unconscious that makes me itch and then scratch. A sort of cerebral athlete's foot. Or, to preserve the birth analogy from *parere*, a monster delivered with much mirth and some puzzlement. Or a square egg laid by a goose who's laughing because it hurts.

"Don't Wash the Carats" was the first one born of term. It came like a hot flash while reading a passage in Henry Miller's *Big Sur and the Oranges of Hieronymus Bosch*. This was, if I remember correctly, "Diamonds are sometimes born during violent storms." Damon Knight, who bought it for *Orbit 3*, wasn't sure what it meant, and neither did, or do, I. But it, and other paramyths, make the same kind of sense that the French "theater of the absurd," which is dominated by Rumanians and Irishmen, does. However, my myths have the quality of being much more intelligible.

The idea for "Only Who Can Make a Tree?" I owe to Ted Sturgeon. At a party at Harlan Ellison's, he told me he'd long thought of writing a story which would reverse the time-(w)ho(a)red Gernsbackian tale of the mad scientist and his beautiful young daughter. What about, Ted said, a story about the beautiful young scientist and her mad daughter? He would, he added, probably never write it. So I asked him if I could use it, since the idea appealed so strongly to me. Graciously, he consented.

Some time later, just after reading an article on ecology, and while watching on TV a Three Stooges short with my granddaughter, the PP (polytropical paramyth) started itching. Hence, the obvious derivation of the names of the three lab assistants, Lorenzo, Mough, and Kerls.

"The Sumerian Oath" certainly came up from the deeps, like an afterbirth from Moby Dick's mother, while I was contemplating, not so quietly, a bill from a Beverly Hills doctor. I have, however, long had a suspicion that the premise of this story is true.

Many of these PP either take place in scientists' laboratories or in hospital operating rooms. I've often asked my unconscious why this is so, but the operator seems to be asleep at the switchboard.

DON'T WASH THE CARATS

A Polytropical Paramyth

The knife slices the skin. The saw rips into bone. Gray dust flies. The plumber's helper (the surgeon is economical) clamps its vacuum onto the plug of bone. Ploop! Out comes the section of skull. The masked doctor, Van Mesgeluk, directs a beam of light into the cavern of cranium.

He swears a large oath by Hippocrates, Aesculapius, and the Mayo Brothers. The patient doesn't have a brain tumor. He's got a diamond.

The assistant surgeon, Beinschneider, peers into the well and, after him, the nurses.

"Amazing!" Van Mesgeluk says. "The diamond's not in the rough. It's cut!"

"Looks like a 58-facet brilliant, 127.1 carats," says Beinschneider, who has a brother-in-law in the jewelry trade. He sways the light at the end of the drop cord back and forth. Stars shine; shadows run.

"Of course, it's half buried. Maybe the lower part isn't diamond. Even so . . ."

"Is he married?" a nurse says.

Van Mesgeluk rolls his eyes. "Miss Lustig, don't you ever think of anything but marriage?"

"Everything reminds me of wedding bells," she replies, thrusting out her hips.

"Shall we remove the growth?" Beinschneider says.

"It's malignant, Van Mesgeluk says. "Of course, we remove it."

He thrusts and parries with a fire and skill that bring cries of admiration and a clapping of hands from the nurses and even cause Beinschneider to groan a bravo, not unmingled with jealousy. Van Mesgeluk then starts to insert the tongs but pulls them back when the first lightning bolt flashes beneath and across the opening in the skull. There is a small but sharp crack and, very faint, the roll of thunder.

"Looks like rain," Beinschneider says. "One of my brothers-in-law is a meteorologist."

"No. It's heat lightning," Van Mesgeluk says.

"With thunder?" says Beinschneider. He eyes the diamond with a lust his wife would give diamonds for. His mouth waters; his scalp turns cold. Who owns the jewel? The patient? He has no rights under this roof. Finders keepers? Eminent domain? Internal Revenue Service?

"It's mathematically improbable, this phenomenon," he says. "What's California law say about mineral rights in a case like this?"

"You can't stake out a claim!" Van Mesgeluk roars. "My God, this is a human being, not a piece of land!"

More lightning cracks whitely across the opening, and there is a rumble as of a bowling ball on its way to a strike.

"I said it wasn't heat lightning," Van Mesgeluk growls.

Beinschneider is speechless.

"No wonder the e.e.g. machine burned up when we were diagnosing him," Van Mesgeluk says. "There must be several thousand volts, maybe a hundred thousand, playing around down there. But I don't detect much warmth. Is the brain a heat sink?"

"You shouldn't have fired that technician because the machine burned up," Beinschneider says. "It wasn't her fault, after all."

"She jumped out of her apartment window the next day," Nurse Lustig says reproachfully. "I wept like a broken faucet at her funeral. And almost got engaged to the undertaker." Lustig rolls her hips.

"Broke every bone in her body, yet there wasn't a single break in her skin," Van Mesgeluk says. "Remarkable phenomenon."

"She was a human being, not a phenomenon!" Beinschneider says.

"But psychotic," Van Mesgeluk replies. "Besides, that's my line. She was thirty-three years old but hadn't had a period in ten years."

"It was that plastic intrauterine device," Beinschneider says. "It was clogged with dust. Which was bad enough, but the dust was radioactive. All those tests..."

"Yes," the chief surgeon says. "Proof enough of her psychosis. I did the autopsy, you know. It broke my heart to cut into that skin. Beautiful. Like Carrara marble. In fact, I snapped the knife at the first pass. Had to call in an expert from Italy. He had a diamond-tipped chisel. The hospital raised hell about the expense, and Blue Cross refused to pay."

"Maybe she was making a diamond," says Nurse Lustig. "All that tension and nervous energy had to go somewhere."

"I always wondered where the radioactivity came from," Van Mesgeluk says. "Please confine your remarks to the business at hand, Miss Lustig. Leave the medical opinions to your superiors."

He peers into the hole. Somewhere between heaven of skull and earth of brain, on the horizon, lightning flickers.

"Maybe we ought to call in a geologist. Beinschneider, you know anything about electronics?"

"I got a brother-in-law who runs a radio and TV store."

"Good. Hook up a step-down transformer to the probe, please. Wouldn't want to burn up another machine."

"An e.e.g. now?" Beinschneider says. "It'd take too long to get a transformer. My brother-in-law lives clear across town. Besides, he'd charge double if he had to reopen the store at this time of the evening."

"Discharge him, anyway," the chief surgeon says. "Ground the voltage. Very well. We'll get that growth out before it kills him and worry about scientific research later."

He puts on two extra pairs of gloves.

"Do you think he'll grow another?" Nurse Lustig says. "He's not a bad-looking guy. I can tell he'd be simpatico."

"How the hell would I know?" says Van Mesgeluk. "I may be a doctor, but I'm not quite God."

"God who?" says Beinschneider, the orthodox atheist. He drops the ground wire into the hole; blue sparks spurt out. Van Mesgeluk lifts out the diamond with the tongs. Nurse Lustig takes it from him and begins to wash it off with tap water.

"Let's call in your brother-in-law," Van Mesgeluk says. "The jewel merchant, I mean."

"He's in Amsterdam. But I could phone him. However, he'd insist on splitting the fee, you know."

"He doesn't even have a degree!" Van Mesgeluk cries. "But call him. How is he on legal aspects of mineralogy?"

"Not bad. But I don't think he'll come. Actually, the jewel business is just a front. He gets his big bread by smuggling in chocolate-covered LSD drops."

"Is that ethical?"

"It's top-quality Dutch chocolate," Beinschneider says stiffly.

"Sorry. I think I'll put in a plastic window over the hole. We can observe any regrowth."

"Do you think it's psychosomatic in origin?"

"Everything is, even the sex urge. Ask Miss Lustig."

The patient opens his eyes. "I had a dream," he says. "This dirty old man with a long white beard..."

"A typical archetype," Van Mesgeluk says. "Symbol of the wisdom of the unconscious. A warning..."

"...his name was Plato," the patient says. "He was the illegitimate son of Socrates. Plato, the old man, staggers out of a dark cave at one end of which is a bright klieg light. He's holding a huge diamond in his hand; his fingernails are broken and dirty. The old man cries, 'The Ideal is Physical! The Universal is the Specific Concrete! Carbon, actually. Eureka! I'm rich! I'll buy all of Athens, invest in apartment buildings, Great Basin, COMSAT!

"'Screw the mind!' the old man screams. 'It's all mine!'"

"Would you care to dream about King Midas?" Van Mesgeluk says.

Nurse Lustig shrieks. A lump of sloppy grayish matter is in her hands.

"The water changed it back into a tumor!"

"Beinschneider, cancel that call to Amsterdam!"

"Maybe he'll have a relapse," Beinschneider says.

Nurse Lustig turns savagely upon the patient. "The engagement's off!"

"I don't think you loved the real me," the patient says, "whoever you are. Anyway, I'm glad you changed your mind. My last wife left me, but we haven't been divorced yet. I got enough trouble without a bigamy charge.

"She took off with my surgeon for parts unknown just after my hemorrhoid operation. I never found out why."

THE SUMERIAN OATH

A Polytropical Paramyth

Caught in the Frozen Foods & Ice Cream aisle, with an assassin coming down from each end, Goodbody leaped upon the top of the grocery cart. With the grace and the flair of Doctor Blood (as played by Errol Flynn), Goodbody dived over the top of Ice Cream Cones & Chocolate Syrups. At the same time, the push of his departing feet sent the cart down the aisle into the nearest assassin.

Though Goodbody soared with great aplomb and considerable beauty, he knocked over tall boxes of ice cream cones and fell down on the other side into the Home Hardware & Fix-It-Urself Supplies. The cataract of Goodbody and wrenches, pliers, screwdrivers, boxes of nails, double sockets, and picture wire startled women customers and caused one to faint into Pet Foods & Bird Cages.

Goodbody dived under a railing and then galloped along the front of the store toward the Liquor Department. A shout caused him to look behind. The fools had actually pulled out their scalpels; they were indeed desperate. It was possible, however, that they did not mean to kill him inside the supermarket. They might be herding him into the parking lot, where others would net him.

He yanked over a pocketbook stand as he went by, whirling it so that *The Valley of The Dolls*, *The Arrangement*, *Couples*, and *Purple Sex Thing from the Fleshpot Planet* flew out like the hyperactive fingers of desperately hungry and desperately typing pornographers. The nearest pursuer, waving his scalpel, found that its tip was embedded in *So You Want To Be a Brain Surgeon?*

How appropriate and how terrible, he thought as he fled through the door. He was the author of that best seller, the royalties of which he could not spend because he might find the AMA agents waiting to pick *him* up if *he* picked up the checks.

In the parking lot, almost as bright as day, a car leaped at him. He soared again, performing three entrechats to gain altitude (reminding him of the days when he had entered the operating amphitheater to the applause of famous surgeons and slack-jawed first-year students). He landed between a Chevy and a Caddy and was off. Tires screamed; doors slammed; feet pounded; voices growled.

"Doctor Goodbody! Halt! We mean no harm! This is for your own good! You're sick, man, sick!"

Cornered in the angle formed by two high walls, he turned to face them. Never let it be said that he would whimper, any more than Doctor Kildare, young god, would have whimpered, even if confronted with a large uncollectable bill.

Six came at him with glittering scalpels, He jerked out his own blade, speedy as Doctor Ehrlich's Magic Bullet. He would go down fighting; they would not get off lightly when they crossed steel with a man whose genius with the cutting edge was surpassed only by that of Doc Savage, now retired.

Herr Doktor Grossfleisch, huge as Laird Cregar when he played the medical student in *The Lodger*, floated forward and cast a hypodermic syringe, .1 caliber. The speed and accuracy with which it traveled would have delighted even crusty (but kindly) old Doctor Gillespie, especially as played by Lionel Barrymore. Goodbody responded with a magnificent parry that sent the syringe soaring over the wall, higher than the legendary intern who drank the embalming fluid.

Two eminent doctors, holding straitjackets before them with one hand and suturing needles with the other, like Roman *retiarii*, advanced. He slashed at them with such speed that five of them cried out with involuntary admiration. They hated themselves afterward for it and would, of course, be reprimanded by the AMA.

Grossfleisch cursed a forbidden curse, for which he would have to pay heavily, though not bloodily. Again he cast a huge syringe with a giant caliber tip, and it sailed over the shoulder of the doctor on Goodbody's left just as Goodbody made a thrust that would have caused Doctor Zorba to go pale with envy. But the needle penetrated Goodbody's extended right arm, and all became as black as the inside of the cabinet of Doctor Caligari.

"Shall we operate, Doctor Cyclops?"

The bright lamp showed six heads in consultation over him. Cyclops' shaven head and thick glasses were not among them. Goodbody had dreamed the words. Coming up from the depths of the dark subconscious, where the only light was the flickering silver of the projector beam on the flickering silver screen, he had brought up with him ancient cherished horrors.

Doctor Grossfleisch, author of *Sponge Counting Techniques* and *Extraordinary Cases of Involved and Involuted Intussusception of the Small Bowel I Have Known*, bent over him. The eyes were as empty and cold as the reflector on the head of a laryngologist. Yet this was the man who had sponsored him, the man who had taught him so much. This was the man who originated the justly famous *When in doubt, cut*.

Doctor Grossfleisch held an ice pick in his goblin-shaped hand.

"*Schweinhund!* First ve do to you der frontal lobotomy! Den der dissection mitout anesthesia alive yet!"

The ice pick descended toward his eyeball. A door exploded open. A scalpel streaked by Grossfleisch's zeppelin hip and stuck in the operating table, vibrating against Goodbody's strapped arm.

"Halt!"

The six heads turned, and Grossfleisch said, "Ah! Doctor Leibfremd, world-famous healer and distinguished author of *Der Misunderstood Martyrs: Burke und Hare!* Vhat gifs for zuch a dramatic entrance?"

"Doctor Goodbody must be kept in good health! He is the only man with the genius to perform a brain operation on our glorious leader, Doctor Inderhaus!"

Goodbody's skin turned cold, and he felt like fainting.

"Zo, our glorious leader has deep tumors of der cuneus and der lingual areas of der brain? Und Goodbody only has der chenius to cut? Mein Gott, how can ve trust him?"

"We stand behind him," Doctor Leibfremd said, "ready to thrust to the ganglia if he makes one false move!"

Goodbody sneered as if he were correcting an intern. "Why should I do this for you when you'll dissect me alive later?"

"Not so!" Leibfremd cried. "Despite your great crimes, we will let you live if you operate successfully on Doctor Inderhaus! Of course, you will be kept a prisoner, but in Grossfleisch's sanatorium, where, need I remind you, the patients live like kings, or, even better, Beverly Hills physicians!"

"You would allow me to live?"

"You will die a natural death! You will not be touched by a doctor!" Grossfleisch said, "And you will get a professional courtesy discount, too! Ten percent off your bill!"

"Thank you," Goodbody said humbly. But he was thinking of ways to escape even then. The world must know the ghastly truth.

The day of the great operation, the amphitheater was filled with doctors from all over the world. The life of their glorious leader, Doctor Inderhaus, was at stake, and only the condemned criminal, the Judas, the Benedict Arnold, the Mudd, the Quisling of the medical profession, could save him.

The patient, head shaven, was wheeled in. He shook hands with himself as his colleagues cheered wildly. Tears dripped down his cheeks at this exhibition of love and respect, not unmixed with awe. Then he saw his surgeon approaching, and the benignity of Hyde changed to the hideous face of Jekyll.

Goodbody slipped on his mask and gloves. Grossfleisch held a scalpel to his back, and a man, who looked like Doctor Casey after a hard night with the head nurse, aimed a laser at Goodbody.

"Stand back! Give me room!" Goodbody said. He was icy cold, calm as the surface of a goldfish bowl, his long delicate fingers, which could have been a concert pianist's if he had gone wrong, flexed as if they were snakes smelling blood. A hush fell. Though the audience hated him to a man, despised and loathed him, and longed to spit on him (with no sterilization before or after), they could not help admiring him.

The hours ticked by. Scalpels cut. The scalp was rolled back. Drills growled; saws whined. The top of the skull came out. The keen blades began slicing into the gray wrinkled mass.

"Ach!" Grossfleisch said involuntarily as the forebrain came up like a drawbridge. "Mein Gott! Zuch daringk!"

There was a communal "Ah!" as Goodbody held up the great jellyfish-shaped tumor in his fist. Despite themselves, the doctors gave him a standing ovation that lasted ten minutes.

It was sad, he thought, that the greatest triumph of a series of blazing triumphs, the apex of his career, was also his black defeat, the nadir. And then the patient was wheeled out, and the surgeon was seized, stripped, and strapped. Grossfleisch and Ueberpreis, well-known proctologist and author of the notorious article *Did Doctor Watson Poison His Three Wives?*, approached the operating table. They were smiling with an utterly evil coldness and abhorrently sadistic pleasure, like Doctor Mabuses.

The audience leaned forward. They had always felt that both the patient and doctor were better off without employing anesthesia. The physician could determine the patient's reactions much more accurately and quickly if his responses were not dulled.

"Doctor X, I presume?" Goodbody said as he awoke.

"What!" said the nurse, Mrs. Fell.

"A nightmare. I thought my arms and legs had been cut off. Oh!"

"You'll get used to that," the nurse said. "Anytime you need anything, just press that plate with your nose. Don't be bashful. Doctor Grossfleisch said I was to wait on you hand and foot. I mean..."

"I'm not only a basket case but a crazy basket case," he said. "I'm sure that I've been certified insane, haven't I?"

"Well," Mrs. Fell said, "who knows what insane means! One man's looniness is another man's religion. I mean, one man's schizophrenia is another man's manic-depressiveness. Well, you know what I mean!"

It was no use telling her his story, but he had to.

"Don't just dismiss what I'm about to tell you as the ravings of a maniac. Think about it for a long time; look around you. See if what I say doesn't make sense, even if it seems a topsy-turvy sense."

He had one advantage. She was a nurse, and all nurses, by the time they were graduated, loathed doctors. She would be ready to believe the worst about them.

"Every medical doctor takes the oath of Hippocrates. But, before he swears in public, he takes a private, a most arcane, oath. And that oath is much more ancient than that of Hippocrates, who, after all, died in 377 B.C., comparatively recently.

"The first witch doctor of the Old Stone Age may have given that oath to the second witch doctor. Who knows? But it is recorded, in a place where you will never see it, that the first doctor of the civilized world, the first doctor of the most ancient city-state, that of Sumer, predecessor even of old Egypt, swore in the second doctor.

"The Sumerian oath—scratch my nose, will you, my dear?—required that a medical doctor must never, under any circumstances, reveal anything at all about the true nature of doctors or of the true origin of diseases."

Mrs. Fell listened with only a few interruptions. Then she

said, "Doctor Goodbody! Are you seriously trying to tell me that diseases would not exist if it were not for doctors? That doctors manufacture diseases and spread them around? That if it weren't for doctors, we'd all be one hundred percent healthy? That they pick and choose laymen to infect and to cure so they can get good reputations and make money and dampen everybody's suspicions by... by... that's ridiculous!"

The sweat tickled his nose, but he ignored it. "Yes, Mrs. Fell, that's true! And, rarely, but it does happen, a doctor can't take being guilty of mass murder anymore, and he breaks down and tries to tell the truth! And then he's hauled off, declared insane by his colleagues, or dies during an operation, or gets sick and dies, or just disappears!"

"And why weren't you killed?"

"I told you! I saved our glorious leader, the Grand Exalted Iatrogenic Sumerian. They promised me my life, and we don't lie to each other, just to laymen! But they made sure I couldn't escape, and they didn't cut my tongue out because they're sadistic! They get a charge out of me telling my story here, because who's going to believe me, a patient in a puzzle factory? Yes, Mrs. Fell, don't look so shocked! A booby hatch, a nut house! I'm a loony, right? Isn't that what you believe?"

She patted the top of his head. "There, there! I believe you! I'll see what I can do. Only..."

"Yes?"

"My husband is a doctor, and if I thought for one moment that he was in a secret organization...!"

"Don't ask him!" Goodbody said. "Don't say a word to any doctor! Do you want to come down with cancer or infectious hepatitis or have a coronary thrombosis? Or catch a brand-new disease? They invent a new one now and then, just to relieve the boredom, you know!"

It was no use. Mrs. Fell was just going along with him to soothe him.

And that night he was carried into the depths beneath the huge old house, where torches flickered and cold gray stones sweat and little drums beat and shrill goat horns blew and doctors with painted faces and red robes and black feathers and rattling gourds and thrumming bullroarers administered the Sumerian oath to the graduating class, 1970, of Johns Hopkins. And they led each young initiate before him and pointed out what would happen if he betrayed his profession.

ONLY WHO CAN MAKE A TREE?

A Polytropical Paramyth

"You'll have to admit that Serendipitous Laboratories cleared away the smog," Dr. Kerls said.

Bobbing, he danced, the toe of his left shoe striking the floor and seeming to catch and pull him backward. He was a very short, middle-aged, and fat chemist. The top of his head looked like the back of a hog, and his voice was high and thin.

"Smog, shmog!" Dr. van Skant said. He snorted as if he had a noseful of nitrogen oxide. "What kind of pollution problem you think a few trillion moths produce, eh? Godalmighty, they're still bulldozing them off the freeways. And I had to stop twice to clean them out of my exhaust pipe! Twice! Godalmighty!"

Kerls grinned and bobbed his head and rubbed his hands together.

"Except for being a failure, the experiment was a success, you'll have to admit that."

The Federal inspector-scientist did not reply. He looked around the huge laboratory. Tubes and retorts were bubbling, booping, and beeping. Colored liquids were racing up and down and around transparent plastic and glass pipes. A control panel was pulsing with lights and squeaking and pinging. Tapes were running this way and that. Generators were hurling wormy sparks back and forth, like robot baseball players warming up before a game.

Two white-coated men were pouring chemicals into tubes, and the tubes were throwing off frosty, evil-smelling, evil-looking clouds.

"Where in hell is the table?" van Skant snarled. He was a very tall and huge-paunched man with glasses and a thick blond moustache, and he spoke from behind, or through, a big green cigar at all times.

Only Who Can Make a Tree?   153

"What table?" Dr. Kerls said squeakily. He cringed.

"The table with the sheet under which is the monster waiting for the lightning stroke to bring it to life, you nitwit!"

Kerls laughed nervously. "Oh, you're joking! It is impressive, ain't it?"

"Should be," van Skant growled. "You jerks set it up just to impress me."

Kerls looked around helplessly.

Dr. Lorenzo smiled and waved at van Skant. He was very short and thin and had a bald forehead with a great Einsteinian foliage of hair behind the baldness to compensate.

Dr. Mough, very short, stern-faced, his hair cut in stylish bangs across his forehead, grimaced at Kerls.

"You jest, of course?" Kerls said. He danced backward while he cracked his knuckles to the tune of *The Pirates of Penzance* overture.

"Does this place hire nothing but psychotics?" van Skant said.

"Serendipitous Laboratories hires nothing but the best," Kerls said.

Van Skant stopped and stared. Dr. Lorenzo had poured the contents of a tall beaker into a rubber boot, and Dr. Mough, holding the top of the boot shut, was shaking it.

"I think they're testing out a new type of vulcanizer," Kerls said.

Mough set the boot upright on the floor, and he and Lorenzo stepped back.

The boot, stiff as a sailor at the end of a three-day leave, rumbled. Then it leaped like a kangaroo down the aisle between tables, hit the wall, bounced, and did not fall but erupted.

The brownish fluid sprayed over half of the huge room. Drs. Kerls and van Skant were caught with their mouths open.

"Coffee!" van Skant howled. "You guys are making coffee! On government time!"

"Gee, is that it?" Kerls said, licking his lips. "Not bad. Better than what they usually make. But they were actually trying to make instant cement. Hyungh! Hyungh!"

Van Skant wiped the brown stuff from his face with a handkerchief.

"I'll shut this place down! Cut off the Federal funds! You're working on a government contract to combat pollution!"

Dr. Mough, the little man with the bangs, said, "Quite true, my dear Dr. van Skant. But we're on our coffee break, and we don't have to account for what we do then."

He turned to Dr. Kerls.

"Clean this mess up."

Kerls looked indignant. "Me? You and Lorenzo made the mess."

Mough made the peace sign with his two fingers, poked Kerls in the eyes with them, rapped him on the head with the butt of his palm, punched him in the belly, and hammered his forehead again when Kerls doubled up.

"Don't talk back to the assistant project director!"

Kerls staggered off while van Skant, goggle-eyed, watched him.

"Not too much trouble with discipline here," Dr. Mough said. "We run a tight ship."

Van Skant followed Mough. Kerls seemed to be alleviating his pain with liquid from a flask he had taken from his hip pocket.

"Inspiration is found in many places," Mough said, noting van Skant's questioning expression. "Dr. Kerls often comes up with an idea after drinking from his fount of wisdom, as he calls it, hah, hah!"

"I wish to see Dr. Legzenbreins immediately," van Skant said.

"Yeah, there she is, just going into her office," Dr. Mough said. "Ain't she too much? I'm in love with her, and so are my two colleagues, the imbeciles! But she's too dedicated to get married as yet. She's a beautiful young scientist."

"And who's that?" van Skant said, pointing at a huge, pimply-faced girl in a laboratory coat who had just waddled out of the office.

"That's her mad daughter."

"Mad? You mean, angry?"

"Nuts," Mough said. "Oh, I don't mean to you, Doctor! She's nuts, out of her skull, real woo-woo, you know. But a brilliant idea man! She's the one thought of the moths."

"That figures," van Skant said.

As he put the handkerchief back in his pocket, he felt something flutter. The insect that he removed and threw away was a large white moth with a scoop-shaped mouth. It flapped around and around the big room until it passed through the steam from an open tube in which bubbled a dark red liquid.

The moth dropped as if it had had a heart attack and fell into the tube, where it disintegrated.

The red liquid turned a bright yellow.

Dr. Lorenzo yelped, apparently with delight, and he motioned for his colleagues and the fat girl to hasten to the tube. Kerls had just picked up a ten-foot-long glass pipe to fit onto a partially assembled setup. He turned when Lorenzo yelled, and the end of the pipe swung around and struck Mough in the back of his head. The cracking noise carried across the huge room.

Kerls dropped the pipe on Mough's head as he struggled to get up from the floor. Kerls ran, ducked behind a table, and reappeared by Lorenzo.

Mough staggered up off the floor, feeling the back of his head.

Van Skant strode up to the group, pushing his big belly as if it contained mail from the President, and he said, "What's so interesting?"

Mough's eyes had lost their glaze by then. He was looking suspiciously at Kerls, who was bending over the tube, rubbing his hands, and humming. Mough said, "Ah, Dr. van Skant, I presume? Yes, the moth undoubtedly contains the missing element, or elements, or combination thereof. We've been looking for a long time..."

"On government time?"

"On our lunch hour," Dr. Lorenzo said.

"It'll be easier just to use moths than to try to analyze a moth and determine the particular stuff responsible for the reaction," Dr. Kerls said. "Hyungh! Hyungh!"

"No trouble there," Dr. Lorenzo said. "We just send the janitor outside with a shovel and a bucket."

"What is that stuff?" Dr. van Skant bellowed, his face red.

"A universal solvent," Dr. Mough said, smiling proudly.

Van Skant struggled for breath and then pointed his finger at the tube. "A universal solvent? But that tube..."

"Oh, the reaction takes time," Kerls said, cracking his knuckles and then looking at his wristwatch, the large white-gloved hands of which were at 12:32. "In fact..."

The tube disappeared, and the yellow fluid splashed over the mica-topped table.

One corner of the table and a leg were gone.

A hole appeared in the floor, and a scream from the room

below came up through it. And then, far below, there was a hiss of severed steam pipes. Presently, intermingled with the hiss, was a gurgle. A moment later, a splash.

"Possibly sheared plumbing," Dr. Mough said, smiling.

Van Skant's face had turned from red to gray.

"My God!" he yelled when he had finally gotten his breath— again. "It'll go all the way to the center of the Earth!"

Dr. Mough passed his hand over his bangs and his face and then cried, "You jerks! You shoulda used less solvent like I told you!"

Kerls was on his right; Lorenzo, his left. His fists caught each in the mouth simultaneously, and they staggered back clutching their faces.

"How deep will that stuff really go?" van Skant screamed.

Mough blinked, rubbed the back of his head, and said, "What? Oh, that! The solvent evaporates within half an hour, so there's no problem there."

A low rumbling noise shook the building, and then the hole in the floor gushed black liquid.

Later on, after much litigation it was established that the oil well was the property of the Federal government. A few days after the suit was settled, very little mattered. But that was some time in the future.

Van Skant, in his report, admitted that he didn't remember much of anything from the moment he heard the rumble. He thought that Dr. Kerls had picked up a big plastic pipe to insert into the hole in the floor as a plug. He thought, but could not swear to it, that the end of the pipe had struck him across the forehead when Dr. Kerls turned around with it on his shoulder. He made a very poor witness for the government, and so the suit against Serendipitous Laboratories and its head, the beautiful young scientist, Dr. Legzenbreins, was dropped.

By the time that Serendipitous had moved into a new building, the oil well had been capped and Southern California was cleansed of its moths. Dr. Mough, during a news interview, said, "How were my colleagues and I to know that one of the atmospheric toxics which the moths were mutated to eat would be a sex stimulant and that the mutants would breed entirely out of hand? Uh, please don't quote that last remark."

Dr. Mough revealed that Serendipitous was mutating bats which could, as it were, vacuum-clean the air. The company was also mutating goats to eat land pollutants and refuse, and

Only Who Can Make a Tree?   157

sharks which would digest oceanic pollutants.

At that very moment, Dr. Legzenbreins was in her office with her daughter.

"I need a man," Desdemona whined.

"Who doesn't?" her mother said.

Desdemona blew out her bubble gum and looked cross-eyed at the iridescent bubble. Her mother became tense. Was Desdemona getting another fabulous idea?

The big bubble collapsed into the big mouth.

"You need a man?" Desdemona said. "You? The most beautiful woman in the world?"

"That's what scares them off," Dr. Legzenbreins said. "And the few that don't scare, the studs with low IQ's, I can't stand. So I'm in as bad a way as you are. Ironic, ain't it?"

"Drs. Kerls, Lorenzo, and Mough would marry you within a minute, and they're Ph.D.'s," the daughter said, drooling.

"They're five feet tall, and I'm six feet two," the mother said. "Besides, I'm not sure they're not punch-drunk."

"They're brilliant!"

"The two states are not necessarily incompatible."

"I don't want big words. I want a man. I'm twenty-five!"

"I have a man for you," the mother said. "A psychoanalyst." She added, "In a very high-class private sanitorium."

But she did not mean it. Her daughter provided the creative genius of Serendipitous. She herself, though a genius, was basically an analytic scientist, and her three assistants were basically synthesizers. Without madness, science would get no place, and Dr. Legzenbreins knew it.

She put on a very tight peekaboo dress and called in the three for a conference.

"I won't marry until my daughter marries and quits bugging me about her sex life or lack thereof. I'd suggest a lover. But she is, as you know, quite insane, and insists on remaining a virgin until she has a husband. Now, each of you goofballs has asked me many times to marry him."

Dr. Kerls stood up, danced backward, cracked his knuckles, and said, "I repeat my offer."

Dr. Mough kicked him in the knee and slapped him twice in the face before he hit the floor. As Dr. Kerls tried to get up, he was hit on the head with the coffee tray, which bent to form a semihelmet.

"Don't interrupt!" Dr. Mough said.

Dr. Legzenbreins told them what they must do.

There was a long silence when she had finished. It was finally broken by Desdemona's "Eureka!" from the laboratory. At any other time, all would have stampeded through the door to find out what new idea she had just stubbed her mental toe on.

Dr. Legzenbreins leaned back and stretched her arms out and arched her back.

"The two survivors, uh, the two that don't marry her, will be permitted to put their names on my marriage lottery list."

Dr. Mough grabbed Dr. Lorenzo's bushy hair and yanked out a fistful. Lorenzo screamed and grabbed the top of his head and moaned.

"Don't ever let me catch you looking at her again like that," Mough said. "It ain't decent."

"Thank you, Dr. Mough," she said. "I can't stand naked lust. Especially in a scientist. It's so unprofessional."

"My pleasure," Dr. Mough said, beaming.

"What I don't like about this," Dr. Kerls said, shrinking away from Mough, "is that the loser has to settle for Desdemona."

"Is any sacrifice too great for Science?" Dr. Mough said, shuddering.

"What's Science got to do with this?" Kerls said. "Unless everything reminds you of Science?"

Dr. Legzenbreins said, "I leave it up to you gentlemen to decide who's going to be put on the, uh, go to the altar with her."

She rose and stretched again, and the three moaned.

"Shall we see what Desdemona has thought of this time?"

"I was thinking," Desdemona said, "that this food tastes more like sawdust every day. So I was going to have to find another delicatessen. And then I thought, sawdust. Termites eat wood and get fat on it. Their guts contain protozoa, you know, them teeny little parasitical animals. Protozoa use enzymes to digest the cellulose in the wood and convert it into stuff fit to digest. OK, so thousands of tons of sawdust and chips of wood are just thrown away every year. Why couldn't these be saved and fed to people? If..."

"If we could mutate protozoa to live in the human gut, right?" Dr. Lorenzo said.

Dr. Mough banged him on the forehead with his fist.

"Imbecile! How do you get people to eat wood?"

Only Who Can Make a Tree?   159

"You make it palatable, indeed, delicious," Desdemona said.

"Just what I was about to say in reply to my rhetorical question," Dr. Mough said.

"I wish you'd just give me rhetorical blows," Dr. Lorenzo said. "Them real blows hurt, you know."

"If I quit hitting you, you'd say I didn't love you no more," Dr. Mough said. "Quit bellyaching; get to work."

Desdemona, being mad, could not be trusted to work with the dangerous chemicals and expensive apparatus. But she was permitted to use cheap chemicals and equipment while searching for something to make sawdust tasty. Dr. Kerls supervised her every move. As Dr. Mough later said, this was a fortunate decision on his part, even though he was criticized for making Dr. Kerls her watchdog.

Dr. Kerls, carrying a long glass pipe to attach to Desdemona's setup, turned around when Dr. Mough called to him. The pipe knocked over a tube of hydrocyanic acid onto Desdemona's experiment for the day. The result was a minor explosion which caused Dr. Kerls to whirl around and bang Dr. Lorenzo across the eyes with the pipe and a salt which, sprinkled over sawdust, would bring tears of joy to a gourmet. Sawdust hamburgers became Desdemona's favorite food.

She forgot that she needed protozoa to convert cellulose into food and that the protozoa had not been successfully mutated yet so it could live in the human gut. She lost weight. But the sad thing was that she was as ugly as ever, if not more so. The fat had hidden a very unaesthetic bone structure.

"Takes after her father," Dr. Legzenbreins said.

One day, Dr. Kerls sneezed into a test tube of protozoa, and the next day the animalcules were turning sawdust into protein. Desdemona drank a cupful of the little beasts and soon began to gain weight on a diet that only a termite should have loved.

A week later, Dr. Lorenzo got mad at Dr. Mough and threw a beaker of protozoa at him. Mough ducked, and the beaker flew through the door of the men's room as Dr. Kerls stepped out. Dr. Mough said there was nothing to worry about, even if the protozoa were circulating in the city's sewage system. The protozoa couldn't get back into the drinking water, and what if they did?

The next day, Dr. van Skant called them all in and asked for a progress report on the antipollution projects.

"Eureka!" Desdemona cried, interrupting the conference.

"How about a virus which you can put into gasoline or any fuels burned in cars and factories? It's quiescent until blown out the exhaust with the gases. Then it combines with the gases to render them physically inert, or it attacks the pollutants and decomposes them rapidly. You kill the toxics at the source. The viruses multiply as they float through the air, and they continue to eat up the combustion products. And we can make aquatic viruses for the rivers, lakes, and oceans."

The three scientists shook hands with each other while the mother beamed at the daughter.

Van Skant said, "That's fine. But I want a report on what's been done, not on what you're going to do in some cloud-cuckoo-land future."

"Certainly, step this way," Dr. Mough said.

He led the Federal man to a large table on which was a complicated array of very busy apparatus.

"My colleagues and I have put in many hours toiling to build this thingamajig. It's designed to make a substance to coat lungs. This coating will filter out the air pollutants and admit only pure air. How's that grab you, Doctor?"

"I don't know," van Skant said slowly. "There's something wrong in your approach to the pollution problem. But I can't quite put my finger on it."

Mough and van Skant put on protective suits and went into the biological room. There Mough showed him the mutated bats, sharks, and winged goats.

"You'll notice the goats don't have any feet," Dr. Mough said. "That means that they have to fly to get from one place to another on land. And while they're flying, being big animals, they're really breathing hard to keep themselves aloft. So they take in vast quantities of polluted air, and their specialized stomachs and lungs burn up the bad stuff. That leaves a swath of clean air behind them. What the winged goats don't get, the bats will. Or maybe it's the other way around."

"Wouldn't flying elephants burn up even more bad air?" van Skant said, sneering.

"Please don't be absurd," Dr. Mough said.

"There's something I can't quite put my finger on," van Skant said, shaking his head.

Dr. Mough didn't tell him, but the thingamajig was also being used as a matrimonial roulette wheel. There were three special chemicals in the setup, each of which was presently colorless but would eventually change into a primary color

Only Who Can Make a Tree?

One would be red; one, purple; one, green. Mough's color was red; Lorenzo's, purple; Kerls's, green. A random selector had dumped the chemicals into the setup, and so the three colleagues did not know which chemical would change color first. It was all up to chance.

The man whose color appeared first would win Desdemona's hand.

"And, God help him, the rest of her!" moaned Dr. Mough.

One day, the winged goats were gone, having eaten through the steel bars and the glass walls imprisoning them.

Several days later, the three scientists and Desdemona were having lunch in the laboratory when Dr. Legzenbreins walked out of her office. She was completely covered with a helmet and suit, being on her way to the virus section to run a late phase of an experiment. She waved at the group as she went by; the men stopped eating to groan and moan.

A moment later, Dr. van Skant, purple-faced, charged into the room.

"You're closed down!" he bellowed. "Your goddamn flying goats ate half my car in the parking lot! This is the last straw! I'm canceling all your government contracts!"

Drs. Kerls, Lorenzo, and Mough sprang to their feet and their heads met. The result was a loud thunk and cries of pain as they reeled back clutching their heads.

The alarm attached to the thingamajig whooped, and a bright orange light flashed.

"Oh, my God!" Kerls screamed. "It's happened!"

"What? What?" van Skant and Desdemona cried. Desdemona had been behaving rather woodenly lately, but she was aroused now.

Dr. Kerls, half-fainting, grabbed Mough.

A green thread was streaking through the mud-brown liquid in the pipes on the thingamajig.

Dr. Mough felt so sorry for his colleague, he did not hit him for having put his hands on him.

Dr. Legzenbreins raced out of the virus section, leaving the door open.

"What is it? What is it?"

Dr. Mough said, "It's the biggest..."

Boom!

Clouds of brown vapor and sprays of green liquid filled the laboratory.

By the time the scientists and Desdemona got back onto

their feet, they could see clearly. The clouds were gone, revealing a wrecked laboratory and ruptured walls behind which had been the virus section and the zoological room.

"The green doesn't count," Kerls mumbled. "I had my fingers crossed when we swore to abide by the decision of the thingamajig."

"You'll marry Desdemona or else," Dr. Mough said.

"Or else what?" Kerls squeaked.

"Or else this!" Mough said, and he broke a beaker of yellow liquid over Kerls's head and then rammed the flaming end of a Bunsen burner against Kerls's rear when Kerls turned away from him.

Desdemona spat out green liquid.

"Gee, I feel funny," she muttered. She walked out of the laboratory as if she were made of wood.

"Think she's all right?" van Skant said. "That virus got blown all over the place, and God knows what the chemicals in the thingamajig will do."

"Won't hurt nothing," Mough said. "I'll stake my reputation on that."

"We're lost!" van Skant said, and he staggered out of the room.

Desdemona wandered around, singing, until she found a vacant lot, one in which the good earth was uncovered. And there she stood motionless, arms extended to the sides, while roots, still half-flesh, sprouted and drove into the ground through her shoes.

The fourth day, she put out buds.

The sixth day, a pigeon spotted her and landed to build a nest.

By then, hundreds of thousands of Southern Californians were undergoing similar metamorphoses.

The polluters were changing into something which could not pollute and which converted carbon dioxide into the much-needed oxygen. Serendipitous had found the ideal solution.

Only one was left unmetamorphosed. She had been wearing a protective suit at the time of the explosion and had not taken it off until she was certain that the danger was over.

She was the only human being left in the world.

The doorbell rang.

She got up and out of bed, walked through the house, and opened the front door.

Only Who Can Make a Tree?

Three man-sized trees stood on the porch.

"Kerls, Lorenzo, and Mough!" Dr. Legzenbreins cried.

Somehow, they had dragged up their roots and tracked her down. Love conquers all.

They tried to get through the door at the same time. Even if they had still been human beings, they would have gotten stuck. But with their extended arms—branches—they could never make it through alone.

Dr. Legzenbreins finally led them around to the backyard, where they took root with a shudder of relief. She went back to bed without closing the window, which was a mistake. She awoke with two branches caressing what she considered to be intimate places.

The other trees were hitting their branches against the one that had hold of her.

She reached up and plucked some of Mough's fruits—she thought it was Mough—and the tree quivered. Then the branches drooped and relaxed their hold.

The others continued to beat him with their branches.

But the next day all three were as rigid and motionless as trees should be, and their skin had become completely bark.

Spring came. Something popped deep within Dr. Legzenbreins.

She wished that she had not eaten Mough's fruit.

THE LAST RISE OF NICK ADAMS

This story has a curious history, but then, don't they all?

A young man named Brad Lang, author of some very good private-eye novels, decided to start a magazine, *Popular Culture*, which would be devoted to just what the title implied. He got hold of me and asked me if I'd write a short story for him. It so happened that I had one on hand, a tale which Ed Ferman of *The Magazine of Fantasy & Science Fiction* had not liked. So I rewrote it and sent it out with the same title and byline I'd sent to Ferman. This was "The Impotency of Bad Karma" by Cordwainer Bird.

The explanation of title and byline may be a little complicated, but bear with me. Cordwainer Bird is the name Harlan Ellison puts on the credits of a movie he's written when he feels that the producer or director or whoever has rewritten his script and ruined it. Harlan insists on a clause in his contracts which permits him to do this.

Now, as you may or may not know, I've written a number of short stories and two novels under bylines which are the names of characters in fiction who are writers. Examples: Kilgore Trout, John H. Watson, M.D., Paul Chapin (a writer in a Nero Wolfe novel), David Copperfield, Leo Queequeg Tincrowdor (one of my own fictional authors), Lord Greystoke (surely you know who he is), and some others. I wanted to write a story by Cordwainer Bird, but the trouble with that was that he was not a fictional author. So, to remedy this, I first put Bird in the genealogy in the appendix to my biography of the famous pulp-era hero, Doc Savage. Then I made Bird a character in a story titled "The Doge

The Last Rise of Nick Adams

Whose Barque Was Worse Than His Bight." Having established that Bird was a character in fiction who was also a writer, I then wrote a story by Bird.

All this was done with Harlan's permission, of course.

At the time, though, I didn't know that Harlan had long before written some stories under the Bird byline.

"The Impotency of Bad Karma" (Harlan's suggestion for a title) appeared in the first and, alas!, last issue of *Popular Culture*. It was interesting, even stimulating, but Brad Lang couldn't get the financing needed to continue it. It also happened that Barry Malzberg had an article, "What Happened to Science Fiction?", in that issue. He read the story by "Bird" and didn't care for the parody of himself (as Michael B. Hopsmount). This, despite the fact that he's parodied others. I only parody those writers whose works I like, so, in a sense, the character of Hopsmount was my tribute to Malzberg.

Sometime later, Roy Torgesson asked me for a story. I explained about "The Impotency of Bad Karma" and the Bird byline and the extremely limited circulation of *Popular Culture*. Roy said he'd take it, and I sat down and rewrote the story again, including removing Hopsmount, and it appeared as "The Last Rise of Nick Adams" in *Chrysalis 2*.

The genesis of the original idea for the story, the basic concept, came one day while I was considering the inflating or deflating effects of good or bad reviews of my works, of good or bad royalty reports, and so on. This story exaggerates the effects, though not very much.

Readers (not very many) have asked me if the Nick Adams in my story could be the son of Hemingway's Nick Adams. I'm not just now in a position to confirm or deny that.

Nick Adams, Jr., science-fiction author, and his wife were having the same old argument.

"If you really loved me, you wouldn't be having so much trouble with *it*."

"There are many words for *it*," Nick said. "If you didn't have a dirty mind, you'd use them. Anyway, there are plenty of times when you can't complain about *it*."

"Yeah! About once every other month I can't!"

Ashlar was a tall scrawny ex-blonde who had been beautiful until the age of thirty-seven-and-a-half. Now she was fifty. A hard fifty, Nick thought. And here am I, a soft fifty.

"It does have a sort of sine-wave action," he said. "I mean, if you drew a graph..."

"So now *it's* dependent on weather conditions. What're we supposed to do, consult the barometer when we make love? Why *don't* you make a graph of *its* rises and falls? Of course, you'd have to have some rises first..."

"I got to go to work," he said. "I'm months behind..."

"I'll say you are, though I don't mean in your writing! All right, hide behind the typewriter! Bang your keys; don't bang me!"

He rose from the chair and dutifully kissed her on her forehead. It was as cold and hard as a tombstone, incised with wrinkles that read *Here Lies Love. R.I.P.* She snarled silently. Shrugging, he walked up the steps toward his office. By the time he reached the third floor, he was sweating as if he were a rape suspect in a police lineup. His panting filled the house.

Fifty, out of breath, and low on virility. Still, it wasn't really his fault. She was such a cold bitch. Take last night, for instance. Ashlar's eyes had started rolling, and her face was falling apart underneath the makeup. He had said, "Did you feel something move, little rabbit?" (He was crazy about Hemingway.) And she had said, "Something's *going* to move. Get off. I got to go to the toilet."

Once it had all been good and true, and he had felt the universe move all the way to the Pole Star. Now he felt as if the hair had fallen off his chest.

He sat down before the typewriter and stroked the keys, the smooth and cool keys, and he pressed a few to tune up his fingers and warm up the writing spirit. He could feel the inspiration deep down within, shadow-boxing, rope-skipping, jogging, sweating, pores open, heart beating hard and true, ready to climb into the ring.

The only trouble was, the bell rang, and he couldn't even get out of his corner. He was stuck on the first word. *The. The...* what?

If only he could see some pattern in his sexual behavior. Maybe the silly bitch's sarcastic remark about making a graph wasn't so stupid. Maybe...

A bell rang, and he sprang up, shuffling, his left shoulder up, arm extended... what was he doing? That was the front

The Last Rise of Nick Adams

doorbell, and it was probably announcing the delivery of the mail. Nick gave the mailman ten dollars a month to ring the doorbell. This was illegal, but who was going to know? Nick could not endure the idea that a hot check was cooling off in the mailbox.

He hurried downstairs, passing Ashlar, who wasn't going to get off her ass and bring the mail to him. Not her.

Since this was the first of the month, there were ten bills. But there was also a pile of fan mail and a letter from his agent.

Ah! His agent had sent a check, the initial advance on a new contract. Two thousand dollars. Minus his agent's ten percent commission. Minus fifty dollars for overseas market mailings. Minus twenty-five for the long-distance call his agent had made to him last month. Minus a thousand for the loan from his agent. Minus fifty for the interest on the loan. Minus ten dollars accounting charge.

Only six hundred and sixty-five dollars remained, but it was a feast after last month's famine. By the time he'd finished reading the fan letters, all raving about the goodness and truth of his works, he felt as if he was connected to a gas station air pump.

Suddenly, he knew that there was a pattern to the decline and fall of the Roman Empire he carried between his legs. In no way, however, was he going to take the edge off his horniness by explaining the revelation to Ashlar just now. He dropped his mail and his pants, and he hurried to the kitchen. Ashlar was bent over, putting dishes in the washer.

He flipped up her skirt, yanked down her panties, and said, "The dishes can wait, but *it* can't."

It would all have been good and true and the earth might have moved if Ashlar hadn't gotten her head caught between the wire racks of the washer.

"You're getting fat again, aren't you?" Ashlar said. "That's *some* spare tire you got. And you missed a patch on your cheek when you shaved. Listen, I know this isn't time to talk about it, but my mother... what's the matter? Why are you stopping?"

Nick snarled and he said, "If you need an explanation, you're an imbecile. I'm pulling out like a train that stopped at the wrong station. I'm going back to my typewriter. A woman will always screw you up, but a typewriter's a typewriter, true and trustworthy, and it doesn't talk to you when you're making love to it."

Two minutes later, while Ashlar beat on the door with her fists and yelled at him, the typewriter keys jammed and he couldn't get them unstuck.

You couldn't even put faith in a simple machine. You could not trust anything. Everything that was supposed to be clean and good and true went to hell in this universe. Still, you had to stick with it, be a man with *conejos*. Or was it *cojones*? Never mind. Just tell yourself, "Tough shit," and "My head is bloody but unbowed. You have to die but you don't have to say Uncle."

That was fine, but the keys were still stuck, and Ashlar wouldn't quit beating on the door and screaming.

He got up, cursing and yanked the door open. Ashlar fell sobbing into his arms.

"I'm sorry, sorry, sorry! What a bitch I am! Here's the whole earth about ready to move all the way down to its core, and I pick on you!"

"Yes, you're truly a bitch," he said. "But I forgive you because I love you and you love me and no matter what happens we have something that is good. However..."

He wasn't going to say anything about his discovery of the pattern. Not now. He'd test his theory later.

An hour afterward, he said, panting, "Listen, Ashlar, let's take a vacation. We'll go to the World Science-Fiction Convention in Las Vegas. We'll have fun, and in between parties and shooting craps, we'll make love. The good true feeling will come back while we're there."

Or should he have said the true good feeling? What the hell was the correct order of adjectives in a phrase like that?

It didn't matter. What did was that Ashlar decided to go to the convention and didn't even complain that she had nothing to wear. Moreover, his theory had worked out. Up to a point, anyway, and that wasn't really his fault. The fans crowded around him, begging for his autograph, and he heard never an unkind word. As if this wasn't heady enough, not to mention the stimulation of his male hormones, three of the greatest science-fiction authors in the world invited him to dinner and paid him many compliments over the bourbons and steaks.

The first, Zeke Vermouth, Ph.D., the wealthiest writer in the field, didn't mention that they were going Dutch until after the meal was eaten. Even this didn't lessen Nick's pleasures. And then, glory of glories, Robin Hindbind, the dean of science-fiction authors, had him in for a private supper. Nick was as happy as a man with a free lifetime pass to a massage parlor. It was fabulous to sit in the suite, which was as spacious as Nick's house, and eat with the creator of such classics as *Water Brother Among the Bathless, I Will Boll No Weevil* and the autobiographical *Time Enough For F***ing*, subtitled *Why Everybody Worships Me*.

Then, wonder of wonders, the grand old man, Preston de Tove himself, asked Nick to a very select party. De Tove was probably Nick's greatest hero, the man who had rocked the science-fiction world in the 40s with his smashing *Spam!* and *The World of Zilch A*.

De Tove, however, hadn't done much writing for thirty years. He'd been too busy practicing a science of mental health originated by another classic author, old B.M. Kachall himself. This was M.P. (Mnemonic Peristalsis) Therapy, a psychic discipline which claimed to enable a person to attain through its techniques an I.Q. of 500, perfect recall, Superman's or Wonder Woman's body, and immortality.

In essence, these techniques consisted in keeping your bowels one hundred percent open. To do this, though, you had to work back along your memory track until you encountered in all details, visual, tactile, auditory, olfactory, especially olfactory, your first bowel movement. This was called the P.U. or Primal Urge.

Kachall had promised his disciples that all goals could be reached within a year through M.P. Therapy. However, de Tove, like the majority of Kachall's followers, was, three decades later, still taking laxatives as a physical aid to the mental techniques. He had not lost faith, even if he did spend most of his time during the party in the bathroom.

De Tove had refused to go along with Kachall's S.P.L. Religion, a metaphysical extension of M.P. Therapy. Perhaps this was because de Tove had to wear a diaper at all times, and attendees at the S.P.L. services were forbidden to wear anything. In any event, the religion required that the worshipper send his C.E. (Colonic Ego) back to the first movement of the universe, the Big Bang. If the worshipper survived that, he was certified to be an E.E. (End End), one who'd attained the Supreme Purgative Level. This meant that the E.E. radiated such a powerful aura that nobody would dare to mess around with him. Or even get near him for that matter.

Aside from having had to sit by an open window throughout the party, Nick was ecstatic. Nothing better could happen now. But he was wrong. The next day, two Englishmen, G.C. Alldrab and William Rubboys, invited him to a party for avant-garde writers. This twain had been lucky enough to be highly esteemed by some important mainstream critics and so now refused to be classified as mere s-f authors. Nevertheless, when the convention committee offered to pay their airfare, hotel expenses, and booze if they'd be guests, they consented to associate, for three days at least, with the debased category.

Alldrab was chiefly famous for stories in which depressed, impotent, passive, and incompetent antiheroes passed through catastrophic landscapes over which floated various parts, usually sexual, of famous people. He was also hung up on traffic accidents, a symbol to him of the rottenness of Western civilization, especially the United States. He sneered at plots and storylines.

And so did his colleague. Rubboys was famous for both the unique content and technique of his fiction. It drew mostly on his experiences as a drug addict and peregrinating homosexual. Otherwise, he was a nice guy and not nearly as snobbish as Alldrab, though some were unkind enough to say that his camaraderie with young male fans wasn't entirely due to his democratic leanings.

Lately, he'd been getting a lot of flak from feminist critics, who loathed his vicious attitude towards all women, though he claimed it was purely literary. They couldn't be blamed. Try though they might to ignore his bias because of his high reputation as a writer, they'd gotten fed up with his numerous references to females as cunts, gashes, twats, slits, and hairy holes.

Rubboys' technique consisted of putting a manuscript through a shredder, then pasting the strips at random for the finished product.

Nick didn't care for either man's works, though he did admit that Alldrab's fiction made more sense than Rubboys'. But then whose didn't? However, to be their guest was an honor in some circles, and these were the critics with clout. Maybe they'd take some notice of him now—glory through association.

Nick was told that, even though he was middle-aged and

wrote mostly square commercial stuff, he had been invited because of his experimental time-travel story, *The Man Who Buggered Himself*. This was great stuff, obscure and unintelligible and quasipoetic enough to satisfy the artiest of the arty.

Nick just grinned. Why should he tell them he had written the story while drinking muscatel and smoking opium?

The party was a success until midnight. Alldrab, pissy-assed drunk by then, tried to get his mistress to take Rubboys' rented car out and drive it at 100 mph into a lamppost. Thus he could witness a real crash and transpose it into sanguinary poetry in his next novel, *Smash!*, get to the root of the evilness in Occidental culture.

His mistress didn't care for this. In fact, she became hysterical. Rubboys wasn't too keen about it either.

Result: a stampede of pale tight-faced guests out of the door, Nick in the lead, while the girl-friend was dialing the police.

Ashlar was curious about why Nick had been so horny during the convention and for some weeks after that, then had quickly reverted to steerhood.

"What's the matter with you?" Ashlar said after one particularly distressing attempt. "Again?"

She dropped her cigarette ashes on his pubic hairs, causing him to delay his reply until he put out the fire.

"I'll tell you!" he roared. "You're always putting me down, literally and figuratively. Criticising me. You deflate my ego and hence my potency.

"The same thing happens when I get bad reviews or fan mail that knocks me or a rejection slip. But when fans and critics and authors praise me, which doesn't happen often, I'm inflated. There's no doubt about it. I've determined scientifically that my virility waxes and wanes in direct proportion to the quantity-cum (no pun intended) -quality of the praise or bumraps I receive."

"You can't be serious?"

"I drew a graph. It isn't exactly a bell-shaped curve. More like a limp cactus."

"You mean I got to say only nice things about you, keep my mouth shut when you bug me? Treat you like an idol of gold? You're not, you know. You have feet of clay—all the way up to your big bald spot."

"See, that's what I mean."

They quarreled violently for three hours. In the end, Ashlar wept and promised she'd quit pointing out his faults. Not only that, she'd praise him a lot.

But that wasn't honest, and so it didn't work out. He knew she was lying when she told him how handsome he was and what a great writer he was and how he was the most fantastic stud in the world.

To make things worse, his latest book was panned by one hundred percent of the reviewers.

"Thumbs down; everything's down," Nick said.

A week later, things got good again. Better than good. He was as happy as Aladdin when he first rubbed the bride given him by the magic lamp.

Dubbeldeel Publications came through with some unexpected royalties on a three-year-old book. The publisher offered to buy another on the basis of a two-page outline. Nick got word that a Ph.D. candidate at UCLA was writing a thesis on his works. The fan mail that week was unusually heavy and not one of its writers suggested that he wrote on toilet paper.

It did not matter now that he doubted Ashlar's sincerity. People with no ulterior motives were comparing him with the great Kilgore Trout.

He was so happy that he suggested to Ashlar that they take another vacation, attend a convention in Pekin, Illinois, which was only ten miles from their hometown, Peoria. Ashlar said that she'd go, even if she didn't like the creeps that crowded around him at the cons. She'd spend her time in the bar with the wives of the writers. She could relax with them, get away from shoptalk that wearied her so when the writers got together. The wives didn't care for science-fiction and seldom read even their husband's stuff. Especially their husband's stuff.

Nick wasn't superstitious. Even so he regarded it as a favorable omen when he saw the program book of the convention. In big bold letters on the cover was the name of the convention. It should have been Pekcon, fan slang for Pek(in) Con(vention). But it had come out Pekcor.

Later, Nick admitted that he'd interpreted the signs and portents wrongly. Had he ever!

At first, things went as well as anyone could ask for. The fans practically kissed his feet, and the regard of his peers was very evident. Some even paid for the drinks, instead of leaving him, as usual, to sweat while he settled a staggering bill.

Ashlar should have been happy. Instead, she complained that she couldn't spend the rest of her life attending conventions just to have a good sex life.

Nick got to talking with an eighteen-year-old fan with long blonde hair, a pixie face, huge adoring eyes, boobs that floated ahead of her like hot-air balloons, and legs like Marlene Dietrich's. Her last name was Barkis, she was willing, and he was overcome by temptation. They went to her room, and the sexual-Richter scale hit 8.6 and was on its way to record 9.6 when Ashlar began beating at the door and screaming at him to open it.

Later, he found out that a writer's wife had seen him and Barkis entering her room. She had raced around the hotel until she found Ashlar, who hadn't wasted any time getting the hotel dick and three wives as witnesses.

All the way to Peoria, Ashlar didn't stop yelling or crying. Once there, she swiftly packed and took a taxi to her mother's house. She didn't stay there long, since she had been so angry that she'd forgotten her mother had recently gone to a nursing home. Unfazed, she moved into an expensive hotel and sent her bills through her lawyer to Nick.

Each day he got a long letter from her—each deflating. Throwing them unread into the wastepaper basket didn't work. He was too curious, he had to open them and see what new invectives and unsavory descriptions she had come up with. So, after long thought, he sold the house and moved from Illinois to New Jersey. Only his agent had his forwarding address, and Nick told him to return all letters from his wife to her.

"Mark them: *Uninterested*."

But he knew that she would find him some day.

Three months passed without a letter from her. Things went as well as could be expected in this world where hardly anybody really gave a damn how you were doing. He did find a young fan, "Moomah" Smith, who was eager to spend a night with him when he got good mail, good notices, and good royalties.

And then, one morning as he was drinking coffee just before tackling the typewriter, the phone rang. His agent's new secretary, one he didn't know, was calling. Her employer was in Europe (cavorting around on his ten percent, Nick thought), but she had good news for him. Sharper & Rake, really big hardcover publishers, had just bought an outline for a novel, *A Sanitary Brightly Illuminated Planet*, and they were going to give him a huge advance. Furthermore, Sharper & Rake intended to go all out in an advertising and publicity campaign.

The first letter was from a member of the committee which

handled the Pulsar Award. This was given once a year by SWOT, the Science-Fiction Writers of Terra. Nick belonged to this, although its chief benefit was that he could deduct the membership dues from his income tax. However, one of his stories, *Hot Nights on Venus,* had been nominated for the Pulsar. And now, and now—the monster felt as if it were the *Queen Mary* heading for port with a stiff wind behind it—he had won it!

"Under no circumstances must you tell anyone about this," the committee member had written. "The awards won't be given until two months from now. We're informing you of this to make sure that you'll be at the annual SWOT banquet in New York."

Nick read the second letter. It was from Lex Fiddler, the foremost American mainstream critic. Fiddler informed him that he had nominated Nick's Novel, *A Farewell to Mars,* for the highest honor for writing in the country. This was the MOOLA, the Michael Oberst Literary Award, established fifty years before by a St. Louis brewer. If Nick won it, he would get $50,000, he would be famous, his book would be a best seller, and an offer from Hollywood was a sure thing even if it didn't get the award.

Nick opened the third letter.

Whooping with joy, he whirled around and around, the end of his mighty walloper knocking over vases and flipping ash trays from tables. He stopped dancing then because he was so dizzy. Leaning on a table for support, gazing at the ever-expanding thing, he groaned, "I've got to get Moomah here. Only . . . I hope she doesn't faint when she sees it."

It was Nick who fainted, not Moomah. The blood spurted from his head, driving downward as his heart constricted in a final massive endeavor to supply what the ego demanded. His blood abandoned the upper part of his body as if the gargantuan paw of King Kong had squeezed it.

Had Nick been conscious, his terror would have halted the process, reversed it, and put the brobdingnagian in its normal state, limp as an unbaked pizza. But his brain was emptied of blood, and he was aware of nothing as he toppled forward, was held for a moment from going over by the giant member, the end of which was rammed into the carpet, and then he pole-vaulted forward, his grayish slack face striking the floor.

He lay on his side while the pythonish member, driven by the unconscious, expanded. It swelled as a balloon swells while ascending into the ever-thinner atmosphere. But balloons have a pressure height, a point at which the force within the envelope is greater than its strength and the envelope ruptures violently.

The mailwoman was just climbing into her Jeep when she heard the blast. She whirled, and she screamed as she saw the flying glass and the smoke pouring out from the shattered windows.

The police found it easy to pinpoint the source of the explosion. The cause was beyond them. They shook their heads and said that this was just one of those mysteries of life.

The police did find out that the third letter, the one from the Swedish Embassy in Washington, D.C., was a fake. Whoever had sent it was unknown and likely to remain so. Why would anybody write Nick Adams, Jr., a science-fiction author, to inform him that he had won the Nobel Prize for Literature?

More investigation disclosed that the letters from the Pulsar Award committee and Lex Fiddler were also fakes. So was the call from his agent's secretary telling him that Sharper & Rake was giving him a huge advance. This was eventually traced to Mrs. Adams, but by then she was in Europe and there to stay. Besides, the police could not charge her with anything except a practical joke.

Ashlar is living in Spain today. Sometimes, for no reason that her friends can determine, she smiles in a strange way. Is it a smile of regret or triumph?

Did she write those letters and make that phone call because she knew what they'd do to her husband? Of course, she couldn't have known how much they would do to him; she underestimated the power of ego and the limits of flesh.

Or did she try to bolster his pride, make him feel good, because she still loved him and so was doing her best to make him inflated with happiness for at least a day?

It would be nice to think so.

THE FRESHMAN

I began reading H. P. Lovecraft's stories about the Cthulhu mythos when I was a young boy. His grim peeps into the Necronomicon and into the shuddery horrors of the extremely ancient elder ones fascinated me. When I got older I still liked to read them, though I wasn't gung-ho about them. But I'd never had any desire to write a story which would be part of the Cthulhu cycle.

Then, one night, some years ago, I had a dream in which I, a 60-year-old man, was a freshman at a strange college and was attending a rush party given by a more-than-strange fraternity. There was something sinister about the whole affair, a sense of mounting danger. Just as the face of one of the frat brothers began to melt and he broke into a cackling laughter and I knew that something horrible was going to happen to me, I awoke.

I remember most of my dreams, and that was one I'd never forget. But it led to this story, "The Freshman," and may lead to others, "The Sophomore," "The Junior," "The Senior," "The M.A. Candidate," "The Ph.D." and who knows what else in the course of degrees.

The long-haired youth in front of Desmond wore sandals, ragged blue jeans, and a grimy T-shirt. A paperback, *The Collected Works of Robert Blake*, was half stuck into his rear pocket. When he turned around, he displayed in large letters on the T-shirt, M. U. His scrawny Fu Manchu mustache held some bread crumbs.

His yellow eyes—surely he suffered from jaundice—widened when he saw Desmond. He said, "This ain't the place to apply for the nursing home, pops." He grinned, showing un-

The Freshman

usually long canines; and then turned to face the admissions desk.

Desmond felt his face turning red. Ever since he'd gotten into the line before a table marked *Toaahd Freshmen A-D,* he'd been aware of the sidelong glances, the snickers, the low-voiced comments. He stood out among these youths like a billboard in a flower garden, a corpse on a banquet table.

The line moved ahead by one person. The would-be students were talking, but their voices were subdued. For such young people, they were very restrained, excepting the smart aleck just ahead of him.

Perhaps it was the surroundings that repressed them. This gymnasium, built in the late nineteenth century, had not been repainted for years. The once-green paint was peeling. There were broken windows high on the walls; a shattered skylight had been covered with boards. The wooden floor bent and creaked, and the basketball goal rings (?) were rusty. Yet M. U. had been league champions in all fields of sports for many years. Though its enrollment was much less than that of its competitors, its teams somehow managed to win, often by large scores.

Desmond buttoned his jacket. Though it was a warm fall day, the air in the building was cold. If he hadn't known better, he would have thought that the wall of an iceberg was just behind him. Above him the great lights struggled to overcome the darkness that lowered like the underside of a dead whale sinking into sea depths.

He turned around. The girl just back of him smiled. She wore a flowing dashiki covered with astrological symbols. Her black hair was cut short; her features were petite and well-arranged but too pointed to be pretty.

Among all these youths there should have been a number of pretty girls and handsome men. He'd walked enough campuses to get an idea of the index of beauty of college students. But here.... There was a girl, in the line to the right, whose face should have made her eligible to be a fashion model. Yet, there was something missing.

No, there was something added. A quality undefinable but.... Repugnant? No, now it was gone. No, it was back again. It flitted on and off, like a bat swooping from darkness into a grayness and then up and out.

The kid in front of him had turned again. He was grinning like a fox who'd just seen a chicken.

"Some dish, heh, pops? She likes older men. Maybe you two could get your shit together and make beautiful music."

The odor of unwashed body and clothes swirled around him like flies around a dead rat.

"I'm not interested in girls with Oedipus complexes," Desmond said coldly.

"At your age you can't be particular," the youth said, and turned away.

Desmond flushed, and he briefly fantasized knocking the kid down. It didn't help much.

The line moved ahead again. He looked at his wrist watch. In half an hour he was scheduled to phone his mother. He should have come here sooner. However, he had overslept while the alarm clock had run down, resuming its ticking as if it didn't care. Which it didn't, of course, though he felt that his possessions should, somehow, take an interest in him. This was irrational, but if he was a believer in the superiority of the rational, would he be here? Would any of these students?

The line moved jerkily ahead like a centipede halting now and then to make sure no one had stolen any of its legs. When he was ten minutes late for the phone call, he was at the head of the line. Behind the admissions table was a man far older than he. His face was a mass of wrinkles, gray dough that had been incised with fingernails and then pressed into somewhat human shape. The nose was a cuttlefish's beak stuck into the dough. But the eyes beneath the white chaotic eyebrows were as alive as blood flowing from holes in the flesh.

The hand which took Desmond's papers and punched cards was not that of an old man's. It was big and swollen, white, smooth-skinned. The fingernails were dirty.

"The Roderick Desmond, I assume."

The voice was rasping, not at all an old man's cracked quavering.

"Ah, you know me?"

"Of you, yes. I've read some of your novels of the occult. And ten years ago I rejected your request for xeroxes of certain parts of *the* book."

The name tag on the worn tweed jacket said: R. Layamon, COTOAAHD. So this was the chairman of the Committee of the Occult Arts and History Department.

"Your paper on the non-Arabic origin of al-Hazred's name was a brilliant piece of linguistic research. I knew that the name wasn't Arabic or even Semitic in origin, but I confess that I didn't know the century in which the word was dropped from the Arabian language. Your exposition of how it was retained only in connection with the Yemenite, al-Hazred, and that its original meaning was not *mad* but *one-who-sees-what-shouldn't-be-seen* was quite correct."

He paused, then said smiling, "Did your mother complain when she was forced to accompany you to Yemen?"

Desmond said, "No-n-n-o-body forced her."

He took a deep breath and said, "But how did you know she . . . ?"

"I've read some biographical accounts of you."

Layamon chuckled. It sounded like nails being shifted in a barrel. "Your paper on al-Hazred and the knowledge you display in your novels are the main reasons why you're being admitted to this department despite your sixty years."

He signed the forms and handed the card back to Desmond. "Take this to the cashier's office. Oh, yes, your family is a remarkably long-lived one, isn't it? Your father died accidentally, but his father lived to be one hundred and two. Your mother is eighty, but she should live to be over a hundred. And you, you could have forty more years of life *as you've known it*."

Desmond was enraged but not so much that he dared let himself show it. The gray air became black, and the old man's face shone in it. It floated toward him, expanded, and suddenly Desmond was inside the gray wrinkles. It was not a pleasant place.

The tiny figures on a dimly haloed horizon danced, then faded, and he fell through a bellowing blackness. The air was gray again, and he was leaning forward, clenching the edge of the table.

"Mr. Desmond, do you have these attacks often?"

Desmond released his grip and straightened. "Too much excitement, I suppose. No, I've never had an attack, not now or ever."

The old man chuckled. "Yes, it must be emotional stress. Perhaps you'll find the means for relieving that stress here."

Desmond turned and walked away. Until he left the building, he saw only blurred figures and signs. That ancient wizard . . . how had he known his thought so well? Was it simply because he had read the biographical accounts, made a few inquiries, and then surmised a complete picture? Or was there more to it than that?

The sun had gone behind thick sluggish clouds. Past the campus, past many trees hiding the houses of the city were the Tamsiqueg hills. According to the long-extinct Indians after whom they were named, they had once been evil giants who'd waged war with the hero Mikatoonis and his magic-making friend, Chegaspat. Chegaspat had been killed, but Mikatoonis had turned the giants into stone with a magical club.

But Cotoaahd, the chief giant, was able to free himself from the spell every few centuries. Sometimes, a sorcerer could loose him. Then Cotoaahd walked abroad for a while before returning to his rocky slumber. In 1724 a house and many trees on the edge of the town had been flattened one stormy night as if colossal feet had stepped upon them. And the broken trees formed a trail which led to the curiously shaped hill known as Cotoaahd.

There was nothing about these stories that couldn't be explained by the tendency of the Indians, and the superstitious 18th-century whites, to legendize natural phenomena. But was it entirely coincidence that the anagram of the committee headed by Layamon duplicated the giant's name?

Suddenly, he became aware that he was heading for a telephone booth. He looked at his watch and felt panicky. The phone in his dormitory room would be ringing. It would be better to call her from the booth and save the three minutes it would take to walk to the dormitory.

He stopped. No, if he called from the booth, he would only get a busy signal.

"Forty more years of life *as you've known it*," the chairman had said.

Desmond turned. His path was blocked by an enormous youth. He was a head taller than Desmond's six feet and so fat he looked like a smaller version of Santa Claus balloon in Macy's Christmas-day parade. He wore a dingy sweatshirt on the front of which was the ubiquitous M. U., unpressed pants, and torn tennis shoes. In banana-sized fingers he held a salami sandwich which Gargantua would not have found too small.

Looking at him, Desmond suddenly realized that most of the students here were too thin or too fat.

"Mr. Desmond?"

"Right."

He shook hands. The fellow's skin was wet and cold, but the hand exerted a powerful pressure.

The Freshman

"I'm Wendell Trepan. With your knowledge, you've heard about my ancestors. The most famous, or infamous, of whom was the Cornish witch, Rachel Trepan."

"Yes. Rachel of the hamlet of Tredannick Wollas, near Poldhu Bay."

"I knew you'd know. I'm following the trade of my ancestors, though more cautiously, of course. Anyway, I'm a senior and the chairperson of the rushing committee for the Lam Kha Alif fraternity."

He paused to bite into the sandwich. Mayonnaise and salami and cheese oozing from his mouth, he said, "You're invited to the party we're holding at the house this afternoon."

The other hand reached into a pocket and brought out a card. Desmond looked at it briefly. "You want me to be a candidate for membership in your frat? I'm pretty old for that sort of thing. I'd feel out of place...."

"Nonsense, Mr. Desmond. We're a pretty serious bunch. In fact, none of the frats here are like any on other campuses. You should know that. We feel you'd provide stability and, I'll admit, prestige. You're pretty well known, you know. Layamon, by the way, is a Lam Kha Alif. He tends to favor students who belong to his frat. He'd deny it, of course, and I'll deny it if you repeat this. But it's true."

"Well, I don't know. Suppose I did pledge—if I'm invited to, that is—would I have to live in the frat house?"

"Yes. We make no exceptions. Of course, that's only when you're a pledge. You can live wherever you want to when you're an active."

Trepan smiled, showing the unswallowed bite. "You're not married, so there's no problem there."

"What do you mean by that?"

"Nothing, Mr. Desmond. It's just that we don't pledge married men unless they don't live with their wives. Married men lose some of their power, you know. Of course, no way do we insist on celibacy. We have some pretty good parties, too. Once a month we hold a big bust in a grove at the foot of Cotaahd. Most of the women guests there belong to the Ba Ghay Sin sorority. Some of them really go for the older type, if you know what I mean."

Trepan stepped forward to place his face directly above Desmond's. "We don't just have beer, pot, hashish, and sisters. There're other attractions. Brothers, if you're so inclined. Some stuff that's made from a recipe by the Marquis Manuel de Dembron himself. But most of that is kid stuff. There'll be a goat there, too!"

"A goat? A *black* goat?"

Trepan nodded, and his triple-fold jowls swung. "Yeah. Old Layamon'll be there to supervise, though he'll be masked, of course. With him as coach nothing can go wrong. Last Halloween, though...."

He paused, then said, "Well, it was something to see."

Desmond licked dry lips. His heart was thudding like the tom-toms that beat at the ritual of which he had only read but had envisioned many times.

Desmond put the card in his pocket. "At one o'clock?"

"You're coming? Very good! See you, Mr. Desmond. You won't regret it."

Desmond walked past the buildings of the university quadrangle, the most imposing of which was the museum. This was the oldest structure on the campus, the original college. Time had beaten and chipped away at the brick and stone of the others, but the museum seemed to have absorbed time and to be slowly radiating it back just as cement and stone and brick absorbed heat in the sunlight and then gave it back in the darkness. Also, whereas the other structures were covered with vines, perhaps too covered, the museum was naked of plant life. Vines which tried to crawl up its gray-bone-colored stones withered and fell back.

Layamon's red-stone house was narrow, three stories high, and had a double-peaked roof. Its cover of vines was so thick that it seemed a wonder that the weight didn't bring it to the ground. The colors of the vines were subtly different from those on the other buildings. Seen at one angle, they looked cyanotic. From another, they were the exact green of the eyes of a Sumatran snake Desmond had seen in a colored plate in a book on herpetology.

It was this venomous reptile which was used by the sorcerers of the Yan tribes to transmit messages and sometimes to kill. The writer had not explained what he meant by "messages." Desmond had discovered the meaning in another book, which had required him to learn Malay, written in the Arabic script, before he could read it.

He hurried on past the house, which was not something a sightseer would care to look at long, and came to the dormitory. It had been built in 1888 on the site of another building and remodeled in 1938. Its gray paint was peeling. There were several broken windows, over the panes of which cardboard had been nailed. The porch floor boards bent and creaked as he passed over them. The main door was of oak, its paint long gone. The bronze head of a cat, a heavy bronze ring dangling from its mouth, served as a door knocker.

Desmond entered, passed through the main room over the worn carpet, and walked up two flights of bare-board steps. On the gray-white of a wall by the first landing someone had long ago written, *Yug-Sothoth Sucks*. Many attempts had been made to wash it off, but it was evident that only paint could hide this insulting and dangerous sentiment. Yesterday a junior had told him that no one knew who had written it, but the night after it had appeared, a freshman had been found dead, hanging from a hook in a closet.

"The kid had mutilated himself terribly before he committed suicide," the junior had said. "I wasn't here then, but I understand that he was a mess. He'd done it with a razor *and* a hot iron. There was blood all over the place, his pecker and balls were on the table, arranged to form a T-cross, you know whose symbol that is, and he'd clawed out plaster on the wall, leaving a big bloody print. It didn't even look like a human hand had done it."

"I'm surprised he lived long enough to hang himself," Desmond had said. "All that loss of blood, you know."

The junior had guffawed. "You're kidding, of course!"

It was several seconds before Desmond understood what he meant. Then he'd paled. But later he wondered if the junior wasn't playing a traditional joke on a green freshman. He didn't think he'd ask anybody else about it, however. If he had been made a fool of, he wasn't going to let it happen more than once.

He heard the phone ringing at the end of the long hall. He sighed, and strode down it, passing closed doors. From behind one came a faint tittering. He unlocked his door and closed it behind him. For a long time he stood watching the phone, which went on and on, reminding him, he didn't know why, of the poem about the Australian swagman who went for a dip in a waterhole. The bunyip, that mysterious and sinister creature of down-under folklore, the dweller in the water, silently and smoothly took care of the swagman. And the tea kettle he'd put on the fire whistled and whistled with no one to hear.

And the phone rang on and on.

The bunyip was on the other end.

Guilt spread through him as quick as a blush.

He walked across the room glimpsing something out of the corner of his eye, something small, dark, and swift that dived under the sagging mildew-odorous bed-couch. He stopped at the small table, reached out to the receiver, touched it, felt its cold throbbing. He snatched his hand back. It was foolish, but it had seemed to him that she would detect his touch and know that he was there.

Snarling, he wheeled and started across the room. He noticed that the hole in the baseboard was open again. The Coke bottle whose butt end he'd jammed into the hold had been pushed out. He stopped and reinserted it and straightened up.

When he was at the foot of the staircase, he could still hear the ringing. But he wasn't sure that it wasn't just in his head.

After he'd paid his tuition and eaten at the cafeteria—the food was better than he'd thought it would be—he walked to the ROTC building. It was in better shape than the other structures, probably because the Army was in charge of it. Still, it wasn't in the condition an inspector would require. And those cannons on caissons in the rear. Were the students really supposed to train with Spanish-American War weapons? And since when was steel subject to verdigris?

The officer in charge was surprised when Desmond asked to be issued his uniform and manuals.

"I don't know. You realize ROTC is no longer required of freshmen and sophomores?"

Desmond insisted that he wanted to enroll. The officer rubbed his unshaven jaw and blew smoke from a Tijuana Gold panatela. "Hmm. Let me see."

He consulted a book whose edges seemed to have been nibbled by rats. "Well, what do you know? There's nothing in the regulations about age. Course, there's some pages missing. Must be an oversight. Nobody near your age has ever been considered. But... well, if the regulations say nothing about it, then... what the hell! Won't hurt you, our boys don't have to go through obstacle courses or anything like that.

"But, jeeze, you're sixty! Why do you want to sign up?"

Desmond did not tell him that he had been deferred from service in World War II because he was the sole support of his sick mother. Ever since then, he'd felt guilty, but at least here he could do his bit—however minute—for his country.

The officer stood up, though not in a coordinated manner. "Okay. I'll see you get your issue. It's only fair to warn you, though, that these fuck-ups play some mighty strange tricks. You should see what they blow out of their cannons."

Fifteen minutes later, Desmond left, a pile of uniforms and manuals under one arm. Since he didn't want to return home with them, he checked them in at the university book store. The girl put them on a shelf alongside other belongings, some of them unidentifiable to the noncognoscenti. One of them was a small cage covered with a black cloth.

Desmond walked to Fraternity Row. All of the houses had Arabic names, except the House of Hastur. These were afflicted with the same general decrepitude and lack of care as the university structures. Desmond turned in at a cement walk, from the cracks of which spread dying dandelions and other weeds. On his left leaned a massive wooden pole fifteen feet high. The heads and symbols carved into it had caused the townspeople to refer to it as the totem pole. It wasn't, of course, since the tribe to which it had belonged were not Northwest Coast or Alaskan Indians. It and a fellow in the university museum were the last survivors of hundreds which had once stood in this area.

Desmond, passing it, put the end of his left thumb under his nose and the tip of his index finger in the center of his forehead, and he muttered the ancient phrase of obeisance, *"Shesh-cotoaahd-ting-ononwa-senk."* According to various texts he'd read, this was required of every Tamsiqueg who walked by it during this phase of the moon. The phrase was unintelligible even to them, since it came from another tribe or perhaps from an antique stage of the language. But it indicated respect, and lack of its observance was likely to result in misfortune.

He felt a little silly doing it, but it couldn't hurt.

The unpainted wooden steps creaked as he stepped upon them. The porch was huge; the wires of the screen were rusty and useless in keeping insects out because of the many holes. The front door was open; from it came a blast of rock music, the loud chatter of many people, and the acrid odor of pot.

Desmond almost turned back. He suffered when he was in a crowd, and his consciousness of his age made him feel embarrassingly conspicuous. But the huge figure of Wendell Trepan was in the doorway, and he was seized by an enormous hand.

"Come on in!" Trepan bellowed. "I'll introduce you to the brothers!"

Desmond was pulled into a large room jammed with youths of both sexes. Trepan bulled through, halting now and then to slap somebody on the back and shout a greeting and once to pat a well-built young woman on the fanny. Then they were in a corner where Professor Layamon sat surrounded by people who looked older than most of the attendees. Desmond supposed that they were graduate students. He shook the fat swollen hand and said, "Pleased to meet you again," but he doubted that his words were heard.

Layamon pulled him down so he could be heard, and he said, "Have you made up your mind yet?"

The old man's breath was not unpleasant, but he had certainly been drinking something which Desmond had never smelled before. The red eyes seemed to hold a light, almost as if tiny candles were burning inside the eyeballs.

"About what?" Desmond shouted back.

The old man smiled and said, "You know."

He released his grip. Desmond straightened up. Suddenly, though the room was hot enough to make him sweat, he felt chilly. What was Layamon hinting at? It couldn't be that he really knew. Or could it be?

Trepan introduced him to the men and women around the chair and then took him into the crowd. Other introductions followed, most of those he met seeming to be members of Lam Kha Alif or of the sorority across the street. The only one he could identify for sure as a candidacy for pledging was a black, a Gabonese. After they left him, Trepan said, "Bukawai comes from a long line of witch doctors. He's going to be a real treasure if he accepts our invitation, though the House of Hastur and Kaf Dhal Waw are hot to get him. The department is a little weak on Central African science. It used to have a great teacher, Janice Momaya, but she disappeared ten years ago while on a sabbatical in Sierra Leone. I wouldn't be surprised if Bukawai was offered an assistant professorship even if he is nominally a freshman. Man, the other night, he taught me part of a ritual you wouldn't believe. I... well, I won't go into it now. Some other time. Anyway, he has the greatest respect for Layamon, and since the old fart is head of the department, Bukawai is almost a cinch to join us."

Suddenly, his lips pulled back, his teeth clenched, his skin paled beneath the dirt, and he bent over and grabbed his huge

The Freshman

paunch. Desmond said, "What's the matter?"

Trepan shook his head, gave a deep sigh, and straightened up.

"Man, that hurt!"

"What?" Desmond said.

"I shouldn't have called him an old fart. I didn't think he could hear me, but he isn't using sound to receive. Hell, there's nobody in the world has more respect for him than me. But sometimes my mouth runs off... well, never again."

"You mean?" Desmond said.

"Yeah. Who'd you think? Never mind. Come with me where we can hear ourselves think."

He pulled Desmond through a smaller room, one with many shelves of books, novels, school texts, and here and there some old leather-bound volumes.

"We got a hell of a good library here, the best any house can boast of. It's one of our stellar attractions. But it's the open one."

They entered a narrow door, passed into a short hall, and stopped while Trepan took a key from his pocket and unlocked another door. Beyond it was a narrow corkscrew staircase, the steps of which were dusty. A window high above gave a weak light through dirty panes. Trepan turned on a wall light, and they went up the stairs. Trepan unlocked another door with a different key. They stepped into a small room whose walls were covered by book shelves from floor to ceiling. Trepan turned on a light. In a corner was a small table and a folding chair. The table had a lamp and a stone bust of the Marquis de Dembron on it.

Trepan, breathing heavily after the climb, said, "Usually, only seniors and graduates are allowed here. But I'm making an exception in your case. I just wanted to show you one of the advantages of belonging to Lam Kha Alif. None of the other houses have a library like this."

Trepan was looking narrow-eyed at him. "Eyeball the books. But don't touch them. They, uh, absorb, if you know what I mean."

Desmond moved around, looking at the titles. When he was finished, he said, "I'm impressed. I thought some of these were to be found only in the university library. In locked rooms."

"That's what the public thinks. Listen, if you pledge us, you'll have access to these books. Only don't tell the other undergrads. They'd get jealous."

Trepan, still narrow-eyed, as if he were considering something that perhaps he shouldn't, said, "Would you mind turning your back and sticking your fingers in your ears?"

Desmond said, "What?"

Trepan smiled. "Oh, if you sign up with us, you'll be given the little recipe necessary to work in here. But until then I'd just as soon you don't see it."

Desmond, smiling with embarrassment, the cause of which he couldn't account for, and also feeling excited, turned his back, facing away from Trepan, and jammed his fingertips into his ears. While he stood there in the very quiet room—was it soundproofed with insulation or with something perhaps not material?—he counted the seconds. One thousand and one, one thousand and two....

A little more than a minute had passed when he felt Trepan's hand on his shoulder. He turned and removed his fingers. The fat youth was holding out to him a tall but very slim volume bound in a skin with many small dark protuberances. Desmond was surprised, since he was sure he had not seen it on the shelves.

"I deactivated this," Trepan said. "Here. Take it." He looked at his wrist watch. "It'll be okay for ten minutes."

There was no title or byline on the cover. And, now that he looked at it closely and felt it, he did not think the skin was from an animal.

Trepan said, "It's the hide of old Atechironnon himself."

Desmond said, "Ah!" and he trembled. But he rallied.

"He must have been covered with warts."

"Yeah. Go ahead. Look at it. It's a shame you can't read it, though."

The first page was slightly yellowed, which wasn't surprising for paper four hundred years old. There was no printing but large handwritten letters.

"Ye lesser Rituall of Ye Tahmmsiquegg Warlock Atechironunn," Desmond read. *"Reprodust from ye Picture-riting on ye Skin lefft unbirnt by ye Godly.*

"By his own Hand, Simon Conant. 1641.

"Let him who speaks these Words of Pictures, first lissen."

Trepan chuckled and said, "Spelling wasn't his forte, was it?"

"Simon, the half brother of Roger Conant," Desmond said. "He was the first white man to visit the Tamsiqueg and not leave with his severed thumb stuck up his ass. He was also with the settlers who raided the Tamsiqueg, but they didn't know who his sympathies were with. He fled with the badly wounded Atechironnon into the wilderness. Twenty years later, he appeared in Virginia with this book."

He slowly turned the five pages, fixing each pictograph in his photographic memory. There was one figure he didn't like to look at.

"Layamon's the only one who can read it," Trepan said.

Desmond did not tell him that he was conversant with the grammar and small dictionary of the Tamsiqueg language, written by William Cor Dunnes in 1624 and published in 1654. It contained an appendix translating the pictographs. It had cost him twenty years of search and a thousand dollars just for a xerox copy. His mother had raised hell about the expenditure, but for once he had stood up to her. Not even the university had a copy.

Trepan looked at his watch. "One minute to go. Hey!"

He grabbed the book from Desmond's hands and said, harshly, "Turn your back and plug your ears!"

Trepan looked as if he were in a panic. He turned, and a minute later Trepan pulled one of Desmond's fingers away.

"Sorry to be so sudden, but the hold was beginning to break down. I can't figure it out. It's always been good for at least ten minutes."

Desmond had not felt anything, but that might be because Trepan, having been exposed to the influence, was more sensitive to it.

Trepan, obviously nervous, said, "Let's get out of here. It's got to cool off."

On the way down, he said, "You sure you can't read it?"

"Where would I have learned how?" Desmond said.

They plunged into a sea of noise and odors in the big room. They did not stay long, since Trepan wanted to show him the rest of the house, except the basement.

"You can see it sometime this week. Just now it's not advisable to go down there."

Desmond didn't ask why.

When they entered a very small room on the second floor, Trepan said, "Ordinarily we don't let freshmen have a room to themselves. But for you . . . . well, it's yours if you want it."

That pleased Desmond. He wouldn't have to put up with someone whose habits would irk him and whose chatter would anger him.

They descended to the first floor. The big room was not so crowded now. Old Layamon, just getting up from the chair, beckoned to him. Desmond approached him slowly. For some reason, he knew he was not going to like what Layamon would say to him. Or perhaps he wasn't sure whether he would like it or not.

"Trepan showed you the frat's more precious books," the chairman said. It wasn't a question but a statement. "Especially Conant's book."

Trepan said, "How did you . . . ?" he grinned. "You felt it."

"Of course," the rusty voice said. "Well, Desmond, don't you think it's time to answer that phone?"

Trepan looked puzzled. Desmond felt sick and cold.

Layamon was now almost nose to nose to Desmond. The many wrinkles of the doughy skin looked like hieroglyphs.

"You've made up your mind, but you aren't letting yourself know it," he said. "Listen. That was Conant's advice, wasn't it? Listen. From the moment you got onto the plane to Boston, you were committed. You could have backed out in the airport, but you didn't, even though, I imagine, your mother made a scene there. But you didn't. So there's no use putting it off."

He chuckled. "That I am bothering to give you advice is a token of my esteem for you. I think you'll go far and fast. If you are able to eliminate certain defects of character. It takes strength and intelligence and great self-discipline and a vast dedication to get even a BA here, Desmond.

"There are too many who enroll here because they think they'll be taking snap courses. Getting great power, hobnobbing with things that are really not socially minded, to say the least, seems to them to be as easy as rolling off a log. But they soon find out that the department's standards are higher than, say, those of MIT in engineering. And a hell of a lot more dangerous.

"And then there's the moral issue. That's declared just by enrolling here. But how many have the will to push on? How many decide that they are on the wrong side? They quit, not knowing that it's too late for any but a tiny fraction of them to return to the other side. They've declared themselves, have stood up and been counted forever, as it were."

He paused to light up a brown panatela. The smoke curled around Desmond, who did not smell what he expected. The odor was not quite like that of a dead bat he had once used in an experiment.

"Every man or woman determines his or her own destiny. But I would make my decision swiftly, if I were you. I've got my eye on you, and your advancement here does depend upon my estimate of your character and potentiality.

"Good day, Desmond."

The old man walked out. Trepan said, "What was that all about?"

Desmond did not answer. He stood for a minute or so while Trepan fidgeted. Then he said good-by to the fat man and walked out slowly. Instead of going home, he wandered around the campus. Attracted by flashing red lights, he went over to see what was going on. A car with the markings of the campus police and an ambulance from the university hospital were in front of a two-story building. Its lower floor had once been a grocery store according to the letters on the dirty plate-glass window. The paint inside and out was peeling, and plaster had fallen off the walls inside, revealing the laths beneath. On the bare wooden floor were three bodies. One was the youth who had stood just in front of him in the line in the gymnasium. He lay on his back, his mouth open below the scraggly mustache.

Desmond asked one of the people pressed against the window what had happened. The gray-bearded man, probably a professor, said, "This happens every year at this time. Some kids get carried away and try something no one but an M.A. would even think of trying. It's strictly forbidden, but that doesn't stop those young fools."

The corpse with the mustache seemed to have a large round black object or perhaps a burn on its forehead. Desmond wanted to get a closer look, but the ambulance men put a blanket over the face before carrying the body out.

The gray-bearded man said, "The university police and the hospital will handle them." He laughed shortly. "The city police don't even want to come on the campus. The relatives will be notified they've OD'ed from heroin."

"There's no trouble about that?"

"Sometimes. Private detectives have come here, but they don't stay long."

Desmond walked away swiftly. His mind was made up. The sight of those bodies had shaken him. He'd go home, make peace with his mother, sell all the books he'd spent so much time and money accumulating and studying, take up writing mystery novels. He'd seen the face of death, and if he did what he had thought about, only idly of course, fantasizing for psychic therapy, he would see her face. Dead. He couldn't do it.

When he entered his room in the boarding house, the phone was still ringing. He walked to it, reached out his hand, held it for an undeterminable time, then dropped it. As he walked toward the couch, he noticed that the Coca-Cola bottle had been shoved or pulled out of the hole in the baseboard. He knelt down and jammed it back into the hole. From behind the wall came a faint twittering.

He sat down on the sagging couch, took his notebook from his jacket pocket, and began to pencil in the pictographs he remembered so well on the sheets. It took him half an hour, since exactness of reproduction was vital. The phone did not stop ringing.

Someone knocked on the door and yelled, "I saw you go in! Answer the phone or take it off the hook! Or I'll put something on you!"

He did not reply or rise from the couch.

He had left out one of the drawings in the sequence. Now he poised the pencil an inch above the blank space. Sitting at the other end of the line would be a very fat, very old woman. She was old and ugly now, but she had borne him and for many years thereafter she had been beautiful. When his father had died, she had gone to work to keep their house and to support her son in the manner to which both were accustomed. She had worked hard to pay his tuition and other expenses while he went to college. She had continued to work until he had sold two novels. Then she had gotten sickly, though not until he began bringing women home to introduce as potential wives.

She loved him, but she wouldn't let loose of him, and that wasn't genuine love. He hadn't been able to tear loose, which meant that though he was resentful he had something in him which liked being caged. Then, one day, he had decided to take the big step toward freedom. It had been done secretly and swiftly. He had despised himself for his fear of her, but that was the way he was. If he stayed here, she would be coming here. He couldn't endure that. So, he would have to go home.

He looked at the phone, started to rise, sank back.

What to do? He could commit suicide. He'd be free, and she would know how angry he'd been with her. He gave a start as the phone stopped ringing. So, she had given up for a while. But she would return.

He looked at the baseboard. The bottle was moving out from the hole a little at a time. Something behind the wall was working away determinedly. How many times had it started to leave the hole and found that its passage was blocked? Far too many, the thing must think, if it had a mind. But it refused to give up, and some day it might occur to it to solve its problem by killing the one who was causing the problem.

If, however, it was daunted by the far greater size of the problem maker, if it lacked courage, then it would have to keep on pushing the bottle from the hole. And....

He looked at the notebook, and he shook. The blank space had been filled in. There was the drawing of Cotaahd, the thing which, now he looked at it, somehow resembled his mother.

Had he unconsciously penciled it in while he was thinking.

Or had the figure formed itself?

It didn't matter. In either case, he knew what he had to do.

While the eyes passed over each drawing, and he intoned the words of that long-dead language, he felt something move out from within his chest, crawl into his belly, his legs, his throat, his brain. The symbol of Cotaahd seemed to burn on the sheet when he pronounced its name, his eyes on the drawing.

The room grew dark as the final words were said. He rose and turned on a table lamp and went into the tiny dirty bathroom. The face in the mirror did not look like a murderer's; it was just that of a sixty-year-old man who had been through an ordeal and was not quite sure that it was over.

On the way out of the room, he saw the Coke bottle slide free of the baseboard hole. But whatever had pushed it was not yet ready to come out.

Hours later he returned reeling from the campus tavern. The phone was ringing again. But the call, as he had expected, was not from his mother, though it was from his native city in Illinois.

"Mr. Desmond, this is Sergeant Rourke of the Busiris Police Department. I'm afraid I have some bad news for you. Uh, ah, your mother died some hours ago of a heart attack."

Desmond did not have to act stunned. He was numb throughout. Even the hand holding the receiver felt as if it had turned to granite. Vaguely, he was aware that Rourke's voice seemed strange.

"Heart attack? Heart...? Are you sure?"

He groaned. His mother had died naturally. He would not have had to recite the ancient words. And now he had committed himself for nothing and was forever trapped. Once the words were used while the eyes read, there was no turning back.

But... if the words had been only words, dying as sound usually does, no physical reaction resulting from words transmitted through that subcontinuum, then was he bound?

Wouldn't he be free, clear of debt? Able to walk out of this place without fear of retaliation?

"It was a terrible thing, Mr. Desmond. A freak accident. Your mother died while she was talking to a visiting neighbor, Mrs. Sammins. Sammins called the police and an ambulance. Some other neighbors went into the house, and then... then...."

Rourke's throat seemed to be clogging.

"I'd just got there and was on the front porch when it... it...."

Rourke coughed, and he said, "My brother was in the house, too."

Three neighbors, two ambulance attendants, and two policemen had been crushed to death when the house had unaccountably collapsed.

"It was like a giant foot stepped on it. If it'd fallen in six seconds later, I'd have been caught, too."

Desmond thanked him and said he'd take the next plane out to Busiris.

He staggered to the window, and he raised it to breathe in the open air. Below, in the light of a street lamp, hobbling along on his cane, was Layamon. The gray face lifted. Teeth flashed whitely.

Desmond wept, but the tears were only for himself.

UPROAR IN ACHERON

This is the only fictional tale which is not science-fiction. I include it because a book which samples the spectrum of my writings should have one non-s-f work and also because of its curious history.

When I wrote it in 1961, while living in Scottsdale, Arizona, I thought that the basic idea, that from which the plot derived, had never been used in fiction before then. As far as I know, that's still true.

I could have set the story almost anywhere on Earth, but, since I was living in Arizona, I used that locale.

At that time, I considered the story to be only one of a series which would be collected for a book. Or perhaps the stories would be rewritten to make a novel about the great conman of the Old West, Doc Grandtoul. Doc, as his name suggests—Grandtoul = Grand Tool—was also a great lover.

I still might write this book someday, but since I've started fifteen series and not as yet finished any, and since I keep getting new ideas at the rate of about three a week, I doubt that I'll finish this long-ago-conceived project. But you never know.

The story here will be extensively and somewhat differently written if I do decide to write a series for a collection.

As it was, I wrote it, and it was published in the May 1962 issue of *The Saint Mystery Magazine*. It was my first printed Western, though I had, during the 40's, written two or three Western short stories which had been rejected and got one-fourth of the way through a novel based on the Johnston County rancher-squatter war.

Two years later, on May 8, 1964, I sat down before

the TV set to watch a *Twilight Zone* show. This was "Garrity and the Graves," a telecast on CBS, teleplay by Rod Serling, based on a story by Nike Korologos. The play had not gone long, perhaps five minutes, when I started swearing, and I told Bette, my wife, "You won't believe this. I can't. But that's based on 'Uproar in Acheron.' Or something like that. I probably said something stronger.

Having watched it to the end, I rose and wrote a letter to my agent. And later I talked to him on the phone. I gave him all the details of the telecast and of my story. He commiserated with me but said there wasn't much to do about it. I could send a photocopy of the story and a letter to CBS, but he doubted that it would do any good.

I did a lot of fuming, but at that time I was having some deep personal problems which made the *Twilight Zone* affair appear minor. Also, my agent, the agent's representative, rather, had not at all encouraged me to pursue the matter.

Then I found out later that my agent was also Rod Serling's. And I quit the agency. I also noticed that after talking to my agent, "Garrity and the Graves" seemed to have been dropped from the reruns. At least, though I looked for it during the reruns, I never saw that it was advertised.

When I moved to Beverly Hills in late 1965, I told several science-fiction and TV writers about my story and the telecast. And I found out that I was not the only writer who had been watching the series and experienced the same trauma.

And now, just this moment, while I was writing this foreword, I experienced an amazing coincidence—or synchronicity, if you prefer that term. I got a phone call from George Scheetz, a friend, fan, and publisher of the *Farmerage* fanzine, of a forthcoming bibliography of my works, and of *Wheelwrightings*, the irregular periodical of the local Sherlock Holmes Scion Society, The Hansoms of John Clayton. He'd just returned from a trip to the West, and he'd found out that, if "Garrity and the Graves" had been dropped from the series, it had been picked up again. It was now included in the reruns.

I suggest to the reader that he compare this story to

"Garrity and the Graves." Consider the basic idea, which had not been used until this story appeared, the locale, the characters, the development of plot.

Everybody in the town of Acheron had been wondering for two weeks whom Linda Beeman favored. Now there was no doubt. The smoke of the revolvers had just thinned away when Linda ran into the Lucky Lode saloon and threw herself, sobbing, on the body of Johnny Addeson.

Skeeter Patton, the Colt still in his hand, stood blinking at her like a cat that'd been suddenly awakened. He was pale and shaking, and no wonder. He'd put two bullets into the chest of his best friend and lost forever his chance of marrying Linda. Yet he could have done nothing to stop what had happened.

The two young men had dropped in at the Lucky Lode after work to have a few. Johnny had been moody for about a week, but tonight he was laughing and joking. That is, he was until Skeeter said that he had to leave soon. He had a date to take Linda for a buggy ride.

Johnny's eyes had widened, and he had said, "Quit your fooling! She has a date with me!"

The men along the bar laughed and watched to see who would win the argument. They didn't expect the argument to be anything except the friendly pretend-mad joshing the two gave each other all the time. Johnny and Skeeter had come into Acheron only three weeks ago on the same stagecoach. They had not known each other before that day. Johnny had come from Tucson, where he'd been studying under a horse doctor. He'd opened his own business next door to the livery stable. Skeeter was fresh into the territory of Arizona from New Orleans, where he'd been a printer's devil. The two had struck it off together like flint and steel. Sparks flew sometimes, but their disputes always ended up with them laughing and backslapping each other. They'd even been agreeable about both courting Linda Beeman, the daughter of the owner of the Beeman Stables.

But Skeeter must have suddenly become serious about Linda. He swore at Johnny and said, "No call for that! And I'm not a liar!"

"This says you are!" shouted Johnny, and he drew his Smith and Wesson .45.

Skeeter struck Johnny's gun upwards with one hand and

started to draw his own with the other hand. But Johnny brought his pistol down and fired. He was so close he couldn't have missed. But his bullet struck the far wall.

Skeeter fired his Colt .44 twice at point-blank range. And Johnny jerked backward from the force of the slugs and fell face up, on the floor. Blood from the two wounds spread outwards on his chest.

There was uproar and confusion. Everybody was paralyzed with shock. A nice young man like Johnny going berserk was the last thing anybody would've thought of.

Old Doc Evans, Acheron's medico, coroner, and undertaker, finished his drink at the bar. Then he felt Johnny's pulse and pulled back one of Johnny's eyelids. When he rose from the body, Doc Evans shook his head.

"Right through the heart," he said. "Deader'n last week's newspaper."

Pedro, the Lucky Lode's janitor, ran to get Linda. He didn't take long. The stables, over which she lived with her father, were only the throw of a horseshoe away. In two minutes she was sobbing over Johnny's body.

Skeeter hadn't said a word. He was too dazed. Even when Sheriff Douglas said, "Don't worry, son. It was a clear case of self-defense," Skeeter didn't talk. Once, he put his hand out towards Linda and then, as if knowing it would do no good, withdrew his hand.

Old Doc Evans gave a few orders. Two men picked up Johnny's body and carried it out of the Lucky Lode. They were headed for the doc's house, which was also the undertaking parlor. But they had not gotten halfway across the street before they stopped.

Everybody else stopped, too, for down the main street was a blaze of lanterns, a squeak of wheels, and the high-walled bulk of a van. It was the kind of van a snake-oil man drives around in and lives in and carries his snake oil and fever pills and tonics in. But this van had no big signs on the side or anything to tell what the owner was selling.

The van pulled up just by the two men carrying the body, and the driver looked down from his high seat.

"Had a shooting, friends?" the man said. "Did this young fellow just die? Perhaps I can do something for him."

It was a strange thing to say, and the man who said it was even stranger. He was dressed in a rusty black suit and wore a black bowler from which hair black as stove polish hung.

His face was as pale as if he'd just seen Death. He had a handsome face, though it was bony with high cheekbones and a Roman nose and deep hollow eyes and dark rings under the eyes. His neck, sticking out of his white collar, was thin as a colt's leg, and his shoulders were narrow as a cat's.

"I am Doctor Grandtoul," he said in a voice that surprised everybody because it was so deep.

"Always nice to meet another M.D. in this unpopulated territory," said old Doc Evans. He took off his Stetson and placed it over his heart. "But there ain't much you can do for Johnny Addeson. He breathed his last five minutes ago, and his soul has winged on to its reward."

Doctor Grandtoul raised a slim pale hand and pointed a slim pale finger. "Ah, my friend," he said, "that is where you are wrong."

He looked around at the crowd, which was rubbernecking as if they knew something out of the ordinary was coming and they weren't sure they were going to like it.

"Yes," said Doctor Grandtoul, "no discredit to you, my worthy Hippocratian comrade. But perhaps you have not heard of the latest scientific advancement.

"Advancement!" he repeated explosively. "No! Miracle, rather! The miracle of electricity, which is both the stuff of lightning and of life itself!"

He swung down off the seat of the van and landed on his feet as lightly as a catamount.

"Bring the late departed to the back of my van," he said, "and help me place the body on my bed. Then I'll do what I can."

He walked around to the back of the van, opened the doors, and leaped into the van like a long lean black cat. Then he took Johnny from the two men who handed him up, and, with a strength amazing in a man with such pipe-cleaner arms, carried Johnny to the bed on one side of the van. Once he'd placed Johnny there, he ripped off Johnny's shirt. Then he cleaned the wounds and from a jar on a shelf he poured out some powder into his hand.

He turned to the buzzing gaping crowd, bowed, flashed white teeth, and said, "Friends, we can't leave an ugly hole in the departed's chest, can we? I think not, for he'd have trouble breathing, what with the air whistling in and out, a ghastly tune. So we'll just place this *soodoplazum,* a secret of the ancient Tibetan lamas, in the wounds. And, once the lightning of the revitalizing machine surges through the body, the *soodoplazum* will become real flesh."

There weren't many who really heard him, and those who heard didn't understand him. They were too busy staring at the big batteries that lined one side of the van. The batteries looked just like the monsters the telegraph companies used to provide electricity for their copper lines. There were many copper wires, very thin wires, that sprouted out of the main cables from the battery terminals. Doc Grandtoul took the wires, one by one, and attached them to Johnny's wrists and ankles and waist and head with thin copper bands.

Then he paused and said, "Would you gentlemen allow your doctor—Evans, is it?—to come up here? I want him to examine the late departed once more and make absolutely certain the ghost is gone."

"Ain't no need," grumbled Doc Evans, tugging at his white walrus moustache and swaying back and forth because, like always, he had a snootful. But at Doc Grandtoul's insistence Doc Evans climbed into the van and felt Johnny's pulse again and looked into his eyes. Then he said, "I'll stake my professional reputation that Johnny's dead as Julius Caesar's mule."

"Wanta buy a drink if he ain't?" somebody called, and the crowd hooted with laughter because they knew how tight old Doc Evans was when it came to buying a drink for anybody except himself.

Nevertheless, not a man or woman there—and everybody in Acheron except the kids and sick in bed was there—didn't believe Johnny was dead. Old Doc Evans might be closefisted, ornery, and too much a tippler, but he'd seen enough corpses to know a dead ringer from a live one.

Doc Grandtoul took a hypodermic syringe from a box, wiped the needle with alcohol, and plunged it into Johnny's chest. After taking the needle out, he said, "The late departed has just been injected with a serum which, coupled with the electricity coursing through his body, should bring the life back."

The crowd gasped. The doctor grinned at them and pulled a huge goldplated watch from his vest pocket. His black eyebrows rose knowingly, and he said, "Three minutes should do it, my friends. The combination of serum and electrical juice in a strong young body as recently deceased as this takes only a short time to accomplish its mission."

Afterwards, there were some that said those were the longest and most terrifying three minutes of their lives. Something about the scene, Johnny's body lying so still in the bed, dimly lit by the kerosene lamp inside the van, the copper wires sprouting from him and running to the huge black batteries, and the calm certain bearing of the mysterious stranger convinced them they were going to see something they'd never seen before, maybe something they shouldn't be seeing.

There wasn't a sound except the hard breathing of the men and women pressing together so they could get closer to the van for a good look.

Then—there was one big gasp, one loud scream, and the sound of running feet. Doc Grandtoul was calling after them, "Come back! There's nothing to be afraid of!"

But he was alone. Even old Doc Evans had bolted.

Not quite alone. Johnny was sitting up in the bed and saying, "What in blue blazes is going on?"

Later, much later, Johnny Addeson, Skeeter Patton, and Doc Grandtoul left the Lucky Lode. Johnny had invited the doctor to stay at the room he shared with Skeeter in Mrs. Lundgren's hotel. The men of Acheron followed the three out of the saloon, for they still hadn't gotten over the wonder of seeing Johnny raised from the dead. They kept touching him and saying, "How was it while you was dead, Johnny?"

And Johnny kept saying, "Just like I was sleeping. I didn't know nothing until I woke up with a strange face looking down at me."

He would laugh and say, "At first I thought it was the devil," and he would whoop with laughter to show how glad he was to be alive.

Skeeter Patton, after making sure that Johnny wasn't still mad at him, was buddies with Johnny again. He swore he didn't have any real interest in Linda Beeman. As far as he was concerned, Johnny could have her all to himself.

That was the strangest thing of all. Linda should have been overjoyed, should have been hanging on to Johnny for all she was worth, shouldn't have wanted him out of her sight. But she hadn't seen Johnny since he sat up and she ran away with the others. Old Doc Evans was with her in her father's house taking care of her. He didn't leave her until Johnny and Skeeter and Doc Grandtoul left the Lucky Lode. He met them just as they crossed the street towards the hotel.

"Doc," said Johnny, "how is Linda? Does she want to see me now?"

Doc Evans shook his head. "Sorry, son. She seems scared to death of you; keeps saying it ain't right you should be living. A dead man ought to stay dead."

"I don't understand that at all," said Johnny, scratching his curly head. "You'd think she'd be thanking God I'm up and jumping."

"She's in a state of shock, son," said Doc Evans. "Why don't you try to see her tomorrow, when she'll probably be recovering? After all, it ain't every day a tender young girl sees her boy friend rise from his death bed."

Doc Evans spoke to Doc Grandtoul. "You've created quite a sensation, to put it mildly. How do you plan to cap what you did tonight?"

Grandtoul lifted his hands, and the crowd fell silent. He looked impressive as Lucifer himself with the light streaming out from a window of the Lucky Lode on his pale handsome face and glistening off his hair and eyes, which were black as malapai rock. His rich baritone boomed out, "Friends, I came to you out of the desert with this miraculous means of revitalizing the dead. I intend eventually to go East. I expect to find fame and fortune there. But I'm in no hurry for it. I don't want to sound like a preacher, but I really am more interested in benefiting mankind than in gaining all the wealth of the world. It makes me happier to think about reuniting you with your beloved dead than in making personal gains. Your happiness is mine.

"So, tomorrow, after I've rested, I'll explain more of what I intend to do. I can't promise you all the dead in your cemetery will be brought back to life. That depends on how they died and how long they've been dead. But I can assure you that if any of those who were taken away from you can be brought back by my revitalizing machine, they will walk once more among you.

"And, to show you my heart is in the right place, I assure you that I will not take one red cent for doing this. I will do everything for free. So you can see that I am not some charlatan who intends to take you for all you have. Good night!"

He walked away with Johnny and Skeeter, leaving behind him, not wild shouts of joy but a silence. Even then, some of the people in Acheron were beginning to see what emptying the graveyard might mean to them.

* * *

Late next morning Linda Beeman walked into the lobby of Mrs. Lundgren's hotel. She wanted to speak to Johnny Addeson, but she was told by Mrs. Lundgren she'd have to wait her turn. Johnny was busy working as Doc Grandtoul's secretary. He and Skeeter were ushering in people who wanted to see the doctor. The doctor had rented a room next to Johnny's and was giving interviews to those who wanted to speak to him in private.

Linda spoke to everybody in the crowded lobby. Half of Acheron seemed to be waiting to talk to the doctor. All seemed to be very nervous. As Linda was the last to come, she wasn't called upstairs until noon.

When she entered Johnny's room, she found Johnny and Skeeter and Doc Grandtoul seated around a table. A large carpetbag was by the doctor's feet.

"Johnny," said Linda, "I'd like to speak to you alone."

"You're not desperate to talk to me?" said Doc Grandtoul. "You're the first."

He rose. "Come along, Skeeter. We'll wet our whistles at the Lucky Lode. Watch that bag, Johnny. It contains all our worldly wealth."

Linda spoke before the doctor could close the door behind him. "Is it true that tomorrow you're going to raise the dead?"

"I'm no miracle-maker," he answered. "Those who are well-preserved will benefit by the scientific means I use. Those who are not, well"—he bowed his head for a second and then continued—"tomorrow I will bring life to the departed and joy into the hearts of the bereaved."

He smiled, bowed, and left. Johnny said, "How're you feeling now, Linda?"

"I'm all over the shock now," she said. She paused, breathed deeply as if to gain strength for what she was going to say, and then spoke. "Johnny, do you think Doctor Grandtoul is doing right by raising the dead?"

"Right?" he said. "Of course! Why, if it wasn't for him I'd be six feet under! You wouldn't like that, would you?"

"No," she said. "Only..."

"Only what? What's eating you? I thought you loved me!"

Linda sat down and frowned as if she were thinking deeply. Finally, she said, "Of course I love you. Didn't I tell you so a week ago? And weren't we going to announce our engagement this Sunday after church? But... well, Johnny, you didn't know this, but I was engaged to Roy Canton only six months ago. We were going to be married, and..."

"What about it?" he said. "You didn't marry him. And you're going to marry me, right?"

"Roy Canton is dead," she said quietly, her wide blue eyes fixed on his face. "He died of fever less than a week after we announced our engagement. He's buried in the cemetery here."

Johnny paled. He swallowed several times and then managed to find his voice. "You don't mean you want him back?"

Suddenly, Linda began weeping. "I don't know what I want!" she sobbed. "When Roy died, I thought I'd die, too. Then I met you. And I fell in love. I wasn't being unfaithful to Roy. You can't be unfaithful to the dead. They're gone; they're never coming back. You're living and can't go on acting as if the dead were just away on a short visit and will be home next week. But now, now, I don't know! I love you, but I never quit loving Roy. And if he comes back, then I won't know what to do! I'll have two living men that I love. And...and I don't know what to do!"

Johnny, choking, said, "Maybe I could talk Doc into not raising Roy."

"No, you don't!" said Linda fiercely. "That wouldn't be fair!"

"What am I supposed to do?" said Johnny. "Wait around while you make up your mind? Who *do* you love, Roy or me?"

"If somebody had asked me that yesterday I'd have told him I love you as I love the living. And Roy as I love the dead. But now..."

"In other words," said Johnny bitterly, "you'll wait until Roy can ask you again, and then you'll make up your mind which of us you want."

Linda began crying again. Johnny's face twisted as if somebody had stuck a knife in him.

And then he shouted, "There's no use crying, Linda! Roy isn't going to come back from the dead!"

Linda rose from the chair and took a step towards Johnny.

"What do you mean?"

Johnny bit his lip and started to turn away. But Linda caught him by the shoulder and, with a strength surprising for such a small woman, spun him around to face her.

"What do you mean by saying he isn't going to come back from the dead?"

"I'll give it to you straight, Linda," said Johnny. "Doc

Grandtoul can't any more put life into a corpse than you or I can!"

Linda gave a little shriek and swayed back and forth for a minute. Johnny caught her in his arms and pulled her to him.

"Oh, Linda, darling, don't be mad at me! I'm a cheat, a liar, a crook! And Skeeter and Doc Grandtoul are cheats, liars, and crooks, too! This whole business is a fraud!"

He dropped his arms from around her and began pacing around the room while he talked loudly and furiously. He would not look directly at her. He seemed to be ashamed and to be afraid he might see scorn on her face.

"I met Doc and Skeeter about six months ago," he said. "In Jumpoff, Nevada. I'd been prospecting and hadn't had any luck. I was broke and hungry. Doc took me in, fed me, clothed me, taught me to be a good poker player. He and Skeeter were dealing for the house in the poker games at the High Stepper Saloon. But Doc wasn't satisfied. He wanted to make more money and faster. He's a great reader, is Doc, well educated. In fact, he's a real doctor, got his M.D. from an Eastern university, though he comes from an old New Orleans family.

"Doc had read something in one of his history books that gave him an idea. It seems that in the Middle Ages there was a band of sharpers that traveled from village to village, announcing they intended to raise the dead from the local cemetery. And things happened there and then just like they did here and now. Nobody was anxious for the dead to come back. In fact, they were determined they wouldn't come back. Why? Because they'd cause too much consternation and turmoil, make too many problems.

"Doc said people hadn't changed a bit since the 13th century. We have gunpowder and steam trains and telegraph and gas lights. But people are just as superstitious and gullible as in the old days. They don't want their lives disrupted any more than can be helped.

"So Doc, who's a smart man even if he is as crooked as a snake's path, made some hollow wax bullets with red dye in the hollows. When they're fired, the wax doesn't hurt the man it hits, just stings. And the wax just spreads out and splatters the red dye so it looks like a bullet wound."

Linda had seated herself on a chair. She had been staring at him as if she could not understand what he was telling her. But when he paused for breath, she said, "What about Doc

Evans? He pronounced you dead. How'd you fool him?"

Johnny, still not looking at her, grinned crookedly. He said, "Skeeter and I always travel ahead of Doc Grandtoul. We stop in a town and look it over. If the local doctor can be bribed or if there ain't no doctors, we stay. Acheron was a setup for us. Old Doc Evans hasn't much money, and he likes his whiskey too well. He agreed to go along with us if we gave him a good cut of the loot. He said he could send his grandson through medical school with the money and have enough to retire on, too."

"Then the whole quarrel over me was arranged by you and Skeeter?"

For the first time since he had started talking, Johnny looked directly at her. Desperately, he said, "Yes! But I wasn't fooling when I said I loved you! I do love you!"

"And just what did you expect me to do when you had to leave town before everybody found out you were a fraud?" she said scornfully. "Go with you? A cheat and a liar!"

"Now, honey," said Johnny, "if you'll think about it, you'll remember that Doc said he'd raise only those that the revitalizing machine can raise. And since it can't raise anybody, well. . . . And he also said he wouldn't take a red cent for raising anybody. He won't, either. He's just taken money not to raise certain dead people. Nothing really dishonest in that. Like Doc says, you can't cheat an honest man."

"I don't know what you mean," she said.

"Here's what I mean," said Johnny angrily as he picked up the carpetbag and dumped its contents on the top of the table. "See all this money? Piles and piles of money? This all comes from the people that saw Doc this morning.

"Here's five hundred from rich Mr. Baggs, the banker. Who'd think he was so anxious to make sure his dead partner didn't climb out of the grave and demand his half of the bank back, hah?

"And here's a hundred from Mrs. Tanner. Her first husband, I understand, died under rather mysterious circumstances. And it wasn't much later that she married her foreman. She must have good reason not to want the old boy to appear and clear up just how he did die.

"And here's two hundred from old Mr. Krank. He's about ready to be buried himself, but he wants his last few days to be peaceful and quiet. Which they wouldn't be if Mrs. Krank's tongue was freed from the silence of the tomb. She was quite a shrew.

"And here's five hundred, a contribution of a hundred each from the sons and daughters of Silas Johnson. He was a tyrant and a hypochondriac. Besides, he might want the inheritance back.

"And here's... well, why go on? It's the same story in every town we've come to."

"It's not a very nice story," Linda said. "But you've not answered me. What did you expect me to do when you had to leave town?"

"I was going to tell you as soon as I could get the nerve. But I was afraid you wouldn't want anything to do with me when I told you the truth."

"What about Doc Grandtoul and Skeeter?" she said. "Did they know you were going to tell me?"

"No. I supposed they'd be mad at me. However, they couldn't do much about it. Anyway, they've got about as much money as they'll get out of Acheron. They could go on and get another partner somewhere else."

"And how," she said sarcastically, "did you expect to keep from being lynched when people found out they'd been cheated?"

"Well," he said slowly, "I was hoping you'd go with me to some other town. We could get a fresh start there. I can't stay here. We'll have to leave tomorrow. Maybe tonight."

"You must be crazy!" she said. "I can't just run off and leave my father like that! I might go away with you, but not before I explain to my father. But I don't think he'd like me to marry a man like you. You might want to go back to cheating people."

"Don't say that, Linda. I'll admit I made a mistake. But Doc was so nice to me, and I really didn't know we'd be hurting people so much."

Linda walked up to Johnny and stood in front of him and looked him in the eye.

"Johnny, if you'll tell everybody in Acheron what you've done, and say you're sorry, and give them their money back, I'll marry you. But if you don't, we're through!"

"Use your horse sense," said Johnny. "If I did that, I couldn't ever settle down here. Who'd trust his horses to a man like me? And you couldn't hold your head high in this town, because you'd be the wife of that sharper Johnny Addeson. Give me a chance to straighten this out. I'll go talk with Doc and Skeeter. We'll fix this up somehow. I swear it! And you and I'll be able to live here the rest of our lives. And I'll be good to you, Linda. Good to you and good for this town. You'll be proud of me."

"All right," said Linda. "I'll give you a chance. I do want to live here. And I don't want anybody scorning you or me. Or our children."

Johnny smiled like a kid who's been given a sackful of candy for free. He picked up the bag and scooped the money into it and said, "I think Doc'll be able to help me out of this jam. He's a sharper, and he likes to take a dishonest sucker. But he isn't mean. He really does have a good heart. If anybody's smart enough to figure this out, he is."

He kissed Linda lightly on the lips and then ran out of the room.

Linda sat down again and waited. After a while she rose and went to the window to look out. She was just in time to see Johnny and Skeeter and Doc Grandtoul come out of the saloon across the street. Johnny was still holding the bag of money, and all three looked grim. Linda couldn't hear what they were saying, but they seemed to be arguing. They were talking and waving their hands when they walked into the livery stable.

Linda didn't leave the window. In about half an hour Johnny and Skeeter came out of the stable. Johnny was grinning. Neither of the two had the bag of money. They walked down the street and stopped in front of the Lucky Lode to talk to Doc Evans. The three talked earnestly for about ten minutes, but when some men joined them they quit talking to each other and joined in the general conversation.

The sound of a shot reached Linda through the half-opened window. The men on the street looked startled, milled around for a moment, and then ran towards the stable. Linda raced down the hall and down the steps to the street. When she was halfway to the stable, she heard what the whole town of Acheron knew by then.

Doc Grandtoul was dead. He had accidentally shot himself.

Some stories have happy endings. Any story of young love should have a happy ending. It means two young citizens settling down in a town and raising more happy young citizens.

Uproar in Acheron

And this was what happened in Acheron after the uproar over Doc Grandtoul's sudden and sad demise had quieted down. Doc Grandtoul was pronounced dead by Doc Evans, and the burial took place next day.

Only Linda thought it was peculiar that, when the coffin lid was closed over Doc Grandtoul, Doc Evans was the sole person present. And she noticed that Skeeter left town the same day. She didn't think it was so peculiar that not a word was said about the money paid to Doc Grandtoul. Those who had paid were not going to raise a fuss. Everybody pulled a long face and said what a pity it was that only Doc Grandtoul knew how to operate his machine. But very few moped around because of what had happened.

For a long time Linda never opened her mouth to Johnny about the incident of the revitalizing machine. She was satisfied that the result had been to make her happy. However, one thing bothered her.

And one night, years later, when she and Johnny were sitting before the fireplace, after putting the kids to bed, Linda said, unexpectedly, "Johnny, what happened to those people who pronounced you dead in all those towns you three scoundrels fleeced? Weren't they left to face everybody and be branded as sharpers just as Doc Evans would have been if Doc Grandtoul hadn't been killed?"

Johnny was startled, but after coughing a few times he managed to say, "I'm sorry to say that we didn't worry about them."

"If Doc Grandtoul had had an 'accident' in every town," she said, "nobody would have been left holding the bag."

Johnny was silent.

Linda looked into the fireplace a moment, and then she said, "I wonder where Doc Grandtoul is now?"

Johnny pretended to misunderstand her.

"I don't know, darling. I'll bet he went to the Good Place. After all, he brought us together, didn't he?"

AN EXCLUSIVE INTERVIEW WITH LORD GREYSTOKE

A subgenre of biographical literature is that which claims that certain people thought to be fictional are, or were, very much living. Splendid examples of this are Blakeney's *Sir Percy Blakeney: Fact or Fiction?* (a biography of the Scarlet Pimpernel), Baring-Gould's *Sherlock Holmes of Baker Street* and *Nero Wolfe of West Thirty-Fifth Street*, Parkinson's *The Life and Times of Horatio Hornblower*, and the Flashman Papers (three volumes so far) by Fraser. In fact, some public libraries stock these in the "B" or biography section. (The Blakeney book is in the "B" section of the Peoria, Illinois, public library.)

I've written two such "lives": *Tarzan Alive* and *Doc Savage: His Apocalyptic Life*. (The former is in the biography section of the Yuma City, California, Library.) I plan to write biographies of The Shadow, Allan Quatermain, Fu Manchu, d'Artagnan, Travis McGee, and a number of others. Fu Manchu, by the way, may have been based on a real-life model, a Vietnamese named Hanoi Shan whose operations in early twentieth-century France were every bit as sinister and fantastic as Rohmer's creation. I was informed of this after I'd made the statement in *Tarzan Alive* that Fu Manchu had no living counterpart.

This form of apologia is a lot of fun and much hard work. It requires as much imagination as the writing of science fiction but more discipline. Historical facts must not be ignored. Baring-Gould, in writing his Holmes biography, had an enormous amount of scholarship, articles published in *The Baker Street Journal* and other periodicals, to draw upon. But he had not only to read all these but to study them and make decisions. He found many conflicting theories, and he had to pick the one that seemed most valid. In addition, where theories or speculations were lacking, he had to generate his own. He had to explain discrepancies, which are numerous in Watson's account of Holmes's life. And, I might add, Burroughs, in his semifictional narratives of Greystoke's career, left many discrepancies for the scholar to reconcile, if he could. There are also gaps in the life of the hero which the biographer must fill in. And if the original writer has neglected the hero's genealogy, the biographer must research this.

Sometimes, a biographer makes a statement which he cannot substantiate. Thus, Baring-Gould said that Holmes was a cousin of Professor Challenger. He has been much criticized by the Sherlockian scholars for this because he presented no evidence from the Canon. Fortunately, in my *Tarzan Alive*, I was able to validate the relationship. The fact that Tarzan's mother was a Rutherford gave me the clue needed to track down the cousinhood.

The following article is part of my interview with "Lord Greystoke" and appeared in the April, 1972, issue of *Esquire* under the title of "Tarzan Lives." It was accompanied by a portrait of Greystoke, a photograph of a painting by Jean-Paul Goude. The staff of *Esquire* went to great lengths and much trouble to acquire this, for which they should be thanked. The report that Goude got the commission to do the painting because he is a relative of Admiral Paul d'Arnot of the French navy, Greystoke's closest friend, is being checked. It is said that Goude, like Holmes, is a descendant of Antoine Vernet, father of four famous French painters.

Editor's Note: For a number of years Mr. Farmer, who recorded the following interview, has been engaged in writing a definitive biography of the man Edgar Rice Burroughs called Tarzan of the Apes. Mr. Farmer's book, Tarzan Alive, *to be published by Doubleday in April of this year, is similar in method to Baring-Gould's* Sherlock Holmes of Baker Street *and Parkinson's* The Life and Times of Horatio Hornblower, *with the very important difference that Mr. Farmer firmly avers that "Lord Greystoke" or "Tarzan" is really alive. In fact, Mr. Farmer was able to track his subject to earth in a hotel in Libreville, Gabon, on the coast of Western Africa just above the equator, where he was granted this interview. "I met him," Mr. Farmer tells us, "in his hotel room—fittingly enough, on September 1, Edgar Rice Burroughs' birthday. He is six feet three and, I suppose, about two hundred forty pounds. I did not have the opportunity to see him in action, of course, but just from the way he moved about the room I could guess at his immense physical strength. As Burroughs said, he is much more like Apollo than Hercules; his power lies in the quality not the quantity of his muscles. I don't hesitate to admit that I was awed. I was concerned, of course, that after all my research I might still have been the victim of a hoax; but from the moment I knocked on the door and heard that deep, rich voice say 'Enter,' I knew I had the right man. And of course I was even more convinced when I saw him move—like a leopard, like water falling." The text of Mr. Farmer's interview follows.*

TARZAN: How do you do, Mr. Farmer.

FARMER: How do you do, Your Grace.

T: If you don't mind, Mr. Farmer, I should prefer simply to be called John Clayton. I own a good many titles, both real and fictional, but John Clayton, is, as it were, my real name. Though not my true *identity*, so to speak. As you apparently know.

F: Excuse me, sir—Mr. Clayton. Mr. Clayton, you told me over the phone that you would see me for fifteen minutes only, so I'd better work fast. I'll start asking questions right now, if you don't mind?

T: By all means. You don't have a tape recorder on you, do you? No? Good.

F: May I ask first, sir, why you were kind enough to grant this interview?

T: Mr. Farmer, my reasons are my own. But I will say that I appreciate the very great efforts you have gone to in researching the details of my life. It is very flattering to me, and I am not entirely immune to that. Besides, you seem to have information about my family that even I myself don't know. Your genealogical researches provoke my own curiosity, which has always been ample. I may ask you a few questions myself.

F: Of course. First, though, may I ask how it happens that

An Exclusive Interview with Lord Greystoke

you seem to speak English as you do, with more or less of an American accent? You speak as though you came from Illinois, which is my own home state. I seem to recall that on the phone you spoke—well, as I imagine dukes speak, the educated British accent.

T: I speak more or less as I am spoken *to*. You will recall that English is not my first spoken language—though it was my first *written* language—very unusual business, that—or even my first spoken *European* language. But the first English-speaking country I visited was the United States, Wisconsin in particular, back in 1909. I was not quite twenty-one years old at the time. So when English was fairly new to me, I had rather a large dose of American. Nevertheless, in Britain I do speak British. I have a gift for mimicry, I suppose you might call it, and I conform pretty much to the dialect of my interlocutors. When I gave my first and only speech in the House of Lords I did speak as dukes speak, or at least as dukes *think* they speak. You seem nervous, by the way. Would you care for a drink? I believe I will join you in a small Scotch.

F: Thank you. But I'm surprised to find you a drinking man. I thought—

T: That I was an abstainer? For many years I was. In my early days among civilized people I not only saw the results of excess but, I'm afraid, committed it myself. For many years I abstained completely. However, I believe the rash impulses of youth are safely behind me now. I can be abstemious without being teetotal. After all, I am—

F: You are eighty-two years old. When this interview is published, you will be eighty-three. But I suppose as far as physical appearance is concerned, you look about thirty-five. It must be true, then, that story about the grateful witch doctor who gave you the immortality treatment—

T: That was in 1912. I was twenty-four then, so as you see I have apparently aged about ten years since. The treatment merely slows down the aging process. Burroughs exaggerated its effects slightly, as he often did. I'll be an old man by the time I'm a hundred and fifty or so.

F: I'd like to return to your physical condition. But since you bring up Burroughs, and since Burroughs is the principal source of information about your life and family—

T: You would like to discuss the accuracy of Burroughs? Go ahead.

F: In *Tarzan of the Apes*, the first Tarzan book, Burroughs says that in 1888 your mother, then pregnant, accompanied your father on a secret mission to Africa for the British government. They hired a small ship, but the crew mutinied and stranded your parents on the coast of Africa. They were left on the shores of Portuguese Angola at approximately ten degrees south latitude, or about fifteen hundred miles north of Cape Town. But it seems to me that many of the scenes in the book could not have taken place in Angola.

T: That is correct. Actually, my parents were marooned on the shore of this very country, Gabon, which was then part of French Equatorial Africa. I was born about 190 miles south of here, in what is now the Parc National du Petit Loango. Any researcher, I believe, could have deduced that from the facts. There were gorillas in my natal territory, but there are no gorillas south of the Congo, and Angola extends far to the south of the Congo. Also, it was a French cruiser that landed near the same spot years later and rescued the party of Professor Porter, including my wife-to-be Jane, but left behind Lieutenant d'Arnot, my first civilized friend. Why would a French warship be patrolling the shores of Angola, a Portuguese possession?

F: Nor are there any lions, zebras, or rhinoceroses in the Gabonese rain forests. What about the lioness whose neck Burroughs said you broke with a full nelson when she was trying to get into your parents' cabin after Jane?

T: The lioness was actually a leopard. It was about the *size* of a small lioness, one of the big leopards that the natives call *injogu*. I did break its neck. As you know, I had independently invented the full nelson a few months before when I fought the big mangani ape that Burroughs calls Terkoz.

F: Well, then, how do you explain the discrepancies between Burroughs and the facts?

T: Mr. Farmer, the relationship between my life and Burroughs' narration of my life is exceedingly complex. I don't choose, for various reasons, to tell you all that I know about Burroughs' methods or my own; but I can tell you a number of his motives, some of which you may have figured out for yourself. First of all, Burroughs was essentially a romancer. He was not obligated to stick to the facts, and even if I had chosen to try to compel him, litigation would have been involved, and I would have had to appear in court and submit to questioning, which I would rather not have done. I entirely appreciate the feelings of your own Mr. Howard Hughes in this

An Exclusive Interview with Lord Greystoke

regard. In fact, after Burroughs wrote *Tarzan of the Apes*, I communicated with him, and I told him he should continue to make the narratives highly romantic, even fantastic. Jane advised that, because she said that if people found out I was not a fictional character, I would never again have a moment of privacy.

In the second place, Burroughs himself was not always fully informed. He first heard of me in the winter of 1911. I had then been known to the civilized world for only perhaps two years, and the records of my existence—including my father's diary, which he kept until his death in Africa—were then in England. By the way, here are some photostats of that diary. You may examine them, but you may not take them with you. In any case, Burroughs had not been to England, much less to Africa, and had his information by word of mouth at several removes. In many cases he had to fill in gaps by sheer guesswork, some of which is accurate, some not. For the sake of verisimilitude, Burroughs pretended to be much closer to his sources than was in fact the case.

Finally, certain facts are disguised in the books because they are best left disguised. Burroughs gives directions for getting to the lost city of Opar, with its spires and domes and vaults of gold and jewels. But those directions will lead the curious nowhere. Not that it matters so much in that case, because I have long since disguised the ruins of Opar completely. You could go there today and never know you were there. But I hope you won't try.

A few of Burroughs' stories are pure fiction. In *Jungle Tales of Tarzan*, I am supposed to have shot arrows into the sky in an effort to stop an eclipse of the moon. But the story happens in 1908, and in fact there was no such eclipse visible from my part of Africa that year. Sheer fabrication.

F: I see from your father's diary that he delivered you himself, though he had nothing but some medical books to go by. You were born a few minutes after midnight of November 22, 1888. On the cusp of Sagittarius and Scorpio. Scorpio the passionate and Sagittarius the hunter.

T: I know that. I have read much about astrology, though I believe in it about as much as I do in the speeches of politicians. Still, Sagittarius, the centaur with the bow, could not be a better symbol of the half-animal, half-man that I have been. And I am a very good archer indeed. And Scorpios are supposed to be ingenious, creative, true friends, and dangerous enemies, all of which I am. We're also supposed to exude sexual power. Hmm.

F: Burroughs gives many instances of women attempting to seduce you. You are certainly not the inarticulate ape-man of the movies. What you say about being a good archer, however, reminds me of some critics who maintain you could not have accomplished this. They refer to Marshall McLuhan's thesis that only literate peoples can produce excellent marksmen.

T: I've read *The Mechanical Bride* and *Understanding Media*. McLuhan forgets the medieval English bowman, who was certainly illiterate but undoubtedly a great marksman. And the critics forget that I taught myself to read and write English. I was not illiterate, though I couldn't *speak* the language.

F: What do you think of the Tarzan movies?

T: I saw the first one in 1920, the one with Elmo Lincoln. I came very near to leaping up onto the stage and tearing the picture apart. That fake jungle, those doped-up, scraggly circus cats! Lincoln was built more like a gorilla than like me, and he wore a headband, which I have never done. All that swinging on a vine is movie invention as well, as is Cheetah the chimpanzee. Nowhere even in Burroughs will you find me swinging on vines, though it's true that he did greatly exaggerate my tree-traveling abilities. I'm too heavy to go skipping along the, ah, arboreal avenues like a monkey. And the chimpanzees would never trust me because they identified me with the great apes who brought me up. We—that is, they—used to *eat* chimps when they could catch them. But later on I began to find the Tarzan movies more amusing than disgusting. Jane helped me to learn to tolerate them.

F: Arthur Koestler wrote an article claiming that you couldn't have escaped being mentally retarded. He said there had been a few authentic cases of children raised by baboons or wolves and then found by humans. These were unable to master any language. Apparently, if the child doesn't experience language before a certain age, it is forever incapable of learning speech.

T: Koestler must not have bothered to read the Tarzan books. Otherwise he would have learned that the great apes *did* have a language. He should have deduced, as many have, that the great apes, or mangani, were really near-humans. Hominids, in fact. Remember what I said about the sketchy information

An Exclusive Interview with Lord Greystoke 217

upon which Burroughs' early books were based? He supplied missing data with imagination or even misinformation. He made up names. He put animals in the Gabonese jungles that did not belong there. He described the mangani as great apes. My father had thought they were apes, and so called them in his diary. But my father was not a zoologist or a paleontologist.

The mangani were a very rare, nearly extinct—even eighty years ago—genus of hominids, halfway between ape and man. They might have been a giant variety of Australopithecus robustus. The fossil remains of this hominid have been found by Leakey in East Africa, you know. The mangani—and I use Burroughs' word for them, since their own term is an unpronounceable jawbreaker—had crested skulls and massive jaws. They had long arms and often used their knuckles to assist them in walking, but they had manlike hips and leg bones. They could walk upright when they chose.

Burroughs later had better information about his *great apes*. However, for the sake of consistency he described them in the later novels as he had done earlier on. He slipped in the sixth book, *Jungle Tales of Tarzan*, when he said they walked upright and were manlike.

I can speak mangani fluently, of course. But I can't pronounce it quite perfectly. The mangani oral structure is different from man's, and many of their speech sounds have no exact equivalent in human speech. So though I can speak English with any of several accents, I always speak mangani with a *human* accent.

F: Did the big mangani, Terkoz, really abduct Jane and try to rape her? And you killed him with your father's hunting knife?

T: Yes. And there you see, by the way, another reason why the mangani should not be classified as apes. They are capable of raping a human being, whereas a gorilla is not. I once read in the memoirs of Trader Horn about a white trader who put a male gorilla in a cage with a native girl. The gorilla did nothing but sulk in one corner while the poor girl wept in the other. Horn said he shot the white man when he found out about it. In any case, gorillas have forty-eight chromosomes, humans only forty-six, so a gorilla-human hybrid is not possible. But Burroughs knew of instances of offspring being born to a human and a mangani.

F: Albert Schweitzer maintained that Trader Horn, aside from some trifling discrepancies, was generally accurate. Did you know that Schweitzer built his house on the site of Horn's trading post?

T: Yes, at Adolinanongo, a little distance above Lambaréné on the Ogowe River. I know it well. There's a Catholic mission there, founded in 1886. That's where Lieutenant d'Arnot and I came out of the jungle on our trek to civilization.

F: Would you care to comment on how you taught yourself to read and write English? As far as I know this is a unique intellectual feat, especially since you had never heard a word of it spoken.

T: I was about ten years old when I discovered how to unlock the door to my parents' cabin, and there I found, as you have read in Burroughs, a number of books, all of them perfectly meaningless to me, of course. But one of them was a big illustrated children's alphabet book with pictures of bowmen and the like, you know, and legends like "A is for Archer, who shoots with the bow," that sort of thing. Finally it dawned on me that the writing had something to do with the picture, and I spent I don't know how long puzzling it out. When I was seventeen I could read a child's primer. I called the letters "little bugs," or the mangani equivalent rather, and I knew how they worked. One detail you may find rather amusing is this: I had to invent, and did invent, my own manner of pronouncing the English words, which had nothing to do of course with real English but was governed by the usages of mangani grammar. Mangani has two genders, indicated by the prefixes *bu* for the masculine and *mu* for the feminine. Now I supposed that the capital letters were masculine, since they were bigger, and the rest feminine. And as children will do when they know the alphabet but don't yet know how to read, I pronounced each letter separately, using arbitrary syllables taken from mangani. Does this seem terribly complicated? For example, I pronounced *g* as *la*; *o* as *tu*; and *d* as *mo*. Now take the English word *God*; adding the prefixes, I pronounced it *Bulamutumumo*. The equivalent in English would be *he-g-she-o-she-d*. Now that's very cumbersome, of course, but it worked. I could read my father's books and know what I was reading.

I had no idea how to write my mangani name, but I had seen a picture of a little white boy, which in Anglo-Mangani, I suppose you might call it, is *Bumudomutumuro*, or *He-she-b-she-o-she-y*. That's what I called myself.

F: Burroughs says that when you discovered intruders had messed up the cabin, you printed a threatening note to them.

You signed it with your mangani name. How could you do that if you didn't know how to write it in English?

T: I didn't. I printed a translation of my mangani name: White Skin. When Burroughs wrote *Tarzan of the Apes*, he had no record of the exact text of the note. He made up the text, and he did not care to take time out from the action to explain that I couldn't use my mangani name. Remember he was first and last a storyteller.

F: Your reading must have given you some strange ideas about the outside world. You had no proper references to give you a full comprehension of the books.

T: My ideas were no stranger than the reality. My initial encounters with human beings were extremely unpleasant. The first human being I ever saw had just murdered my foster mother. To him she was an ape, but to me she was the most beautiful and loving and lovable person in the world. The first time I saw white men, one was murdering another. I am fortunate that that didn't make me shun mankind forever. Otherwise I'd never have known human love.

F: When you matured and discovered that you were not an ape but a man, didn't you think of turning to the native tribes for companionship?

T: No. I hated them all for a long time, because I blamed them for my foster mother's death. Also, they were cannibals, and anybody not of their tribe was meat to them. And they had had unfortunate experiences with white men. In addition to that, the women coated their bodies and hair with rancid palmnut oil. I have an unusually keen sense of smell, and consequently they repelled me. Still, if Jane hadn't come along—

F: Burroughs portrays you as free of racial prejudice.

T: Like Mark Twain, I have only one prejudice. That is against the human race.

F: Let me not pursue *that* further. Many readers have found your behavior with Jane when you were alone in the jungle incredibly chivalrous. Burroughs attributes this to heredity, but no one today would accept this explanation.

T: Remember, I read all the novels—Victorian novels, mind you—in my father's library. And I read Malory's book about King Arthur and the knights and the fair ladies. I believed in chivalry quite literally. And I was in love with Jane and did not want to offend her. Besides, the mangani have a code of ethics, you know. They are not apes. They do not copulate in public; they demand, though they do not always get, marital fidelity; they punish rape with death, if the injured party wishes it. Consider all the factors and you'll find my behavior credible enough.

F: You became chief of a black tribe which Burroughs called the Waziri. Are you aware that Robert Lewis Taylor, in his biography of W. C. Fields, says that Fields once went with Tex Rickard on a world tour? And that Fields entertained a tribe of naked Waziri? That would have been in 1906 or 1907, several years before you encountered the Waziri. Did your Waziri ever say anything about Fields?

T: I have no comment on that, I'm afraid.

F: How much of Burroughs' *Tarzan and the Lion Man* is true? It seems to me that Burroughs wrote it mainly to satirize Hollywood.

T: Yes, nearly everything in that book is fiction. But I did visit Hollywood once, though I told no one except Burroughs who I was, of course.

F: Did you actually try out for the role of Tarzan in a movie? And were you rejected because the producer said you weren't the type?

T: No, though I wouldn't be surprised if such a thing were to happen. In any case, I went there too late to try out for the Weissmuller movie *Tarzan the Ape Man*, and too early for the Buster Crabbe movie *Tarzan the Fearless*. I did meet Burroughs, secretly of course. I liked him very much. He was gentle and broad-minded and he didn't take himself or his works too seriously. He saw many things wrong in civilization, many sickening things, and he satirized them in his books, you know, but his mockery was Voltaire's, not Swift's. He was never soured or snarly. But since we are now discussing authors, let me indulge my curiosity a moment. I gather that you have been led to me by a fairly elaborate trail. Would you mind explaining to me how you first caught my scent, as it were?

F: I had long suspected that Burroughs, Arthur Conan Doyle, and George Bernard Shaw had all written stories about your family. Each, however, used more or less sophisticated systems of code names for your various relatives. If these codes could be cracked, and used as guides to the right places—Burke's *Peerage*, for instance—they would lead me right to you. And as you see, they have. The reasoning I have employed is long and complex, and I hope you'll be willing to delay a full understanding until I can send you a copy of my book, since our time today is short. Suffice it to say that I have shown

An Exclusive Interview with Lord Greystoke

you are closely related to the men who were the living prototypes of Doc Savage, Nero Wolfe, Bulldog Drummond, Sherlock Holmes, Lord Peter Wimsey, Leopold Bloom, and Richard Wentworth (also known as G-8, the Spider, and the Shadow), and a number of other notable characters in nineteenth- and twentieth-century fiction.

T: Indeed.

F: I have also found the explanation for the remarkable, almost superhuman powers exhibited by yourself and many members of your family. As you know, a monument marks the spot where a meteorite hit Wold Newton, Yorkshire, in 1795. It just so happened that three coaches were passing by when the meteorite struck, and in them were the third Duke of Greystoke and his wife, the rich gentleman Fitzwilliam Darcy of Pemberley House and his wife Elizabeth Bennet—the heroine of *Pride and Prejudice*—Sherlock Holmes's great-grandparents, and a number of others. All the ladies were pregnant. Everybody was exposed to the radiation from the meteorite. Ionization accompanies the fall of these, you know. And the radiation must have caused favorable mutations in the party. Otherwise how do you explain the nova of genetic splendor in the descendants of these people, including yourself?

T: I will not say that I am entirely convinced. Nevertheless yours is a very probable theory. My own skeletal bones are half again as thick as normal, which might well indicate that I am a mutant. Moreover, even before I received the immortality treatment from the witch doctor, I was developing oddly, though I had no one of my own race to compare myself with at the time. I was six feet tall at eighteen years of age, and grew three more inches in the next two years. I did not have to shave until I was twenty. I have never been ill or had a toothache. So your mutation theory seems likely enough. And now, I'm afraid, our interview is over. May I have the photostats back, please?

F: My time's up? But—

T: I don't need a watch to know how many minutes have passed. Good-bye. I won't be seeing you again. May I ask you to remain in this room a few minutes and allow me to leave first? I have already checked out and shall soon be gone.

F: May I ask where you're going?

T: To arrange a seemingly fatal accident. Too many people are wondering why I look so young. One reason I gave you this interview is that I'm disappearing. Your book won't help anyone find me. But I hold you to your promise not to reveal my true identity for ten years. I'll be living incognito with Jane in various countries under various names. Occasionally I'll return to the jungle. There are still vast tracts in the rain forests of Gabon and the Ituri where the only men are a few pygmies. The rain forests may disappear someday. But I think that the worldwide pollution is going to result in a collapse of civilization and a drastic reduction of population. Perhaps the forests will be spared after all, and many of the species now threatened with extinction will come back. In any case, I intend to survive. If I don't, well, death gets us sooner or later, and I won't be able to worry about its being sooner if I'm dead. As I told you, I'll be old anyhow when I'm a hundred and fifty. Send your book to my bankers in Zurich.

Then, Mr. Farmer tells us, he left the room and was gone.

(Author's note: For security reasons, I stated in this interview that I met "Lord Greystoke" in Africa. It's safe now to reveal that the meeting actually took place in Chicago.)

SEXUAL IMPLICATIONS OF THE CHARGE OF THE LIGHT BRIGADE

This is an extract from "Riders of the Purple Wage," which won a Hugo in 1967. Some might think it a satire on Freudian analysis. Believe me, it's not a bit exaggerated.

Sexual Implications of the Charge of the Light Brigade is so fascinating a book that Doctor Jespersen Joyce Bathymens, psycholinguist for the Federal Bureau of Group Reconfiguration and Intercommunicability, hates to stop reading. But duty beckons.

"A radish is not necessarily reddish," he says into the recorder. "The Young Radishes so named their group because a radish is a radicle, hence, radical. Also, there's a play on roots and on red-ass, a slang term for anger, and possibly on ruttish and rattish. And undoubtedly on rudeickle, Beverly Hills dialectical term for a repulsive, unruly, and socially ungraceful person.

"Yet the Young Radishes are not what I would call Left Wing; they represent the current resentment against Life-In-General and advocate no radical policy of reconstruction. They howl against Things As They Are, like monkeys in a tree, but never give constructive criticism. They want to destroy without any thought of what to do after the destruction.

"In short, they represent the average citizen's grousing and bitching, being different in that they are more articulate. There are thousands of groups like them in LA and possibly millions all over the world. They had normal life as children. In fact, they were born and raised in the same clutch, which is one reason why they were chosen for this study. What phenomenon produced ten such creative persons, all mothered in the seven houses of Area 69-14, all about the same time, all practically raised together, since they were put together in the playpen on top of the pedestal while one mother took her turn baby-sitting and the others did whatever they had to do, which... where was I?

"Oh, yes, they had a normal life, went to the same school, palled around, enjoyed the usual sexual play among themselves, joined the juvenile gangs and engaged in some rather bloody warfare with the Westwood and other gangs. All were distinguished, however, by an intense intellectual curiosity and all became active in the creative arts.

"It has been suggested—and might be true—that that mysterious stranger, Raleigh Renaissance, was the father of all ten. This is possible but can't be proved. Raleigh Renaissance was living in the house of Mrs. Winnegan at the time, but he seems to have been unusually active in the clutch and, indeed, all over Beverly Hills. Where this man came from, who he was, and where he went are still unknown despite intensive search by various agencies. He had no ID or other cards of any kind, yet he went unchallenged for a long time. He seems to have had something on the Chief of Police of Beverly Hills and possibly on some of the Federal agents stationed in Beverly Hills.

"He lived for two years with Mrs. Winnegan, then dropped out of sight. It is rumored that he left LA to join a tribe of white neo-Amerinds, sometimes called the Seminal Indians.

"Anyway, back to the Young (pun on Jung?) Radishes. They are revolting against the Father Image of Uncle Sam, whom they both love and hate. Uncle is, of course, linked by their subconsciouses with *unco*, a Scottish word meaning strange, uncanny, weird, this indicating that their own fathers were strangers to them. All come from homes where the father was missing or weak, a phenomenon regrettably common in our culture.

"I never knew my own father... Tooney, wipe that out as irrelevant. *Unco* also means news or tidings, indicating that the unfortunate young men are eagerly awaiting news of the return of their fathers and perhaps secretly hoping for reconciliation with Uncle Sam, that is, their fathers.

"Uncle Sam. Sam is short for Samuel, from the Hebrew *Shemu'el*, meaning Name of God. All the Radishes are atheists, although some, notably Omar Runic and Chibiabos Winnegan, were given religious instruction as children (Panamorite and Roman Catholic, respectively).

"Young Winnegan's revolt against God, and against the Catholic Church, was undoubtedly reinforced by the fact that his mother forced strong *cath*artics upon him when he had a chronic constipation. He probably also resented having to learn his *cat*echism when he preferred to play. And there is the deeply significant and traumatic incident in with a *cath*eter was used on him. (This refusal to excrete when young will be analyzed in a later report.)

"Uncle Sam, the Father Figure. *Figure* is so obvious a play that I won't bother to point it out. Also perhaps on *figger*, in the sense of 'a fig on thee!'—look this up in Dante's *Inferno*, some Italian or other in Hell said, 'A fig on thee, God!' biting his thumb in the ancient gesture of defiance and disrespect. Hmm? Biting the thumb—an infantile characteristic?

"Sam is also a multileveled pun on phonetically, orthographically, and semisemantically linked words. It is significant that young Winnegan can't stand to be called *dear;* he claims that his mother called him that so many times it nauseates him. Yet the word has a deeper meaning to him. For instance, *sambar* is an Asiatic *deer* with *three*-pointed antlers. (Note the *sam*, also.) Obviously, the three points symbolize, to him, the Triple Revolution document, the historic dating point of the beginning of our era, which Chib claims to hate so. The three points are also archetypes of the Holy Trinity, which the Young Radishes frequently blaspheme against.

"I might point out that in this the group differs from others I've studied. The others expressed an infrequent and mild blasphemy in keeping with the mild, indeed pale, religious spirit prevalent nowadays. Strong blasphemers thrive only when strong believers thrive.

"Sam also stands for *same*, indicating the Radishes' subconscious desire to conform.

"Possibly, although this particular analysis may be invalid, Sam corresponds to Samekh, the fifteenth letter of the Hebrew alphabet. (Sam! Ech!?) In the old style of English spelling, which the Radishes learned in their childhood, the fifteenth letter of the Roman alphabet is O. In the Alphabet Table of my dictionary, Webster's 128th New Collegiate, the Roman O is in the same horizontal column as the Arabic Dad. Also with the Hebrew Mem. So we get a double connection with the missing and longed-for Father (or Dad) and with the overdominating Mother (or Mem).

"I can make nothing out of the Greek Omicron, also in the same horizontal column. But give me time; this takes study.

"Omicron. The little O! The lower-case omicron has an egg shape. The little egg is their father's sperm fertilized? The womb? The basic shape of modern architecture?

"Sam Hill, an archaic euphemism for Hell. Uncle Sam is a Sam Hill of a father? Better strike that out, Tooney. It's possible that these highly educated youths have read about this obsolete phrase, but it's not confirmable. I don't want to suggest any connections that might make me look ridiculous.

"Let's see. Samisen. A Japanese musical instrument with *three* strings. The Triple Revolution document and the Trinity again. Trinity? Father, Son, and Holy Ghost. Mother the thoroughly despised figure, hence, the Wholly Goose? Well, maybe not. Wipe that out, Tooney.

"Samisen. Son of Sam? Which leads naturally to Samson, who pulled down the temple of the Philistines on them and on himself. These boys talk of doing the same thing. Chuckle. Reminds me of myself when I was their age, before I matured. Strike out that last remark, Tooney.

"Samovar. The Russian word means, literally, self-boiler. There's no doubt the Radishes are boiling with revolutionary fervor. Yet their disturbed psyches know, deep down, that Uncle Sam is their ever-loving Father-Mother, that he has only their best interests at heart. But they force themselves to hate him, hence, they self-boil.

"A samlet is a young salmon. Cooked salmon is a yellowish pink or pale red, near to a radish in color, in their unconsciouses, anyway. Samlet equals Young Radish; they feel they're being cooked in the great pressure cooker of modern society.

"How's that for a trinely furned phase—I mean, finely turned phrase, Tooney? Run this off, edit as indicated, smooth it out, you know how, and send it off to the boss. I got to go. I'm late for lunch with Mother; she gets very upset if I'm not there on the dot.

"Oh, postscript! I recommend that the agents watch Winnegan more closely. His friends are blowing off psychic steam through talk and drink, but he has suddenly altered his behavior pattern. He has long periods of silence, he's given up smoking, drinking, and sex."

THE OBSCURE LIFE AND HARD TIMES OF KILGORE TROUT

A Skirmish in Biography

This is another specimen of the "biographical." It originally appeared in a fanzine, *Moebius Trip,* December, 1971 issue, edited and published by Ed Connor of Peoria, Illinois. Later on, I suggested to the editor of *Esquire* that he might want to publish this "life." Regretfully, he rejected the idea. He did not think that Kilgore Trout was as well-known as Tarzan. This is true, but the majority of *Esquire*'s readers are probably readers of Kurt Vonnegut's works and would be acquainted with Trout. So it goes.

I identify strongly with Trout.

The editor and readers of *Moebius Trip* thought that the letter from Trout and the letter describing Trout's interview in the *Peoria Journal Star* were made up by me. No such thing. These letters actually appeared in the letter section of the editorial page of Peoria's only local newspaper, and I can prove it.

Since I wrote this, I have been fortunate enough to read the galleys of Vonnegut's novel *Breakfast of Champions*. It contains many new facts which have enabled me to amplify and to correct the original article. Even so, some things are still in doubt because of contradictions in the three books in which Trout figures. Mr. Vonnegut evidently regards consistency as the hobgoblin of small writers.

Internal evidence in *God Bless You, Mr. Rosewater,* the first book about Trout, implies that Trout was born in 1890 or 1898. *Slaughterhouse Five,* the second, implies that he was born in 1902. But *Breakfast of Champions* makes it clear that he was born in 1907.

There are other discrepancies. *God Bless You, Mr.*

Rosewater says that no two of Trout's books ever had the same publisher. In *Breakfast of Champions* the World Classics Library publishers have issued many of his books.

Rosewater states that Trout's works can only be found in disreputable bookstores dealing in pornography. Yet the same book has Eliot Rosewater picking up a Trout novel from a book rack in an airport.

Trout's novels are supposed to be extremely difficult to find. Rosewater is an avid collector of Trout (in fact, the only one), and he has only forty-one novels and sixty-three short stories. Yet the crooked lawyer, Mushari, goes into a Washington, D.C., smut dealer's and finds every one of Trout's eighty-seven novels.

Breakfast of Champions says that until Trout met a truck driver in 1972 he had never talked with anybody who'd read one of his stories. But Eliot Rosewater and Billy Pilgrim had read his stories and had met him some years before.

Trout's sole fan letter (from Rosewater) reached him in Cohoes, New York, according to *Breakfast*. But Rosewater says that Trout was living in Hyannis, Massachusetts, when he got the letter.

The description of the extraterrestrial Tralfamadorians in *The Sirens of Titan* differs considerably from that in *Slaughterhouse Five*.

And so it goes.

Who is the greatest living science fiction author?

Some say he is Isaac Asimov. Many swear he's Robert A. Heinlein. Others nominate Arthur C. Clarke, Theodore Sturgeon, Harlan Ellison, Brian Aldiss, or Kurt Vonnegut, Jr. Franz Rottensteiner, Austrian critic and editor, proclaims the Pole, Stanislaw Lem, as the champion. Mr. Rottensteiner may be biased, however, since he is also Lem's literary agent.

None of the above can equal Kilgore Trout—if we can believe Eliot Rosewater, Indiana multimillionaire, war hero, philanthropist, fireman extraordinaire, and science fiction connoisseur. According to Rosewater, Trout is not only the greatest science fiction writer alive, he is the world's greatest writer. He ranks Trout above Dostoevski, Tolstoi, Balzac, Fielding, and Melville. Rosewater believes that Trout should be president of Earth. He alone would have the imagination, ingenuity, and perception to solve the problems of this planet.

Rosewater, drunk as usual, once burst into a science fiction writers' convention at Milford, Pennsylvania. He had come to meet his idol, but he found, to his sorrow and amazement, that Trout was not there. Lesser men could attend it, but Trout was too poor to leave Hyannis, Massachusetts, where he was a stock clerk in a trading-stamp redemption center.

Who is this Kilgore Trout, this poverty-stricken and neglected genius?

To begin with, Kilgore Trout is not a nom de plume of Theodore Sturgeon. Let us dispose of that base rumor at once. It is only coincidence that the final syllables of the first names of these two authors end in *ore* or that their last names are those of fish. The author of the classical and beautifully written *More Than Human* and *The Saucer of Loneliness* could not possibly be the man whom even his greatest admirer admitted couldn't write for sour apples.

Trout was born in 1907, but the exact day is unknown. Until a definite date is supplied by an authoritative source, I'll postulate the midnight of February 19th, 1907, as the day on which society's "greatest prophet" was born. Trout's character indicates that he is an Aquarian and so was born between January 20th and February 19th. There is, however, so much of the Piscean in him that he was probably born on the cusp of Aquarius and Pisces, that is, near midnight of February 19th.

Trout first saw the light of day on the British island of Bermuda. His parents were citizens of the United States of America. (Trout has depicted them in his novel, *Now It Can Be Told*.) His father, Leo Trout, had taken a position as birdwatcher for the Royal Ornithological Society in Bermuda. His chief duty was to guard the very rare Bermudian ern, a green sea eagle. Despite his vigilance, the ern became extinct, and Leo took his family back to the States. Kilgore attended a Bermudian grammar school and then entered Thomas Jefferson High School in Dayton, Ohio. He graduated from this in 1924.

Though Trout was born in Bermuda, he was probably conceived in Indiana. His character smells strongly of certain Hoosier elements, and it is in Indianapolis, Indiana, that we first meet him. This state has produced many writers: Edward Eggleston *(The Hoosier Schoolmaster)*, George Ade *(Fables in Slang)*, Theodore Dreiser *(Sister Carrie, An American Tragedy, The Genius)*, George Barr McCutcheon *(Graustark, Brewster's*

Millions), Gene Stratton Porter *(A Girl of the Limberlost)*, William Vaughn Moody *(The Great Divide)*, Booth Tarkington *(Penrod, The Magnificent Ambersons)*, Lew Wallace *(Ben Hur)*, James Whitcomb Riley *(The Old Swimmin'-Hole, When the Frost is on the Punkin')*, Ross Lockridge *(Raintree County)*, Leo Queequeg Tincrowdor *(Osiris on Crutches, The Vaccinators from Vega)*, Rex Stout (author of the Nero Wolfe mysteries), and, last but far from least, Kurt Vonnegut, Jr. *(Player Piano, Cat's Cradle, The Sirens of Titan*, "Welcome to the Monkey House," *Mother Night, God Bless You, Mr. Rosewater, Slaughterhouse Five, Breakfast of Champions, Slapstick, Jailbird*, and others.)

Mr. Vonnegut is the primary source of our information about Kilgore Trout. We should all be grateful to him for bringing Trout's life and works to our attention. Unfortunately, Vonnegut refers to him only in the latter three books, and these are popularly believed to be fictional. They are to some extent, but Kilgore Trout is a real-life person, and anybody who doubts this is free to look up his birth record in Bermuda.

Vonnegut has brought Trout out of obscurity and has given us much of his immediate life. He has not, however, given us the background of Trout's parents, and so I have conducted my own investigations into Trout's pedigree. The full name of Kilgore's father was Leo Cabell Trout, and he was born circa 1881 in Roanoke, Virginia. Trouts have lived for generations in this city and its neighbor, Salem. Leo's mother was a Cabell and related to that family which has produced the famous author, James Branch Cabell *(Figures of Earth, The Silver Stallion, Jurgen)* and a novelist well-known in the nineteenth century, Princess Amélie Troubetzkoy. The princess was the granddaughter of William Cabell Rives, a U.S. Senator and minister to France. Her first novel, *The Quick or the Dead?*, was a sensation in 1888.

Trout inherited a talent for writing from his mother's side also. She was Eva Alice Shawnessy (1880–1926), author of the Little Eva series, popular children's books around the turn of the century. She wrote these under the nom de plume of Eva Westward and received only a fraction of the royalties they earned. Her publisher ran off with his firm's profits to Brazil after inducing her to sink her money into the firm's stock. Her unpublished biography of her father was the main source of information for Ross Lockridge when he wrote *Raintree County*.

Her father was John Wickliff Shawnessy (1839–1941), a Civil War veteran, country schoolteacher, and a frustrated dramatist and poet. Johnny spent much of his life thinking about and seeking the legended Golden Raintree, an arboreal Holy Grail, hidden somewhere in the Great Swamp of Raintree County. Johnny never finished his epic, *Sphinx Recumbent*, but a great-grandson has taken this and rewritten it as a science fiction novel. Leo Queequeg Tincrowdor (born 1918) is the son of Allegra Shawnessy (born 1898), daughter of Wesley Shawnessy (1879–1939), eldest son of John Wickliff Shawnessy. Kilgore's cousin, Leo, is primarily a painter, but he has written some science fiction stories which have been favorably compared to Kilgore's.

Johnny's father was Thomas Duff Shawnessy (died 1879), farmer, lay preacher, herbalist, and composer of county-famous, but awful, doggerel. He was born in the village of Ecclefechan, Dumfriesshire, Scotland, and was the illegitimate son of Eliza Shawnessy, a farmer's daughter. Thomas Duff revealed to his son Johnny that his, Thomas', father had been the great Scots essayist and historian, Thomas Carlyle (1795–1881). Eliza (1774–1830) had taken Thomas Duff when he was a boy to the state of Delaware. After his mother died, Thomas Duff Shawnessy and his nineteen-year-old bride, Ellen, had settled in the newly opened state of Indiana. Thomas Duff thought that his father's writing genius might spring anew in his grandson, Johnny. Surely the genes responsible for such great books as *Sartor Resartus, The French Revolution*, and *On Heroes, Hero Worship, and the Heroic in History* would not die.

There is, however, strong doubt that Thomas Carlyle was T.D. Shawnessy's father. Eliza Shawnessy would have been twenty-one years old in 1795, the year Carlyle was born. Even if she had seduced Carlyle when he was only twelve, Thomas Duff would have been born in 1807. This would make him thirteen years old when he married the nineteen-year-old Ellen. This is possible but highly improbable.

It seems likely that Eliza Shawnessy lied to her son. She wanted him to think that, though he was a bastard, his father was a great man. Probably, Thomas Duff's father was actually James Carlyle, stonemason, farmer, a fanatical Calvinist, and father of Thomas Carlyle. The truth seems to be that Thomas Duff Shawnessy was the half-brother of Thomas Carlyle. Thomas Duff should have been able to figure this out, but he never bothered to look up the date of his supposed father's birth.

Johnny's mother, Ellen, was a cousin of Andrew Johnson (1808–1875), the seventeenth president of the United States.

Johnny's second wife, Esther Root (born 1852), was of English stock with a dash of American Indian blood (from the Miami tribe, probably).

With so many writers in his pedigree, it would seem that Kilgore Trout was almost destined to become a famous author. However, his talents were marred by his personality, which had been soured and depressed by an unhappy childhood. His father was a ne'er-do-well, and his mother was embittered by her husband's drunkenness and infidelity, and by the theft of her royalties. Trout was prevented from going on to college by his parents' long and expensive illnesses, resulting in their deaths a few years after he graduated from high school.

Trout had three great fears that rode him all his life: a fear of cancer, of rats, and of Doberman pinschers. The first came from watching his parents suffer in their terminal stages. The second came from living in so many basements and tenement houses. The third resulted from several attacks by Doberman pinschers during his vagabondish life. Once, out of a job and starving, he tried to steal a chicken from a farmer's henhouse but was caught by the watchdog. Another time, he was bitten while delivering circulars.

Trout's pessimism and distrust of human beings ensured that he would have no friends and that his three wives would divorce him. It drove his only child, Leo, to run away from home at the age of fourteen. Leo lied about his age and became a U.S. Marine. While in boot camp he wrote his father a denunciatory letter. After that, there was a total lack of word about Leo until two FBI agents visited Kilgore. His son, they told him, had deserted and joined the Viet Cong.

Trout moved around the States, working at low-paying and menial jobs and writing his science fiction stories in his spare time. After his final divorce, his only companion was a parakeet named Bill. Kilgore talked a lot to Bill. And for forty years Kilgore carried around with him an old steamer trunk. This contained many curious items, including toys from his childhood, the bones of a Bermudian ern, and a mildewed tuxedo he had worn to the senior dance just before graduating.

Sometime during his lonely odysseys, he fell into the habit of calling mirrors "leaks." Mirrors were weak points through

The Obscure Life and Hard Times of Kilgore Trout   233

which leaked visions of universes parallel to ours. Through these four-dimensional windows he could see cosmos occupying the same space as ours. This delusion, if it was a delusion, probably originated from his rejection of our universe. This was, to him, the worst of all possible worlds.

Our planet was a cement mixer in which Trout had been whirled, tossed, beaten, and ground. By the mid-1960's, his face and body bore all the scars and traumas of his never-ending battle against the most abject poverty, of his unceasing labors in writing his many works, of a neglect by the literary world and, worse, by a neglect from the readers of the genre in which he specialized, science fiction, and of an incessant screwing by his fly-by-night publishers.

Fred Rosewater, in *God Bless You, Mr. Rosewater*, picks up a book by Trout. It is *Venus on the Half-shell*, and on its paper back is a photograph of Trout. He's an old man with a bushy black beard, and his face is that of a scarred Jesus who's been spared the cross but must instead spend the rest of his life in prison.

Eliot Rosewater, coming out of a mental fog in a sanitarium, sees Trout for the first time. He looks to him like a kindly country undertaker. Trout no longer has a beard; he's shaved it off so he can get a job.

Billy Pilgrim, in *Slaughterhouse Five*, is introduced to Trout's works by Eliot Rosewater, his wardmate in a veterans' hospital near Lake Placid, New York. This was in the spring of 1948. In 1964 or thereabouts, Billy Pilgrim runs into Kilgore Trout in Ilium, New York. Trout has a paranoid face, that of a cracked Messiah, and he looks like a prisoner of war, but he has a saving grace, a deep rich voice. He is, as usual, living friendless and despised in a basement. He is barely making a living as a circulation manager for the *Ilium Gazette*. Cowardly and dangerous, he succeeds in his job only by bullying and cheating the boys who carry the papers. He is astonished and gratified that anyone knows of him. He goes to Pilgrim's engagement party, where he is lionized for the first time in his life.

In 1972, according to *Breakfast of Champions*, Trout is snaggletoothed and has long, tangled, uncombed white hair. He hasn't used a toothbrush for years. His legs are pale, skinny, hairless, and studded with varicose veins. He has sensitive artist's feet, blue from bad circulation. He doesn't wash very often. Vonnegut gives a number of physical statistics about

Trout, including the fact that his penis, when erect, is seven inches long but only one and one-fourth of an inch in diameter. Just how he found this out, Vonnegut does not say.

In *God Bless You, Mr. Rosewater*, Mushari, a sinister lawyer (or is the adjective a redundancy?), investigates Trout. He is not interested in him as a literary phenomenon. Trout is Rosewater's favorite author, and Mushari is checking out Trout's works for his dossier on Rosewater. He hopes to prove that Rosewater is mentally incompetent and unable to administrate the millions of the Rosewater Foundation. No reputable bookseller has ever heard of Trout. But he does locate all of Trout's eighty-seven novels, in a tattered secondhand condition, in a hole-in-the-wall which sells the hardest of hardcore pornography. Trout's *2BR02B*, which Eliot thought was his greatest work, was published at twenty-five cents a copy. Now it costs five dollars.

2BR02B has become a collector's item, not because of its literary worth but because of the highly erotic illustrations. This is the fate of many of Trout's books. In *Breakfast of Champions* we find that his best distributed book, *Plague on Wheels*, brings twelve dollars a copy because of its cover art, which depicts fellatio.

The irony of this is that few of Trout's books have any erotic content. Only one has a major female character, and she was a rabbit *(The Smart Bunny)*.

Trout only wrote one purposely "dirty" book in his life, *The Son of Jimmy Valentine*, and he did this because his second wife, Darlene, said that that was the only way for him to make money.

This book did make money but not for Trout. Its publisher, World Classics Library, a hardcore Los Angeles outfit, sent none of the royalties due to Trout. World Classics Library issued many of Trout's books, not because the readers were interested in the texts but because they needed his books to fill out their quota. They illustrated them with art that had nothing whatsoever to do with the story, and they often changed Trout's titles to something more appealing to their peculiar type of reader. *Pan-Galactic Straw-boss*, for instance, was published as *Mouth Crazy*.

Vonnegut says that Trout was cheated by his publishers, but *Breakfast of Champions* reveals that Trout's poverty and obscurity was largely his own fault. He sent his manuscripts to publishers whose addresses he found in magazines whose main market was would-be writers. He never inquired into their reputation or the type of literature they published. Moreover, he frequently sent his stories without a stamped self-addressed return envelope or without his own address. When he made one of his frequent moves, he never left a forwarding address at the post office. Even if his publishers had wished to deal fairly with him, they could not have located him.

Actually, Trout was a prime example of the highly neurotic writer whose creativity is compulsive and who could care less for the fate of his stories once they'd been set down on paper. He did not even own a copy of any of his own works.

Vonnegut calls Trout a science fiction writer, but he was one only in a special sense. He knew little of science and was indifferent to technical details. Vonnegut claims that most science fiction writers lack a knowledge of science. Perhaps this is so, but Vonnegut, who has a knowledge of science, ignores it in his fiction. Like Trout, he deals in time warps, extrasensory perception, space-flight, robots, and extraterrestrials. The truth is that Trout, like Vonnegut and Ray Bradbury and many others, writes parables. These are set in frames which have become called, for no good reason, science fiction. A better generic term would be "future fairy tales." And even this is objectionable, since many science fiction stories take place in the present or the past, far and near. Anyway, the better writers spend most of their time trying to escape any labels whatsoever.

In fact, there is a lot of Kilgore Trout in science fiction writers, including Vonnegut. If I did not know that Trout was a living person, I'd think he was an archetype plucked by Vonnegut out of his unconscious or the collective unconscious of science fiction writers. He's miserable, he wrestles with concepts and themes that only a genius could pin to the mat (and very few are geniuses), he feels that he is ignored and despised, he knows that the society in which he is forced to live could be a much better one, and, no matter how gregarious he seems to be, he is a loner, a monad. He may be rich and famous (and some science fiction authors are), but he is essentially that person described in the previous sentence. Millions may admire him, but he knows that the universe is totally unconscious of him and that he is a spark fading out in the blackness of eternity and infinity. But he has an untrammeled imagination, and while his spark is still glowing, he can defeat time and space. His stories are his weapons, and poor as they may be, they are better than none. As Eliot Rosewater says, the mainstream writers, narrators of the mundane, are "sparrowfarts." But the science fiction writer is a god. At least, that is what he secretly believes.

Trout's favorite formula is to describe a hideous society, much like our own, and then, toward the end of the book, outline ways in which the society may be improved. In his *2BR02B*, he shows an America which is so highly cybernated that only people with three or more Ph.D.'s can get jobs. There are also Ethical Suicide Parlors where useless people volunteer for euthanasia. *2BR02B* sounds like a combination of Vonnegut's novel, *Player Piano*, and his short story, "Welcome to the Monkey House." I'm not accusing Vonnegut of plagiarism, but Vonnegut does think highly enough of Trout's plots to borrow some now and then. Trout's *The Big Board* is about a man and a woman abducted and put on display by the extraterrestrials of the planet Zircon-212. Vonnegut's *Slaughterhouse Five* tells how the Tralfamadorians carried off Billy Pilgrim and the movie star, Montana Wildhack, and put them in a luxurious cage.

It may be that Trout gave Vonnegut permission to adapt some of his plots. At one time Trout lived in Hyannis, Massachusetts, which is very near West Barnstable, where Vonnegut also lived.

Vonnegut admires Trout's ideas, though he condemns his prose. It is atrocious and Trout's unpopularity is deserved. (By the way, I'd characterize Vonnegut's own prose, and his philosophy, as by Sterne out of Smollett.) A specimen of Trout's prose, taken from *Venus on the Half-shell*, sounds like that of the typical hack semipornographer's. Most of the science fiction writers, according to Eliot Rosewater, have a style no better than Trout's. But this doesn't matter. Science fiction writers are poets with a sort of radar which detects only the meaningful in this world. They don't write of the trivial; their concerns are the really big issues: galaxies, eternity, and the fate of all of us. And Trout is looking for the answer to the question that so sorely troubles Eliot Rosewater (and many of us). That is, how do you love people who have no use? How do you love the unlovable?

Vonnegut lists Trout's known residences as Bermuda, Dayton, Ohio, Hyannis, Massachusetts, and Ilium and Cohoes of New York. To this I can add Peoria, Illinois. A letter from Kilgore Trout was printed in the vox pop section of the editorial page of the *Peoria Journal Star* in 1971. In this Trout denounced Peoria as essentially obscene. It suggested that the natives quit raising so much hell about dirty movies and books and look in their own hearts for the genuine smut: hate, prejudice, and greed. Trout gave his address as West Main Street. Unfortunately, I no longer have the letter or the address, since I clipped out the letter and sent it to Theodore Sturgeon, who lives in the Los Angeles area. Before doing this, however, I did ascertain that the address was genuine, though Trout no longer lived there. And he had failed, as usual, to leave a forwarding address.

I do have a letter which appeared on the editorial page of the *Peoria Journal Star* of August 14th, 1971. This gives us some information about Trout's activities while he was in Peoria. The letter was signed by a D. Raabe, whom I met briefly after I'd given a lecture at Bradley University. Some extracts of the letter follow.

"... Eminent scatologist, Dr. K. Trout, W.E.A., in an interview outside the public facilities in Glen Oak Park, had some things to say about the Russian-Indian pact... On the subject of internal disorder, Dr. Trout noted that if Indian food becomes a fad in Russia, the Russians may 'loosen up a bit' although they might become a little touchier in certain areas...."

Apparently, Trout had a job with the Peoria Public Works Department at this time, and he claimed to have a doctor's degree. I don't know what the initials stand for, unless it's Watercloset Engineering Assistant, but I suspect that he sent in fifty dollars to an institution of dubious standing and received his diploma through the mails. Despite the degree, he still had a menial and unpleasant job. This was to be expected. One whom the world treats crappily will become an authority on crap. He knows where it's at, and he works where it all hangs out.

Trout's last known job was as an installer of aluminum combination storm windows and screens in Cohoes, New York. At this time (late 1972), Trout was living in a basement. Because of his lack of charm and other social graces, Trout's employer had refused to use him as a salesman. His fellow employees had little to do with him and did not even know that he wrote science fiction. And then one day he received a letter. It was the harbinger of a new life, a prelude to recognition of a writer too long neglected.

Trout had an invitation to be a guest of honor at a festival of arts. This was to celebrate the opening of the Mildred Barry

Memorial Center for Arts in Midway Center, Indiana. With the invitation was a check for a thousand dollars. Both the honor and the check were due to Eliot Rosewater. He had agreed to loan his El Greco for exhibit at the Center if Kilgore Trout, possibly the greatest living writer in the world, would be invited.

Overjoyed, though still suspicious, Trout went to New York City to buy some copies of his own books so he could read passages from them at the festival. While there, he was mugged and picked up by the police on suspicion of robbery. He spent Veterans' Day in jail. On being released, he hitchhiked a ride with a truck driver and arrived in Midway Center. There, unfortunately, the joint of his right index finger was bitten off by a madman, and the festival was called off. This made Trout hope that he would never again have to touch, or be touched by, a human being.

Breakfast of Champions is, according to Vonnegut, the last word we'll get from him on Trout. I'm sorry to hear that, but I am also grateful to Mr. Vonnegut for having first brought Trout to the attention of the nonpornography-reading public. I am also sorry that Mr. Vonnegut indulges in sheer fantasy in the last quarter of the book. The first three parts are factual, but the last part might lead some to believe that Kilgore Trout is a fictional character. The serious reader and student of Trout will disregard the final quarter of *Breakfast of Champions* except to sift fact from fantasy.

Though the Midway Center Art Festival was aborted, Kilgore Trout is nevertheless on his way to fame. I've just received word that Mr. David Harris, an editor of Dell Publishing Company, is negotiating for the reprinting of *Venus on the Half-shell*. If the arrangements are satisfactory to both parties, the general public will have, for the first time, a chance to read a novel by Kilgore Trout.

The following is a list of the known titles of the one-hundred-seventeen novels and two thousand short stories written by Trout. It's a tragically short list, and it can only be lengthened if Troutophiles make a diligent search through secondhand bookstores and porno shops for the missing works.

NOVELS

The Gutless Wonder (1932)
2BR02B
Venus on the Half-shell

The Obscure Life and Hard Times of Kilgore Trout

Oh Say Can You Smell?
The First District Court of Thankyou
Pan-Galactic Three-Day Pass
Maniacs in the Fourth Dimension (1948)
The Gospel from Outer Space
The Big Board
Pan-Galactic Straw-boss (Mouth Crazy)
Plague on Wheels
Now It Can Be Told
The Son of Jimmy Valentine
How You Doin'?
The Smart Bunny
The Pan-Galactic Memory Bank

SHORT STORIES

The Dancing Fool (April, 1962 issue of Black Garterbelt, a magazine published by World Classics Library)
This Means You
Gilgongo!
Hail to the Chief
The Baring-gaffner of Bagnialto or This Year's Masterpiece

(Author's Note: Since this was first written, Mr. Vonnegut's novel *Jailbird* has come out. In this Mr. Vonnegut claims that it was not Trout but another man who wrote the works which Vonnegut hitherto had claimed to be Trout's. Nobody believes this disclaimer, but the reasons for it have been the subject of much speculation. Several people have wondered why the initial letter of the surname of the man Mr. Vonnegut claims is the real Trout is also mine. Is Mr. Vonnegut obliquely pointing his finger at me?

I really don't know. In one of many senses, or perhaps two or three, I am Kilgore Trout. But then the same could be said of at least fifty science-fiction writers.)

THANKS FOR THE FEAST

This is the only item in this collection which I did not write. I was, however, responsible for its being written. I did not ask that it be written. I did not even know that it was being written until I got a long-distance call from Digby Diehl, editor of the *Los Angeles Times* Book Review section. He informed me that Leslie A. Fiedler, the distinguished critic and author *(An End to Innocence, The Nude Croquet, Getting Busted, The Stranger in Shakespeare, Freaks,* and others) was writing an article on me. Fiedler wanted me to send him some of my works which he lacked so that he could complete his critique.

I was surprised, because I had no idea that Fiedler was the least interested in science-fiction, let alone in me. I had the same reaction that Kilgore Trout did when he ran into Billy Pilgrim, the antihero of Vonnegut's *Slaughterhouse Five*.

The article was printed in the *Times* of April 23, 1972. Ostensibly, it was a review of my *Tarzan Alive* but was, in actuality, a bird's-eye, or perhaps a worm's-eye, view of my career. It was accompanied by an illustration of a goofy-looking Tarzan riding astraddle a rocket, obviously a phallic symbol. Its title was: "Getting into the Task of Now Pornography." I could take the illustration, but I did not care for the title. I found out later that it was an editor's, not Fiedler's. The editor had also emasculated the text and inserted some mismating of titles and their publishers.

The work at hand is Fiedler's original article with the original title. This was first printed in *Moebius Trip;* the quotations in double parentheses are the comments of the editor, Ed Connor, and one of my own.

Fiedler is a dyed-in-the-wool Freudian, but most of his analyses are valid—from my viewpoint. There is also much that is Jungian and Reichian in my works, and these aspects are neglected in the article. Freudian, Jungian, Reichian, are terms I don't really like to use to apply to literary works. The term Farmerian should be good enough.

Some of my friends, on reading the *Times* article, commiserated with me. They did not read it aright. I was pretty happy with it. It's by no means a denigration, though not all laudatory, and it's a hell of a lot more insightful than anything most of the specialized science fiction critics have written about me.

I hope there's no deep significance in the fact that Fiedler wrote this on April Fool's Day.

NOTES ON
PHILIP JOSÉ FARMER
by Leslie A. Fiedler

Philip José Farmer seems now to have reached the point of public recognition, and I for one am feeling a little dismayed. I don't suppose that publication in *Esquire* alone is enough to make an unfashionable writer a *chic* one, but it is a real, perhaps irrevocable, step in that direction. I liked it much better when a taste for Farmer's fiction could still seem a private, slightly shameful pleasure, or a perverse affectation on the part of a scholar, an eccentric vice. In those days, he belonged chiefly to readers who did not even suspect that the novel is dead— to an audience which took him off the racks in drugstores or supermarkets or airports to allay boredom—and with no sense certainly that they were approaching "literature." Beyond them, there were, of course, a few others, some themselves more highly touted writers of Science Fiction, who knew that he was something very special; but they wanted to keep it a secret.

To be sure, Farmer had won a Hugo Award or two, one for his earliest work and another a decade and a half later. And a third, in 1972, for the novel, *To Your Scattered Bodies Go.*" But he was never the object of cult adoration, like Robert Heinlein, for instance, after the appearance of *A Stranger in a Strange Land;* nor was he regarded, like Kurt Vonnegut, by *his* group of the faithful, as a hidden "great writer." To tell the truth, Farmer does not behave much like an aspirant to "mainstream" greatness. With all the modesty of a hack, he inclines to throw even his best conceptions away—writing hastily, sometimes downright sloppily; so that we are likely to be left with the disconcerting sense that his work, especially when it aspires to novel length, runs out rather than properly finishes. ("To preserve the Freudian tone of this article, I would have said 'peters out.'")

Nonetheless, he has an imagination capable of being kindled

by the irredeemable mystery of the universe and of the soul, and in turn able to kindle the imagination of others—readers who for a couple of generations have been turning to Science Fiction to keep wonder and ecstasy alive in times apparently uncongenial to those deep psychic experiences. That wonder and ecstasy, wherever it is found in Science Fiction, is ultimately rooted in our sexuality; and the best writers of the genre during its period of flowering after World War II, appear to have realized instinctively that to succeed in their enterprise they had somehow to eroticize machines, gadgets, and the scientific enterprise itself—or at least to exploit the preexistent erotic implications of the paraphernalia of a technological age.

Philip Farmer was, however, during the 50's, the only major writer of Science Fiction to deal *explicitly* with sex. He constituted, therefore, a singular exception, an eccentric case—in a genre whose leading authors created protagonists themselves apparently desexed, though they and their adventures implicitly symbolized or projected sexuality; since they constitute, as it were, the communal dreams of a technological, urban civilization. And that civilization knows in its sleep, what it denies waking, that at this point, it must eroticize the Industrial Revolution or perish; just as it thinks it knows waking, what it denies in its sleep, that sex must be reimagined as machine technology or rejected out of hand. The latter is the task of modern pornography, even as the former is that of Science Fiction.

It was inevitable, therefore, from the start that Farmer would, at the climax of his career, produce two works at once fantasy and bald, explicit pornography—"hardcore pornography," as the cant phrase has it: *The Image of the Beast* and *A Feast Unknown*. Both books were published by the same sub-respectable firm and distributed through channels ordinarily unsympathetic to any work not aimed exclusively and directly at simple-minded titillation, "jerk-off literature," in short. Never mind that *A Feast Unknown* begins with a quotation from May Swenson's poetry and ends with an apologetic Afterword by Theodore Sturgeon, in which he insists that this piece of sado-masochistic porn, whose hero can only have an orgasm over the bleeding body of his victims, represents somehow "the very core of the healthy truth expressed in the slogan, 'Make love, not war.'"

A Feast Unknown is a hilarious parody of the pop literature of super-heroic adventure; but its essential characteristic is a shamelessness beyond all possible apology. To speak of the imagination which informs it and its predecessor (in whose key scene an extraterrestrial girl with sharp iron dentures goes down on an unwary cop) as "healthy" is an inadvertent error or a deliberate lie. They are about as healthy as the works of the "divine" Marquis de Sade himself; which is to say, they may function therapeutically, but only by releasing in us, or exploding out of us, fantasies in themselves sick. And they have, in fact, helped pave the way for a new brand of Science Fiction, which deals frankly with human passion, "sick" and "healthy"; providing us with real phalluses and wombs, against which we can measure their symbolic projections in spaceships and underground cities on unknown planets. The paperback periodical, *Quark*, for instance, in which Farmer himself has been published, has also printed the work of younger writers, his debtors and descendants—in the form of candidly-worked-out genital fantasies, often by recently liberated women, eager to excel him in the candor of their language and the brutality of their images. But Farmer was there first.

I remember reading many years ago my first Farmer story, which was called "Mother," and being astonished and gratified (a little condescendingly, perhaps) to discover certain Freudian insights into the nature of family relationships, ingeniously worked out and made flesh, as it were, in the world of intergalactic travel and an endlessly receding future. My surprise and delight were not only cued by the prejudice which then possessed me utterly—my conviction that pop fiction was necessarily immune to the insights of depth psychology; but arose also because the mythology of Freud was based on the belief that the neuroses were rooted in the past, and that, therefore, the revelation of sexual secrets depended on retrospection. It needed a writer like Farmer, committed to the anticipation of the future, to turn psychoanalysis in the direction of prophecy. The concerns first explored in "Mother" and the other tales later collected in a volume called *Strange Relations* have continued to obsess him, reaching their culmination in his Hugo Award winning story, "Riders of the Purple Wage." In that tale—whose title puns on Zane Grey, of course (as he is always punning on names out of earlier literature, popular or elitist), and whose not-so-secret motto is "the family that blows is the family that grows"—he has taken advantage of the greater linguistic freedom of the past decade. And he has thus been able to render even more explicitly the vision of a cloying and destructive relationship between Mothers and Sons, with which he began nearly twenty years ago.

One of Farmer's major obsessive themes, as a matter of fact, is precisely the theme of Mother as a threat to freedom, a temptation to regression, a womb turned prison. And closely connected to it is the second of his major themes, the discovery of new religions in a new world; for those religions always turn out to be matriarchal and are presented as an overwhelming challenge to the patriarchal faith of Christianity. Yet it is a Roman Catholic padre, more son than father though he is called Father John Carmody, who in various short stories and the extraordinary novel, *Night of Light,* somehow comes to terms with those alien mythologies and rituals; or even manages to defend them and his own *machismo* simultaneously with gun and fist.

In any case, the Cults of the Great Goddess have always obsessed Farmer; and, indeed, there seems something deep within him that yearns for a time, real or imagined, in which the male was not a Hero but a Servant of that great principle of fertility, as in the bawdiest of his subpornographic novels, *Flesh.* Yet Farmer's third obsessive theme comes into direct (and perhaps irreconcilable) conflict with this fearful nostalgia for the matriarchal security each of us has known in infancy. And this is the myth of The Hero With a Thousand Faces, the lonely phallic *übermensch* triumphing by his ability not to create but to kill. Farmer's favorite name for the extravagantly male super-Hero is "Tarzan"; a killer presumably suckled by a she-ape rather than a mere female woman; but really created out of his own head by a god or devil called Edgar Rice Burroughs, and endlessly recreated by a subsidiary deity or demon called Philip José Farmer.

In five major books at least, he has returned to that key figure—who also flickers in and out of his other fictions, sometimes quite irrelevantly: in *Lord Tyger, A Feast Unknown, Lord of the Trees, The Mad Goblin,* and most recently in *Tarzan Alive.* The first of these deals with a boy brought up in the jungle by a mad scientist (a caricature of Farmer himself?) eager to save Burroughs' honor by proving that a Savage Noble can indeed survive under the conditions described by Tarzan's original biographer. The second is a sado-pornographic account of a struggle to the death between "Lord Grandrith" (the *true* Tarzan) and "Doc Caliban" (the *true* Doc Savage): a struggle which reaches an initial climax when the two super-heroes duel with erect phalluses on a knife-edge of stone bridging a chasm, and ends with both of them deballed. The third and fourth, issued as a double paperback—this time without the warning, "ADULTS ONLY"—represent, in Farmer's own words, "something unique... the only spinoff of 'clean books' from a 'dirty' book."

In all of them, however, "clean" or "dirty," Farmer insists not only on Tarzan's virtual immortality, but—even more strongly—on his extraordinary sexual endowment: his superiority in this respect to his primate pals and his Black neighbors (though he argues heatedly that Tarzan is no "racist")—as well as, one presumes, to his author and his readers. The same themes obsess him still in the fifth, to be published April 28—but already excerpted in *Esquire*. It is in all respects the culmination of the others: a delightfully monomaniac attempt to "'prove' through the use of quasi-scholarly tools..." that Tarzan is (a) "a close relative of such modern heroes as Professor Challenger, Holmes and Wolfe, Lord John Roxton, Denis Nayland Smith, Bulldog Drummond, Lord Peter Wimsey, Raffles, Leopold Bloom, and Richard Wentworth (who is not only the Spider but was once G-8 and is at the same time the Shadow)..." and (b) "that Tarzan is the last of the Heroes of the Golden Age, Nature's final expression...."

But Tarzan, for all his encyclopedic comprehensiveness, represents only a small part of Farmer's larger attempt (at once absurd and beautiful, foredoomed to failure but, once conceived, already a success) to subsume in his own works *all* of the books in the world that have touched or moved him. For him, the traditions of Science Fiction provide a warrant for constructing Universes of his Own: worlds whose place names turn out inevitably to demand as many footnotes as T.S. Eliot's *The Waste Land*—Dante's Joy, Baudelaire, Ozagen (Oz again!); and which are inhabited not only by new species but old friends, fictional or real—Hiawatha, Alice in Wonderland, Sir Richard Burton, Ishmael (Melville's), and Herman Goering.

Particularly in his "pocket universes" series and in his more recent Riverworld Books, *To Your Scattered Bodies Go* and *The Fabulous Riverboat*, all that seemed to have died here on Earth (everywhere at least except in the head of one voracious reader) is resurrected—or at least reconstructed in quasi-immortal form by omniscient computers in Worlds Out There. Obviously, it is the deepest level of childhood response which

Notes on Philip José Farmer

Farmer has reached in this pair of novels, in the first of which Sir Richard Burton pursues amorously Lewis Carroll's chastely loved Alice Lidell; while in the second, Mark Twain searches with equal passion for his lost wife, Livy, and for iron ore deposits rich enough to make possible the building of a paddlewheel steamer. The primary images seem erotic, even genital; but in the Riverworld there turns out to be more detailed description of eating than of sex. And, indeed, the most important gadget in its extraterrestrial technology is the "Grail," a kind of portable short-order kitchen provided by the invisible masters of a warmed-over universe.

But this is fair enough; since throughout Farmer's work he demonstrates himself to be the most oral of men—his heroes being more typically blown than laid; his image of ultimate horror a bitten-off penis; and his vision of utopian bliss a kind of not-quite-kiss, in which the partners (functionally neither totally male nor female) move their lips ecstatically around a pale snakelike organ which wriggles out of the mouth of one into that of the other. In this light, it seems appropriate to describe Farmer's cultural imperialism as a gargantuan lust to *swallow* down the whole cosmos, past, present, and to come, and to spew it out again.

Farmer wants even to eat and regurgitate himself; the industrious hack who writes his books, plus that hack's fantasies of what he secretly is or might be. And in the end, he does manage to mingle almost unnoticed among super-heroes and mutants and monsters, as if the character Philip José Farmer were as real as any fiction: the writer without real fans, who, for twenty-five ((*five* is correct)) years, tried to make it in Southern California, baffled by apartment house living among Jewish neighbors, improbably married for the whole time to the same wife—and fleeing at last back to Peoria, Illinois, where he was born ((correct place of birth: North Terre Haute, Indiana)). Usually his self-portraits are betrayed by the initials, P.J.F., as he himself points out: "Kickaha (Paul Janus Finnegan) is me as I would like to be. Peter Jairus Frigate *(To Your Scattered Bodies Go)* is me as I (more or less) really am."

Finally, I suppose, Farmer must dream of swallowing down his readers, too, or at least of "taking them in," as the telltale phrase has it, with jokes and hoaxes and "scholarly" proofs. And there is something satisfactory, after all, about imagining ourselves, complete with wives, kids, and worldly possessions, disappearing into an utterly fictional world along with Alice and Tarzan and Kilgore Trout, the Scarlet Pimpernel and Jack the Ripper and Samuel Clemens. But not before we have managed to say, as I am trying to say here: *Thanks for the feast.*

—Leslie A. Fiedler
Buffalo, New York
1 April 1972.